Sangria

Sunsets

Edward R Hackemer

Sangria Sunsets

(Book 6 - Throckmorton Family Novels)

~ a novel ~

Edward R Hackemer

ISBN 13: 978-1542615945

ISBN 10: 1542615941

Other titles by this author:

(The Throckmorton Family Novels)

In A Cream Packard

(Book 1)
© 2011, 2013
ISBN-13: 978-1482662801

The Katydid Effect

(Book 2)
© 2013
ISBN-13: 978-1482669831

A Bridge To Cross

(Book 3)
© 2014
ISBN-13: 978-1494972820

Dollar To Doughnut

(Book 4)
© 2014
ISBN-13: 978-1505245110

The Flying Phaeton

(Book 5)
© 2015
ISBN-13: 978-1518707858

Titles are available in print and electronic format at online booksellers.

Visit the author's web page:
edhackemer.info
"Elvis reliquit aedificium[*]*."*

Acknowledgement

for:

My friend & checker – Edny.
My pen pal & editor – Letitia.
My advocate & reader – You.
The songwriters, musicians, and vocalists.

Dedication

to:

The legend.

The Legend & Fine Print

Sincere effort has been taken to ensure that this novel contains the straight stuff for 1937 to 1960. Please realize that much of this novel is fiction; the exception being the specific enigmatic parts that are not. The needle and names were changed to protect the record and only the record, because although daunting, lie detector tests are generally unreliable.

A novel is a work of fiction therefore, many of the featured characters in this book are fictional. Any resemblance in the description or name to any real person, living or dead is purely coincidental and unintentional. No endorsement is given or implied for the surreptitious activity of any character, organization or institution described in this novel. Any dialogue, comments or opinions expressed or indicated by any character acting individually or on behalf of an organization either actual or fictional, are used solely for descriptive and entertainment purposes. Please note that Dick Tracy two-way wrist radios are no longer available.

Any lyrics, songs or music annotated in this book are the intellectual property of individual copyright holders and are referenced only for descriptive purposes. The reader is encouraged to purchase the music, listen and feel free to tap either a hoof or foot. Except for the most experienced users, finger snapping while texting is strongly discouraged.

Governmental, military or ecclesiastical institutions mentioned in this book, actual or fictitious, are included neither as an endorsement nor as editorial rejection of their function or doctrine. The descriptions of military organizations or governmental agencies within these pages, either actual or apocryphal, are included with literary license and no negative inference or implication to any past or current entity is intended. Civil, military or personal violence is recounted solely for editorial reality. The reader is encouraged to research the history. It can be multi-faceted, complicated and certainly, not always nice.

☞ Verbiage used in this novel is contemporary to the story except what ain't. Mid-20th Century terminology, slang and colloquialisms are indicated with a *single* superscript asterisk (*) and can be found in the GLOSSARY at the back of the book. ☞

☞ Incidentals, curiosities and footnotes are indicated with by *double* superscript asterisks (**) and indexed as handnotes at the back of the book in the section titled THE END NOTES. ☞

The Jazz

The Players:

Jovita Maria (Vasquello) Throckmorton,
Nora (Sterescu) Throckmorton, Alexander Throckmorton,
Katherine Ann Dobbs, Nicholas Throckmorton,
Eloisa (Ashworth) Throckmorton

The Stage:

America
(North, Central & South)

The Story:

Personal, emotional and geopolitical conflict.

The Quotes:

"I just needed a breather. It had little or nothing to do with a woman."
~ Nicholas Throckmorton

"I don't think I could trust a man who didn't cheat or drink."
~ Jovita Vasquello

"Live American. Dream Puerto Rican."
~ Carilla Pérez de Vasquello

"They would have overthrown us even if we had grown no bananas."
~ Manuel Fortuny

From the author

I've spent six years chronicling the history of the Throckmorton family and the events that influenced their lives. It's been an enjoyable and rewarding experience. After the barley crop was harvested, winnowed from the chaff and milled, the finished product became a heady brew of novels that neatly fit into a six-pack.

After lengthy character interviews and careful study of photograph albums, family archives and public records, I discovered a few hidden tidbits of personal history that I felt obliged to include in this edition. From the far side of the gallery the picture may look complete, but I think every brush stroke counts. Therefore, for this edition of the Throckmorton family saga, I invited the characters to spatter some of their personal insights into the hidden corners of the finished portrait. The reader will find these colorful additions at the end of the book in the section titled 'SINCERELY'. Because they may contain 'spoilers', I suggest that these are read last.

The actors on life's stage enjoy unscripted roles and are free to rewrite the screenplay and send the story in unknown directions. At any given time, a character may even forget his or her lines and improvise.

Throughout the fabric of all families, there are threads that tie everyone together. Occasionally, these connecting fibers are worn threadbare by distance, or so badly blurred by time that they can be difficult to see or touch. Yet, every now and again, these fibers can unexpectedly reappear. Like the filaments running through a spider's web, you are surprised each time you walk into one. They are invisible until reflecting sunlight, shimmering moonlight or the morning dew causes them to glisten.

With help from my wife, my editor, my readers and every character in the Throckmorton novels, I have endeavored to illuminate as many silky threads as possible.

Enjoy the story and have fun. I did. Thank you all.

What's Inside

AND SO IT GOES ...

JOVITA ... 1937 – 1946

A Tisket, A Tasket ...
Sunday, market day:
Plaza del Mercado, Ponce, Puerto Rico, March 21, 1937

Walking among nearly overflowing produce stands and past scores of loud, boisterous vendors hawking their fruits, vegetables, tinwork and bric-a-brac, Carilla Vasquello and her daughter Jovita managed to bob, weave and gracefully bump along the narrow walkways. They were just two of hundreds of shoppers leisurely making their way through Plaza del Mercado and all of the hustle and bustle of the Ponce marketplace.

Carilla grew up in a two-room shack on a sugar plantation in Manatí, on the northern coast of Puerto Rico. She met her husband, Army Private Simón Vasquello on New Years' Eve, 1918, in San Juan, barely one month after World War I[**] had ended. They married after a whirlwind romance that rivalled a Caribbean super hurricane. Their daughter Jovita was born in April of 1920.

Carilla, aged 37, and Jovita, a month shy of 17, did not present the everyday image of mother and daughter on market day. They treated the market as if it was a holiday destination. Going to the Merchant Plaza was a weekly ritual that was celebrated as a day off from the work-a-day life and a chance to dress up. Mother was teaching daughter to celebrate life and appreciate everything it provides.

Carilla wore her long, dark brown locks braided and pinned back into a bun, with small, tight curls falling down over her ears and temples from under a soft rose, floppy-brimmed silk hat. A light pink scarf crossed her shoulders and a multi-colored dress followed her form softly to mid-calf, ending in delicate, deeply pleated flounces. Jovita's piano black hair curled and fell across the puff shoulders of her cream keyhole blouse. Her long sunflower-yellow skirt barely revealed the tops of her new burgundy boots.

For them and hundreds of others, this particular day was much more than a weekly shopping trip or market day. It was Palm Sunday, a day of religious high celebration that was observed as a social event. Shoppers, merchants and visitors, all shared the opportunity to enjoy the festive atmosphere, excitement and frivolity that pulsed through the streets.

A four-piece brass and percussion band performed in the slivers of shade underneath a half dozen acrocomia palms at the corner of Calle Atocha and Victoria. Dressed in carnival-colored slacks and white, puffed shirtsleeves, they played a stylized bolero. A yard or two away, two lovely señoritas stepped to a lively mazurka, flashing white lace underskirts, flaunting bouncing bosoms and fingering rhythmic castanets. The entire plaza was a resonating mass of humanity engaged in a festive, managed mayhem that only vaguely resembled commerce.

Not only fresh citrus and pineapples, but also crates of avocados, guavas, guineps, mangos, papayas, plantains, red bananas, and soursops were stacked, sorted and displayed throughout the produce market and open-air bazaar. Scattered among the farmers and grocers were crude storefronts made of used pallets and bits of scrap lumber, painted in flashy enamel or decorated with bits of bright fabric. From behind temporary countertops, tinkers and traders hawked all things imaginable, either tangible or edible.

The marketplace was a bulwark of individual enterprise in Ponce and acted as a commercial magnet, drawing small independent tradesmen, farmers and tinkers from miles away.

As two o'clock neared, Carilla and her daughter decided to stop at one of the vibrant outdoor cafés before they returned home. They set their multi-colored woven grass shopping baskets down next to their chairs and decided to enjoy a snack of fresh bacalaíto[**] cod cakes and share a bottle of Coco Rico coconut soda.

La Borinqueña (The Puerto Rican Girl) ...

A curious distraction arose partway through their meal. An out-of-tune marching band could be heard approaching from the south, and the brash sounds of tubas, drums and trumpets began to drift through Plaza del Mercado. It intensified, becoming louder and more spirited as the band neared. Within a few seconds, it became apparent that a parade was approaching.

The march had been coordinated by the Puerto Rican Nationalist Party[*] and had begun as a peaceful independence demonstration four blocks south on Calle Atocha, outside the Bank of Ponce. About one hundred revolutionary Cadets of the Republic, dressed in black uniforms, paraded alongside scores of field hands and dockworkers. Many of them came directly from the wharf and sugarcane plantations and wore short, wide-brimmed hats, and were dressed in the soiled and sweat-stained clothes of field hands. As they approached the market place, armed officers of the Insular Police Force blocked their path and closed ranks on the connecting streets and alleyways. The police had been ordered to prevent the demonstration from expanding beyond Calle Victoria and further into the city.

The marketplace became overspread with nervous, yet curious anticipation.

The black-shirted marchers in the front line carried their flags on high and proudly pointed them forward. The revolutionary flag of the Nationalist Party flew front and foremost: black with a centered, double-inverted swastika. The second line carried the outlawed red, white and blue flag of Puerto Rico.

The drum major proclaimed proudly and vehemently in English and Spanish, "Liberty and independence! ¡Independencia y la libertad!" Those words signaled the band to begin another raucous, revolutionary off-key canticle. The marching order had been well scripted.

As the music became louder and more intense, so did the protests demanding revolution and the liberation of Puerto Rico from the colonial rule of the United States.

Carilla stood, reached across the table and covered Jovita's hand, "I think we should leave."

In the two seconds that followed, the palm fronds and olive branches of Palm Sunday were set aflame. No sooner had the first stanza of *la Borinqueña*[**] begun, than the sound of gunfire silenced the music and closed the gates on the parade. In those singular instants, hundreds of lives were jostled and jolted upside down. Angry shouts, cries of alarm and screams for help boiled upward to a deaf sky. The frightening sounds of revolution and its violence had extinguished the band's rousing, patriotic march. The music of brass instruments was muted by the cracking thunder of lead bullets. Bats, bricks, sticks, machetes and pistols were no match against the automatic weapons and machine guns of the Insular Police.

Heart And Soul ...

Shoppers scrambled for refuge under carts, crawled on the cobbles or, like Carilla and Jovita, ran for their lives. Carilla grasped her daughter by the hand and fled the café, leaving their colorful baskets and market bounty behind.

A half dozen steps beyond their table, Carilla stumbled and fell to the ground like a sack of rocks, pulling Jovita down with her. Jovita dropped to the street next to her mother, her arm across her mother's back, her eyes scouring the bedlam surrounding them; searching, hoping for an end, a calm, a peace.

Fear began to worm its way into the mind of young Jovita. Dread began to flood and surge through her thoughts. She turned her head and whispered desperately into her mother's hair, "Mamá?"

The initial blaze of bullets had quieted, and changed to isolated bursts of Thompson machine guns, sporadic rapid-fire from automatic weapons and singular rifle shots. The trumpets were quiet. The drums were silent. The music had ended. There were calls for help, cries of anger and profane screams of protest. Men cursed. Women wept. Children cried. The acrid, ammonia-like smell of gunpowder rose over the marketplace like the mist off a pond. What was to become known as the Ponce Massacre[**] had ended nearly as quickly as it started. Senses were numbed. Palm Sunday was bloodied.

A heavy cloak of fear fell over Jovita. She felt a terrifying void, an eerie emptiness expanding deep within her bosom.

She fought back and dared to ask again, "Mamá?" Gently, she tried to jostle her mother. There was no response. Jovita cautiously, slowly raised her head, noticed blood, the torn dress and placed her mother's scarf over the wound. Cries of grief, anger and horror painted Palm Sunday black. Jovita looked around, and counted scores of bodies across the marketplace. She sat up and slowly, tenderly turned her mother over.

"¡Mamá, mi Mamá!"

Jovita's arms, wet with blood, cradled her mother's head to her breast. She wept. Her sobs cut so deep, so hard that her chest ached. Her breath tore through her lungs. The deepest love of Jovita's young life had been ripped from her heart.

Hours later, the Red Cross[**] was able to contact her father at the Punta Salinas Army base, which was located about thirty miles east of Ponce. Granted off-post privileges, Simón was able to take his daughter home to their two-room walkup on Calle las Flores just past two o'clock in the morning.

Aunt Agnes and Uncle Horado...

More than two hundred people died on Palm Sunday, March 21, 1937, in Ponce, Puerto Rico: men, women and one child. Governor General Blanton Winship kept the city under marshal law for two weeks following the violence.

On Holy Thursday, March 25, Carilla Pérez de Vasquello was buried at the Playa Methodist Church of Ponce on Calle Villa. For days after her mother's funeral, Jovita fought to maintain mental balance and endured a personal anguish that teetered between the emotions of youth and maturity. She struggled with the placement of blame, and wondered why such brutal consequence could be solely dependent on simple coincidence.

With some additional help from Army Special Services, her father, a staff sergeant in the Army Signal Corps, was able to get one week of Emergency Family Leave. *Emergency Leave* was just that: emergency. Simón had a year and two months remaining on his current enlistment and he was bound to the Army for the duration. Something needed to be done. Tragedy turns everyday life upside-down, and Jovita's father recognized that his wife's death had left a vacancy that he alone could not fill. The problem required an immediate solution. His closest blood relative provided one.

Simón's sister Agnes and her overbearing husband, Horado Pedreira, willingly offered to provide shelter and watch over Jovita until a more permanent solution could be found. The Pedreira family lived in Juana Díaz, a few miles east of Ponce where they operated a small bodega and a three-table sidewalk café on Calle Primo. It was agreed that Aunt Agnes and Uncle Horado would take on the role of guardians and Simón would contribute five dollars a month and cover any unforeseen expenses. Without any children of their own, Agnes and Horado welcomed their niece into their modest home situated above their colonial delicatessen and patio restaurant. Jovita could finish high school and learn the trade while helping with the day-to-day operation of the food shop and eatery.

Aunt Agnes was a practical, buxom woman of forty-three. She was straightforward, honest, had the laugh of a child and could swear and roll cigarettes like a sailor. Over the years, Jovita had enjoyed many family dinners, holiday and birthday celebrations at Aunt Agnes' small but efficient, second-story home above the store. Whether she was flipping fry cakes, scrambling eggs or cooking plantains on the griddle, serving coffee, or guava pastry, or wringing laundry in the back alley, Agnes always wore a smile. Jovita grew up believing that Aunt Agnes was a master in the kitchen and fun to be around. Her father oftentimes would refer to his sister as *Saint Agnes*, while inferring that she lived under Horado's thumb.

Fifty-year-old Uncle Horado was a massive, round man that Jovita pictured as the *Jack and the Beanstalk* giant. He had a pockmarked face, hands as big as baseball mitts, a huge protruding belly and a nose that rivaled a ripe mango. Jovita never paid much attention to him or his slanted opinions, because everything he said came sounded like *Fee-Fi-Fo-Fum*. Her mother was partly to blame for the opinion Jovita had of her uncle, having once said, 'I've never liked or trusted that man. He can't hold his rum and his eyes don't focus even when he's sober'.

Despite these character faults, Horado had a few redeeming qualities: a sense of humor, nothing but praise for his wife's cooking and he only smoked his short, stinky cigarillos outside.

After her mother's funeral, Jovita's father went back to the Army base and everything immediately changed. In particular, two days after Jovita moved in, uncle Horado laid claim to Carilla's tabletop radio, and began to sell her clothes and shoes on the sidewalk in front of the bodega. Horado loaded most of the Vasquello furniture and household goods onto a two-donkey wooden wagon and delivered them to a pawnshop in Castello.

After Easter Week, Jovita attempted to re-start her life. She soon realized how much she missed that radio and the way things used to be.

Daddy, Won't You Please Come Home? ...

Although nearly everything was new to her, Jovita's daily routine quickly became predictable, mundane and tiresome. The bus ride to and from Ponce high school in barrio Tercero, was a dusty, rough forty-five minute trip that was not just for commuters and school students. The bus was cheap, five cents per round trip municipal transportation that was available to all passengers, including farm hands, cane cutters, chickens and the occasional goat. Jovita left the apartment at six in the morning and completed the return trip ten hours later. When she returned in late afternoon, she had time to help out at the café or bodega, either sweeping the tile floors and sidewalk or washing dishes.

The apartment above the store was cramped, dated and full of street noise. Jovita was relegated to a tiny six by eight foot windowless room off the kitchen that had a multi-colored, woven cotton blanket as a door. It was large enough for one small, square, open bedside table with capacity for a few folded clothes. Her narrow bed had a two-inch straw mattress atop a handmade wooden frame. A small kerosene lamp hung on the wall near the doorway.

On Saturdays after dinner, Agnes would go downstairs and prepare sweet custards, mantecadito* cookies and quesitos* for sale on Sunday noon. It was a decades-old ritual that she had claimed as her own. The café kitchen was her private getaway.

Uncle Horado would then take the opportunity to walk to his private retreat, a bar called *Cantina Toledo* on Calle Dorado. There he would play a few hands of pinochle, talk about baseball, the independence movement, how the Americans controlled their lives and the communist revolutionaries. He would also drink his belly full of spiced coquito, a potent punch of coconut milk, vanilla and sugar cane alcohol.

On one particular Saturday evening in early May, Jovita sat at the kitchen table under the limited light of a single 40-watt bulb that hung from the ceiling. She sat in the company of her daydreams, sadly aware that only one week of school remained before summer recess. In years past, she and her parents would take small trips to the shore, or spend a day or two camping in the wild, rugged interior of the island. She allowed her thoughts to drift away through time, back to when she could laugh aloud. Although her father was about a half-hour away in Punta Salinas, he was only able to get off-post privileges one weekend per month. She had decided to write and ask if they could do something special together the next time he came home.

Two sentences into her letter, uncle Horado opened the kitchen door, locked his eyes on her and walked to the table like a cat stalking a mouse. Jovita was surprised, wondering what could be amiss, and set her pencil down. She hadn't heard him trudging up the steps as he normally did. He had returned home early, and didn't appear to be quite as tipsy as he usually was after a visit to Cantina Toledo. He grinned wide and flashed his tobacco-brown teeth as he spoke, "Jovita, my lovely girl. You bring back my youth. You look so much like your mother, you excite me."

He bent at the waist, and put a big hand on the table to steady himself. He leaned in and tried to place a wet kiss on his niece's lips. She turned away, repulsed not only by his words and actions, but also his putrid breath that stunk like a wet dog and cigars.

In an instant, he grabbed her with one gigantic arm across her shoulders and chest, pulled her away from the table and jammed his filthy red kerchief into her mouth. She kicked backward at him, her legs flashing out in a frenzy. Horado scooped her up, locked her thighs to him with his free arm and carried her to her little room. It was unimaginable horror. Her heart felt like it was about to fly from her breast. She writhed, struggled and twisted in vain against his brutish strength. His whisper was a muffled growl that came from deep within his chest, "I love you, my darling Carilla. My lovely little Carilla Jovita de Vasquello." The last thing she could recall was his closed fist smacking the side of her head.

When Jovita awoke from what she hoped was a nightmarish dream, her muscles tensed with defiance and her thoughts became electrified. In a nervous frenzy, her eyes scanned the walls, ceiling and floor of her dark little room. She was alone. She shuddered from her shoulders to her toes and saw that her blouse had been unbuttoned. Her white cotton brassiere was on, but pulled up and off her breasts. Except for the muffled street noise of Saturday night, it was quiet. Her trembling hands went to her thighs and she discovered that her skirt had been lifted above her knees. She looked around the room again and discovered that her socks and underpants were off and lying on the floor beside her bed. Jovita whispered her torment, *"Oh my God."*

She had a pulsating headache. She glanced at her Westclox alarm clock on the small table. The soft green, luminous hands indicated seven-thirty. She thought, *"Aunt Agnes will be coming up the stairs soon."* She was worried, not about herself, but what her aunt might see and imagine.

Her eyes nervously scoured her room one more time. She thought about Horado's handkerchief in her mouth, gagged and somehow withheld the urge to retch. She vowed that she would not be his victim again.

She fixed her eyes above her bed, somewhere on the fuzzy shadows of the ceiling. Her body quaked to her core as she started to slip a hand up and under her skirt. She calmed as she moved it closer and softly, slowly felt around her femininity, pressing, checking, for what she could not know. Jovita didn't hurt or find anything that didn't belong. She took a breath, mustered courage and dared to feel just inside with two fingers. She had no idea what she could be searching for, only that she had heard that men could leave an awful wet mess when they spill their seed. Jovita found nothing and nothing can be very disconcerting when you are searching for something. In this case, she felt only confusion mixed with horror. It was worry she had never known.

Her head spun with revulsion, fears and wicked thoughts. In spite of her fear, she strained to remember what had happened, hoping it would quiet her raging imagination. But, try as she might, nothing came to mind. Her mental turmoil receded and she thought, *"Thank Heaven I can't remember anything."*

She knew for certain that she needed a way to protect herself from any further unwanted attention from Horado, and had a flash of an idea. With frantic determination, she readjusted her brassiere, skirt and blouse, pulled on her socks and underpants and got out of bed. She stepped to the doorway, pulled the blanket aside and peeked outside to the kitchen.

With relief she discovered, *"He's not here."* Cautiously and on tiptoe, she took five steps into the kitchen. She scooped up a paring knife from the drawer, two light bulbs from the cupboard under the sink, then scurried back to her room and squirreled her bounty under her pillow.

She walked to the restroom and placed her hand on the white porcelain knob. She held her breath, opened the door, stepped inside and locked it behind her. Jovita frantically brushed her teeth with Ipana paste and spat into the toilet. She then eased down, sat on the wobbly seat and peed. She let out a deep sigh, pulled the chain on the water closet and watched the swirling water gurgle down and away. She felt relief, as if she had completely flushed away his touch and rancid breath.

The right side of her head felt warm to her touch and it hurt. She held her face in her hands and quietly wept, wondering, *"Oh, God ... what do I do now? What will happen?"*

Moments passed unnoticed before she stood staring into the brown, stained mirror at her reflection. She saw the smeared, red Coty lipstick and dried tears on her cheeks. She worried, *"Maybe I brought this on myself"* but quickly discounted that idea as rubbish. Carilla had told her, "You are beautiful and men will want you. But you have the right to choose who will touch you." Her mother was right. But Horado was not only an oaf, Jovita now knew him to be the devil incarnate.

She rolled off a wad of toilet tissue to wipe her face clean and concluded that without a doubt, her uncle was a filthy, old sewer rat and what had happened could not be blamed on two cents worth of makeup from a Rexall drug store.

She didn't have the time or patience to heat up a pot of hot water for the sink. Jovita remained in the tiny lavatory and let the tap run until the wash basin began to fill. The violated young woman hurriedly washed and rewashed in cold water with a sliver of Ivory bar soap, rinsed and rinsed again until she heard someone coming up the stairs.

She further tormented herself, *"I can't say anything about this. I just can't. I can't tell anyone. No one would believe me, even if I become pregnant. Maybe he just looked and felt and touched."*

Her aunt called out, "Jovita! I'm home, my darling!"

Aunt Agnes always brought some fresh-baked sweets up from the café.

Running a brush through her hair, she answered, "I'll be out in a minute, Aunt Agnes. Just one minute." Her stomach churned. Her skin crawled with the thought of the lies and disgusting deceptions to come.

That evening, Jovita ate only one small guava and cream cheese quesito for her snack. Agnes did notice that something was amiss and accepted her niece's excuse of a headache. It wasn't a lie.

By nine o'clock, Jovita was back in her bedroom preparing her defenses. She put the light bulbs inside a pair of socks, smashed them to bits and spread them on the floor next to her bed. The plan was to clean them up in the morning, and repeat the routine every day until she was able to leave. She wanted to leave, badly. She hid the knife just under the edge of her mattress and resolved that if it should happen again, she would at least wound him.

Horado stumbled up the stairs about half past ten. He was undoubtedly pickled* on a belly full of coquito. Jovita noticed that he had changed to his other pair of trousers.

Jovita didn't sleep well that night, if at all. She tossed and turned, wiggled and squirmed, stared at the ceiling, silently wept and used a hand towel to wipe away what felt like an ocean of tears.

"This is Hell. Pure Hell." She surrendered to the concept of total silence, accepted the hole in her heart and knew she would likely take this private horror to her grave.

Jovita feigned a stomach ache the following day and skipped Sunday services at First Methodist. Instead, she finished the letter to her father. She found it not only distressing, but painful to refrain from telling her father everything.

The three weeks that followed her spoiling at the hands of Horado were indeed hell for Jovita to bear. She avoided his feeble attempts at conversation, refused to make eye contact, and tried her best to give him ten yards of elbow room. Her assessment of life as a lie was correct: it was hell. She could only hope that somehow, someday her torment would come to an end. The days dragged by drudgingly and the words between Horado and Jovita were limited to short, terse exchanges. Early on, Agnes had recognized the tension between them and asked what the problem was.

Jovita blandly replied, "I'm still upset about my mother's radio."

Horado needed to retort, "You don't even have electric in that rat's nest that I keep for you. And besides, you don't know how to dance, do you?"

Her skin crawled. Jovita couldn't remember the exact words she used to express herself in the letter she had written to her father weeks earlier. She could only continue to plot and plan her imagined escape and pray, *"Papa, oh Papa, please come home soon."*

The first week of June arrived with some sense of relief for Jovita. She had her monthly flow.

Panama ...
June, 1938 – May, 1942

On Friday, June 18, Simón Fernando Vasquello walked into the bodega on Calle Primo, dropped his duffle and hugged his daughter. Emotion overflowed and tears of relief rolled down Jovita's cheeks.

They sat at one of the outdoor tables with iced bottles of malta[*] and a lunch of mortadella[*] on fresh rolls. When her father said he had news, her heart fluttered and her hopes took flight.

"When your mama was killed, you knew I had to do something. Your stay here was necessary, but temporary. Things change, they always do, and sometimes, good things and good change takes more time. I had to think about everything that I could possibly do for us, and I think that I have made the right decision, Jovita, my daughter. I think you will like what I have done. We will go to Panama and we will be together. Together. You and I. I know you cannot stay here, and I do love my sister, but this place is no bigger than a closet with a toilet. And he may seem harmless, but I think your uncle Horado is pendejo[*]. I don't know why Agnes agreed to take him for a husband."

"Horado's not pendejo, Papa. He is very pendejo. And he kept Mama's radio from me." Jovita's ardent tone troubled her father.

They looked at one another for a moment. Simón smiled and chuckled, "I'll buy you a new one, my daughter."

His reassuring voice comforted Jovita and momentarily tempted her to confide in him. She thought, *"If he only knew, Papa would kill him. He would go inside, grab him by the throat and kill him."* She decided to say nothing, to spare her father the torment and the consequences. She stood and stepped to her father. She dropped to a knee and held him, "Papa, oh Papa, thank you! Tell me about Panama, please tell me!"

Simón went on to explain that he had reenlisted and received an overseas assignment to the Canal Zone** with on-post dependent housing. Their new home would be at the joint forces base on the Caribbean side of the canal at Cristóbal, Colón, Panama. Since 1914, the War Department had recognized the importance of a secure passageway between the Atlantic and Pacific Oceans and because of recent rumblings in Europe, the Army's Signal Corps outposts were being updated.

The Spanish Civil War was being fought throughout the Iberian Peninsula with fervor, stirring up war clouds all over Europe and spreading worldwide concern of another Great War. The presence of a strong United States military in Latin America became an important part of President Roosevelt's foreign policy. The Signal Corps and military personnel fluent in Spanish, were quickly recognized as valuable assets. Staff Sergeant Simón Vasquello's new duty station was the largest listening post for German, Spanish and Italian chatter in the Western Hemisphere.

The American base at Cristóbal was much newer, cleaner, refined and urban than her childhood home of Ponce, Puerto Rico, and sat isolated like an island of civilization surrounded by a sea of tropical rainforest.

The next year flew by. Jovita did very well at school and received a diploma with high honors from the Army's highly accredited Cristóbal American High School in August, 1938. She was accepted into the winter semester freshman class at Louisiana State University, Baton Rouge. Jovita's high school standing, Canal Zone scholarship and the Department of the Army all had significant influence on the admissions decision. A childhood dream of setting foot on the continental United States had come true.

Baton Rouge, Louisiana gave Jovita a cultural shock she could not have imagined. When she saw Billy Ray Wilkins' Ford dealership on Perkins Road, she realized how much her world and her role in it had changed. Growing up in Puerto Rico or going to school in Panama, she never dreamed of a store with gigantic picture windows that sold automobiles.

Jovita kept her life at Louisiana State strictly academic, and she purposely limited her social exposure. The incident with her uncle Horado was the driving force behind her lifestyle choice. She kept herself within a tightly wrapped cocoon of self-imposed social isolation at the university and kept very few friends, none of them close.

In the spring of 1940, her junior year at LSU, Jovita was recruited by the Army Intelligence Service. Without doubt, her father's duties in the Signal Corps had triggered the initiation of a background check, her preliminary interview and resulting procurement. She was fast-tracked and received a degree in Social Sciences from the university in October, 1941, two months prior to the entry of the United States into World War II. Simón hopped a military transport to Shreveport and attended her graduation. Afterwards, Jovita had a brief two-day reunion with her father before he had to return to duty at the joint Army-Navy base in Colón, Panama.

Upon her graduation from LSU, Jovita was assigned to Army Intelligence School at Fort Polk, Louisiana, where she would spend the following six months in basic service training. Jovita experienced only a slight measure of culture shock when she moved from Panama to LSU and on to Fort Polk. More than the heat and humidity had followed her. She had finished her high school education in Panama, on an American military installation and she was quite familiar with Army life. Besides tedious classroom, cryptograph and ciphering work, the Fort Polk trainees attended seemingly never-ending service orientations, seminars, mission overviews, briefings, motivational workshops and viewed captured Axis propaganda films. She and the others in her platoon were soon running five miles daily, swinging on monkey bars and swimming fifty meter laps. Inspiration and ability varied among the cadets, but wartime patriotism sustained their efforts.

There were life lessons learned, but no lasting friendships made. So much needed to be mastered so quickly, that there simply was not enough time for socializing. However, Captain Angus Munson was the singular cadre instructor who left an impression that she would never forget. Less than a week into the training, Munson dramatically influenced the young woman's life as he burned a brand upon her that she would carry from that day forward. Initially, he had nicknamed her *José*, but it wasn't long before he changed it to *Joey*. Jovita disliked both nicknames at first, but gradually accepted *Joey*. She pointedly refused to respond to *José*.

At Fort Polk, the rigid routine and focused curriculum of a cloistered military school was not an unfamiliar experience for Jovita. Although the base was situated about 1600 miles north, Louisiana's climate did not vary much from that in Panama. She adjusted well during her training, likely due to her life at the Joint Base, Colón. She was an exceptional trainee and put concerted effort into every lesson assigned and every task ordered. Her segregated[**] entry class of 30 cadets (26 men and 4 women) consisted of six squads: five male and one female. Housing was segregated also, but weapons familiarization was the singular difference between the training of the men and women. While every cadet received safety orientation, basic maintenance and hands-on instruction with various types of firearms, it was men-only at the shooting range. At graduation, 20 men and 3 women advanced to specialized intelligence training.

After the commencement ceremony there was an informal gathering for the class at the Officers' Club with hors d'oeuvres and drinks – the first social event of any kind in six months. Jovita casually mentioned to her cadre advisor that statistically, the women had outperformed the men, and if given the chance, they could do the same on the firing range and boldly challenged Captain Angus Munson to a target shoot. She was teasing, of course, but it appeared that her off-the-cuff remarks offended him. He moved one step closer and stood nose-to-nose with her. Jovita curled her lips into a coy smile. Munson signaled that he wasn't amused. The clock seemed to have stopped.

She heard the squish. Instantly, she knew that she had stepped in a big, steaming pile of crap, and every eye in the room saw it happen. Silently, the room gasped. Her classmates knew that she was knee-deep in muck.

Standing at five feet, eleven inches, Munson was perhaps two inches taller than Jovita, thirty pounds heavier and at least five years her senior. He had curly, dark brown hair and cold, steel-hardened eyes. Over the previous half-year of training, he had proven himself to be a by-the-book, straightforward instructor and barracks sergeant. Jovita thought she was about to receive a stern verbal retort. She certainly did not expect a harsh rebuttal to her innocent statement of fact and playful supposition. She was about to get one.

He spoke loud enough for every ear in the room to hear his words, "I appreciate your candor, Graduate Cadet Vasquello. You were, in fact, correct when you pointed out that women have some ability to compete equally alongside and, on a rare occasion, outperform their male counterparts. My male cadet trainees, however, DO outshine at following orders and respecting their superiors." Everyone in the room awaited more.

Munson gave them what they wanted, "Even today, after training has ended, there is a lesson to be learned here. It's simple, Cadet Joey: braggadocio is not an admirable trait for a young woman OR a Graduate Cadet. For example, if Joan of Arc were born as a man, she would be just another mediocre French soldier and not flashy footnote in history books. Furthermore, throughout my years of experience, I have discovered that there are indeed, several things that a woman simply cannot do. One of them is the ability to piss their name in the dirt, Joe."

A wave of whispers calmed to a murmur, then silence. She still respected Angus Munson, but at that moment, she decided that she didn't like him or her newly abbreviated nickname. He had always made her feel uncomfortable, but now he became a sharp rock in her shoe rather than an annoying pebble.

She learned an important lesson that day: don't pick a fight with a mouth breather, feral pig or any other creature with a vocabulary limited to grunts or bodily sounds. She believed that Angus Munson fit at least two of those categories.

The following morning, Jovita left Army Intelligence School as a commissioned First Lieutenant in the Military Intelligence Service. She was proud of her Army pink and green** uniform and its shiny silver bars, but unhappy with the fit. An unforeseen remedy was in the wind, and she wouldn't be wearing it for long.

Change was coming.

Hot And Anxious …
Area RTU-11, OSS training facility,
(near) Alexandria, Virginia,
June, 1942

Upon her graduation from Fort Polk, Jovita alone was issued orders for further training at RTU-11, the newest OSS[**] facility. Affectionately known as *The Farm* because of its rural setting, the exact location of Area RTU-11 remained unknown to those who had never been there and factually, to some who actually had.

Her orders simply stated that she would fly via Army Air Corps transport to Langley Army Air Field, Virginia, where she was to receive specialized training for Intelligence Services, Personnel Analysis and Procurement. She was relieved to discover that Captain Angus Munson would not be at The Farm.

The remainder of her graduating class was spread with the wind to other OSS training sites scattered across the country, many of which were also isolated installations hidden away in the vast wilderness of America's national parks[**].

Jovita was excited beyond words, beaming with pride, yet still disappointed. She knew her mother would have been very proud of her, and unfortunately, her father couldn't witness her commission ceremony either. The war had put him in a new duty station half a world away in Hawaii. Her sadness and loneliness quickly gave way to scalp-tingling anticipation. The mystique surrounding her next assignment, the undisclosed location and inspiration she experienced after graduation fed her fantasy of becoming America's answer to Mata Hari[**].

The bone-rattling, noisy transportation from Alexandria Army Air Field, Louisiana, did not dampen her spirits, nor did the thunderous, weather-jostled flight. She sat alone inside the aluminum and steel shell of a twin engine, six-passenger Beechcraft C-45 Expeditor[**]. The solitude was soothing, and allowed her thoughts to wander. She could barely catch a glimpse of the pilot and copilot at their seats in the cockpit. She wondered if they really were pilots or merely bus drivers on unmapped roads of air. A memory brought a smile. Her father once joked that pilots were nothing more than little boys trying to throw their paper airplanes the furthest. Jovita sat alone with her daydreams for six hours.

Upon arrival in Virginia, she was met with darkness and drizzle. At the foot of the boarding ladder, two figures in dark raincoats and fedoras awaited. One took her bags and the other said, "Welcome to Langley Army Air Field, ma'am. We have a few more miles to go, so please follow me, Lieutenant."

She was whisked away in the back of a windowless, olive green, 1940 Ford panel truck. It was at that moment that she positively knew her destination.

It was a secret.

At daybreak, the day following her arrival in Virginia, Jovita discovered that she was no longer on an Army base. The Farm was literally Main Street, USA: drugstore, five-and-dime, grocery, delicatessen, butcher, movie house, hardware, dry goods, bakery, department store ... everything America. The storefronts were generic, but all the wares were brand name. She was no longer in barrack housing, but assigned a second-floor room in a two-story women's dormitory that could compare to be a hotel without staff. The food was markedly better than cadet school at Fort Polk, the level of privacy increased a thousandfold, and she was told to *ditch the GI* duds and given a clothing allowance. Her rank of Lieutenant 02 became pay grade Agent L9. She had worn army green for six months and two days.

Notwithstanding textbook and lecture hall dissertations on ethics and personal codes of conduct, her time in Virginia wasn't bare-boned instruction, but rather functional training in the efficient tasking, apportionment and delegation of assignments.

Her surroundings were no longer austere, olive drab or strictly military. Life at The Farm was much like that at LSU, but unlike the real world* outside, there were no wartime ration books. Everything from butter to beef and soap to silk was available.

Two months after her arrival, Jovita forged a casual twenty-four hour friendship with a French woman, Aspirant Renée-Ffion Delacroix, one of a group of Free French DGER**, who had just finished intense covert insurgency training. The group had ended their secretive quarantine at Area 16 and for the first time in three months was allowed to mingle with other residents of The Farm.

Their eyes met while they were standing in the ticket line at the Silver Star Cinema. Smiles led to conversation. They bought their tickets, learned to pronounce each other's name, laughed and found seats in the center of a middle row inside the darkened theater. Between sips of Royal Crown cola and nibbles on Baby Ruth candy bars, they exchanged whispers of gossip and talk of movie stars.

After a fifteen-minute Castle Films newsreel of the April, 1942 Doolittle Raid** over Tokyo, the comedy feature *Her Cardboard Lover*, starring Robert Taylor and Norma Shearer, flickered across the silver screen. Ninety-three minutes later, when the final credits were rolling, Renée placed a warm hand on her neighbor's knee and smoothly slipped her fingers just under the hemline and onto the inner thigh. Jovita found it surprisingly pleasant. The gentleness of the touch bore no resemblance to Horado's brutish pawing. Jovita's heart throbbed and her thoughts raced into a taboo erotic adventure.

They ordered milkshakes and burgers at the City Diner and were barely able to hurriedly finish half. By eight-thirty they were alone and sharing Renée's bed at the dormitory. For Jovita, it may as well have been Paris. She was on an adventure, visiting somewhere she had never been before.

The following morning, they awoke together and opened their eyes to find one another. Renée's lips glistened; her scent spilled off her shoulders, across the pillows and onto Jovita's being. Their lips barely touched when, with enlivened desire, Jovita smoothed a hand gently across her lover's breasts. They were modest in size and each could scarcely fill a champagne glass. Renée's nipples stood firm and proud, like the cut stem of a pomegranate.

Renée kissed Jovita softly on the lips, got out of bed and walked to the bathroom. In that moment, Renée appeared as sensual as Aphrodite and moved with the grace of Diana. Her skin was as smooth, white as Tuscan alabaster and her legs as long, and fresh as the first day of spring.

For the first time ever, Jovita was aware of her own sexuality and affirmed she was able to experience passion. She had never felt this way before, and toyed with the idea that this must be infatuation. It was satisfying to feel good, refreshed; to wake up and feel alive, vibrant and renewed. Thinking of the redhead in the next room made her fingertips and toes tingle. Her senses sparkled, but she couldn't explain the chill that suddenly and strangely caused her to shudder. She worried they would be discovered and immediately scolded her foolish thought, but the dread remained.

Jovita looked around. The bed sheets lying across her breasts and belly were twisted, tangled and askew. Her bare legs were outside the covers. The morning sun sliced through the vertical window blinds and made a shadow on the far wall that resembled prison bars. She heard the water running in the bathroom, and imagined the smell of Ivory soap and the freezing chill of cold water from years earlier.

The old nightmare returned; a sense of fear blanketed her and completely darkened the room. It covered her fading ecstasy, and she could not be sure if the fantasy had ended or her memory failed. Her retention of what had occurred during the night became fragmented. Bits and pieces of lust and loving were scattered like dandelion tuft in a warm breeze. Jovita fought the fear of forbidden hunger and illicit thirst. She felt torn by joy, guilt and painful memories.

For the second time her consciousness had failed her, and again she became traumatized by what she refused to recall. She worried if this was normal, or if she was somehow flawed. This morning-after, marshmallow-soft, spongy feeling terrified her. What bits she remembered were nothing like the poetry or novels she'd read and they had an uncomfortable fit.

She slowly moved her hand under the sheet, along her belly and cautiously between her legs. She felt her dewy warmth, remembered Renée's kisses, then Horado, shuddered again with a mixture of joy and dread, and sprang from the bed. Hurriedly she pulled her dress over her head, jostled her hair and scooped up her shoes, socks, brassiere and panties. She scurried on tiptoe across the wooden floor and out the door. She gave no time to consider who or what could be in the hall, and desired only to leave her lurid slivers of memory behind with Renée-Ffion Delacroix.

Although she was barefoot, she was cautiously quiet and felt extremely uncomfortable walking on tip-toe back to her room. She felt pressured and pinched, as if she was wearing a new pair of shoes, one size too small and on the wrong feet. As soon as she got inside her sanctuary and locked the door behind her, she vowed to never again spend the night with a Renée-Ffion. Those shoes just didn't fit and she couldn't remember when, where or why she got them. However, no one could ever say she didn't at least try them on.

For the next five days, Jovita went out of her way to avoid seeing Mademoiselle Delacroix. She made a game of it, wore dark glasses and kept her hair up and under a large brimmed hat. Jovita considered it good undercover training.

One week later, Aspirant Delacroix finished her concealment, ordinance and tactical weaponry training. She and six other French agents left The Farm for New York City and a troop/supply ship convoy steaming to the United Kingdom. In spite of a promise to write, Jovita would not hear from Renée until more than a decade later.

Jovita spent the next eighteen months at The Farm, perfecting her skills in Spanish linguistics, dialects and regional colloquialisms. In February, 1944, she got a three-grade promotion to L-12 and her first field assignment. She was stationed at the American Consulate, Via Blanca, Havana, Cuba until the Japanese surrender in August of 1945.

Her eighteen-month tour of duty in Cuba coincided with Operation Bolívar, the allied effort to destroy Nazi Germany's extensive spy ring and radio network in Central and South America. The end of the war and the success of Operation Bolívar earned Jovita a generous bump in grade and an assignment to Chicago, Illinois.

She was tasked as Deputy Operations Supervisor, Latin American Enterprise. When she discovered that Senior Field Agent Angus Munson was her immediate subordinate, she was exuberant. Her education had paid off, in a way that she'd never considered possible.

On Monday, April 1, 1946, Jovita met her first recruit, Colonel Nicholas Throckmorton at the Twin Anchors bar; a front for Central Intelligence located on South Canal Street, Chicago, Illinois. Three days earlier, he had been discharged at the rank of major after eight years in the Army Air Corps; the last five and a half as a fighter pilot in the Southwest Pacific.

After brief introductions and a preliminary briefing, Jovita gave him his initial assignment orders and instructed him to report to 537 Corinth Street, Jacksonville, Florida, no later than noon Sunday, April 14. She explained that she would fill him in on the details after he arrived.

South America, Take It Away …
Jacksonville, Florida
Wednesday, April 10, 1946

Nicholas took one last draw on his cigarette, dropped and twisted it into the sidewalk. The warmth of the spring sun radiated onto his shoulders.

Three cars were parked on Corinth, and a half dozen more around the corner on Doris. He pushed the heavy green, wooden door and took a few steps inside Fernando's Havana Hideaway, stopped, removed his sunglasses and stuck them in his jacket pocket. He waited a few seconds for his eyes to adjust to the murky, smoky shadows of the barroom and wondered why the bright Florida sun was so unwelcome inside this particular den of drink. More from habit than necessity, he glanced at his watch. The olive-green hands pointed at one o'clock ... on the dot.

Inside, the place was drenched with the smell of beer, cigarettes and Spic and Span. There were five other men in the drinkery – four at the bar and one behind it. His leather soles tapped across the tile floor to the bar. The Wurlitzer jukebox was running a needle through Bob Wills' version of 'Sitting on top of the World'. Nick stood at the end of the bar.

The bartender blandly prodded, "What are you having, buddy?"

"I'm looking for Joey. I'm Nick."

The barman nodded and said, "I'll tell her you're here." He turned, took ten steps and disappeared through a doorway.

Nick studied the place, his eyes covering every board, tile and corner. The four at the bar were scattered: two apart, two together and promptly classified as: one Sears and Roebuck suit, one mechanic's coverall and two work-a-days. His eggshell white, summer linen suit didn't fit in. He loosened his tie and resolved, *"I suppose it makes some sort of business sense to run your spy operation from a gin joint, be it either Chicago or Jacksonville."*

The bartender motioned him down to the end, lifted the hinged pass-through, pointed down a short, narrow hallway and added, "Second door on the right ... knock and go right in."

Nick was looking forward to seeing Jovita at least one more time. He knew she was younger than he by at least ten years. Back in Chicago, she pointed out that at thirty-seven, he was the silverback gorilla in the room. She had woven a mystic tapestry at their last meeting, and had left him with more questions than she had given him answers.

He walked down the hall pondering his immediate fate and what she could have planned for him. He knocked twice then heard, "Come in."

The brass knob turned with precision under his grasp. The door shut firmly behind him with a decisive click of hardware. She stood behind a polished black desk and watched him step across the aged pine floorboards toward her. She motioned to the larger of two wooden chairs in front of her desk, "Have a seat," and gave a brief, firm handshake before she sat. She watched intently as he set his frame into the wooden armchair. She studied his weathered complexion, steely eyes and dark curly hair. From his appearance and manner, Jovita assumed that he would be a formidable opponent in any physical confrontation. Additionally, from her study of his personnel file and military record, she believed that he could be a trusted and reliable asset in her growing team of agents.

Nick studied his surroundings. Her office was about fifteen feet square, painted in a flat, dark, rich, indigo blue. It could have been a waiting room, or doctor's office. It was full of deep shadows; there were no windows and the only light came from the desk lamp. An 11 X 17-inch photograph of President Truman and gigantic map of the Western Hemisphere hung on the wall behind her desk. The map was full color, in super detail, and showed everything from Barrow, Alaska to Tierra del Fuego, Argentina. Her workstation had a wide desk lamp, a cup with a few pencils, Biro and Eversharp ballpoints**, a pen and inkwell, and a large leather and felt desk pad. There was a large sofa against the wall with a matching chair cocked at an angle. Next to the divan was an end table with a lamp. A freestanding floor lamp stood guard in the far corner. The near corner was home to a file cabinet with a Big Ben wall clock hanging proudly above it.

It was less than two weeks since they first met and of course, she hadn't changed. Just as he remembered, her jet-black hair gently fell over her shoulders and cocoa eyes glistened. She had Mediterranean features, soft bronze skin and a presence that oozed confidence. "How was your trip from Detroit?"

"Fine. No bumps, no bruises. I got in last night."

"Last evening to be correct. 1830 hours to be exact."

He retained his thought, "*This is outstanding. I got a broad for a chief and already she's looking over my damn shoulder.*" He followed that errant thought with, "That's right, Joey. I know specifics are important. I know that. I got lost in the semantics, that's all."

He paused and asked, "How do I address you?"

"My official, paper title is *Deputy Operations Supervisor Vasquello*. Unofficially, it's *Boss*. Here in the outside world, it's either Jovita or Joey. Unless you or I are outside in legend[*] ... undercover or with a false identity. Got it?"

"Yes, Boss. How do I know when you're addressing me?"

With only a hint of a smile, she answered, "You'll know ... but right now I have a couple things to go over, just to make sure you, me and the Group are on the same page, OK?"

"Sure. You're the boss." Nick noticed that her Latin accent had disappeared. It was as if she could turn the faucet on or off and let it run hot, cold or middling.

It was their second meeting, and she needed to let him know straightaway who the boss was, "Like we discussed in Chicago, the Group has arranged for the Army to notify your wife, Nora, on June the first, in a few weeks, that you were reported as 'missing air crew' and are listed as Missing In Action. And I continue to assume you're OK with that?"

"Yes. That way she'll keep drawing my pay and allowances. And I do not have any intention of making contact. I have made my peace with the situation as it is."

Her tone was formal, almost mechanical, "Well, that's fine, well and good, Nicholas, but understand that you're still married ... you, indeed, seem to have broken completely away from your family ties ... and if you're comfortable with that ... well ... that's a good thing. The absence of strong bonds to a former life is generally considered prerequisite for field work in Central Intelligence.

"I've studied your profile, your dossier, your personnel folder, if you will. And, long before I met you, long before you were first recruited, the Group knew that your fly-by-night marriage had been stuck in the Ice Age since your wedding vows. They also knew that your brother, Leopold, both parents and your three sisters had passed. And they further discovered that ten years ago, back in 1936, you happened to be in Buffalo when an old Mafioso[*] was murdered ... the same Mafioso who was implicated in the deaths of your mother and sisters."

He teased her, "You've been reading my mail, haven't you?" He could feel her eyes peering inside him, searching for secrets, studying his features and memorizing the lines on his face. He assured himself, *"Nothing gets by this woman."*

She was straightforward, "I haven't been reading your mail, Nick, but I'm sure Central Intelligence has. It's their job. You're here where you are, sitting in front of me, because of who you are. They picked you.

"When you were in Burma and smuggling jade from Siam into Hong Kong, who did you think you were working for? Yourself? The Air Corps? The Brits?

"I'll tell you a few things you don't know, Agent Throckmorton ... those British officers who paid you cash for the stones weren't running a smuggling operation; they were Section D, British Intelligence. The stones that you and your wingman McElvoy snuck into China helped finance their Hong Kong espionage network. What's more, you flew around with a sophisticated Army Intelligence camera in the cockpit of your fighter plane. Every single photograph of every Jap position, Jap aircraft, Jap or Chinese airfield that you snapped ended up on the desks of Allied analysts all over the Pacific Theater.

"You've been acting as an agent for years, and didn't know it. And now that you've found out about it, and agreed to it, you're in deeper than ever. I discovered early on that the Group knows more about us than we know about ourselves. It goes without saying. It's their business. *Intelligence* is their middle name. You need to settle into your new life.

"So, I simply need to make sure that you're still agreeable to the *Missing In Action* telegram to your wife."

"I am. She'll get paid. Nora's been a good mother to our son."

She pressed him, "And what about your son, Alexander?"

A second or two passed, "He's eighteen ... a grown man. His mother did a good job and he'll be fine. His whole life ... if you add it all up and string the days together ... I've been with him, maybe, for six months ... a year ... tops. He don't know me."

There was another pause before he continued, "I'm not making any bones about it … I'm giving it to you straight ... the Service is my home … whether I'm spying or flying ... it's been all I've known since I signed on back in '38. I left my life in Detroit to serve my country and I've been happy doing just that ever since. At one time, I thought I could use the wind and clouds to build a home for my wife and son, but a problem arose when I tried to nail down the roof.

"It's hard to explain, but I think everybody needs a foundation to build upon; a sense of permanence … a feeling of security ... a feeling of purpose. For me, for years it was the Air Corps, and now it's the Group ... and serving my country. That's what I do ... this is where I live ... and this is who I am."

She stood. He stood. She extended her hand, "Good. We understand each other. Pleased to meet you, Field Agent Throckmorton."

"Thank you, Boss."

"A drink?" Her eyes motioned toward the wall.

"Sure, thank you." He stood and watched her walk to the filing cabinet. She was wearing a tailored red, square-shouldered blouse with a wide revere collar, and a navy blue skirt. The seams along the back of her hose ran straight and true. *"Perfect,"* he thought.

She set a nearly full bottle of Don Q Añejo rum and two glasses on the desk. He watched her pour and noticed the top two buttons of her blouse were undone. He scolded himself for being presumptuous, but continued to enjoy the view.

She toasted, "To the Group."

He replied, "To the mission, Boss." He waited for a reaction, and got one.

"Yes, to the mission." The corner of her mouth curled ever so slightly upward before she spoke, "Yes, indeed, Agent Throckmorton. The mission. But first, let's appreciate this rum."

"Puerto Rican, isn't it? Are you Puerto Rican, Joey?"

The time between his question and her answer was razor thin.

Her strictly-business demeanor returned, but she toyed with him. She formed her words from crimson lips, "Yes, it's Puerto Rican rum. And to your second question, I've spent some time in Puerto Rico, but I'm an American. I'm not from anywhere. I'm here. I've also spent time in Panama and Cuba and Columbia and Costa Rica. And I've been to Baton Rouge and Chicago. Now I'm here in Jacksonville. And, no, I will not let you read my mail." She nodded in resolute affirmation and finished her drink.

He knew she was daring him. He emptied his glass, set it down and sent a smile across the desk, "I've been to Louisiana and Illinois, too. And I've flown over most of them other places, and I don't want to read your mail. I don't have the time to read mine."

She allowed their little back-and-forth to briefly cut the tension. She poured another two fingers into each glass, sat down and crossed her legs. He heard her stockings delicately whisk across her thighs.

She quickly got back to business, lifted her glass and barely wet her lips on the rum before she set the glass back down.

She needed Nicholas to know she was serious, "Right now, this is classified 'Ears Only', and stays in this room. Something came up and your original mission to Guatemala has been put on the back burner."

"The war surplus** fighters for their air force?"

"Yes, that's got to wait ... I'll read you through the complete new mission brief tomorrow morning, but right now I'll give you a quick overview. Listen up. It's all part of something they're calling Operation Paperclip**.

"On Monday, you will leave for South America ... Argentina, to be exact. There you will meet up and work with Senior Agent Angus Munson ... you remember him ... you know him from the Philippines, during your initial training and orientation. This operation is part of something that's been going on since the end of the war. 'To the victor goes the spoils of war', they say ... well, we're grabbing their brains ... the Nazi scientists ... physicists, chemists, spies, rocket men, doctors ... all of them. We've been catching as many as we can before the Russians do. We were comrades-in-arms with them during the war, but they're sure as hell not our comrades now and we don't want them in-arms. These old Nazis down in Argentina will help us win this arms race with the Commies*.

"We've already rounded up quite a few in Europe, and now we're starting to pick them off the underground Nazi escape routes to South America. You and Munson are going to escort a handful of these special ex-Nazis to Fort Bliss, Texas, Agent Throckmorton. Think of yourself as a highly trained babysitter*, a very strict nanny, or an armed chaperone, Agent Throckmorton. There's always a few of these Germans who need some specialized treatment and if it becomes necessary, you'll give it to them. That's what you and Munson are going to do ... by any means necessary."

"Any means?"

"I didn't stutter. Munson will fill you in. You'll meet him in Argentina ... Bariloche[**], Argentina to be exact. He's been in-country about a month and working on the extractions. Like Santa ... making a list and checking it twice.

"Tomorrow morning I'll give you all the particulars and your identification."

"Identification?"

"Yes. You'll have a moniker[*] down there. You'll be someone other than Nicholas Throckmorton, a Grade 12 Field Agent, or an Air Corps colonel. And you don't know me until you lay eyes on me again."

Down Argentina Way ...
Bariloche, Argentina
Monday, April 22, 1946

One year and one month after the Allied victory over Nazi Germany and nine months after the surrender of Japan, Nicolás Tavarez arrived in Bariloche. Jovita had selected this false identity for him, knowing that the first time answering to an assumed name can be tricky. As it turned out, Nick had plenty of time to get used to his assumed name.

It took him six days to reach his destination and his journey proved that it was impossible to go nowhere fast. And Bariloche was right in the middle of *nowhere*.

Nicolás caught a taxi outside the San Carlos de Bariloche train station for a ten-minute taxi ride across brick and cobblestone streets to the city center and the Hotel de Casa Mia. The driver laughed at his Caribbean Spanish, and called him a turista[*]. Nick laughed along with him, and explained that he was indeed a tourist from the Dominican Republic and was there to meet his friend and countryman, Jorge Andrade.

The town was well hidden by Mother Nature, secluded by the towering Andes Mountains to the west and isolated on the east by thousands of miles of desolate Patagonian steppes. It was a perfect, picturesque holiday getaway in the Andean Alps, only a few miles from the Chilean border. It was full of Germans, Austrians and Czech immigrants, and since the beginning of the 19th century, it had earned an honest reputation as being South America's Alpine tourist center. In the 1930's it became known as *Little Berchtesgaden*[**] and a Nazi sanctuary.

Nicolás Tavarez checked in at the hotel desk and asked after his friend, Jorge Andrade.

"I believe he is in the bar, sir."

Nick paid the desk clerk and handed his worn, beat-up leather suitcase to the bellhop. "Thank you," he said, dropped some loose silver into the man's outstretched palm and walked across the dingy lobby to the small canteen.

His memory whisked back to the Philippines when he recognized Angus Munson sitting at the bar. He stayed in legend, walked over, put an arm across Angus' shoulder and man-hugged the supposed Jorge Andrade. They each fit the carpet bagger mold: crumpled slacks, wrinkled shirts and three-day stubble.

"Jorge! So glad to see you again!"

Angus stood and returned the hug. They shook hands. "Good job, Nicolás, but we're alone. And English is OK between us. Just keep it low."

"Got it." The place was empty. An aged, rotund and whiskered bartender was at the far end with a thin, tattered newspaper in front of him. He spotted the newcomer, and waddled down the bar.

The barkeep greeted his new customer with a nod and spoke, "Ah, Jorge! I see your friend has finally arrived. Would you like another beer, and one for your friend?"

Nick answered for Angus, "Yes, another for my friend and one for me ... what Jorge's having ... a bottle of that Szot."

They moved away from the bar and took a small table near the door to the lobby.

"So, Nick, the trip went OK?"

"Slower than I expected, but I made it. It's a little out-of-the-way, this place, ain't it?"

"Sure is. But tell me, how'd our gal Joe treat you this time around? Getting to know her at all? That broad's a hotsy-totsy* ball-buster, as good-looking as she is. Could be a dyke. Or maybe just a man-eater. Who knows? I haven't been able to read her at all. I'll tell you what ... I'd like a sip of that ... I've tried, believe me."

Nick knew better than to talk out of school, and took the high road, "She treats me fine, so far anyhow. I got no beef. She seems straight-arrow and no bullshit. To me, anyway. But then again, I'm fresh meat, ain't I? I'm the new kid on the block, so what do I know?"

He paused and looked around the bar. He wasn't looking for anything in particular, just looking. Nick never did like yapping about higher-ups, and thought he should take the conversation in another direction, and talk about the job at hand. "What's the story with this town, anyhow? Seems like we're in Switzerland, or the Alps, or someplace." Nick put a match to an Argentine Nobleza cigarette, inhaled, coughed and crushed it out. "Good God Almighty, these things are bad. They're almost bad enough to make me quit smoking."

Angus offered no opinion, took a swallow of beer and added a comment, "If you don't like the smokes, then you better steer clear of the cuy*." Nick didn't ask, and Angus needed to feed the silence. He appeared distracted and disappointed that his gossip had curled up and died. He took a deep breath, "Tell you what ... if anybody offers you cuy on a plate, you sure as hell won't eat it. It looks like a sprawled out, fried rat ... I'll tell you ... the crap some people eat. After I was here for two days, I said to myself, *Who the hell can live like this? Jesus H. Christ, there's nobody in this place here but Incas and goddamn Nazis!*

"I'll tell you what, Nick ... I can't figure out why they just don't send in the Marines and wipe them all out. I mean, they're all over the place ... hiding, always staying deep in the shadows, lurking on the other side of the street, talking in whispers and dodging glances. And they're still coming. Seems like at least once a week a couple more Nazi krauts[*] come off the train."

He took another swallow of beer, and lowered his voice a notch, "But you and me are going to lower the kraut population a little bit. Joey ... Washington actually ... got a list of five high-interest individuals who arrived here two weeks ago after running the Ratlines[**] out of Böblingen[**], Germany for the last six months. They were designing and building rockets and jets for the Reich before they got out and Washington wants them bad. Once the Company discovered that these five Nazis were on their way, they put out the word to nab the five of them. The plan is to, let's say, extradite them to the United States with as little fanfare as possible. You, me and a tough old Columbian named Héctor are going to snatch them up and take three of them stateside. Fort Bliss, Texas, to be exact.

"Our Moroccan branch fixed them up with Argentine papers, gave them a pep talk and tightened the screws and told them that their families were already in Columbia and waiting for them. With some persuasion and a wheelbarrow load of Pesos, the Columbian was able to get hold of a beat-up, 1930's German Siebel[**] light transport, eight passenger, bone-

---

shaker aircraft from the Argentineans ... and he had it all painted in green jungle camouflage with real kraut, Iron Cross fuselage markings, then had it sandblasted so it looked as worn and beat-up as lipstick on a two-dollar whore. Tell you what ... them Nazis will see that and think that they're going home sweet home and won't suspect a thing. It's parked about ten clicks east on hard-scrabble grassland ... gassed up and ready to rattle."

Angus stopped for another taste of beer, lit one of his Nobleza and added, "These smokes are all right once you get used to them. But, lucky for you, Nick, we should be out of here tomorrow noon at the latest."

Nick had been listening closely to Angus' fast-paced narrative. "Who's flying the bird?"

Angus taunted him, "You're the pilot, right? That's what your gal Joe told me. She said you could fly anything with wings or wheels ... a regular wiz-bang in the air. Now's your chance to grandstand your stuff, hotshot."

Nick was enduring a slow burn.

Angus exhaled cigarette smoke across the table and grinned, "I was just yanking your chain, buddy. The Columbian's a jungle pilot and he's flying us up the backbone of the Andes to Meneses Air Base, a secure government strip outside of Bogotá. The Columbians got it locked up tighter than a bull's ass. It's all cleared with them and we got the flight plan and maps. The plan is that you're going to right-seat the Columbian to Bogotá and fly us home from there. Worse come to worse, one of them krauts was a test pilot. We'll gas up in Lima, Peru and then on to Meneses. Then out of Columbia to Punta Gorda, British Honduras[**], and then San Luis, Mexico and on to Fort Bliss."

Nick pressed him, "You said we're grabbing five, but I heard you say only three were going to Fort Bliss. What is it? Three or five?"

"Sorry about the three and five screw-up. I double-talked. I meant to say five. All five are going. For now."

Nicholas decided then and there that he didn't particularly like this man, but had to ask, "What happens when we get to Columbia? They're going to figure it out then, won't they?"

Angus sneered, "That's when we hogtie them." He then swallowed the rest of his bottle of Szot and set it on the table with a hollow clunk, "Rest up tonight, Nicolás. We got a day and a half of flying ahead of us."

Das gibt's nur in Berlin (This only happens in Berlin) ...
Tuesday, April 23, 1946, 0930

Héctor Quintero, their Columbian pilot, arrived at the airstrip an hour earlier to prepare for the flight to Bogotá. From the cockpit, he watched with detached curiosity as his human cargo approached. The Siebel's exhaust temperature, oil and manifold pressure gauges were significantly more important to him and held his attention. Both engines were grumbling at idle, with wide-open cowl flaps and feathered propellers.

A canvas-covered, one-ton stake truck rattled to a stop fifty yards from the aircraft. Nick and Angus began acting full time as Nicolás Tavarez and Jorge Andrade. They exited the truck cab, walked to the rear, folded back the canvas flaps and dropped the tailgate.

Jorge stammered in broken German, "Here we are, gentlemen. You're on your way to your families and new home." His words formed vanishing clouds of frost in the mountain air of an Argentine autumn.

Five men dismounted and stood bewildered, awestruck and anxious at the back of the truck, studying the surrounding landscape and their winged transport. They each had very limited baggage; tattered suitcases, railroad bags and sailcloth sacks. Their clothes were hanging, clinging to their frail frames with the sweat and dirt of six months on the run.

The German passengers were: physicist Bernt Dahmbadt, metal engineer Heinrich Herglotz, chemist Oskar Langbein, Luftwaffe test pilot Gerhardt Blikslager and doctor Hartmut Planck. Washington's dossiers on Dahmbadt, Herglotz, and Langbein indicated that they had worked at the Luckenwalde rocket research center and were deemed valuable assets. Evidence was strong that the remaining two abductees were of no critical interest. Doctor Planck had spent two years stationed at Mauthausen labor camp, and Blikslager had helped develop and flew the Messerschmitt 262[**] jets during extensive research and test flights.

One of the Germans recognized the mottled Iron Cross insignia on the Siebel, "We're not far from home!"

Nicolás added in Spanish, "You're going home, my friends."

Another German translated for the other four, who were already all in smiles.

The flight north was uneventful despite an uncomfortable bout with air sickness from Herglotz, the metallurgist.

Nick sat in the navigator/copilot seat next to Héctor during the first thousand miles, takeoffs and landings to familiarize himself with the Siebel. Planned refueling stops were at Iquique, Chile and Lima, Peru, prior to arrival in Bogotá at 0400 the next morning.

Nick radioed the tower from ten miles out and got clearance for their approach. When the flickering landing lights of Meneses Air Base came into sight, Héctor gradually reduced altitude, checked his horizon and adjusted the trim. The Siebel's massive windscreen squeezed water droplets out of the humid air and they danced across the glass. Without any fuss or flourish, Héctor set the plane down and directed the rattling, vintage aircraft along the runway to the taxiway and toward the terminal.

It was time to introduce the five Germans to the truth.

Nick got out of the right seat, exited the cockpit and bobbed through the narrow door into the passenger compartment, his Colt in hand. Angus was standing with drawn pistol, holding onto his seatback and glaring at the five Germans. In bad German, he ordered them to remain in their seats until the plane came to a halt and the engines were cut.

Angus continued, "Gentlemen, we have arrived in Columbia, but you will stay in your seats until Nicolás or me say otherwise. You are going to the United States, my Nazi friends, where you will be guests of the American government. To make sure we have a good flight, I ask that you listen very carefully. We now have a one-hour stopover here in Bogotá for fuel and food. A squad of Columbian military will come aboard the aircraft and escort you off the plane for a meal and bathroom break. Once you have come back aboard the aircraft, you will be handcuffed and secured to your seats. We don't want any trouble, and want to make this trip as pleasant as possible. We will have at least two more stops before we reach the United States."

He lowered his voice and switched to English, "Please take full advantage of your comfort stops. We really don't want your Nazi shit on American soil."

The Germans looked at each other, to Nicholas, to Angus and back to Nicholas. Hartmut, the doctor stood and bolted toward Nick and Angus. Nick discharged his Colt 1911 into the man's abdomen, throwing him backwards. Angus stepped sideways and fired a bullet through the fallen man's skull.

The others froze, some agape, some trembling, all afraid. Nick and Angus glared at them with pistols aimed at their target of choice.

"Good reflex, Nick. Teamwork, I'll tell you what ... that's what it takes. One to the gut and one to the skull. He's dead and just as well. Washington said he was one of them concentration camp Nazi Frankenstein doctors."

The chemist pleaded, "No more. No more Nazis. My friends are not Nazis. Only him. He was the only one."

Nick scowled, "It's always the other guy, ain't it Heinie[*]? It's funny how all the living krauts ain't Nazis. Just the dead ones. That's real convenient, Heinie." It was questionable if any of them understood what he'd said.

Nick and Angus stood with weapons drawn, swaying, jostling, holding onto the ceiling rope like strap-hanging passengers on a bus, waiting for the aircraft to brake to a stop. They strained their eyes into the blackness outside, looked for Columbian troops, and managed to keep watch on the remaining four passengers for signs of another possible mutiny.

Héctor parked the Siebel a few steps from a maintenance hangar, opened the cockpit hatch, hopped down onto the tarmac, tipped his hat, lit a cigarillo and walked toward the hangar. Angus commented, "Look at that. That sonuvabitch can just park it and walk away. I want his job."

A detail of twelve Columbian military in jade green uniforms appeared from the dark, humid shadows, approached the plane with bayoneted rifles at the ready and stood at the Siebel's belly door and watched as the Germans deplaned onto the asphalt. Munson detailed two of the Columbians to remove the body of Doctor Hartmut Planck.

A second group of four soldiers with brushes and paint cans hurried to the aircraft and used black paint to obliterate the German iron cross on the fuselage.

Upon completion, the Columbians scurried like monkeys onto the wings, walked along the top of the plane, and painted *91*

BG in large white letters on each side of the tail stabilizer, and added a huge white triangle as a border. The markings indicated US Army Air Force, 1st Bomb Wing, 1st Air Division. The paint crew hopped off the wing and vanished as quickly as it appeared.

Nicolás Tavarez, Jorge Andrade and four German expatriates arrived at Biggs Army Air Field near El Paso, Texas, at 0100 hours, April 25.

Nick received a flight plan and orders to fly the Seibel to Montevideo, Uruguay and await further instruction.

It was difficult, but Angus kept his orders to himself. He nearly burst his buttons when he discovered that he had received a bump to Operations Supervisor, Midwest Division, Latin American Enterprise and was assigned to Chicago. To his knowledge, the woman he had once nicknamed *Joe* had been in charge of the Chicago office. Munson wondered what had become of her.

Jacksonville, Florida
Noon, Friday, May 31, 1946

The storm pulled sheets of rain across the city, unleashing torrents of water through the streets. Raindrops as large as quarters pelted everything natural or manmade. Jovita had returned from San Juan two days earlier and she'd experienced nonstop rain since.

The past week had been traumatic for her, and although she was coping as well as could be expected, the weather certainly did nothing to boost her spirit.

It's said that *when it rains, it pours.* Jovita was not able to find an umbrella big enough to be of any help.

Her father, Sergeant First Class Simón Vasquello was killed in action on Luzon, Philippines, April 14, 1946. He was riding in a motorcade of six Army jeeps* and four government vehicles en route to a cease-fire conference in Quezon City when it was ambushed by Hukbalahap** communist guerillas. Her father was one of five fatalities. Eight others had been wounded or injured in the crash that followed. The number of guerilla casualties was not reported.

Simón's remains were shipped back to Puerto Rico at Jovita's request, and buried with military honors next to her mother, Carilla, at the Playa Methodist Church in Ponce. The funeral was excruciating, but otherwise uneventful. She had managed to completely avoid her uncle and was able to break Aunt Agnes away from the other mourners. Jovita considered telling her of Horado's transgression, but decided against it, telling her aunt instead that Simón had often spoken tenderly of his sister. When she left Ponce the following day, she felt she had no reason to return. She had decided that mourning black wasn't her favorite color and she'd never wear it again. The two people who she had loved most were dead and buried side by side, along with her childhood innocence.

Sorrow and grieving were not new to her. Loneliness to this degree was. She no longer had an emotional bond with anyone. She didn't like it.

One good drink deserves another ...

When Nick walked into Fernando's Hideaway he did not expect to see Jovita sitting at the bar in a skirt, smoking and with a drink in her hand. Jovita's hair, shoulders, hips and legs betrayed her identity. He had seen enough of her rear view to burn her figure forever into his memory.

There was one other person sitting at the bar: a scruffy character, slouched and staring into his glass of beer and the dancing lights that reflected off the dinging, blinking Brunswick bowling machine behind him. Jovita did not notice, hear or care if anyone had walked through the door. "May I buy you another round, Miss?" As those words left his lips, he expected a sharp retort.

She welcomed the sight of him. Her first smile in weeks signaled that she was pleased to see him. Nick was someone she knew, however briefly. Perhaps it was his official folio and her comprehensive knowledge of his life history that allowed her to consider him a trusted acquaintance. After all, weeks earlier Agent Throckmorton acknowledged that she must have been *reading his mail.* Her spirit brightened and her response mirrored it, "No thank you, but I'll buy you one. How's that? Pick your poison."

He noticed that she had turned off the faucet and her Latin lilt had curiously returned. He removed his raincoat, dropped it over a chair at the table behind him, and took the stool to her left. "I'll have what you're having, Boss."

She motioned for the bartender. He set down the glass that he had been wiping, slung the towel over his shoulder and moved down the bar. "Nicholas, meet Oliver. I haven't had the chance to introduce him properly, but he is my trusty, faithful assistant, barman, backup, bar-back and all-around fix-it man. I trust him ... Oliver, bring Nick a scotch and some more ice for me, please."

Nick graciously nodded. "Nice to meet you, Oliver. I'll have a double. Neat."

She placed her elbow on the bar, her chin resting on the back of her hand. There was a twinkle of drink in her eye. Oliver set Nick's drink and a glass of cubes in front of them and silently disappeared. Jovita crushed out her cigarette, dropped an ice cube into her glass, and began, "I knew you were on your way back, but couldn't know exactly when you'd show up. It's good to see you ... and know that you're safe and sound. We'll finish our drink and cover the details in private ... in the back. I just heard that Munson got himself promoted ... and moved right into my old slot."

This was news to him. Munson had proved himself in the field, but Nick just didn't like the man, and considered him crass and overbearing. Nick gulped half his scotch.

She paused, and allowed her thoughts to catch up, "Let's go into the office, like I said. Everything's too out in the open out here ... too public to be comfortable. Everybody and anybody shouldn't be able to hear our whispers, right?" She surprised herself. She was loosening up.

She grabbed her glass of ice and slid off the stool with as much grace as permitted after two glasses of scotch, "Thank you, Ollie. We'll be in the office." The bartender didn't look up, only nodded. The noon news was crackling through the vacuum tube radio behind the bar.

"And leave your drink, Nick. I'll pour you another ... a fresh one in the back." Oliver kept polishing his glassware.

Nick didn't listen. He finished the drink with one swallow, thinking, *"Waste not, want not."*

Jovita's heels clicked across the floor, and Nick followed one step behind. She could feel his eyes. Strangely, she wanted him to see all of her. The lone customer watched them disappear down the darkened, narrow hallway. His lewd thoughts brought a grin to an otherwise miserable face.

The door to her office closed with its familiar, precise thump. With measured, memorized steps, she walked through the darkness, directly to her desk and snapped on the gooseneck lamp. "Take a seat. Pick one. Any one. Another drink?" She wondered if he'd move to the leather sofa at the far wall. He didn't. She didn't hear the telltale swoosh of air escaping the cushions.

"Yes, thank you. I was expecting rum, but another scotch is perfect."

"Scotch it is, then ... The Famous Grouse." She continued as she poured, "Lately, I've lost my taste for Puerto Rican rum. All rum, actually."

They spent the next hour and a half alone, along with one glass of scotch apiece, hashing over the cabled mission reports and assessments. The wooden chair burned and bit his backside. He tensed his legs, wriggled his toes inside his oxfords, flexed and relaxed his stiffening muscles. Nothing helped. He hated this part of the job.

She sat remarkably still behind her desk, making little notes on the decrypted cablegrams, occasionally looking up at him from under her ebony lashes. She studied him closely, just as a fastidious perfectionist would examine the pieces of a jigsaw puzzle. The gray at the temples, the little wrinkles at the corners of the eyes, the broad shoulders, the tight curls in the black hair, the strong hands, powerful fingers and the glint of his deep brown eyes captured her imagination. Regardless of how much she knew about him, he was rapidly becoming the biggest enigma ever presented to her. She briefly considered that perhaps it was she, not he, who was creating the mystery. Her assumption was correct. She also found it shocking that she could neither stop nor scold herself. She did not understand.

The debriefing and mission evaluation was over by two o'clock. However, Jovita's personnel evaluation of Nick secretly continued. For her, it was getting personal.

"It seems that you can handle yourself in a pinch, Agent Throckmorton."

She leaned back in her chair, resting her palms on the edge of the desk. She locked her eyes onto his and began, "Munson said that you performed well, and once again you proved your skills in the air. And about those ten days in Uruguay ... what you encountered and how you dealt with it ... well, frankly, it came as an unexpected, yet informative and lucrative operation to Washington. Don't get a fat head, but I've got to say that you did an outstanding job and proved that you can make the correct decision. You insured the success of the mission under difficult circumstances without loss of equipment or assets. Most importantly, you didn't leave any footprints. That's impressive for a new field operative or a veteran. Very good, Nicholas. Very good. And you made me and the rest of the team look good. Your first two field assignments got you noticed. Again." She came across as sincerely as she intended.

Jovita leaned forward and teased, "And finally, here's the latest news flash, hot off the wire."

She began to clarify Munson's promotion and station to Chicago as well as her newly named duty slot as Supervisor, Atlantic Division. She explained, "The Company's getting serious about Latin America. They split up into three divisions now, Atlantic, Midwest and Pacific. It's me here in the Atlantic, Munson in the Midwest, Carlisle on the West Coast, and my boss, someone I've never met, Allen Dulles, the Assistant Chief of Latin American Operations, in San Francisco."

She stood, stretched and let out a sigh. Nicholas fought his tight muscles, stood straight up, twisted, tensed and bent, all the while watching her every move. She didn't need to see his eyes to feel them.

"We're done. One last drink before we call it a day ... sound good?" She was nervously confident and worried that it showed. It didn't.

"Sure. A double. Neat, if you will. Thanks."

She smiled, turned and stepped to the file cabinet for the whiskey and glasses. She was aware that all of the ice had melted. "Take a seat on the easy chair behind you; it's softer than that oak antique you've been stuck to." She brought The Famous Grouse and glasses to the end table and took a seat on the sofa, slowly, carefully crossing her legs on the way down. Her hemline dashed above the knee. The leather stretched, strained and released a whoosh of air. They were close, he in the chair and she on the divan.

Jovita poured the drinks, handed one to Nick and raised her glass, "Happy days."

"Back at you, Boss." Their glasses answered with a clank.

She had a brief, soft giggle. "It's Jovita or Joey in the outside world, Nick." It was the first time he heard her laugh. "I know, I know. We're inside ... but we're outside. Does that make sense?" She tried to hold back another little laugh.

"It does. You're Joey now. Got it."

Her tone became serious. "I'm sure you remember my father, Simón." Her words found an alcohol-fueled freedom, and came out unchained, unshackled. She needed to tell someone. Even Oliver didn't know. She had told her deputy that she was visiting her aunt. Only she and Washington knew why she quickly left Jacksonville for Puerto Rico. Someone else had to know. Something inside had to be set free.

"Yes, of course I remember your father. He gave me my first Spanish language lessons during the war, back in the Philippines."

She looked deep into his eyes, searching for some link to his humanity, and some release of empathy toward her. "He was killed in action there in the Philippines ... ambushed ... the middle of last month. I'm alone now. Alone. I lost my mother when I was seventeen." She could have squeezed a tear, but held back, "I'm alone now."

Nick set his drink on the floor, took two steps to the sofa, sat close and put an arm around her. She welcomed his touch, turned toward him, held him, and put her head to his chest.

She feared an emotional breakdown, but there wasn't any. Her emotions had tried to cheat her, but she fought back an avalanche of grief. The loudest sounds were his heartbeat and the wall clock ticking the seconds away.

She held him tighter, closer, "I've got two more days of Compassionate Leave, and then it's back to ... back to ... work." She felt robbed, yet relieved. She had opened herself up and nothing came out; only words, no broken sobs, forced breaths or rivers of tears. The release she sought was dammed up by her stubborn loneliness and isolation.

Her head was on his shoulder. He whispered, "Take the time they give you, Joey. It's there for a reason: to help you deal with your loss and sorrow. And to sort things out in your life and your mind." Her hair tickled his lip.

"You don't think I'm being too non-compassionate, do you?"

"People grieve in different ways, Joey."

She trembled in his arms, "I feel so damn alone. I feel cheated. Ransacked. Violated and angry."

He continued to hold her, "You have to deal with that, Joey. The anger ... it can eat you up. I was angry when my mother and sisters were killed by senseless mob violence. Time heals the grief but you alone need to deal with the anger. For almost ten years, I kept my anger wrapped up inside me like one of them Egyptian mummies. It took me awhile, but I found a way to open King Tut's tomb and I dealt with it.

"You have to let it out, Joey. Let it out any way you can. The sooner the better."

Moments of silence passed. She sat up. Nick lit a Camel and picked up his glass.

"Thank you, Nicholas. You've helped."

"I've done bupkis*. I only relayed what I went through. You can share your grief with anyone who's close to you ...

anyone you're comfortable with ... and then you deal with it. But anger is different ... it's personal and only you can fix that."

She reached for her drink and stared into the golden liquid, "Are you in the billets at the Naval Air Station across the street?"

"No. I got a room at the Swansea. I didn't want military."

Jovita had a thought, "How about we go to dinner? I'll shower and change and I can meet you at your hotel about six. How's that? I'll have the desk call your room." No sooner than her words left her lips, she questioned her motive, then her wisdom.

"No need for that ... I'll meet you in the lobby ... six o'clock. We'll go to the Blue Oyster."

Bésame Mucho (Kiss me a Lot) ...
Room 214, Swansea Hotel, Jacksonville, Florida
May 31, 1946, 10:30 PM

Nick locked the door behind them and kicked off his shoes. Joey was standing at the bed. He dropped his linen jacket and tie on the dresser.

The light of a million twinkling stars peeked through the sheer muslin drapery liners. Soft red light pulsed from the rooftop neon sign across the street and bathed the room in warm, undulating color.

Her fingers tore at his shirt buttons, then his belt. He pressed her hips to him and kissed the nape of her neck. At no other time in her life had she known wanton passion. Her thoughts were whirling, her heart raging and her body burning. His trousers dropped to the floor and her dress fell onto the end of the bed.

Jovita pulled him backward onto the bed, cast off his shirt, kissed a nipple and slid her tongue across his chest.

He slowly, methodically moved a hand around each thigh, releasing the garter grips one by one until he could unhook the belt. He slid her panties below her knees and off.

"Abrázame ... bésame ... quiéreme, Nicolás. Hold me, kiss me, love me."

He whispered, "You don't need to say it twice, my dear. I will love you all night. I will love you forever." He murmured into her ear; she quivered and pushed her hips to him.

She whimpered. Again, he whispered. He couldn't know that he was entering unexplored, virgin territory.

Jovita was pushed toward the unfamiliar, the unknown. She wanted to share herself and become part of someone. She desired to soar higher and discover love on its highest possible plane. Love at that altitude was something she had never experienced. Brutality, uncharted novelty and an unreliable consciousness had all spoiled her appetite for intimacy.

It was different with Nicholas. Tenderness put aside carnal abuse and natural order replaced experimentation. This time she would remember. To seal her certainty, she welcomed an encore.

Sorrow, grief and loneliness had created a vacancy deep inside that brought her to room 214. She allowed a fantastic new passion to unlock the door and let her in. She wondered how difficult checkout could be.

Please Don't Talk About Me When I'm Gone ...

They were sitting up in bed, their backs against the headboard. His arm was around her, and her head against his chest. He exhaled the last of his cigarette, reached to the bedside table and snuffed it out. His watch read 2 AM.

Jovita sat up and took his hand. She had been thinking about what she was about to say for the past half hour. It needed to be said, but still, she struggled to find the right words. She looked into his brown eyes, "We work together, Nick ... I'm your boss ... and I can't sleep here. We can't do this and work together. I have to go back to the Hideaway."

"Why? Who's going to know?"

"Oliver comes in at six, and Leonard's always there at seven and pulling the overnight cables off the teletype and checking the radio. I have to go back. "

"You live there?"

"Yes, I do. I've go my own cozy little nest, right next door to my deep blue office."

"How about Ollie and Lenny then?"

"They're down the block and across the street at NASJAX[**]. And you're not the only field agent in my charge. There are two more in Argentina and another in Columbia. All four of you keep me busy." She winked, puckered and gave him an air kiss.

He kissed her forehead, "Another secret revealed."

"Stop it, Nicholas. Stop it. Please understand. This never happened. We're living in a legend. Both of us. A Company legend ... that's all this is. We can't do this and be part of that. This and that don't mix."

He knew that, but this was new to him. Never before had he played the role of bed warmer, and did not know how to respond. A full minute of silence began building an impenetrable wall between them. Joey broke it down, "Please understand. I needed you. And I wanted you. And what you said about dealing with anger helped me more than you can know ... and ..."

He interrupted and gave a retort to avoid appearing wounded, "You're right, Joey. You're absolutely right. We're living a scripted life. We're living like actors on a stage and playing a role, aren't we? We come out, say our lines and exit stage left."

"I'm not throwing you away, Nick. I need to put tonight on a shelf for later ... later, when we can be honest. Face it, what happened here tonight is against regulation. You're still married to Nora and I'm still your boss. That's the way it is."

"Yeah, right. But we both knew that going in."

"Please, Nick, let me finish. While you slept, I realized that I allowed anger to smother my grief. Tonight you helped me catch my breath and deal with things in my past. Terrible, sorrowful and crazy mixed-up things. My father was a veteran of two world wars and was only a month away from a decent, thirty-year Army retirement. And what really churned my stomach, just like bad shrimp, is that both of my parents are dead because of communists. Maybe not directly, but one way or another it's their fault. A violent parade or a jungle ambush. It's all the same. The result is death because of false political ideology.

"I now realize that I can't allow the past to control my emotions. I refuse to wallow in sorrow. If I can't fix it, to hell with it. You helped me breathe again and put my anger where it belongs. The Company can handle the communists. I just follow orders. Did I explain myself? And please, please understand about us."

"I do. You made it clear. Your Compassionate Leave is over. And my lips are sealed. Only my pillow will know, Boss."

She kissed his lips, slid out from under the sheet and put on her brassiere, "One more thing." She stepped into her white cotton underwear.

She was back in form, and all business, "Come to the office before noon. I've got your next assignment: Guatemala."

"They're building a pea-shooter air force?" He was aggravated and felt a slow burn. Like an Army shower, she went from hot to cold to hot. He watched her drop her dress over her head, wiggle it down over her hips and fasten four buttons up from the waist. Nick reached to the bedside table, finished the last swallow of scotch from a lipstick-smudged glass, grabbed his Zippo and lit a smoke.

"Yes, they're building an air force. Your last two stations weren't typical, Nick. I believe you have a special finesse, and I will use it, but right now, I need you primarily as a technical agent, not as a muscleman or enforcer. Your abilities to adapt to any situation are exemplary and are what got you noticed in the first place, but your experience as a pilot and flying skills are critical the Group's mission in Latin America. I've already mentioned that the extraction from Bariloche was an unexpected development, and out of nowhere that damaging hiccup in Uruguay happened ... and needed to be dealt with ... and you took the necessary action and handled it. But long story short: you were brought back mainly because of my temporary absence. Munson was busy in Chicago with his assets in Mexico and Costa Rica besides picking up the leftover slack that my emergency funeral leave created.

"When you leave for Central America on Wednesday, you could very well be headed for an extended station. It's likely that our only contact will be cablegrams or through channeled chatter. You'll be walking a tightrope*, but I cannot always be your safety net. That's another reason why what went on in this room stays in this room."

Nick gave a stinging reply, "Roger, Boss. Message received."
He was burned, but not bruised.

NORA ... 1946

I Can't Begin To Tell You ...
Mount Clemens, Michigan
Saturday, June 1, 1946

The noon fire whistle sounded just as Nora and Alexander sat down for their lunch of cream of tomato soup and grilled cheese sandwiches. It was a pleasant early summer day, and Nora had decided to enjoy their meal on the front porch. Song sparrows and chickadees chattered and danced among the sprawling branches of sugar maples. A pair of black squirrels was playing tag in the pin oak across the street.

Eighteen-year-old Alex had already lined up his afternoon's entertainment. Earlier that morning, he'd brought out the Philco table radio from the kitchen and plugged it into a twenty-foot extension chord. He had four bottles of Vernors ginger ale in the Kelvinator and a can of Planters redskin peanuts at the ready. At one o'clock, he and his pal Bobby Weeks planned to tune the radio to 760 and listen to Harry Heilmann[**] call the play-by-play on WJR radio. The Detroit Tigers were away from home and playing the Senators at Griffith Stadium, Washington, DC.

Nora would miss everything: the national anthem, first pitch and the last out due to standing obligations. On Saturday afternoons, she, Alice Wetherby, Gloria Himmel and Deloris Deerfield sweep and mop the floors, polish the pews and lower the kneelers, thereby readying the nave[*] of Saint Peter for Sunday Mass.

Alex finished off his last bit of sandwich after he used it to wipe up the final drops of his soup from the bowl. He checked his watch: twelve-thirty, half an hour to first pitch.

Bobby was always prompt, so his grey 1936 Chevy should pull up to the curb in about fifteen minutes.

Just as Nora began to gather the dishes, silver, cup and glass off the Cape Cod table, a brief metallic screech and mechanical clatter put the brakes on her cleanup. She looked to her left, out across the front lawn and noticed that an unexpected visitor had pedaled down the street and come to a stop on the sidewalk in front of the house.

A Western Union[**] messenger propped his black, sleek English racing bicycle against the privet hedge and started up the fieldstone walkway to Throckmorton home. He sprung up the wooden porch steps, reached into his satchel and dutifully announced, "Telegram for Missus Nora Throckmorton."

His voice had the embarrassing crackle of puberty. The courier was a young, long and lanky fellow with an uncomfortable, ruddy teenage face accented with acne and freckles. His ears supported an oversized garrison cap atop his head and a brass-buttoned, navy-blue uniform disguised his skinny frame. A heavy blanket of dread suddenly darkened number 12 Second Street, Mount Clemens, Michigan. Nora simply signed the receipt book, took the envelope from the messenger, nodded and stared at it. Her heart was pounding. She took a breath. The courier and his bicycle squeaked away unnoticed toward their next stop.

Alexander anticipated the message contents. A telegram wasn't known to bring good news. It was the type of dispatch that had become feared and despised by nearly five brutal years of World War. He moved to the edge of his wicker chair, and watched nervously as his mother opened the flap to read the message.

Her eyes moved rapidly across the telegram. Her hand began to tremble, as the disheartening news seemed to jump off the page and burn its way into the reader's marrow.

The Telegram

JUNE 1 1946

MRS NORA THROCKMORTON
STOP
THE SECRETARY OF WAR DESIRES
ME TO EXPRESS HIS DEEP REGRET
THAT YOUR HUSBAND MAJOR
NICHOLAS J THROCKMORTON USAAC
HAS BEEN LISTED MISSING IN
SERVICE AND MISSING AIR CREW
SINCE APRIL 29 1946 IN THEATER
SOUTHEAST CHINA
STOP
IF FURTHER INFORMATION OR
DETAILS ARE RECEIVED YOU WILL
RECEIVE PROMPT NOTIFICATION
STOP
LETTER OF CONFIRMATION FOLLOWS
STOP
SIGNED   CAPT JA ULIO
STOP
ADJUTANT GENERAL
STOP
END OF TRANSMISSION

Without a word, Nora handed the dispatch to her son, turned, opened the wooden screen door and allowed it to slam behind her. She walked into the front room and sat on the green divan. Despite her husband's frequent and prolonged absences, Nora found the news unsettling.

Alexander looked at the yellowish, 6X8-inch piece of paper and instantly found the words "missing air crew" in the text.

He folded it once, followed after his mother and sat next to her on the sofa. Nora fixed her eyes on the portrait of Christ on the opposite wall, crossed herself, bowed her head and whispered, "Bless him". Several silent minutes passed before she raised her head and opened her eyes. She then placed her hands over the gold crucifix around her neck and pressed it to her chest. She had received the necklace as a gift from Nick two months earlier.

The possibility of a deadly air crash or ground accident had haunted the furthest reaches of Nora's thoughts since her husband began his career as a crop duster in 1931. When he later joined the Air Corps in 1938, she had grown fully accustomed to his absence and accepted the inherent dangers of his job. Over the previous nineteen years, Nora had grown accustomed to her husband's flighty lifestyle and her son Alex had long ago accepted his father's absence as the norm. Still, they were not prepared for the shocking text they discovered in the telegram, nor how deeply it affected them both.

Alex quickly read the complete dispatch he held in his hands. He attempted to soothe his mother, "Don't worry yourself, Mom. I'm sure that he'll show up ... he always does. And after all, this is nothing new. It's old hat, and he's good at what he does or they wouldn't let him keep doing it. He always comes back after he takes off. Always. He'll show up."

"You're a good son, Alex. You always have been." Nora knew it to be true. Her words helped soothe his anguish but not her worry.

She dutifully remembered her obligation to Saint Peter Parish. "Alex, please telephone Alice and tell her I can't help today."

He put an arm around his mother's shoulders, "Sure. OK, Mom. Don't worry about this. We'll get through this all right. We'll get through it together, no matter what."

Alexander called Alice Wetherby and explained why his mother would not be at the church. He was about to call his friend Bobby and cancel their front porch baseball party when he heard him bouncing up the steps.

He stepped outside and quietly closed the screen door. "Sorry, pal, but we can't listen to the game today. Mom and me just got a telegram and it wasn't good news. They just reported my old man as missing air crew over China."

After the telegram, it appeared that life would continue as usual on Second Street, at least on the surface. Mother and son continued to go about their daily routine without the presence of a husband or father. This time, however, there was a foreboding uncertainty. An official military transmission had cemented the possibility that Nicholas would not return. Although he had been absent for long, extended periods even before the war, a single telegram created a chill in the air that was entirely uncommon in June.

It's Been A Long, Long, Time ...

Within a few hours, the news about Nicholas had spread throughout Saint Peter Parish. Support and expressions of sympathy came from telephone calls and knocks at the front door. A pot roast and strawberry-rhubarb pie appeared on the porch that evening.

Nora's early visitors were Sister Anna Maria of Saint Mary school and Father John. The teaching nun and parish priest had been Nora's pillars of support for the better part of nineteen years.

In the days that followed the news, despite her best efforts to carry on, the tapestry of Nora's life began to unravel. Worries arose over things that she had always taken for granted. Three days after the telegram, Nora rode the Inter-Urban trolley to 21-mile Road and Selfridge Army Air Field. She inquired at the Personnel Office about Nicholas' pay status and discovered that, although her monthly dependent's allotment would end, she would continue to draw his pay until her husband's status changed. It was a relief to hear she would not immediately lose her only source of income. Even so, she considered it peculiar that the thought of forever losing a husband who she never really had created a relentless, hollow anguish within her. She remembered her father's scorn for Nicholas, and felt personal guilt for shunning her husband in the early months of their marriage. She worried whether she was to blame for his wayward decisions. For days, she struggled in vain, trying to understand. As usual, her husband wasn't there, and yet, it took a telegram to make her feel alone. She longed for consolation.

Of all the teaching nuns, aides and volunteers from Saint Mary School and Saint Peter, Father John visited Nora the most often. He walked or bicycled the five blocks from the rectory and made the trip to Nora's Second Street home whenever he could. He shuffled his schedule at Saint Peter enough to afford him nearly daily visits to Nora. He became a steady, quieting influence and graciously provided the shelter of Providence for Nora. He professed that he had tasked himself with helping her withstand the tornadic emotional storm she was experiencing.

Father John and Nora had first crossed paths in 1929, immediately after Nora's parents left Detroit for Oshkosh, Wisconsin. He was known as *Brother John* back then, just 20 years old and a first-year seminarian at Sacred Heart. Together, he and the eighteen-year-old, newlywed Nora studied the *Lectio Divina*, the Divine Readings. They developed a trusting, personal bond. Other than a brief six-month station to the Dominican Republic in 1934, he'd had an exclusive posting at Saint Peter Parish in Mount Clemens. In 1939, he left Saint Peter again, this time for a twelve-month mission to Rome. He explained to Nora that it was a *devotional immersion* sabbatical. He returned to Mount Clemens in June, 1940 and became the Parochial Vicar for Father James Patrick of Saint Peter. Conjectures arose, and occasional whispers passed among the faithful, but the real reasons behind Father John's foreign postings were never clear.

For nearly seventeen years, Father John and his spiritual guidance enabled Nora's triumphant-appearing run against the challenges of familial derision and trepidation, an empty marriage, loneliness and the exclusion of intimacy which she, herself had imposed. In fact, Father John and Sister Anna Maria were at Nora's bedside during her nearly fatal bout with appendicitis in 1936.

After the telegram, Father John became Nora's bastion of support and the center of her spiritual encouragement, more than ever before. He visited often, if only for a few minutes and usually during the hours that Alexander was in school, busily finishing his senior year at Mount Clemens High. The priest discovered a convenient, short walk to Nora's back door when he began parking his bicycle in the alley behind her Second Street home.

Just past nine o'clock on the morning of June 7, Father John's unique knock signaled his arrival. He had a personal rap-rap-triple-rap. Nora welcomed him into the kitchen with a smile, and invited him to the living room where she had coffee and sliced apple bread waiting on the sideboard. He followed closely behind as she led him to the parlor. Since the telegram, she had begun to anticipate his arrival and had looked forward to his company. His smile and soft, steady voice calmed her beyond explanation.

As they entered the room, she turned and greeted him with a contented smile and outstretched arms, palms up, expecting the warm touch of his hands in return. Rather, he reached out and held her, one arm across her shoulder and the other snuggly around her waist. She was startled only for an instant and allowed a quick surrender. She returned his embrace, her heart pounding.

Father John whispered that he could feel the hand of God resting upon him, and wanted to share His touch.

She whispered, "I welcome Him."

They were standing behind the green brocade sofa that her husband had purchased years earlier. He kissed her softly on her mouth and within seconds, she responded in kind, signaling that she welcomed his presence in her lonely world. It was her first impassioned kiss in nearly two decades and it thrilled her from head to toe.

She didn't care whose heavenly hands were upon her. She was encouraged and warmed by an inexplicable, virtually forgotten passion. What she was experiencing was real and present, not fanciful and departed. The amorous *here and now* completely subdued the revered, avowed *never ever*. The question of divine or demonic did not cross her mind. Desire subdued reservation. She surrendered.

He slowly, methodically unbuttoned her housedress, unhooked her brassiere and smothered her breasts with kisses and soft caresses. His touch explored abandoned and forgotten places.

An unfamiliar excitement pulsed through her veins and she had Father John to thank. She felt a thrilling flush pass through her and fresh new desires flooded her senses. She stepped out of her dress and pushed it aside with a foot. Forgotten emotion had taken control. Lust rendered her helpless and drew her to submission. She yielded to her weakness, dropped her glasses onto the armchair, pulled her underwear down and off, kicked off her shoes and pulled the cleric's hips to her. Longing replaced years of barren restraint and self-imposed celibacy. His touch and kisses aroused her passion and teased forgotten desire. She quivered under the touch of his hand and allowed his fingers to explore her deepest secret. She became lost in his kiss and whimpered, "Love me. Love me."

He didn't answer, but gently turned her around, deftly pulled her thighs backward and leaned her over the divan. She bent at the waist and pressed the palms of her hands against the seat cushion. She felt his hot breath against her back, moving slowly down across her buttocks and his hands on her thighs, between her legs, teasing her warmth and pulling down her cotton stockings one inch at a time. Waves of daring and lustful expectation began to pound her thoughts. Her dreams swirled in frothing eddies on forgotten shores. There were no sounds other than her murmurs and his breaths.

She barely heard the rustle of cloth, and realized that he had stood, lifted his frock and set much of it across her bare back. It covered her. His flesh burned onto hers. She raised her head and glanced at the portrait of Christ on the opposite wall just as Father John became fully consumed by her warmth. He whispered, "Redemption is yours, Nora."

Minutes later, a fully appeased Nora collapsed in a dizzying culmination, trembling like aspen leaves in a spring breeze. She gathered her senses, stood, turned and held him close. His tenderness, kisses and soft caresses revived her. His pressing hands set her afire again. Like vanilla ice cream in

July, one small taste was not enough. For Nora, one scoop would not suffice, and licking the bowl just wouldn't do. Father John could not allow her insatiable hunger to go unrequited, and they spent the next hour upstairs in her bedroom.

Thirty-four-year-old Nora could not have dreamed what she experienced that morning. It was an acceptance, a revelation, a total surrender and a connection of living beings that she had perceived at no other time. She could not remember ever feeling so complete. There were no more than two dozen words whispered during that first heated encounter, yet they understood one another perfectly. Nora felt she had approached at least the first doorstep to Heaven.

Nora fell asleep that night comfortable in the bed she had made. She dared to indulge in self-recrimination and thought, *"A single apple was enough to tempt Eve."*

How Can You Say No? ...
(When the whole world is saying yes)

When Nora awoke the next day, the sun shone brighter. The birds sang more sweetly and the whole world sparkled. Her life had changed drastically overnight; her passion for life was renewed, and she hoped for a bright new future. She decided that she was long overdue for a break from her duties at Saint Mary school, and that after more than a decade of emotional drought, it would be refreshing to spend some time and effort on herself.

After Alexander went off to school, she rode the trolley downtown and purchased a new, colorful print housedress and a pair of nylon stockings at Hudson's. A block away on Macomb Street, outside Bergenfield and Ross, she recognized that the shoes on her feet looked like a beat cop's service oxfords. Somehow, she garnered the courage to venture inside and buy a pair of T-strap Cuban heels. Crowley's on Gratiot Avenue was her next stop, where she replaced her F.W. Woolworth^{**} five-and-dime cotton brassiere for an uplifting 34D Maidenform. Her five-foot, two-inch form hadn't looked so pert and perky since her teenage years. Nora was back in Mount Clemens by eleven and bravely walked into the Gold-n-Hair salon. She had her below-the-shoulder, coal black hair cut, curled and styled into a short bob for the first time since her marriage at age seventeen. While sitting in the stylist's chair, she thumbed through a tattered copy of Woman's Weekly and noticed one particular ad that prompted her to consider a pair of cat-eye eyeglass frames. She considered them a possible future purchase along with a long overdue eye exam.

Back home, she applied a touch of lipstick, tried on her new brassiere and dress, studied her hairdo, rejuvenated form and the new reflection in her dresser mirror. She didn't even consider her little belly pouch, but smiled and knew that John would be pleased on his next visit. As things turned out, she was more than correct. The priest was ravenous and smothered her with his attentions.

Nora was so pleased with his reaction, she felt obliged to ride the trolley downtown one more time. On Saturday, she purchased one more new housedress and another pair of Mojud stockings before the shops closed at noon.

During the week that followed, Nora had several more boudoir rendezvous with Father John. She felt and behaved like a woman reborn: reinvented and revitalized.

Alexander noticed his renewed mother but made no comment other than, "You look snazzy[*], Mom." He was puzzled, yet happy for her. He considered that, perhaps, she had discovered something that was able to resuscitate her dark, dingy Puritan existence. It pleased him, but he didn't give it much more thought than that. He was too involved with his upcoming graduation and the end of school.

The next morning, on his way out the door for graduation rehearsal, Alexander discovered someone had pushed an envelope through the mail slot. It was an offering envelope from Saint Peter Church with *Nora* written in neat, block letters. Little back-and-forth messages from the church were commonplace and he simply set it on the kitchen table, knowing his mother would find it soon enough.

Five minutes later she did. Inside, she found a note written in Father John's bold script: *Receive the Sacrament of Confession today to seek Contrition.* In that instant, her world crumbled around her like a tower of building blocks with the noise and dust of a thousand brick. Her hands trembled and her heart panged as if pierced by Lucifer's trident.

All By Myself ...

Nora had no doubt that the author of the note was also the voice behind the screen: Father John. She laid bare her soul within the sacred privacy of the confessional.

After her thirty-minute exhortation, Nora, the penitent rose from her knees and took one wobbly half-step outside. Standing at the threshold, she asked between sobs, "Father, will you please convey to Father John that I asked for him to visit me?"

From the within the darkened stall she heard, "He cannot. The demands of his ministry are too great. Rather, you must pray to the Saints Monica and Anastasia. Prayer will unite you with God so you may then unite with all members of the Mystical Body to ask for forgiveness. Go with the knowledge that when you confess your sin, He is faithful and just to forgive you your sin and to cleanse you from all unrighteousness. The transgression may not be forgiven but the transgressor may."

It took Nora twenty minutes, rather than the usual ten, to walk home from Saint Peter Church back to Second Street. By the time she got back to Second Street, her white cotton, lace-trimmed hankie was wet with tears. She left a note on the kitchen table for Alex that she was upstairs in bed with a headache. She suggested that he either warm up some leftover pea soup or make a meatloaf sandwich for his dinner.

Upstairs in the safety of her bed, she curled up like an infant, her arms around her chest in an empty hug. It was after her tears had stopped and dried up that she recognized his scent. The thick, spicy smell of incense had permeated the sheets and pillow shams. She desperately stripped the bed and spent a night of torment on her cotton tick mattress.

Nora was alone, and knew it to be true. She felt deserted, and realized she was.

In the first light of morning, she sat up in bed and studied the Sacred Heart of Christ portrait above her dresser. Nora's lips formed her quiet words. She muttered silently to her shame, *"Lord Jesus, am I the only woman who ever felt this way? ... I feel so cold, so lifeless ... have I been cast to stone? ... Why, oh why did I not deny myself? ... Did I share my bed to spite the Saints? ... Am I cursed to a life of sackcloth and ashes? ... Who shall guide me to the righteous path?"*

She then held her rosary close to her bosom and asked her phantom priest, *"How could you truly know what I felt, Father? Do you understand the emptiness, the hurt, the burning and twisting pain that you created within the depths of my soul? You could not possibly feel what was inside me, despite your false witness. You have darkened my spirit, tarnished my soul and caused me to doubt my faith.*

"I trusted you and accepted you and together we sinned. I believed that you were moved by heavenly vision and that you

could renew me as clean as a dove. But instead you blackened me with falsehoods and then deserted me in my time of need and indecision.

"I have sinned and sought redemption. I pray our Lord Jesus gives me the courage to forgive you, the strength to graciously forget and the wisdom to learn."

For the better part of an hour, Nora questioned her faith and future. Somehow, she recalled an obscure Bible passage, and believed it to be an answered prayer, helping her find encouragement in the Holy Word. She found it in First Corinthians, Chapter Ten, Verse Thirteen: "No trial has overtaken you that is not faced by others. And God is faithful: He will not let you be tried beyond what you are able to bear, but with the trial will also provide a way out so that you may be able to endure it."

For the first time in ten years, Nora did not attend Mass on Sunday. Rather, she prayed and vowed that the following week she would begin attending the early Latin Mass with Father Anthony.

Bad things come in threes ...

Nora received a telephone call from her younger sister Marie on the day preceding Alexander's graduation. Marie was married with two children and taught elementary school in Fond du Lac, Wisconsin. Nora suspected that her sister had called to congratulate Alexander on his graduation or announce another pregnancy. She was wrong.

Her sixty-year-old father, Dominik had suffered through an apoplectic* incident while working a double shift at Oshkosh Truck** corporation. He was alive and in the hospital, but paralyzed on his right side. Nora kept that latest bit of painful news to herself, not wishing to disrupt her son's big day.

ALEXANDER ... 1946 – 1951

Pomp And Circumstance ...

June 19 was graduation day for the senior class of Mount Clemens High School. Nora had graciously raised a respectful, honorable son and could not have been prouder. She carried that distinction proudly and no one could deny her achievement. Eighteen year-old Alexander was her polished badge of pride. He was about to become the second member of her immediate family to receive a diploma. Her sister Marie had been the first.

Despite all the upheaval and heartache that had been cast her way over the past two decades, and especially the previous two weeks, the one great thing Nora had been able to accomplish was about to be put on display.

Nora and her guests arrived early at the auditorium and sat together; second row, center. She was sitting in the middle of good company with Sister Anna Maria on her left and Sister Mary Alice of Saint Mary School on the right. Nora and the nuns have known one another since Alexander was an infant. Of course, there was the familiar chatter about the school, their work and the students, yet there was a strange, eerie quiet hanging over the second row. Neither mentioned or questioned Father John's absence, nor spoke his name. Rather, they sat in their seats much like grade school students waiting in the principal's office: silently ignoring the incident, nervously smiling and expecting the shoe to drop at any moment.

The auditorium of Mount Clemens High School filled quickly to its capacity of slightly over two hundred audience members. Behind the heavy, royal blue stage curtains, two twenty-foot, four-level sections of tiered wooden bleacher seats awaited their occupants. Faculty advisor and Librarian Constance Hedsturm had all eighty-four presumptive graduates of the class of 1946 assembled in the adjoining gymnasium, awaiting her direction. Alexander was one of thirty-two young men ready to receive a diploma. The class of 1946 was the fifth successive group of graduating seniors where the girls significantly outnumbered the boys.

The effects of World War were still evident. The young men who did not lie about their age to enlist in the armed forces often took advantage of the wartime industrial push and quit high school for the assembly lines. For the past five years, the Mount Clemens baseball Bengals had struggled to keep a team of 13 players on the field.

Right-fielder Alexander made every effort to keep his mind on baseball. The end of World War II led Alex to consider how much the absence of his father had influenced his entire boyhood, forcing him to assume responsibilities generally relegated to fathers and husbands. Lately, the task had become markedly more difficult. Now his father was not only gone, and not just *in theater* or *in action*, but *missing*. It was crystal-clear that his father would not be sitting in the audience. Additionally, over the past weeks he had witnessed his mother's mood change radically. She quickly went from mournful dismay to revitalized youth before an abrupt fall into demoralized melancholy. He refused to obsess about it, but it worried him. He blamed his father.

For a full week, the senior class had rehearsed marching into the auditorium again, again and over again. Each time, Principal Willis Hurford found fault with one or more supposed missteps. For Alex, it was overstated, overacted pomp and circumstance. He considered the graduation march itself to be nothing more than collected noise of hollow substance; every note meaningless twaddle and nothing like the timely hits of Bob Crosby or Jimmy and Tommy Dorsey.

Alex was dealing with plenty of distractions other than his life at home or the imminent musical mess in the auditorium. His thoughts were drifting elsewhere. Specifically, he was thinking about seeing his girl Audrey at Bobby Weeks' graduation party. She and Alex had been sharing smiles and glances all morning.

Pomp and Circumstance[**] crassly interrupted his daydreams about dancing with Audrey to the latest records on the hit parade. Miss Hedsturm clapped her hands, giving the signal for the class to gather in the hall and line up in reverse alphabetical order as rehearsed. The pomp began just as circumstance allowed the public address system to play a certain well-worn, squawky and scratched record.

The students paraded down the aisles, took the stage and filed onto the waiting stage and bleachers. With wanton disregard for precision, eighty-four pairs of feet caused the wooden bleachers to crack, creak and moan enough to override the scratchy sounds coming from the Western Electric phonograph. Predictably, the entire procession was much more of a memorable event to the audience than to the participants onstage. The seniors just wanted to forget the pomp and get to the parties. Miss Hedsturm and Principal Hurford however, were quite pleased with how the production was progressing.

Alexander was standing in the second row, surrounded by his alphabetical homeroom friends, Jeffrey Tatelford, and Paulette Tuttle. His buddy Bobby Weeks, a six-foot-three-inch standout, towered in the back row between Noreen Van Knoren and Alex's steady girl, Audrey Young. Their mortarboard hats with the swaying, wiggling nylon tassels played no favorites and equally annoyed every graduate on the heavily shellacked bleacher. Like the slick, silky feel of their rayon graduation gowns, the maroon fabric seemed to promise the students a smooth transition from high school to the adult world.

When the music ended, the talking began. The valedictorian had her say, the salutatorian seconded the valedictorian's remarks in a nearly word-for-word replay, and the class president outlined his hopes for everyone's future prosperity and happiness.

Finally, it was Principal Willis Hurford's turn at the podium. He used his sterile monotone to summon each graduate by name in plodding alphabetical order. Methodically, one by one, each graduate filed off the bleachers, across the stage and received a diploma to restrained applause. The entire affair turned out to be just as Alexander had expected: choreographed boredom and scripted mumbo jumbo. The auditorium emptied markedly faster than it filled.

When Alex tossed his mortarboard and gown into the laundry hamper in the entry vestibule, his high school experience yielded to his excited expection. He was going home for a shower, change and dinner before heading over to Bobby's house for the party. He could hardly wait until he could hold his Audrey.

To Each His Own ...

As he got ready to celebrate, Alex could smell dinner on the stove. After some deep breaths, he was able to control his earlier nervous jitters. The graduation and dance party at Bobby's house over on Clinton River Road was a big deal to Alex. Audrey was a catch.

His mother had made a pot of chicken with dumplings, one of his favorites. He checked the knot of his tie in the bathroom mirror, dropped a splash of Old Spice into his palms and rubbed the sting into his freshly shaven face and the back of his neck. He slipped on his two-tone brown and white oxfords, snapped on his suspenders and dropped his sport jacket over his arm. He bounded down the stairs like a kid running for the Good Humor^{**} man.

Nora stood at the kitchen stove, ladling the soup into bowls and carefully dropping two dumplings into each. Alexander's pent up excitement and bubbling anticipation blocked his perception of his mother's dark mood. She brought dinner to the table, carrying a bowl in each hand, and carefully set them down onto the table.

When he looked up, Alex couldn't help but notice his mother's bloodshot eyes. Her cheeks were flushed with emotion and stained with dried tears. He thought he had discovered the problem when he spotted the morning mail and a Bank of Detroit passbook lying at the corner of the table. On top of the Detroit Edison bill was on open letter from the War Department. He hurriedly pulled the correspondence out of the envelope it and discovered that it was an identical, word-for-word copy of the June 1 telegram. He then assumed it was the reason behind his mother's distress. It was the promised confirmation letter of his father's status.

He tried to soothe her, "Don't let old news get you down all over again, Mom. We've come this far, and it seems so foolish to let a hiccup of old news throw a monkey wrench into our lives all over again. We went through all this weeks ago. This ain't nothing new. And besides, we're stronger now."

Nora sat, covered her face with her hands and began to cry. This level of torment was new to Alex. It was disturbing. His heart ached with hers. It was the first time he had seen his mother surrender to grief.

Speechless, he moved his chair next to hers and sat as close as he could without trying to smother her release of anguish. He gently laid his arm across her shoulders and uttered, "Sshussh. It's all right, Mom."

She tried desperately to control her sobs, and struggled to catch her breath. She fought back at her misery, dabbed at her tears, broke the bonds of her torturous heartache and talked through her wheezing. She formed her words between labored gasps, "It's not your father I'm upset about. It's everything else. I feel so damn alone. Forgotten and alone."

She took a minute to compose herself and started again, "Please don't worry about me, Alex. This is my problem and not yours. Not yours in the least bit. Today is your day, so pay no mind to my troubles. They're all mine. Every single bit of it is mine. All damn mine."

Overridden by obligation ...

Hearing his mother utter a curse word was akin to Martians landing a spaceship in downtown Detroit ... it just doesn't happen. Hearing her say the same word twice meant that the Martians were landing in Mount Clemens as well. Alex knew something serious was troubling his mother.

His earlier good mood crashed and burned to cinders. The dream of a good time and dancing close with Audrey disappeared like cottonwood tuft in a spring breeze. He couldn't and wouldn't leave her alone like this. He promised, "I'm not leaving you alone tonight, Mom. I don't want to leave you alone."

"I won't hear of it. You go to your party and have fun. I just hit a little rough patch, that's all. You were right, the letter did it. It threw me for a loop all over again, but I'll be fine. You go to your party. I mean it." She regained her breath, calmed her nerves and could speak with some authority, "You're going to Bobby's and you're going to have fun. That's the end of it."

Alex was familiar with his mother's resolve. Had they heard his mother using that tone of voice, the Martians would start up their spaceships and take off for outer space.

She straightened her shoulders, slid the bankbook across the table, and dabbed at her eyes again. "That's from your father. It's your graduation present."

Alex was curious but puzzled, "When did he do that?"

"He left it here in April when he reenlisted. It's for your college, he said. He also said that he didn't think you'd go."

Alex opened the passbook and saw a single, initialed, handwritten entry with a little red date stamp next to it that indicated a balance of five thousand dollars. He closed the little book and shoved it back across the table.

"You know that I really haven't given college any serious thought, Mom. I said that a million times and the Old Man knew it. I'm not that kind of guy. I'll be happy just working for a living and getting my hands dirty."

"Eat your supper and go to your party, Son. We can talk about college tomorrow." Nora knew better.

He patiently finished his bowl of chicken stew, two dumplings and a slice of rye. He was able to sneak a few glances his mother's way. She caught him once and cast a brave-but-weak smile, but neither said a word. The silence was finally broken with the clink of his spoon into the empty bowl.

His mother had regained her composure by the time the second dumpling disappeared. The old, time-tested 'chicken soup' cure must have worked its magic yet again. She gave her son a peck on the cheek on his way out the front door. Halfway down the front walk, he turned around, waved and blew his mother a kiss. He noticed that she didn't advise him to 'be home before the streetlights come on' and considered that perhaps it was her way of silently granting him passage into adulthood. Then again, it was still a little more than two hours before sunset.

He gave his mother a smile and sent another little wave, "Goodnight, Mom."

As he started for Bobby's, it hit him. *Five thousand was a wad of cash.*

Alexander's Ragtime Band ...

Bobby Weeks had been planning this party in slapdash fashion since the beginning of the school year. Month by month, the anticipation and the accompanying expectations grew. Bobby's height, flashy red hair, freckles and an ostentatious, almost bawdy laugh brought him the attention that powered his outgoing personality. The planned party brought him more.

Alexander's friendship with Bobby was built around their mutual interest in girls, cars, gasoline engines and the Detroit Tigers. Bobby could be obnoxious, but when he was alone with Alex, he exercised some self-restraint. There were whispers that Bobby was dishonest, but there wasn't enough evidence to convince Alex. Once however, he overheard Bobby's mother, Myrtle Weeks protest, "Bobby Weeks! You little black snake!"

The party's guest list grew during the last few weeks of school, especially after Bobby started to brag about the liquid menu. His father, Charles R. Weeks, was Senior Brewmaster at Stroh and had facilitated a supply of Stroh's non-alcoholic Bohemian 'near beer' in addition to the usual Vernors and Canada Dry. Twenty graduates, nearly one-forth of the Class of '46, were invited to help fill the back yard of 214 Clinton River Road with raucous, teenage antics.

Alex hopped the 19 Mile Road streetcar, dropped a nickel in the slot, and rode to Bobby's house on Clinton River Road, believing that his six o'clock arrival would be acceptably late. On his way into the yard, he counted three cars in the driveway, another on the lawn and a few more on the street. In the backyard, his eyes quickly found Audrey and at least two dozen more of his classmates. He paid attention to his surroundings as he began to work his way across the yard toward Miss Audrey Young. He noticed Bobby's father, Charles was at the charcoal brazier, fanning the smoke and flames with a folded copy of the Detroit Free Press. Myrtle Weeks was on the patio holding a cocktail, well within eyeshot of the sodas, pretzels and popcorn. An open bottle of whiskey sat alongside a quart of soda water on a folding tray table. Bobby's father had a stack of big band, jazz and swing records piled next to a substantial ten-pound, Bendix Super-phonic record player. Four strings of light bulbs dangled over the back yard and flagstone patio in no particular pattern or order. They hung suspended from the maple trees, over to the eaves and back to the porch roof. Bobby's younger siblings Alan, Tommy and Carol were nowhere in sight. The weather was also cooperating with mild temperatures, calm easterly breezes off Lake St. Clair and a starlit sky. Overall, it was crystal clear that a fun night was in store.

Audrey spotted Alexander and took him by the arm as quickly as she could. She bumped his hip with hers and flashed a flirty smile, "Hey, Alex! I was almost worried that you weren't coming!" She wore a dark blue skirt that came just below her knees, white socks, loafers and an ivory, snugly-fit cardigan over a crisp white blouse.

Alex explained his delayed arrival, "I got held up a little bit and lost track of the time when I was talking with my mom. She's still upset about my old man." Before Alex finished his last sentence, she started walking him toward the patio. Audrey was eager to dance and champing at the bit like a brood mare. She drew Alex onto the flagstone patio and once there, she pulled his arm around her waist and waltzed him into Les Brown's 'Sentimental Journey'.

A demure smile wasn't the only Lana Turner quality that Audrey could claim. She had a fine figure, strawberry blonde hair, blue eyes and the soft, fluffy personality of a bunny. She was friendly, mildly daring, and seemed to have a carefully selected inner circle. She was a good dancer, too. Audrey remained on the patio and stubbornly kept Alex busy shuffling his shoes for seven records.

Bubbly Audrey didn't need Alex to tell her that something was on his mind. She knew there was something troubling him. No matter how close she was or where she touched him, his thoughts were elsewhere.

"I'm sorry, sweetheart. My mother is in distress and I really need to go home. I just don't feel right staying here and after that telegram and the letter today, it was too much for her. I'm sorry."

She tried to be sympathetic, but sounded discouraged, "I understand." Audrey was an only child and had lost her Marine Corps father in 1943 somewhere in New Guinea. She remembered her mother's anguish when they got the news. Still, it was so long ago that she couldn't really understand why Alex felt that way.

He tried a compromise, "How about the pictures on Friday? A Friday night movie? How's that? I think 'Spellbound' is at the Odeon, with Gregory Peck and that Ingrid Bergman. And we could grab a hot dog and soda at Fergusson's."

"Sure." She was disappointed, and knew she was playing second fiddle. Still, she tried to deny, or at least disguise her jealousy.

"I'll call tomorrow, Audrey. And Friday too, of course. Thanks for understanding."

They shared a gentle kiss, a cuddle, and one more kiss. Audrey was merely going through the motions. Alex realized it and felt torn.

He refused to rethink his decision, fought emotional temptation and turned away. He didn't waste any time getting out of Bobby's back yard and down the street to the trolley stop.

While he stood under the streetlight, his thoughts drifted back to Audrey, the dancing and their planned Friday movie date. He fantasized about the intimate secret he'd discovered as he and his flirtatious Audrey danced. He held her close during their first dance and allowed his curious touch to reveal that there wasn't a brassiere under her sweater. He wondered if she realized he knew and if she wanted him to know. The mystery started a fire that would burn for the rest of the night.

He remembered how fresh and beautiful his Audrey looked, the taste of her kiss and the scent of Elizabeth Arden perfume at the nape of her neck. He worried if his departure had disheartened or tarnished the sparkle of their relationship.

He imagined an embrace, a waltz while his Audrey presses her body close, surrenders, kisses him and asks him to stay. He would return her kiss and they would hold one another throughout the night.

For a fleeting moment, he considered turning back, but his love-struck stargazing was abruptly spoiled by a different kind of electricity. The 19 Mile streetcar was rattling into view and throwing wild sparks from its trolley pole to the overhead power line.

I've Got Rain In My Eyes ...

Alex walked softly up the porch steps and turned his key in the lock. He expected that his mother would be upstairs in bed, but found her lying on the front room sofa and suspected that she had been waiting for him to come home.

Nora's voice passed through the gloom, "Alex, is that you?"

He was relieved that her tone telegraphed curiosity rather than alarm.

His eyes adjusted to the dim light. "Yeah, it's me, Mom. I left Bobby's early. The whole party was off the cob* and not for me. And I got bored."

The only light in the house was coming from the kitchen ceiling lamp down the hall, and the smell of candles lingered. Alex noticed the pewter candlestick on the sideboard held the remnants of a burned out taper. He sat in the armchair, leaned forward, elbows on thighs and asked, "Are you all right, Mom? Want me to get you something? A glass of water, maybe?"

Nora sat up, but kept the cotton wrap up under her chin and covering her. "No, nothing. I'm fine. Really, I'm OK. Just tired and worn out, I guess."

It made him uncomfortable to see his mother in such a state of distress. Her afternoon blue mood had returned, worsened and turned deep violet. He tried again to change her darkened frame of mind, "That bank passbook from the old man ... I think you should go ahead and use it for yourself, Mom. Get some nice things and maybe cheer yourself up a little bit. Turn over a new leaf, like they say."

"That account is yours, Alexander Throckmorton, not mine. It yours and you can do what you like, but your father left it for your college."

Alex tried to convince himself more than his mother, "You know by now that I'm not thinking about college, Mom. Not yet anyway. Books just don't float my boat. Trade school, maybe. Not college. I'd rather work with my hands, like a man should."

Nora let out a deep sigh. Her son rightly perceived that it came from distress more than frustration. "What's the matter, Mom? The letter from the Army? It was old news, that's all."

She looked up, holding the coverlet close. "It's more than that, Son. I found out yesterday that your Papa Dominik had an apoplectic* fit at work ... and he's paralyzed on his whole right side."

"Jesus ..."

Nora didn't say a word, and let her eyes scold him for a moment before she continued, "I don't feel at home here any longer, Alexander. So much has changed in my life. And your life. I don't feel at home here and I'm not comfortable with my standing at the church. I feel that I'm not able to devote all that I should after everything that has happened. It's impossible to explain. There is no longer a path here that I can follow and everywhere I look I see a dead end. I'm boxed in. I feel the need to move to Oshkosh. I need to leave, not just to be with Papa and help Mutti, but I have to get out of here and leave my darkened past behind. And I think it would be better for you, too. A fresh start. A new life. And I would feel better if you would accompany me."

Alexander didn't answer. He did not see this knuckleball coming. His shock over the proposed move completely displaced his curiosity about how his mother could have a darkened past.

Nora read his expression, allowed the blanket to fall from her shoulders onto her lap, and continued her plea, "You're young, and you'll be able to adjust to new surroundings and find new friends. Your aunt Marie said that there's a college right there in Oshkosh, and one in Fond Du Lac and one in Appleton, too. You can stay here, but I would like you to come with me. You are the only light in my dismal world.

"We can leave Detroit and start again in Oshkosh. It will be the fresh air I need, Son. I feel so alone, so cast off and so soiled. I can take care of Mutti and Papa and you can go to school and make a dozen of new friends. Please come with me. There's nothing to tie us here.

"When I look back on my life, I know I was harsh with both you and your father. Your father was harsh too, but for reasons I still question ... I know that he needed to be ... in order to survive in his gray world, but I'll never know why.

"There are things that you and I don't know ... your father was a haunted man. He was haunted by evil things from his past.

"I think when he left Buffalo ... I think he was trying to escape from something. Maybe he had a fear. He had an older brother that left at the same time ... Leopold ... but he never talked about him. Not to me. Your father kept secrets. Too many secrets.

"Understand this, Alexander ... your father was barely eighteen when we married and I was not yet sixteen. We were young and dumb and I was a child. My father never accepted him and Nicholas considered himself banished from my family and my faith. My great uncle Dmitri in Hungary saw my future on the day I was born, and he cautioned my mother that I would live two childhoods. The first would be happy and the second would not. Now I pray that I could have a third."

Nora's eyes looked up to the portrait of Christ. She bowed her head and crossed herself before she continued, "That was then. This is now. I never wished your father any ill will, nor did he on me. I hope that your father ... that my Nicholas has found peace. I really do. May Jesus save his soul.

"My Nicholas, your father ... was absent but honorable. He provided for us, Alex. And he made certain that neither you nor I would want for anything."

Nora stood, folded the coverlet and set in down on the sofa. She put a hand on her son's shoulder and said, "Your father stole my essence and flew away on aluminium[*] wings, but he provided sustenance. That much I can say. He left me alone, but he did not forsake me. Or you."

"I'm not going to college."

"Good night, Son."

With those three words, his mother ended her sermon. To his relief, his mother stopped rambling, kissed him on the cheek and went upstairs to bed. Alexander felt that he had successfully made his point about college, but the discussion about Oshkosh would have to wait. He had a date on Friday.

Yes, Oshkosh could wait. He couldn't. He was afraid Audrey wouldn't.

Perhaps his mother wasn't serious about Oshkosh.

He thought, *"It's not easy being the man of the house."*

Let Me Call You Sweetheart ...

The Friday movie date with Audrey didn't come to be. She telephoned two hours before show time, canceled, apologized and blamed a headache. She promised that she would be in touch when she was feeling better.

Alex did receive a telephone call on Saturday evening but it wasn't Audrey on the other end of the chord. It was Myrtle Weeks, with news that Bobby had crashed his car on Friday night and was at Harper Hospital with broken bones. Alex held the handset closer and tried to guess the rest of the story. He couldn't see what was coming down the line, but wasn't surprised or totally devastated when he found out. Myrtle told him that Audrey Young was also in the car with Bobby but she had fared much better, suffering a laceration on her left leg and some cuts and bruises. Audrey was also admitted to the hospital, received some stitches and spent the night, but was sent home on Saturday afternoon. Bobby was expected to recover, but the duration of his hospital stay remained uncertain.

After Myrtle hung up, Alex placed the handset back on the receiver, and remained seated on the sofa. The news about Bobby and Audrey served up a spicy stew of mixed emotions. Alex weighed his options and decided not to visit or telephone. Instead, he rode the streetcar to the post office on Cass Avenue, purchased a penny postcard and wrote a short, get-well note to Audrey's home on Moross Street. After he dropped it into the local delivery letter slot, he decided that since he was already there, he might as well spend another penny and send a note to Bobby also.

Alexander wasn't nearly as angry or devastated over the accident as he was disappointed by his judgment of character. Something his father told him before he left for the Orient hit home, "The road always goes both ways, so make damn sure you're headed in the right direction."

Things in Mount Clemens slowly began to fall back into place and within a week, Nora resumed her staff work at the Saint Mary School. Summer recess had started and her schedule was reduced to three hours a day; a welcome respite. Culling textbooks, polishing desks and washing windows was plodding work, but the routine helped soothe her anxiety.

Mother and son had a number of discussions and heartfelt conversations after the telegram, the graduation and Bobby's accident. Alex briefly considered enlisting in the Army or entering a machinist trade school like the Packard Institute, but ultimately dismissed such ideas as pure folly. He knew recent events had been pounding his mother like a blacksmith's hammer. Alex knew they needed to leave.

The news about Nicholas and Dominik weighed heavily upon Alex's decision to support his mother's move to Wisconsin. Although she never disclosed the true reason behind her bleak mood, she couldn't hide her demeanor. Privately, her shame weighed ten times heavier than the uncertainty over her husband's status or the anxiety over her father's health.

Twice during the week after Alex's graduation, Nora visited a local attorney and put 12 Second Street up for sale. She informed Saint Mary School of her impending move to Oshkosh and received unexpected assistance. Sister Anna Maria promised that she would contact the Green Bay diocese and check for any comparable teaching assistant or helper positions in or near Oshkosh.

A few days later, Sister Anna Maria handed Nora a letter of recommendation from Bishop Fuller to the Parish Priest of Saint Joseph Church, Oshkosh, Wisconsin.

Alexander quit his Saturday job at the Kroger grocery and resigned himself to life in Wisconsin, at least for the immediate future. He helped his mother pack a six by six foot wooden crate with household goods and arranged its shipment to New York Avenue in Oshkosh with Midwest Motor Express. Nora donated her furniture and the remaining odds and ends to Saint Peter Parish.

They purchased coach tickets on the Milwaukee Road and left Detroit for Oshkosh at six o'clock in the morning on July 4, Independence Day.

Whoa, Sailor ...

An otherwise smooth trip ended with an unexpected bump when they stepped off the train and onto the platform in Oshkosh. Nora's sister Marie met them at the station with the news that Dominik had experienced a second stroke at home in his bed. He did not survive.

Notwithstanding the dark clouds that she left behind in Mount Clemens and the sudden storm that she faced when she arrived in Oshkosh, Nora's mood gradually brightened. Five hundred miles of steel rail somehow made a world of difference. Leaving behind a soured and spoiled life seemed to be the change that Nora needed for a fresh start. It heartened Alex that his mother had found a measure of contentment in her new surroundings. It was gratifying, but baffling.

Bishop Fuller's letter of introduction helped Nora find a sense of community in her new environment. By the third week, Nora was hired as a teaching assistant at Most Blessed Mother School. It was a modest position with not much more than token compensation. Fortunately, the sale of the home in Mount Clemens, along with her husband's continued military allotment, provided Nora with financial security.

Over the months that ensued, Nora's resolve and resilience reflected her inner strength. Whether it was her confident tenacity or dogged determination, she privately fought through her intimate degradation and personal loss to remain a bastion of strength. Nora's elderly mother gave her a sense of purpose and her sister Marie provided emotional support when needed. The Church still played an important role, but not first and foremost as it did in Mount Clemens.

Try as he might, Alex found it nearly impossible to feel at home in Oshkosh. His grandmother Gabi was a sweet soul chained to tradition and blackened by the recent death of her husband. Moreover, she was two generations older and entrenched in a patriarchal Old World, Austro-Hungarian culture that found change almost unthinkable. He imagined that his situation mirrored the icy reality that his father had experienced in 1927.

Alexander landed a job as a stock clerk at Krambo Grocery downtown but due to vast numbers of returning GIs and the post-war recession, he was unable to find meaningful employment in or around Oshkosh. Fresh out of high school and plucked from his hometown, he felt like a fish out of water.

He thought about his options and concluded that reading college textbooks was about as appealing as a night out with Sophie Tucker**, and a career of stocking shelves with Wheaties, Campbell's soup and cans of Crisco would be as tedious as counting feathers on a chicken.

All things considered, he enlisted in the United States Navy in February 1947. Alex had his head in the clouds until the entry physical and eye exam put the kibosh on his preferred enlistment option. A Navy optometrist discovered that he was partially color blind and unable to identify luminous, vivid reds or high-spectrum greens. A small, twenty-page picture book of little colored dots ruined his chance to become a Navy pilot. He settled for Aircraft Technician.

Since World War I, the US Navy had been recruiting new sailors with the slogan, *Join the Navy and see the world*. He didn't expect it, but when Alex joined the Navy, he received an education that no university or college could offer. During the first three years of his enlistment, he saw quite a bit of the United States from Naval installations, coast to coast. He had his hands on steel and his nose in books. He began with recruit training at Port Deposit, Maryland, followed by engine mechanics school in Ypsilanti, Michigan and aircraft technical school in Norman, Oklahoma. Upon completion of the first three assignments, Lieutenant Commander Morris Betterman recommended him for further training in Naval Aviation Administration at Oak Harbor, Washington.

In November, 1949, he was assigned to the aircraft carrier USS Valley Forge** as an Aircrewman, Aviation Specialist X with the rank of Petty Officer Third. On December 6, 1950, the Valley Forge and its crew of three-thousand-plus sailed from San Diego, California for deployment to the Korean War Command, East China Sea area of operations.

Shortly after the carrier arrived in theatre, Alex was assigned as a senior enlisted crewman aboard a Sikorsky HO-3S[**] helicopter unit for emergency medical transport and fleet messaging service off the Valley Forge.

Ten months later, in early September, 1951, Fleet Command sought a volunteer for Temporary Duty at Fleet Activities, Sasebo[**], Japan. The Navy had essentially hung the carrot in front of the right horse. Alexander was in the middle of his second deployment and nearing his expiration term of service and discharge in February. He struggled to make a timely decision, knowing that volunteering for anything in the military could end up as fool's folly, and accepting an extended new assignment could require a renewed enlistment. The pros and cons that weighed on his choice bounced back and forth like ping-pong balls in a championship table-tennis match. He did, however, have an ace in the hole: if the duty didn't appeal to him, he could simply get out of the Navy in February and return home to Oshkosh. Within an hour, Alex had stopped second-guessing his decision, threw caution overboard like a barrelful of rusty rivets and volunteered.

Four days later, it did not come as a complete surprise when the Navy exercised its standard operating procedure of *hurry up and wait*. The on-again-off-again, cease-fire and armistice negotiations at Kaesong were off again, as was Alex's temporary assignment.

In late September 1951, the peace talks resumed, thereby facilitating his temporary transfer to Sasebo. In order to accept the Navy's offer of a TDY[*] station to Headquarters, United Nations Command, Joint Services Signals Section, he agreed to extend his enlistment for one year. It was common knowledge that an off-ship assignment to a Naval Base Headquarters was like living the life of Riley[**]. At age twenty-four, Alexander believed that he had nothing to lose and only experience to gain.

Although it was a year since his last shore leave in The Philippines, he had no deal-breaking complaints about the Navy. Like most of the crew aboard *Happy Valley*, Alex believed that a bitching sailor was a happy sailor. However, lately he was experiencing symptoms of a fleeting condition that was common among sailors and soldiers alike: the effects of a serious, but treatable physical affliction: the lack of female companionship.

There were no drops of scuttlebutt[*] or mess[*] deck intelligence to indicate that Sasebo, Japan offered the same fringe benefits as Subic Bay[**] in the Philippines did, but he held out hope that he could find some relief on shore.

On October 1, he stepped off the carrier deck, shuffled down the gangway and touched dry land at Sasebo. Once ashore, an ensign immediately directed him toward the Arrivals Briefing and Orientation Center. Inside a nondescript Quonset hut, he learned that his duty classification was as a Communications Yeoman assigned to Headquarters, Joint Services, Signals Section, located in the Victor Sector of the base.

KATHERINE ... 1951 – 1952

As Time Goes By ...

Katherine Ann Dobbs grew up as an only child in Solvay, New York, a suburb on the west side of Syracuse. Her family lived in a brick and frame, two-and-a-half-story Tudor on a two-acre pastoral lot in the Craig Lang Estates neighborhood. The Southwicke Country and Tennis Clubs were a short, three-minute, one-mile drive away on Preston Pointe.

During her formative years at 100 Sedge Row Crossing, young Katherine wanted for naught, but because of the numerous professional and charitable commitments of her adoptive parents, oftentimes she found herself in the care and supervision of others. With exception of her seat at the dinner table, Katherine was seldom in the company of either her mother or father and rarely together with both at the same time. Her parents employed a bevy of well-qualified surrogates to provide their daughter with guidance and education throughout her formative years. She grew up educated and proficient in everything except forming bonds of trust and affection.

She spent the summers of her childhood at Camp Fire Girls nature retreats or Girl Scout camps in the Catskills. As an adolescent, she attended Anglican Summer Youth programs in Cobleskill, Saratoga or Saranac Lake, New York. Partly driven by the horse-themed novels *My Friend Flicka, Black Beauty* and the movie *National Velvet*, she developed an infatuation with horses, and like countless other girls, wished for a pony of her own. After her thirteenth birthday, the Adirondack church retreat at Saranac Horse Camp became her only destination because of their riding lessons, instruction in basic dressage, equine care and simple husbandry. She would never know it, but her fascination for horses would affect the lives of several people, some unknown to her, far into the future.

She had dozens of private tutors and several nannies over the years, but her favorite was also her last, Elspeth Keiley, an immigrant au pair from Dromgarriff, Ireland. Together, they built and shared a relationship that was new to Katherine: a close, personal bond. Like sisters, they shared stories, little secrets, fantasies and created nicknames for one another. Katherine's father allowed *Peth* to move into the upstairs bedroom adjacent to *Kitty Kat*, a shift that further tightened the girls' friendship. For the first time in her young life, Katherine built a close connection with someone who was dear to her and enjoyed a closeness that resembled familial love. She cherished Elspeth's understanding, words of encouragement and gentle hugs. The Irish miss became a surrogate sister.

Katherine turned sixteen during the final six months of Elspeth's two-year tenure with the Dobbs family, and during that time, nineteen-year-old Elspeth went beyond her prescribed duties and enlightened the young, blossoming American about the birds, bees and young men. Beneath the ornate plaster ceiling of the family study, colleen Keiley glamorized every sensuous detail that she and young Katherine gleaned from decades-old copies of John Cleland's erotic *Fanny Hill*[**] and D.H. Lawrence's *Lady Chatterley's Lover*[**], and used the 1930 home edition of Encyclopedia Britannica as a full-color, illustrated textbook of human anatomy and biology. Elspeth's embellished tales and romanticized descriptions of her personal escapades in County Cork sent Katherine's imagination sailing far beyond the oak-paneled walls of the extensive Dobbs' family library.

She longed for the idyllic affection she discovered within the pages of romantic novels.

Driven by fascination, curiosity, youthful daring and a hunger for intimacy, Katherine had her first rousing, fully physical sexual experience at the age of seventeen. She was away at summer horse camp; it was 1945, World War II had just ended and the country's mood was at a full gallop. She allowed a twenty-something stable hand to steal away her virginity on the grassy shores of Moody Pond. The deed left her heart empty, but her senses longed for more.

Prophetically, it was her last summer camp at Saranac Lake, New York. In the fall, she would begin her senior year at the Essex Preparatory Montessori School in Skaneateles and would not have the time for more riding lessons. Rather, she would prepare for college.

Katherine's intimate education accelerated during her senior year at the Montessori school. She discovered that she could be judiciously selective with her male companions and acquired the skills needed to steal a kiss or hide away for a secret tryst. Her ability to cherry pick a few promising suitors from a senior class of more than fifty young men allowed her to temporarily swim in a sea of self-confidence that seemed without depth or bounds. In August of 1946, she left Skaneateles, high school, Craig Lang and Solvay behind. She headed off to Ithaca, New York and Cornell University with a bucketful of hopes and expectations, a boatload of daring experience and a sinking hole in her heart. Her father informed her that Elspeth was no longer needed at 100 Sedge Row Crossing and that the young lady from County Cork would be leaving the United States on a passenger steamer for Galway, Ireland.

Likely because of her connection with the Montessori school, a member of Cornell's Theta Alpha chapter of the Chi Omega** women's Pan-Hellenic Conference contacted her within days of her arrival on campus. After her recruitment and initiation into the sorority, she became hopeful and enjoyed a renewed affinity with the world around her. She developed a sense of belonging that enabled her to collect more new friends than ever before. The structured culture of Greek Life at Cornell proved to be a positive and gratifying experience.

Very early in the semester, a sorority sister introduced Katherine to redheaded, rough-cut, twenty-year-old Roland Hilliard of Tulsa, Oklahoma, a junior-year undergraduate majoring in biology with aspirations toward Veterinary Medicine. Their relationship blossomed over the fall and winter but began to wilt with the warmth of spring.

Katherine experienced her first broken heart. Tragically, her soaring love life crashed and burned before her first year at university ended. Roland told her, "A kiss is just a kiss, Sweetheart. In the heat of the moment, and when all is said and done, everybody says *I love you*, but nobody really means it. As time goes by and you get older, you'll realize that."

She collected her emotions quickly and realized that Roland had treated her exactly as she had handled her brief, hectic liaisons during her high school years. She vowed that an embarrassing break-up wouldn't happen again, and from that day forward, she would be the one who picks, plucks and tastes the fruit off the apple tree.

Each successive September at Cornell's ivy-covered Ithaca campus, Katherine received different professors, new class schedules, updated syllabi and textbooks. She became an active member of the university's Equestrian Club during her sophomore year and, next to Chi Omega, it became her second-most rewarding social experience on campus. During her remaining three years at the university, she continued be in the company of young men enrolled in Equine Medicine at Cornell's Veterinary College. She reverted to her Montessori *modus operandi* and collected her suitors like butterflies, with a flash of colorful, sweet nectar. Katherine kept them all pinned neatly inside her crystal-clear, dreamy display case of memories.

She graduated with honors from Cornell University in May of 1950, and received a neatly rolled sheepskin secured with a bright orange ribbon tied into a bow. Inside was her Bachelor's Degree in design, but it did not come with an instruction book, map to the future or a written guarantee. She was leaving college with no direction and no idea which road to take. The soirées and intimate tête-à-têtes were over.

At the age of twenty-two, she discovered that a university diploma did not ensure employment. The post-war recession, industrial migration, plant closings, and corporate mergers took their toll on job opportunities in Upstate New York. Moreover, the need for wartime munitions production had disappeared, and the newly discovered high levels of industrial pollutants in some of the Finger Lakes created ecological concerns. Several chemical and fertilizer plants throughout the region began closing their doors against of the winds of an environmental scandal. Although her immediate future looked bleak and the prospect of securing meaningful employment was next to nil, unforeseen change was coming for the young Cornell graduate.

Rocking, Rolling, Ocean ...
All ahead full ...

Roger Dobbs, Katherine's father, was Managing Director at Condor Chemical and her mother Mabel held the title of Office Superintendent at the Oneida Street offices of Solvay Salt. Mabel's father, Ignatius Lumpkin had been Plant Manager and Vice President of Drying Operations up until his retirement in early 1949.

Her father's executive position at Condor Chemical was in serious jeopardy. After fifty years in Syracuse, there were rampant rumors that the plant was closing soon to avoid environmental embarrassment. Furthermore, her mother's employer, Solvay Evaporated Salt, was considering a move to Elmira. Katherine's dreams of finding meaningful professional employment in Central New York and maintaining her independent lifestyle were disappearing faster than the smoke from her father's Meerschaum pipe.

In the months that followed her graduation, her search for employment in and around her hometown of Syracuse proved fruitless. Katherine's quest resulted in disappointment and frustration. During an interview at Carrier Corporation[**], she learned firsthand that Upstate New York was overflowing with highly qualified job seekers and that a design degree was useless if there were no new products to design. Before the door closed behind her, her interviewer mentioned that technical design applicants did not generally wear skirts or nylon stockings. Insulted and disgruntled, she brazenly considered returning to Cornell for a secondary degree in Veterinary Medicine. She felt dejected and lonely; separated from her Chi Omega clutch of friends and without the emotional distraction of male companionship. For some unknown reason, she unwittingly postponed her rash decision to return to university.

Days later, while returning home from an unsuccessful job hunt in Canastota, she received renewed inspiration from an unlikely source: an outdoor advertisement. In a remote, fallow farm field along NY Route 5 in Chittenango, New York stood an unconventional yet eye-catching and colorful United States Navy recruitment[**] billboard. It pictured a battleship steaming full speed ahead, with all of its young, masculine, muscular hands on deck and ready to serve. An attractive young woman was standing at dockside, winking and proclaiming, *'If I were a man, I'd sign up!'*

For nine months, she searched in vain for employment in her field of study. The roadside advertisement was whimsical enough to convince Katherine Dobbs to enlist. There was nothing tying her to Upstate New York and she certainly had nothing to lose. Desperate for change, she didn't struggle with her decision and audaciously chose her path away from Syracuse. She was ready to take the silver spoon out of her mouth and return to its velvet-lined drawer in the china cabinet. She had grown tired of her surroundings and dared to leave the mowed lawns and manicured fairways of Craig Lang Estates for the rocking, rolling ocean.

She was about to embark on a journey that would result in a head-on collision of culture that she could not imagine. Her parents weren't at all comfortable with her hasty decision and tried in vain to change her mind.

Katherine had set her course. Her ship was about to sail.

After eight weeks of Navy boot camp at Great Lakes, Illinois and twelve weeks of Officer Candidate School at Newport News Naval Station, Katherine received her commission. She spent an additional eight weeks at the Naval Services Academy, graduated as a Lieutenant Junior Grade and received shiny, new lapel brass for Naval Information Systems. Her Montessori and Cornell experience helped Lieutenant Dobbs excel at the Academy and light her way forward. She had a Navy commission, a specialty diploma and a set of orders under her arm that were about to create a tidal wave and eventually turn four lives upside down. Lieutenant Katherine Ann Dobbs would be sailing for Korea.

She returned with her parents to Syracuse after graduation and spent two unavoidable, torturous weeks at home. She knew she was about to be harangued, but couldn't prepare for what was coming. There was one day of defiance, two days of debate, three days of disagreement, four days of deference and five days of reconciliation. It was a long-overdue exercise in family relationships delayed by years of detached existence. She and her parents didn't see it coming. Katherine certainly wanted to see it go.

By the time Lieutenant Dobbs ended her two-week liberty and boarded a Greyhound bus for New York City and LaGuardia Airport, she was anxiously anticipating dropping anchor at a new duty station, meeting new people, forging a career and settling into her role as a Naval officer. For all it mattered, Korea may as well have been Kalamazoo. She was starting anew and ready for her journey with two silver bars on her shoulders. She was expecting the time of her life.

She experienced her first airplane ride on a non-stop transcontinental, New York-to-Los Angeles TWA** flight aboard a Lockheed Constellation**. From Los Angeles, the Southern Pacific Railway gave the Navy Lieutenant first-class, scenic passenger rail service to San Francisco aboard the Coastal Daylight diesel streamliner. It was then up to the United States Navy to carry her from California the rest of the way to Korea. Her initial experience on the high seas would not to be aboard a battleship such as the romantic enlistment poster had promised, rather, she would receive her sea legs and transportation across the Pacific on a re-commissioned, refurbished WW II hospital ship, the USS Haven**. Lieutenant Dobbs steamed from San Francisco, California, to Pearl Harbor, Hawaii, and to Inchon, Korea in August, 1951.

She was one of three female officers who were in transit and awaiting orders for their specific assignments to 7th Fleet, Korea Operations. During the passage of the USS Haven across the Pacific, the women lived belowdecks in a billet section reserved for the ship's twenty-one nurses and two female sailors. The quarters were cramped, restricted and on the dingy, dungeon side of glamorous. Privacy was unknown other than visits to the head*. Off-duty, she shared a ten-by-eight-foot berth with Ensign Florence Clubb, the ship's Junior Galley Officer, who hailed from Meridian, Mississippi and really did curse like a sailor. Even after a shower and wearing clean socks, Mississippi Flo's feet smelled like a pailful of crawfish in the July sun.

Katherine was uncertain of where her permanent[*] duty station would be once the Haven reached port in Korea, and she could only guess if it would be aboard a ship or somewhere on the base at Inchon. Her initial assignment orders were written in military-speak and number codes. She tried to decipher the naval mumbo-jumbo and her best summation was that her duty assignment was to the Seventh Fleet, Task Force 73, Logistic Support and Personnel Staging. She didn't dare ask whatever or wherever that could be, but she didn't really care.

Aboard ship, for twelve hours a day, Katherine occupied an uncomfortable, armless, steel swivel chair behind a two-foot square, gray metal desk. Transport on wartime Navy ships never was gratis and without exception, passengers worked for their suppers. Her duty station was in a row of tiny, two-person offices on the lower bridge deck and alongside the midship helicopter deck. Her desk was equipped with a top-of-the-line Remington *Quiet-Riter,* a note pad and a cupful of ballpoint pens and pencils. Beneath the desk, and fighting with her feet for equal space, were a dozen reams of Hammermill typewriter paper. For hours, Katherine sat with her ears glued to headphones and her fingers plinking out the latest fleet dispatches and authorized news. It was during those hours of monotonous isolation crossing the Pacific that she had daydreams of those men aboard that battleship pictured on a certain distant recruitment billboard in Upstate New York. She discovered that living among seven hundred assorted aboard-ship personnel doesn't protect the lonely from loneliness.

Although the four-week passage across the Pacific was more drudgery than duty, Lieutenant Dobbs survived the crossing in the manner that all good sailors do: she remained aboard ship until it arrived in port. The first cruise casts a lasting impression on fresh recruits, and it throws the longest shadow on those who had never seen the ocean prior to enlistment. Katherine was looking forward to the moment that she could once again place her service oxfords on terra firma.

Nearly two fortnights* after the USS Haven left San Francisco for its second Korean deployment, the ship moored at Inchon Harbor. Lieutenant Dobbs was genuinely happy to be in port and anchored starboard at berth A4. After a month of splash and dash hygiene, she could finally take a Hollywood* shower.

The next day, she held a fresh set of orders in her hands, and could feel her fingers tingle as her eyes moved across the paper. Her heart sailed over the moon. She had a report date of September 5 to Seventh Fleet Headquarters, Operations and Communications Command, Naval Fleet Services, Sasebo, Japan. Her new duty station would be on dry land; Japanese land, but an American military base in Japan was by law, American land.

On September 2, 1951, Lieutenant Dobbs left Inchon, Korea aboard the USS Graffias, a supply and stores ship. She sailed as a passenger for the sixteen-hour passage across the Yellow Sea toward her first duty assignment and permanent posting.

Once the Graffias moored at dock the following morning, she could see that Sasebo was a busy place. Across the quarterdeck, through the gangway and off the ship, Katherine and fourteen other transferred personnel were met dockside by a bus, its driver and a Navy Staff Corps warrant officer. Like the others, Lieutenant Dobbs stood at attention, moving her eyes over the docks, taking in her surroundings and glancing up and down the line of transferees standing in makeshift formation on either side of her. There was one other woman on line. All of them, men and women, held onto one common thread: they were complete strangers.

Katherine sensed her knees wobbling with excitement, and heard, "I am Warrant Officer Briggs. The United States Navy and I welcome you to Fleet Services, Sasebo: your gateway to career enrichment, the Orient, Japan and the Korean Peninsula. This bus will be your transportation to the Transit and Welcome Center. Before you leave the dock area for the bus, please be doubly certain that you have all of your belongings with you." His voice and greeting were as sharp and sterile as a surgeon's scalpel. He stood without expression and watched as thirteen men and two women struggled with full seabags[*] and boarded the bus.

What followed was a woefully bumpy, twenty-minute ride off the docks and into the base. The women shared a seat during the bus ride and introduced themselves. Ensign Ellen Thompson of Wichita, Kansas and Lieutenant Katherine Dobbs found themselves immersed in nothing less than orchestrated pandemonium. They witnessed a naval installation that was bursting at its seams with ships, vehicles, troops and supplies taking part in a strange new type of warfare: a United Nations *Police Action*. There were some flags flying that they recognized from high school social studies, foreign military personnel in unfamiliar uniforms, busy foot traffic on wobbly boardwalks and jeeps bouncing off the paved road, onto gravel side streets or darting between buildings. The troop bus jolted its passengers to a halt outside a single-story wooden structure with the words *Transit Hall* neatly painted in deep blue letters, and centered directly above the portico. Once inside, CWO Briggs segregated Lieutenant Dobbs and Ensign Thompson from the remaining thirteen men and politely directed the women down a hallway and into a separate room. Thirteen pair of eyes watched from the main hall.

Inside, they discovered yet another Warrant Officer seated behind a desk in what appeared to be a small classroom. There was a wall of windows with shades drawn halfway down, about a dozen student desks, a portable blackboard, folded movie screen, a film projector and large instructor's desk. Chief Warrant Officer Alistair Higgins stood up from the instructor's desk and cleared his throat. His voice started pitchy, but he quickly managed to gather some balance, and introduced himself as their sole instructor for five hours of the Navy's mandatory *Newly Arrived Personnel Orientation*. He was a tall, thin man in his thirties, with sandy hair, pale hazel eyes, very fair skin and long, slim fingers.

He provided emotionless, monotonous instruction, word-for-word, directly from the handbooks that included detailed familiarization and inter-agency politesse for varied United Nations forces. Katherine and Ellen also watched two thirty-minute films that were essentially geography lessons identifying the nations involved in the Korean conflict. Halfway through their classroom work, they were given a half-hour break and presented with a nasty bag* that consisted of an egg salad sandwich, four vanilla wafers, a pull-top paper cup of chocolate pudding, a napkin, plastic spoon and a four-pack of Wings** cigarettes. Higgins had a good-natured laugh and offered a half-hearted apology on behalf of the Navy. He explained that it was standard treatment of incoming personnel and promised that the galley food on Sasebo was top-notch. With a bent sense of humor, he gave them pocket-sized copies of the Uniform Code of Conduct and the Geneva Convention Rules for Prisoners of War, explaining that the handouts were a United Nations gourmet dessert. After four and a half hours of classroom toil, the women hoped that they could finally set their careers in motion.

Higgins stepped out from behind his desk, came to attention, snapped a salute, and said, "It was a pleasure to meet you, Lieutenant Dobbs, Ensign Thompson." Perhaps his words were some type of signal, or Naval Code, because at that exact moment, there was a quick, resounding knock on the classroom door. The brass knob turned and in walked a Navy

Lieutenant Commander. Following an exchange of salutes between commander, warrant officer, lieutenant and ensign, Higgins stepped out of the room.

Katherine and Ellen felt prickles at the back of their necks and assumed their Sasebo experience was about to genuinely begin. They were correct.

Lieutenant Commander Morris Nuttall was a tall man, with black hair and the type of heavy beard that always appears as five o'clock shadow. His voice was deep, imposing, and authoritative. Following brief generic pleasantries and hollow *how-do-you-do's,* he introduced himself as their immediate commanding officer.

He became the third Navy officer to welcome them to Sasebo, and explained they were part of a new information division that the Navy set up in conjunction with the Army, Air Force[**], Marines and the United Nations Command especially for the resumption of the peace talks with North Korea and the Peoples' Republic of China. Lieutenant Dobbs and Ensign Thompson received their specific duty stations, assignments and the chain of command for Joint Services. Nuttall then gave a tedious, detailed explanation of their Security Clearance and the responsibilities that went with it.

Last on the agenda was their quarters assignment. He began, "Lieutenant Dobbs ... Ensign Thompson ... as commissioned officers in the United States Navy, there are additional responsibilities that are charged to you. As part of your assignments to Joint Services, you will also act in the role of Billet Officers, in two newly assembled Nissen[**] huts, courtesy of Her Majesty Queen Elizabeth II and the British Commonwealth Forces, Korea. Currently, there are sixteen Navy enlisted women occupying those new huts across the base in the new Victor Sector on Kittanning Avenue. You are assigned Billet One, Lieutenant, and Ensign, you are the Billet Officer in Number Two. You will each have the charge for the supervision and oversight of up to twelve sailors in your respective hut. Female enlisted sailors. I understand that most of these sailors are young, eager-to-learn Seaman Apprentice or Seaman enlisted personnel, and a few could soon be eligible for promotion to Petty Officer Third with an appropriate time-in-grade waiver. As of now, I don't know how many may be in your specific duty section, or directly under your command, but they are all assigned to Headquarters, Joint Services, Signals Section for duty in varied parameters of clerical Occupational Specialties. I'm certain they are fully trained and ready to serve. Clearly, the important thing is that they are young, enthusiastic and malleable. That said, you should be able to mold them how you want them. And you want them to be sailors."

Lieutenant Dobbs and Ensign Thompson shared glances.

Katherine began to wonder exactly what message Lieutenant Commander Nuttall intended to convey with his last few sentences. She didn't believe that he meant to demean women sailors or the work they do, but he certainly wasn't describing a crack, spit-and-polish fighting unit. Nonetheless, his closing remarks gave the impression that Lieutenant Dobbs and Ensign Thompson could be taking on the additional role of baby sitter, den mother or dormitory monitor.

"Get yourselves settled in and get a good night's sleep. You will report to your duty stations tomorrow morning at zero-six-hundred. Any questions?" Two seconds of silence passed before he continued, "Fine. Then I think we're finished here. Good luck with your assignments and career. There should be a jeep and a motor pool monkey outside waiting to drive you to your quarters."

After handshakes, nods and a few parting pleasantries, their welcome, orientation and instructional exercise ended without further fanfare.

As promised, there was a jeep and a driver waiting outside the building. A young marine snapped a salute and spoke, "Corporal Freeborn Wilson, Ma'ams. I'll be driving you to your quarters." The marine quickly loaded their seabags and ditty* cases onto and in front of the passenger seat. He walked around the vehicle, offering his hand as support, assisting them up and into the back of the jeep. His movements were precise, perfect. He hopped into the front seat behind the wheel and pushed the gearshift into first. During the ensuing ten minutes, they traveled around chuckholes and standing water. The passengers in Marine Corporal Freeborn Wilson's jeep bounced, skipped and jerked as if they were a batch of chitterlings and fatback bacon in a hot, cast iron fry pan.

They arrived at their billets none the worse for wear, stood on the boardwalk and watched as the jeep drove away, down the dirt and gravel road and out of sight.

Their little plot of Sasebo Naval Base consisted of groomed, freshly laid pea gravel interspersed with a few isolated patches of newly seeded grass. New concrete sidewalks led from the front entrance of two adjacent Nissen huts and out to the gravel street. Fifty yards East, there was an intersection that revealed more new construction to the North and South, evidenced by airborne dust and the noise of machinery. Their new residence was located on Kittanning Avenue, as promised and further verified by the hand-painted street sign in front of their buildings. The huts were shiny, new galvanized sheet metal, about 10 X 24 feet, with four dormered windows along the sides. There was no sign of human activity, and Ellen and Katherine could only assume that the other residents were either sound asleep or on duty.

Katherine stood in shocked disbelief. She was jostled not by the bumpy ride or her new open, barren neighborhood, but by Lieutenant Commander Nuttall's remarks, especially his last.

She purposely withheld her comments until they arrived at their billets.

"I don't want you to take this the wrong way, Ensign, but I believe our commanding officer is a class-A nitwit. Maybe I'm talking out of turn, and making too much of it, but during our briefing back there, I got the distinct impression that he straight up believes that female sailors are undisciplined little girls and it will be up to us to crack the whip. Then he gave us insincere, bilge water best wishes, took the helm, and went ahead full speed and called that Negro US Marine a monkey. That's the kind of thinking that boils my blood, especially from a career officer. I have no idea how long he has been in the Navy, but he still carries a strong, Deep South inflection and probably all the prejudices that he grew up with."

Ensign Thompson had just met Lieutenant Katherine Dobbs, and decided to choose her words carefully, "I noticed it too, and I picked up on how he was referring to our fellow sailors. But maybe that 'monkey' comment was meant to be something like 'grease monkey'. You know how men like to talk about mechanics and such."

Katherine set her ditty bag down, pulled her little pack of Wings out of her jacket pocket, lit one, passed it to Ensign Thompson and lit another for herself. She drew on her cigarette and thought aloud, "Maybe you're right. But can I trust you to keep this between you and me, Ellen?"

"Absolutely, Katherine. Your words went from your lips, to my ears and into the lockbox. They'll go no further. He's our commanding officer, and I really want to respect him, but he also gave me the impression that he was a nitwit."

"It's OK for me to call you Ellen out of company?"

"Sure."

"You can call me Kate. Or Katy."

They shared more than a cigarette and a secret. Katherine hoped that she was building a friendship as strong as those she knew at the Chi Omega sorority house. There was the excitement of a new duty station, a new job and a fresh set of untested responsibilities. It was challenging and exhilarating.

"Did you see the arms on that driver we had, Kate? My God, they were as big as fence posts."

"They were. You weren't the only one who noticed. I can imagine how much muscle he keeps hidden under that shirt. You do know what they say about men with arms like fence posts, don't you, Ellen?"

"No, what?" Ellen was coyly curious.

"I don't have the slightest idea. I thought perhaps you did."

East of the Sun and West of the Moon ...
Late September 1951

The newness and unfamiliarity of her new assignment kept Katherine busy for the first few weeks in Building One, Signals Section. However, as the days dropped off the calendar she began to suspect that Lieutenant Commander Nuttall may have unduly embellished the importance of her position and its responsibilities. She was weighed down with ostensibly inconsequential requests for outdated, nonexistent or unavailable reports. Adding to her frustration, the so-called armistice and peace talks were on-again, off-again three or four times a week. What she deemed as her most meaningful transmissions had all but dried up.

The various national commands of the British Commonwealth of Nations began to send daily assessments back and forth about their specific status in the conflict. The Canadians would send a message to the Australians that the British sent to the New Zealanders and ring-around-the-rosie until the circle was complete. The replicated messages were directed everywhere east of the Sun and west of the Moon. The reports were generally the identical, overstated versions that were dispatched the night before from the US Army, Air Force or Marine Corps to United Nations Command HQ. There were days when the casualty reports were the only new information.

By the end of September, the stone had fallen out and the shine had worn off the dime-store ring. The work was largely redundant with only enough developing news to keep it marginally interesting. The daily grind at Joint Services was beginning to wear on Lieutenant Dobbs so much so that she dared to type a memo to her Section Chief, Lieutenant Commander Nuttall, that she was working below her capabilities, needed challenge and that her work was largely redundant with just enough developing news to keep it minimally significant. Afterwards, she scolded herself and nervously expected some sort of discipline. She began to wonder if Nuttall had any authority to put a rifle in the hands of a woman and send her to the forward lines. If worse came to worse, she would simply face the music. He was far too repulsive to consider swaying him personally.

Ensign Thompson however, was quite content with her duty assignment in Dispatch Section. During her ten-hour duty tours, she accepted hard copy communiqués from Joint Services couriers of all services and ranks, sorted and relayed them to her dedicated detail of four Seamen for chronicling, transcription, and in-house redistribution. It was a two-here, one-there, six-over-there pigeonholing and sortation system that was as outdated as the pony express, but worked just fine for the United Nations Command.

Surprisingly, Katherine's appeal to her commander yielded a positive response. He promptly returned a hand-written reply on the bottom of her memo stating that her 'duty assignment is in a state of flux and additional responsibilities are forthcoming'. The message was so short and so generic that it brought a shiver across her shoulders and did nothing to ease her anxiety or the monotony of her job. She could only speculate exactly what his brusque reply meant. It was then that she decided that silence is golden and that worry is vanity's reward.

She was never sure and didn't dare presume that Lieutenant Commander Nuttall knew exactly what was about to happen. Two days after his terse reply, she received approval from the Naval Aviation Command for something she hadn't asked for and had no knowledge of: a Navy HO3S helicopter and its dedicated pilot. Moreover, she paid no particular attention when she received notice of approved Temporary Duty for a Communication Yeoman and arrival orders for an additional two new permanent clerical positions. At the bottom of the page were the names of three incoming personnel who would be in her charge. The first two were women: a Seaman, and a Seaman Apprentice. Underneath, one name popped off the page and greened her imagination like a field of rye after a spring rain. The name belonged to a man.

The moniker itself was enough to fuel fantasy and feed speculation. *Alexander Throckmorton* conjured up an image of a tall country gentleman with a neatly trimmed mustache, tailored show coat, fitted breeches, and riding crop. Her fascination with horses combined with burning memories of the Chittenango recruiting billboard stoked the flames of her erotic dreams.

She held out hope that this newly assigned sailor would have more personal appeal than the few servicemen she had already met at Sasebo. Perhaps this Throckmorton fellow could be worth some effort.

A helicopter, a dedicated pilot and an assigned Yeoman sent her into a flight of fancy. She dared to anticipate that she would soon be experiencing her first vertical take off, and to daydream that her Yeoman would spend some time in the saddle with her.

Between The Devil And The Deep Blue Sea ...

At 0600 hours on Monday morning, October 1, Lieutenant Dobbs received a full briefing about the new operational procedures at Joint Services. It was a certainty that the Navy helicopter came with a specific mission. During her detailed meeting with Lieutenant Commander Nuttall, she discovered that her Signals Section would soon begin ferrying documents between United Nations Field Commands on the Korean Peninsula and Headquarters, Sasebo. Before she left the conference room, Katherine learned that the incoming Communications Yeoman would double as an in-fight Aircrewman and she would act as Dispatch Commander.

Cautiously optimistic and looking forward to her expanded role, Katherine held out hope that from that day forward, her tour of duty would no longer be a humdrum experience. She filled her spare moments daydreaming about exciting and romantic missions. There was a spring in her step for the first time in months.

Petty Officer Second Class Alexander Throckmorton held orders to report for duty at Joint Services, Signals Section, no later than two o'clock. Temporary Duty oftentimes involved a vague chain of command and muddied accountability. Alexander's arrival orders assigned him to Headquarters, Joint Services, attached him to Naval Helicopter Utility Detachment HU-3, and detailed him exclusively to Signal Services. The day before, he learned that his living quarters were a corner room in the Non-Commissioned Officers' Transit Billets of Leroy Sector, on the East Port. He felt as if he were in the middle of no man's land** without a road map. He would soon discover that his premonition was spot-on.

The Signals Section building was a long, narrow, windowless, unassuming structure fronted with manicured foundation plantings of Japanese Yew. He hoped that within the brick and cinderblock walls of the building, he would get a clear definition of his duty assignment.

He stopped briefly at the door, grasped the doorknob and wondered what was on the other side. He imagined a roomful of sailors sitting at desks in front of shortwave radios, wearing headsets and scribbling notes on yellow pads of paper. He took a breath, turned the knob, stepped inside and immediately was unsure of his eyesight and footing. At the door, a blonde Seaman glanced at his orders, welcomed him and directed him to the far end of the building. The picture he created in his mind's eye wasn't too far from the truth. Nevertheless, he was dumbstruck by this particular form of "no man's land". He had not seen so many women wearing sailor uniforms in one place, at any time during his career. A few women did, in fact, wear headsets, some were typing and others were on telephones, but very few acknowledged his presence and all of them continued to work. He was the single man in a segregated sea of female sailors.

He walked down the center of the building, between rows of desks and women, under a ceiling of flickering fluorescent lights, toward an office with the words *Section Commander* painted on the door. He knocked and heard the reply, "Come in." He was surprised yet again. He heard a woman's voice coming from behind the door, entered, stuck his watch cap in his pocket, snapped a salute, stood squarely in front of her desk and introduced himself, "Petty Officer Third, Alexander Throckmorton, reporting for duty, Ma'am."

The clean-shaven sailor presented a good first impression. His dungarees** were starched, pressed and crisp, and his jump boots spit-shined. The lieutenant guessed that he stood a bit over six feet tall, and took special note of his dark brown, wavy hair and brown eyes. He was clean-shaven, mustache-free and didn't have a riding crop in his grasp or looped around his wrist. The missing equestrian accessory was her only disappointment.

"Welcome to Sasebo Fleet Services, Petty Officer. I am Lieutenant Dobbs, your Unit Commander. "

Alexander made a concerted effort to control his eye movement as he simultaneously tried to survey his new his surroundings and commander. He assumed that her vanilla voice was too smooth to belong to a John Wayne[*] officer and she was too young to be Victorian. He would come to realize that fluorescent lighting is harsh and washes out a healthy complexion. She was a dark brunette with a gently curled, bobbed hairdo like Doris Day. He couldn't be certain, but from where he stood, her eyes appeared as the lightest blue. Her dress khakis cheated him out of a good look at her form.

It was unavoidable; their eyes met. They didn't realize it, but at that moment, they shared their first secrets. Separately, they felt their souls touch and knew their story was about to begin. It was undeniable. The open-ended question was: when would their adventure begin?

What followed were two days of preparation and procedural review coupled with a handful of mission compliance flights between UN commands in Sasebo and Kitakyushu, Japan. Katherine discovered that seated near an open door in a helicopter flying at eighty miles an hour was a much bigger thrill than horseback riding. The noise, vibration and altitude primed her pump, and the swinging safety straps and body harnesses fueled her fancy. However, it was the flight jacket, headset and boots worn by Aircrewman Throckmorton that revved her engine.

Although he steered the helo[*], Warrant Officer Charles Coupland left Katherine's flying fantasies grounded. He was in his early forties, blue-eyed, blonde, fair-skinned and soft-spoken. He confessed that, after his graduation from Ball State, he'd made several bad decisions and that his young, ill-conceived marriage ended a month later with an annulment. As an age-old escape, he joined the Navy, left Muncie, Indiana and never looked back. From the various bits of additional information that Coupland volunteered, Katherine deduced that women were not on his radar.

On the other hand, her new Yeoman presented a fresh and challenging course of study for his commanding officer. She casually gathered a few tidbits of his history without being overtly inquisitive. In return, she offered him a limited amount of her background and explained her interest in horses and horseback riding.

The Petty Officer noticed his Lieutenant's subtle signals early on. At the onset, he assumed that she was just being curious and studying him as a subordinate. Things changed after their first few flights. She began to cast subtly flirtatious glances his way with come-hither eyes, smile and turn her head away. She dared him and enjoyed it. For a sailor unaccustomed to such suggestive behavior coming from the opposite sex, it was unsettling. Temptation from a commanding officer is dangerously exciting. To a sailor who is five thousand miles away from home, such teases are as irresistible as honey is to a bear. Although there were more than thirty female sailors in Signals Section, Lieutenant Dobbs alone piqued his interest. They had met a few days earlier, and already it appeared that they were racing toward the finish line. Her bottomless, sky-blue eyes, cottony soft voice and unassuming gestures had roped him in. He fantasized and toyed with the possibility that she knew a good deal about horsing around. When he was alone with his thoughts, she had him kicking in his stall.

While they were airborne, Alexander would watch her from the corner of his eye like a high school kid. When he caught her smiling and looking his way, he of course, was obliged to smile back. During their last orientation flight from the aircraft carrier Essex to Pusan, Korea and back over open water to Sasebo, she dared to lean forward and squeeze his shoulder just as CWO Coupland banked the helo hard left. It was the first of many lingering touches to his arms, neck and shoulders.

Lieutenant Dobbs was playing with fire and flying dangerously close to the flame that was riding in the forward jump seat. Petty Officer Throckmorton recklessly stoked the burning embers and harbored fantasies of his own. Both of them were certainly aware of the Navy's strict General Orders** against fraternization among the enlisted and officer ranks, yet they continued to fly without parachutes.

Although they never discussed their out-of-bounds behavior, individually they believed that their deering-do, flying flirts were as harmless as sticking one foot over a cliff edge. Back on the ground at Sasebo, the sexual tension between them continued to tighten like an over-wound clock spring. Two weeks after Katherine first cracked the ice and placed a hand on his shoulder, she realized that it was circumstance that blocked their union, not an abundance of caution. Alexander was ready and she was willing, but the world's social taboos and the Navy's Code of Conduct weren't able to accommodate them.

Katherine could only dream. She endured frustration and suffered in burning silence. The Kingdom had forbidden their love. She felt as if she was the beautiful, young scullery maiden, banished by the wicked, jealous Queen and locked away in the tallest, most impenetrable watchtower: the Keep. The overbearing King decided to further her punishment and ordered Alexander, the stable master, to be shackled and locked away in the darkest, deepest dungeon, far beneath the palace courtyard. Katherine desperately needed someone to come riding to her rescue and free her and her lover. Her fantasy was about to come true.

Stormy Weather ...

As if a wizard recognized her peril, Mother Nature was about to grace the stage, knock down the castle gates, and save Katherine from the bonds of convention. Typhoon Ruth[**] would empty the moat, topple the watchtowers and unlock the dungeons. The approaching Category Four storm was forecast to wreak havoc across the Japanese island of Kyushu.

The super storm transformed an international war machine into purposeful, organized chaos. On the morning of October 14, warships of the American, Australian and New Zealand navies exited Sasebo harbor into the Sea of Japan to escape the expected fifty-foot waves and storm surge. Land-based command personnel and senior non-commissioned officers assigned to headquarters, supply, logistics, transport, communication, and medical units were to remain at their secured duty stations and all others were to shelter in quarters. Lieutenant Dobbs tasked Ensign Thompson to requisition emergency rations, first aid kits and muster the sailors of Kittanning Billets 1 and 2 into one Nissen hut.

The typhoon created an unexpected opportunity for Katherine and Alexander. He was confident that his absence from quarters would go unnoticed, and explained to Katherine that the Transit Billets in Leroy Sector had no organization whatsoever. Sailors came and went from the barracks like fleas jumping off a wet dog. Additionally, the confusion created by Ruth would provide the perfect cover for their dalliance. Emergency preparedness activities on the base began kicking up dust ahead of the storm's forecast impact of over one hundred mile an hour winds. The bough was about to bend just enough to put the forbidden fruit within reach. The lieutenant and petty officer plotted and schemed that they could hunker down, where else, but at their duty station, just as they were ordered.

As all good sailors do, Katherine and Alexander prepared to batten down** the hatches, face the storm's fury and sail into the wind. They cleared the desks and stashed the radios, teletypewriters and telephones underneath. Alexander set the codex machine on the floor and set a metal table over it. They boxed all the loose papers they could find, locked the file cabinets and laid them down on their backs. The office that was normally full of clicks, clacks, bells, ticks and the constant undertone of human voices was as silent as Mona Lisa's smile. They worked quickly and by six o'clock in the evening, it was strangely still. There were no howling winds or raging squalls of rain. It was the 'calm before the storm'.

Relieved of obligation and satisfied with their efforts, they shared their first full-body embrace and held one another close as long as the moment allowed. There was an ominous, silent foreboding inside and out. They couldn't hear it, but they felt it. A storm was approaching. She kissed him and quivered inside. He kissed her back and felt her tremors.

He reluctantly broke her hold on him, moved away and forced the words, "We need to secure the door."

She forced a little smile, and stepped back into character, "Yes. We must."

They walked the length of the building to the door and she stopped, looked into his brown eyes, stood squarely in front of him and kissed him as if it were her last chance. The uncertainty of Mother Nature's script drove the drama and played into their roles.

She whispered playfully, "Let's see what ancient ghosts could be creating all this unbearable silence and causing so much disruption without making a sound."

Katherine unlocked and opened the door. Hand-in-hand, she and Alexander stepped outside, onto the concrete pad and boardwalk. They looked to the skies above them, and saw a pale, cream-colored moon glowing gloriously alone and gracing the Eastern sky. Stars twinkled like fairies dancing across an ebony stage. The eerie stillness stirred feelings of haunting anticipation in the minds of Lieutenant Katherine and Petty Officer Alexander. Certainly, they were cautiously aware of the remote possibility that the forecasters, Air Force reconnaissance flights and Pacific-island storm reports could all be wrong, but they were also realists. There was still some work to do. Together they turned and went back inside to finish securing the main deck. They pushed and shoved three desks across the asphalt-tiled floor and bulwarked shut their only way in or out of Signals Section, Building One.

They brought candles, flashlights, rations of food and water out of the storage closet and into her office. Alexander lit a single candle and set it inside a china coffee cup from Katherine's desk. They placed one skinny mattress on the floor, next to an interior wall and sat close, huddled together. They were sitting with their backs against the wall; she with her legs and feet covered in a dark blue, wool blanket marked with the initials *USN*. They stayed as close as they could to one another, listening for weather bulletins, and waiting in apprehension for the expected storm. The typhoon was about to make the improbable possible.

A few minutes past seven o'clock the command telephone came to life. Its little red light flashed and an obnoxiously loud ring pierced the temporary silence and bounced off the walls of Katherine's office. She sprang to her feet, took a step off the mattress, and instantly became all Navy. She reached to the floor beside her desk, picked up the heavy black telephone receiver, and answered, "Joint Services, Signals Section, Lieutenant Dobbs speaking, sir." The chord was stretched nearly to its limit.

She listened intensely for about twenty seconds before she replied, "Yes, sir, understood, sir. Will do. Thank you, sir," and hung up.

"That was Damage Headquarters, the Officer of the Day on the Telephone Tree[*]. The storm wall is sixty miles out. We got maybe thirty minutes. It just hit Kumamoto to the east. I'm calling Ensign Thompson. Then we sit and wait for all Hell to break loose, I guess."

Her fingers twirled the dial as fast as it would go around. She spoke briefly with her Ensign, informed her of the oncoming storm and once again verified the health and welfare status of the sailors in Billet Two. After she ended the call, Katherine hung up and returned to the mattress. Alexander was silent, and allowed her the time and space for the reality outside. Together, they waited. A few minutes passed before she leaned into him and he put his arm around her shoulders once again.

During the previous four hours, non-stop emergency radio alerts had promised that the storm would strike before midnight. Typhoon Ruth forcefully announced her arrival at half past seven and shattered the silence. Everything crashed. The wind howled and screamed as if the bowels of Hell had opened. Alexander and Katherine believed that they felt the concrete floor shudder beneath them. Their pulses raced and their eyes flew around the room. They noticed that the little red pilot light on the command telephone went out. Every fluorescent ceiling light flashed, flickered and went dark in unison. The steady stream of storm warnings and command updates gushing from the radio speakers clicked, snapped, dried up and disappeared into the darkness.

Outside Signals Section, angry skies full of heavy black clouds swirled counter-clockwise and smothered the creamy moon and sparkling stars. Sheets of punishing rain and wind-driven debris attacked everything in their path like stampeding bison.

Inside Signals Section, the storm could not extinguish the burning desire inside the Commander's Office. The sounds of billiard-ball-sized raindrops and growling gusts of wind fell on deaf ears. The storm was upon them. They got closer.

Take It Easy, Greasy ...

In the flickering candlelight, passion rapidly surmounted fear. Two weeks after they first met, they dared to breach the taboos and share out-of-bounds intimacy as soon as the lights went out. Their boots and shoes were the first cast aside. Locked in kisses, Alexander slowly worked on opening her blouse, and her right hand clumsily found and struggled with the thirteen buttons of his dungarees. After she managed the top four, she decided to take her time with the remaining nine. Slowly, they popped open one by one, assisted by the building pressure inside his bellbottoms.

Without a word, Katherine made certain that the way forward was 'steady as she goes' and 'all ahead slow'. Her blouse came off her upraised arms and onto the floor. He discovered that unlike his uniform, her skirt had no buttons and zipped down the back. Each bit of clothing that they removed revealed inches of skin that ached to be touched, caressed and kissed. She removed his white undershirt, pressed her face to his naked chest, swallowed his scent, and ran her tongue down his breastbone. He unhooked her brassiere and garter belt, and pushed them off the mattress and onto the cold floor. She raised her hips and allowed him to slide off her cotton panties. The winds were growling, hearts were pounding and his patience was wearing thin. She taunted him with her fingers and helped with the condom.

He started to roll down her stockings. She silently protested and abruptly moved aside, turned around, and guided him onto his back. She slowly, purposely, set her hands on his shoulders, straddled him and delicately clamped his hips between her knees. "If we're going to ride out this storm together, we've got to work together as a team, Yeoman Alexander."

"I'm willing to do that." He knew his words were wobbly but didn't care. He could only smile at her; anxious to start riding out anything. His hands were at her hips, gently tugging, trying to bring her closer and onto him. She bedeviled him further and ignored his persuasive pressure.

Again, she signaled she wasn't ready, waggled under his touch and continued with her admonition, "Listen to me. This isn't going to be just once around the track or a single furlong. No, sir. I want this to last as long as this damn storm can keep us locked up in here ... so, pace yourself, Sailor."

She didn't allow him time to answer, but leaned forward, kissed him and nimbly settled in for the ride. The candlelight threw indiscernible, soft, dancing shadows onto the wall.

Alexander tried to think of things that could delay the approaching gust. Katherine's apparent interest in horses didn't help, and thoughts of his high school sweetheart Audrey didn't provide the least bit of distraction. His memories of Suhail, the Philippine USO** girl he kept on his arm for five days and four nights at Subic Bay, were no help whatsoever. She taught him much more than how to dance. Their experience and everything about her was unforgettable. The thought of surging, rocking and rolling seas didn't help either. He could only surrender and allow his Lieutenant to hold the harness, and consider his current predicament to be a command evaluation of his willpower and stamina.

Two passion-starved souls came together again and again on the thin, 30 X 75 inch, cotton-batting mattress that they had requisitioned from the Emergency Supply and Preparedness closet. Wind-driven sheets of rain couldn't drown the sounds of lustful whispers, whimpers, kisses and coos that they shared. Alexander and Katherine braved the raging storm and darkness with the warmth of body heat, the light of a flickering field candle and sustenance from two boxes of C-rations^{**} and a two-quart can of drinking water. Lieutenant Dobbs' office had never seen such a storm of activity. For nearly twelve hours, they remained behind windowless brick and block walls and a locked, barricaded door. They rode out the raging storm entangled in reins of rapture. They managed to catch a precious few hours of anxious sleep during the night.

Alexander woke first, and opened his eyes to blackness and quiet. He was jolted back into reality, weighed by emotion and unsettled by the storm that passed. The candle he left burning inside the coffee cup had burned out. Blinded by the void of light, he could only rely on his touch and smell. Time was a forgotten concept. The usually luminous green dial of his watch was black and there was a woman lying next to him.

He awoke on his back with her head on his arm, an arm over his chest, and her leg over his. She had owned him. He believed that he fell asleep in that position and had spent hours wrapped between her arms and legs. He stretched underneath her weight and kissed her forehead. It was the morning after and she still smelled delicious. *Good God, she was delicious.*

She awoke, blinked the sleep out of her eyes, surrendered to the darkness and kissed him passionately. "Good morning, Alexander."

"Good morning. I think it's morning. I think it's over," he said.

He gently slid out from under her arm and reached to his left. His hand and fingers searched alongside the mattress and found his Zippo. A blue flame followed the little flash of flint.

He lit one of the three remaining field candles, stuck it into the coffee cup of melted wax and burnt wick, and looked to his watch. It was seven o'clock. Certainly, it was morning. It was October 16. Typhoon Ruth blew out of Sasebo and the race results were in. Katherine and her mount shared the winning purse. *Steady Pacer* came first, *Exuberance* placed, *Lust* showed and the loser was *Restraint*.

Katherine sat up next to him with her back against the wall. She pulled the blue, woolen Navy blanket up over her knees, to her waist, and studied his face. She leaned in, kissed him and repeated, "Good morning, Alexander."

It was the morning after, and she was happy, satisfied and warm in his company, yet the dim light of a single candle cast a restless shadow of doubt over them. She knew that they could cover up their tracks, but not erase the line they had crossed.

Before she fell asleep, she'd thought about what words she could say when they awoke in the same bed. She needed to explain her feelings for him without an overdose of drama or pathos. It was necessary for the Lieutenant to rewrite the code of conduct for the Petty Officer. When the storm ended, she knew she would have to plead her case.

She gathered her thoughts, sailed into his eyes and said, "The typhoon might be over, but please ... Alexander ... tell me what we shared last night doesn't end now ... and that the rising sun won't shrivel or dry up what we shared. I want to feel near someone, and to keep someone close to my heart. I need that ... that feeling of being close to someone."

Alexander was relieved that he didn't need to initiate such an appeal. He was also a bit bewildered. What Katherine said seemed to be the terms for an unconditional surrender, and he considered it odd that such a forceful woman would use such words. He felt special and didn't understand why.

He sat up, kissed her lips, and answered, "Hell, no. I enjoy the sunshine. I'll especially enjoy it with you."

Regardless of Ruth's violent indignations and no matter what they could say about it, the calm, unnatural quiet that descended upon them after their own personal, emotional storm was greater. Without another word between them, they knew what the other was thinking. They were satiated in lust but starved for peace of mind. Their uneasiness however, was temporary; tender human togetherness has the ability to ease worry just enough to make it bearable. They shared one more loving kiss before their return to normal, and began picking up their scattered pieces of clothing.

He thought about a parallel analogy, "This morning, I was thinking about our pickle. I know this is not identical to our situation and it isn't going to change things, but I think it might help put things in a different light and make it clearer for us.

"When I was a kid, maybe ten years old, my old man caught me in the alley behind our house smoking one of his cigarettes and he told me something that I didn't understand right away, because I thought for sure he was going to ball me out, tan my backside and take my bike away. But he didn't ball me out, give me the belt or take my bike away. He said, *'It ain't what you do that gets you in trouble, Alex. It's what you get caught doing.'* I think it took me a week to figure out what he meant."

"Really? He let you off the hook scot free?"

"Yep, he did ... in a big way. Then he told me to go into the house and drink some milk so my breath didn't stink and my mother couldn't find out. And he never mentioned it again.

"So, I think the Old Man was telling me not to get caught the next time I wanted to sneak a smoke ... and if I could live with my conscience, it was no skin off my nose."

She lit a cigarette off the candle, inhaled and wondered, "Were you and your father close?"

"No. We couldn't be. As far back as I can remember, he was a barnstorming crop duster before he joined the Army Air Corps, and honestly, I grew up without a father. He would come and go and was hardly ever home. Sometimes my mother called him a *fly-by-night*. I guess she was right."

She thought a minute and looked into his eyes. "Do you keep in touch with your father at all?"

"No. He was lost in the Pacific Theater of the War. The Army sent a telegram back in '46, and I figure he was killed in some jungle in Indochina."

"Oh. I'm sorry." It wasn't often that she felt compassion, but she empathized with his deep sense of loss. It was an unsettling feeling.

A brief, uncomfortable silence settled around them until Katherine broke it with official business, "We still don't have electricity, so grab the portable telephone ... please ... the field phone. I've got to call in." Reality needed to replace the moony morning.

Alexander cranked the growler[*] and passed the handset to Katherine. They shared glances, each waiting for the telephone to come to life and connect them with the topsy-turvy world outside.

She gave Alexander a quick thumbs up signal, smiled, nodded and listened. Suddenly, she was all business, "Joint Services, Signals Section, Lieutenant Dobbs requesting Orders of the Day, sir."

Alexander heard only silence as she listened to the voice inside the olive drab, Bakelite handset. He watched as she answered, "Yes, sir. All is well at first assessment, sir. Will secure and send updated Resource and Morning Report, sir. Copy, sir."

She handed the receiver back to Alexander, and said, "Orders are to report to duty station, assist injured personnel, secure duty station, evaluate damage, remain at duty station and await further orders."

"I think we already did all that except for the *'await further orders'* part, don't you think?"

They shared smiles like teenagers after a first kiss and cuddle.

"When we have our hats and shoes off, and mind you, only when we have our hats and shoes off, please call me *Kate* or *Katy*, OK? I prefer *Katy*."

"Pleased to meet you, Katy. I'm Alex."

"I know. Believe me, I know."

She leaned in and kissed him on the lips, and ordered, "Good. Let's hit the deck and clean this mess up, Yeoman. Then we'll check the sailors over on Kittanning."

All's well that ends well ...

The new Nissen huts faced the fury of Ruth well and suffered only minor damage. There were a few lifted corners of corrugated steel and one broken window in Ensign Thompson's building. The sole human casualty in all of Signals Section was one case of shattered nerves: a young sailor from Abilene, Texas. She was admitted to the hospital and returned to duty after five days of restrained bed rest and an anti-psychotic** regimen.

Slipping Around ...

Fleet Services was fully functional one day after the storm. During the days following the typhoon's departure, Alexander spent most of his time in the air, hand-carrying dispatches between commands in Korea that were isolated by the storm and suffered power outages and radio blackouts of their own. Katherine had a full plate with the added responsibilities of a Section Commander after a natural calamity. Their jobs kept them too busy to allow any unfounded worry about their transgression. The dust would settle without any outside help. They relished the passion that they shared and stealthily, yet separately, plotted their next union.

Days later, when asked about their typhoon experience, Alexander and Katherine led everyone to believe that she weathered the storm alone in her office and that he spent the turbulent night sprawled on a medical evacuation stretcher at Heliport 1A, inside Navy helicopter #AM1-B4U. Their stories were both reasonable and plausible enough not to raise any eyebrows. Those who were curious enough to listen, seemed a hundred percent convinced. There were plenty of typhoon war stories that garnered much more attention.

When the new lovers had the opportunity to talk privately, they made a concerted effort to do it in the open, albeit well out of earshot. On occasion, when whispers of passion were desired, they would parley in the Section Commander's office with the door wide open. Like all couples who dare to share secret intimacy, the initial cover-up is the most important. If the first lie is believable, it generally eliminates or reduces the need for secondary lies.

About a month after their tryst, the Navy and not cyclones or high tides assisted Alex and Katy in their constant pursuit of carnal connections. Fleet Headquarters indicated that the workload was expanding for various reasons, including more participation from the United Nations Command and progress with the armistice negotiations.

The Treaty of San Francisco officially ended the Occupation of Japan^{**} in April of 1952, and many of Sasebo's facilities began to return to Japanese civilian control. Headquarters issued an announcement that a fresh allotment of additional administrative slots was about to boost the ranks of Signals Services. The rumor of an influx of female sailors was likely the underlying reason that the Kittanning billets of Victor Sector gained the nickname of *Kitty Cat City*. A week later, an Ensign and six fresh-faced sailors arrived and were given quarters on Kittanning Avenue in Billet One. In less than twenty-four hours, Billet Three was assembled to accommodate additional sailors en route from San Diego.

Lieutenant Dobbs was moving out of the Nissen hut and into junior officers' temporary housing at the Bayside Sunny Hotel, a half-mile from her Signals Section office. Initially, she believed that the move was a downgrade from the new Nissens and their proximity to her work from Kittanning Avenue.

The Bayside was one of many hastily built, slap-dash construction projects that popped up immediately after World War II to accommodate the influx of the American occupation forces. It was a two-story, no-frills concrete block construction, with crank-open, steel frame windows only on the front side of the building. When the United Nations military and diplomatic delegations appeared in early 1951, a fresh coat of turquoise blue paint was applied to the exterior, and the metal window frames had their first-ever coat of white enamel. While the Japanese owned and managed the hotel, the Navy had contracted the first floor for overflow housing. Katherine selected a room at the end of the hall, on the hotel's left side.

Although the Bayside was recently remodeled and upgraded, it had a carry-over reputation of ill repute that it acquired during the earlier occupation years. The whores, Saki and drunken sailors disappeared off the base and deeper into

Sasebo City, but Katy's move to Bayside Sunny was a degradation that she was willing to accept. On the positive side, the move meant that she would no longer play the role of dormitory monitor for twelve sailors that were still wet behind their ears. Additionally, the possibility of conjugal visits from a certain Petty Officer could offset the longer walk to her office at Fleet Services. Bicycle taxis were also an option for her half-mile commute.

More experienced dalliers might call it an overabundance of caution, but in the beginning, Katy and Alex checked around corners and stayed yards ahead or behind of one another when they walked down Pacific Boulevard toward the Bayside. At first, it was a thrill equal to stealing a kiss in the back row of a movie theater balcony during a Randolph Scott western matinee.

The Lieutenant and Petty Officer quickly grew accustomed to their new situation. No more than a month after Ruth, the intrigue of stolen moments had worn off without so much as a close call or a suspicious glance. It was so easy to dodge detection that it no longer warranted worry and allowed their dalliance to go unnoticed for a year after the typhoon. The exclusivity and regularity of their encounters were the word-for-word dictionary definition of 'slipping around'.

They spent twelve months on the sly. She offered him gratuitous sex and he provided her with the type of sterile, uncommitted companionship she had grown accustomed to in New York.

Katy influenced Alex in a way that would change the course of his life. Her interest in horses ignited a spark within him that he couldn't explain. He began to visit the post library and read everything he could about horses. From books about the breeding and care of horses to cowboy films at the movie tent, he spent hours studying the animals. Alex also held onto his private erotic fantasies about how Katherine first rode him as her exclusive mount.

Don't Fence Me In

Although circumstance gave free range to their love affair, it bridled their romance. They could only pace within the bounds of a paddock that was fenced in by regulation and protocol. The freedom to prance in a sunny pasture and proudly display their love to the world was nonexistent. However, Thanksgiving, 1952 was one of the very few occasions that allowed them to socialize, sit at the same table and carry on a conversation without looking over their shoulders or whispering.

Katherine and Alexander were among more than two hundred officer and enlisted personnel who enjoyed a traditional holiday meal with all the trimmings at the Duquesne Annex, NCO Navy Mess. They imagined that it would be an opportunity to share some time together without hiding in the shadows. It didn't work out that way. Although the large hall and table arrangement afforded them some privacy, their predicament soured the mood.

Halfway through their turkey, gravy and baked Idaho potatoes, Alexander felt the need to explain his pent-up frustration, "Sitting here in the daylight, without ducking behind corners or checking over our shoulder is nice, Katy, but I wish I could take your hand, stand up, and tell all the world what I feel for you. I wish I could ditch this monkey-suit tomorrow, wear a shirt and tie, take you by the hand and dance the night away to Frank Sinatra and Dinah Shore records on the jukebox. I wish we could sit at a Woolworth lunch counter and order vanilla phosphates and banana splits. I wish we were five thousand miles from this godforsaken hell hole and we could walk together down Main Street,

Anytown, USA. It would be wonderful to hold your hand and not worry who's watching or who even gives a damn."

She let his words settle for a moment or two, and answered, "So do I, Alex. But this here, all this, all around us, this war ... it's us. It's our lives. This is who we are right now. We can't escape the cold, hard reality of our situation."

"I know that, Katy. But it pains me that we can't visit a corner café, share a glass of wine, hold hands across the table and whisper promises to one another. I want to do that so badly, it hurts."

Cautiously, she glanced around to see if anyone was listening or paying close attention. Out of habit, she kept her voice low, "I know how you feel, because I feel the same now and again. But like I said ... this ... the Navy is our life right now. I can't see any pathway out rather than letting time run its course. I've resigned myself to the facts.

"And realistically, your TDY is almost over and your term of service is coming up. You're a short-timer. On the other hand, I'm tied to the Navy for the next four years. We knew this going in, Alex. All good things come to an end. We made a promise and we need to keep it. You remember. I know you do. You told me that you could stay close but keep your distance. Please don't make a fool of me. Please keep your promise."

Her words reminded him that an enduring commitment was not in the playbook or part of their unwritten pact. The pang in his chest gave emphasis to what Katy said, and credence to the adage: the truth hurts. The hurt that Audrey caused years earlier proved to be insignificant, compared to how deeply Katy's words cut into his soul. Katy, however, had simply pointed out the handwriting that was already on the wall.

Now And Then There's A Fool Such As I

Another type of storm struck after Thanksgiving. It wasn't a typhoon, but an outbreak of nausea and fever. United Nations troops from Great Britain unwittingly brought the 1951 European influenza pandemic with them to the Korean War. Katy was one of many who were sickened and hospitalized at the Base Hospital Clinic at Sasebo. For the first two days, Alex sat at her beside every minute the hospital staff allowed. Her treatment was an IV drip of codeine for cough and discomfort, aspirin, Smith Brothers cough drops, and throat and chest wraps slathered with Vicks VapoRub[**]. For much of her first day and half in hospital, Katy was incoherent and unable to keep her eyes open. Each visit, he brought either a copy of *Life* magazine or *The Saturday Evening Post*, thinking he could read to her if she wished. She was in a room with six other coughing, moaning and nauseated female patients. The smell of turpentine and chlorine bleach permeated his clothes.

Not just a show pony, but a thoroughbred ...

Tuesday morning, December 2, 1952 was the third day of Katy's nausea, dehydration and 101° plus temperatures. When Alexander arrived to visit her that morning, he sensed something was out of the ordinary. The Ward Nurse limited his time to fifteen minutes and told him that the clinic staff decided to transfer Lieutenant Dobbs and two additional patients to Yokosuka Naval Hospital, Tokyo. They would leave Sasebo via medical airlift before noon.

She also said that not only was Katherine being transferred to Yokosuka, she also had orders rotating her out of theater and back to the United States as soon as she was strong enough for the move.

The flu hastened the inevitable; a British virus infected Katy and ended her clandestine, yearlong fling with Alex. The Department of the Navy cut a set of orders that confirmed it. It was over, but the news didn't hurt him as much as her condition. He sat at her bedside, and for the first time in mixed company, he held her hand. Alex felt about ending things with Katy the way he'd always felt about the last day of summer. He couldn't believe it was ending.

"You get better, Katy girl. When I'm out, the first thing I'm going to do is get a ticket. I'm getting a ticket on a plane, a bus or a train ... any old way at all I can get to you, Katy Dobbs, I will. I promise."

Her complexion was ashen; her eyes and mind cloudy with opiates. She gently squeezed his hand and spoke between breaths. Her broken sentences bore witness to her foggy state of mind and disconnected thoughts, "You're a good man, Alex. I needed you ... you were reliable ... steady ... strong and thorough ... yes ... a thoroughbred."

She paused, renewed her breath, and continued, "Yes, that's right. That's exactly ... what I meant to say. You weren't just my show pony, Alex ... you were my thoroughbred ... I have always believed in you and trusted you. Nothing can steal ... you or that away from me. Not the influenza ... not anything." She wriggled her shoulders, adjusted her upper body on her stack of pillows and looked at him through glassy eyes.

She sipped some iced water, licked her lips, and carefully formed her words, "When you knocked on my door, you launched a lifeboat. I was drowning in a sea of women and wishy-washy men. Your presence inspired me, and gave me hope ... you threw me a lifeline and pulled me from an ocean of mediocrity ... your kisses resuscitated me ... and you brought life back into my veins, but listen to me ... and listen close: You deserve your own, private future, Alexander. You don't need me pull your bridle. You cannot waste your life away waiting for me ... it's not acceptable. Cut the reins and run free, Alex. You need to face the fact that I don't want you cluttering up my life anymore."

Alex was dumbstruck.

The Ward Nurse appeared at the foot of her gray metal bed, softly cleared her throat and said, "You need to end your visit, Petty Officer. We need to ready the Lieutenant for her transfer to Yokosuka." For a second, the nurse stood feigning a smile, then turned on a dime and disappeared into the ward.

Alexander was suffering with the hole that his lover's goodbye had dug into his chest. As soon as his words left his lips, he knew they were foolish, "Get well, Katy, girl. Listen to the nurses and get better. I'll write to you and I can wait for you as long as it takes."

She pulled her hand from his and her tone inexplicably hardened, "Stop it, Alexander! You're rather new at this aren't you? Haven't you ever had a relationship end? Ever?"

She covered her mouth with the bed sheet and coughed.

Alex couldn't be sure if she intended to be cruel, but her indignant response burned further into the pit of his opening chest wound. He felt insult on top of injury. Any young man would. His reply reflected his pain, "When we met, I wasn't the only one in the room that was suffering from lack-a-nookie*. I'm not a boot*, Lieutenant, and you weren't my first time ashore, if that's what you mean."

His pride forced him to get up and walk away.

He left his heart and a copy of *Life* magazine on her bed.

ELOISA ... A New Year ... 1952 –1953

What's New? ...
*96 Cayuga Avenue, Balboa Park, San Francisco,
California, Tuesday, December 30, 1952*

Startled, and thinking she had answered the knock of a ghost, Eloisa took a quick breath. She studied the visitor across the doorway of her heather-green, one and a half story bungalow. From the other side of the street, a flock of a half dozen Stellar Jays loudly protested the unexpected arrival of her guest. The mid-morning sun was starting to melt the fog and silently warm the western shores of San Francisco Bay.

The black, shiny new automobile parked in front of her home added to the mystery. A visitor at her door was a rarity; she didn't lead a sheltered life, but one largely relegated among her job at Mission Bakery, housework and her children.

At first glance, Eloisa thought that her late husband Leopold had somehow cheated death and returned to her. It was only a second before she realized that the tall stranger standing at her door was her late husband's brother, Nicholas. She had met him once, thirteen years earlier, and spent a few fleeting hours in his company over Thanksgiving dinner. She remembered that he had arrived unannounced on that occasion as well. Her thoughts were racing across long abandoned roadways of dusty recollection and allowed a welcoming smile to cross her lips.

Mysteriously, she felt that Fate had orchestrated this reunion, and that one way or another, their paths were destined to cross again. She searched through thirteen years of memories, hunting for an explanation for her spontaneous, curious excitement.

She stood in silence, suspended in the moment and looking at her visitor like a teenager on a first date, unsure of what to do or say next.

It was uncertain who was first to move, but they opened their arms and unconsciously merged into one. They engaged in an clinging hug that could be likened to one shared by long-lost lovers. After more than a decade on the shelf, Eloisa's stale, forgotten feelings came alive in his arms.

She was at a loss to explain why she held him so tight, and decided not to tease her moral sense. It felt good to allow years of pent-up emotion to flow from her bosom to his. She didn't understand, but was happy knowing that she felt refreshed. She refused to question her lack of guilt. It didn't bother her that it was her brother-in-law in her arms and she allowed his presence to invigorate dormant sensations. For nearly a half generation, she had considered that she could never again be close to a man. Apparently, she was wrong.

Eloisa hadn't held a man that close since she lost her husband in early 1942, five weeks after Pearl Harbor. San Francisco Police patrolman Leopold Throckmorton was shot dead in the line of duty while answering a domestic disturbance call. At the age of thirty-five, she became a widow with two young children.

She could not remember fantasizing about Nick or granting him anything more than a passing thought. True, driven by a sense of duty and kindness, she felt compelled to write to him once, but only to inform him about his brother Leopold's sudden death. Instantly, she worried if Nick ever received that letter, and if it could have been forever lost to the spoils of war. The fact that she never received a reply further tortured her memory.

The knock on her door had washed away years of emptiness. Eloisa and her field of fantasies had lain fallow too long.

She boldly pushed her fanciful dreams aside and ended their impassioned clutch, "Nicholas! It's so good to see you after all these years ... how'd you find this place again? The telephone directory?"

Nick remembered that her eyes were blue, but he could not recall the stunning shade of lavender that he saw looking back at him. He studied her and confirmed that his recollections served him well. She was as boldly blonde, built and buoyant as his imagination and memory had sculpted her.

"To be honest, I didn't consider looking you up in the telephone book, Ellie ... I thought that it wouldn't have done me any good anyway ... because I figured that at the least, you could have moved away or remarried and have a different last name."

His reply affirmed to her that he must have received her letter and knew that his brother was dead. "No, no ... Nicholas. I'm still a war widow and probably always will be." She took him by the hand, "Come on in, Nick. Come on in and out of the doorway."

He followed her down the short, narrow hall to the living room and allowed his eyes to wander over her form. He watched countless little blue blossoms of forget-me-nots dance up, down and sideways over her pale green, brushed cotton housedress.

She motioned to the davenport, "Sit. Sit down, Nick." He sat on the near end and smiled up at his sister-in-law. It was Eloisa's turn to study him. He wasn't in uniform, so she was uncertain if he was still in the military. His brown wool suit was summer weight, fresh, clean and not wrinkled from travel. It didn't appear new, but neither was it tired from wear. He wore a cream silk shirt, burgundy tie and clean, polished but not shined, oxblood oxfords. His appearance wasn't what she would have expected. He looked like a professional, but did not carry a valise or suitcase full of samples, so it was unlikely that he was selling insurance or anything else door-to-door.

"Goodness, Nick. The last time I laid eyes on you was a couple years before the war."

"It was Thanksgiving, 1939."

"You remembered."

"I couldn't forget that visit, Ellie. Of course, it was the first time we really met and talked to one another but it was the last time I saw my brother."

She needed to break an uncomfortable silence, "Would you like something to drink? There's a few bottles of root beer in the Frigidaire or I could make a pot of coffee. Anything?"

"A coffee would be great. Black, thank you."

"I'll put the pot on and be back in a flash." She was elated with the thought of mixed company, be it inconsequential or relative.

"How about I come with you into the kitchen and at least keep you company in the meantime, Ellie?"

"You know what, Nick? That's a good idea. Thank you, I'd welcome the company."

They traded innocuous, inquisitive smiles, Nick stood and they walked to the kitchen. He sat at the table and watched as Eloisa filled the coffee pot, put it on the stove and took a seat across from him. Their wooden chairs squeaked in protest. The walls were pale yellow, faded with time and soiled from years of cooking, frying and the activities of life. The linoleum floor was showing its age as well. The pattern was wearing thin from foot traffic and exposing the black, tarpaper core.

She asked, "Nick, you must've got my letter, didn't you? I wrote as soon as I collected myself after Leopold was shot and killed."

Eloisa moved her glance away, afraid that she sounded forlorn and lonely. She looked across the room, focusing beyond the wall, searching for direction, and a pathway for the countless conversations roaming through her mind. She wanted to capture her wayward thoughts and point them in a direction that made sense. She did not want to come across as a pitiful, aging widow.

"I'm sorry, Ellie. I got your letter about six or seven months after the fact, when I was in Australia and about to get stationed to New Guinea, but I guess I can't make excuses for not writing. I must have read your letter a couple dozen times and I memorized everything, even the blacked-out censored parts and your address, thinking that someday I would stop in and see you and your kids after the war. I thought I owed it to you. I'm sorry that it took me so long to get here, and I'm not making excuses, but I never really got out of the service, and I've been busy ever since the war ended, but I do think about you and little Shirley, though. Where is she? And her brother? I remember that the last time we met, back in '39 if I'm not mistaken, you were in the family way and you mentioned in your letter that you were blessed with a son, Albert, and he should be about ... about eleven years old by now."

Nick's questions fell to the floor. She didn't answer them, but stood, stepped to the range and turned off the burner so the pot could steep down. She had allowed her thoughts to wander far away to places she'd never been and imagine things that could have been.

She returned to her seat at the table and asked him, "You're still in the Air Force, then, Nick? What brought you to my doorstep after all these years?"

"No, I'm sorry, Ellie. Maybe I misspoke. I'm not in the military, but I'm working for the Department of the Air Force, and going on all sorts of little snafu* missions. I just got back from Washington State, where I was checking last week's crash of a Douglas C-124[**] transport plane. The Air Force and the FBI are working together on the investigation and maybe you heard about it; the rattletrap crashed right after takeoff and killed about eighty airmen and soldiers. I'm sort of an inspector, arranger and fixer. And since I'm in San Francisco anyhow, and I got a couple days off before I need to get back to work, I thought I'd stop in and see you, my niece and nephew. You might say that I was in the neighborhood and decided to stop in."

After his words settled, there was silence. Eloisa remembered hearing something on the news about a plane crash, but she only heard Nick say that he decided to pop in and that he worked for the Air Force as an inspector, nothing more. She had no way of knowing that Nick was doing what he had been trained to do: disguise and protect the mission with the purposeful misdirection of information.

He found his eyes locked onto her stare and forced them away, and searched around the room. He wasn't accustomed to a woman's eyes holding his. Apparently, her steady gaze had distracted him and made him antsy, "Got an ashtray nearby, Ellie?"

She stood, took a few steps to the sink and brought one over to the table.

Nick had a Camel lit before she set it down, "So, you didn't answer me. Are your kids at a friend's house or what? Does Shirley still have those curly blonde locks?"

Eloisa had turned, opened a cabinet, grabbed two coffee cups and brought them and the pot to the table. She spoke as she filled the cups, "You said you like your coffee black, didn't you?"

Stubbornly, Eloisa wanted to be the one to ask the questions and direct the conversation. She was hoping to start mouthing those incomplete sentences and unfinished stories that were swirling around in her head. Eloisa lightly brushed her fingers over the curls at her temple, thankful for her Toni home permanent. She was generally comfortable in her skin and not concerned about her age, but at that moment, there was a bee in her bonnet. She remembered that she wasn't wearing any makeup and only applied a touch of lipstick. At forty-five, she knew the clock was ticking and wondered if her visitor believed that the hands of time had treated her well.

Nick interrupted her worry, "Yes, black is perfect."

She returned the pot to the stove and explained, "I'm sorry, I didn't mean to keep you hanging out on a limb, Nick. I'm not trying to avoid your questions, I'm just so excited to have some company ... I mean when I saw you standing at my door ... of all the people in the world and after all this time, goodness gracious ... it's just that you being here sort of knocked the wind out of my sails and got my mind traveling every which way. To tell the truth, you favor your brother so much, I got completely discombobulated when I saw you.

"It's taken me a while to pull myself together, I guess. I was daydreaming and I apologize for not answering straight away ... you're right, I do have two children, Shirley and Albert. Shirley, you've met her, on that Thanksgiving years ago, and she's still blonde, like me, but she's lost most of those little girl, natural curls. She'll be seventeen next month and Albert, he was ... he was just six months when Leopold was killed. He's twelve now and he's the spitting image of his father, and he looks a lot like you, too, in fact. Black hair, dark eyes and good-looking. It must be something in that Throckmorton blood of yours.

"Ever since I lost my Leopold, most every year the kids and I spend Christmas up in Sacramento with my elder sister Ginny, her husband Geoffrey and their brood of four holy terrors. No ... forgive me ... I shouldn't say that ... they're good kids, really. They run from twenty to ten years old ... a real full house, and not the card playing kind. The twenty and eighteen-year-old don't live there, they're usually both away at college, but they're home visiting for the holidays, too. I drove back home here on Sunday, a few days after Christmas, and Shirley and Al will take the noon commuter train back home on Friday after New Year's. I can't stand Geoffrey's endless gabbing and opinions, to tell the complete truth. And he knows it, and it's fine with me. I don't know how my Ginny puts up with his opinions and constant complaining. No matter who gets elected, who wins the baseball game or what union goes on strike, he has something negative to say about somebody or something. But Shirley and Al like it up there in the capital, and hanging around with their two younger cousins, though. I think it must be the change of scenery and the different day-to-day routine. And it's not near as foggy or rainy as it is here."

Although Eloisa's soft voice sounded as fresh as a woodland stream, she withheld her soul and seemed to be preaching to empty pews. The emotional dam she had reinforced over the years kept all her passion and sorrow walled up behind her personal, private levee.

Nicholas crushed out his cigarette. He watched her expressions closely as she talked and while it seemed that she was telling all there was to tell, he sensed that her words were sterile and without feeling. She seemed cautious.

"How about I take you out to dinner tonight, Ellie? We can catch up some more and maybe fill each other in on what's been going on with our lives, and where we've been and where we're going."

His last words baffled her and sounded like a riddle. She wasn't sure if he was talking about a planned conversation or a dinner destination. She sipped at her coffee, studied him over the brim of her cup and asked, "Where we have been and where are we going?"

He understood that his double-talk confused her and simply answered the last part of her question, "I'll surprise you. I'll pick you up at six o'clock, how's that?"

Eloisa attempted to answer immediately, but her voice cracked a bit and her cheeks began to flush, betraying her initial excitement. "Sure. Six is good. And will you be picking me up in your black Cadillac that's parked out front?"

"It's not a Cadillac and it's not mine by a long shot. I have it on loan until I fly out of Travis Air Base on Friday."

He bobbed his head and pointed with his thumb, "That's a government car out there, an Olds Rocket 88. The name almost fits my job description. I've been traveling so much lately; it feels like I got rockets strapped to my shoes. But to tell that story I would need more time than I got right now."

He rarely turned down an opportunity to talk about things powered by aviation fuel or gasoline, but somehow Nick felt that cars and aircraft wouldn't be a topic of conversation over dinner. He recognized Eloisa's lonely isolation and detected her apparent desire for a temporary fix. Briefly, he studied his conscience.

Their visit lasted about an hour. They said their goodbyes on the front porch and shared a firm but abbreviated hug. He held her close, his arms around her waist, and spoke softly through her curls and into her ear, "Pick you up at six, Ellie," and he left her with a peck on the cheek. She couldn't be positive, but she believed she felt his arousal while entwined and she couldn't be sure who pressed into whom. She stood there wondering, waving and watching him drive off.

The mystery of exactly where they would sit down for their evening meal was secondary only to her anxious anticipation of the outcome. There were so many possibilities powered by so many variables that everything in her world was spinning around like pinwheels in a hurricane.

Eloisa had no idea where Nick was staying, so any suggestion for a restaurant was limited not only to his budget, but also to his willingness to drive around in an unfamiliar city. Because he had a government car and said that he worked for the Air Force, she assumed he was staying in government quarters. She felt comfortable with her decision to leave everything entirely up to him and she would only offer a choice if asked. Her personal knowledge of dinner spots was limited, anyway.

She had about seven hours to get ready for her night out.

Till The Real Thing Comes Along ...

Eloisa didn't need a lot of time to ponder the modest collection of dresses in her bedroom closet. In short order, she made her choice and set it neatly on her bed. She smoothed the material, straightened the shape, stood back and thought about her choice. It needed to pass one more critical test. She bent at the waist, and put her nose to the shoulders, bodice and waist. She decided that all it needed was a light brushing with a little bit of Cheer laundry powder mixed in some warm water and the stale closet smell would disappear.

It was a lace-trimmed, coral pink dirndl dress, with a sewn-in white blouse, tailored puffy sleeves, a definitive bust line, waist and soft, billowy skirt. She last wore it a bit more than a year earlier, for her niece Sally's confirmation at Trinity Episcopalian. Eloisa rationalized that if the dress was good enough for church it would certainly pass for dinner. Furthermore, if Nick dressed in his brown suit, the color wouldn't clash with her dress and no one could fault her fashion sense.

She brought out a pair of sandalwood beige, t-strap pumps with two-inch heels from the back of her closet, and set them on the floor next to her bed for examination. First, they would need a brushing followed by a touch-up and a buff with some Johnson's paste wax.

She opened her dainties drawer, picked out her best under things, sorted through her stockings and was able to arrange a slightly mismatched pair without runs or snags.

Eloisa returned to her closet for the last item. She retrieved a cropped cape out from under the paper wrap of a dry cleaner's hanger, and set it on her bed next to the dress. The cape, like her dirndl dress, was a veteran of Sally's confirmation. It was made of brown and white, curly knit wool that from fifteen or twenty feet away, appeared beige. No matter the color, it could keep the chill of night off her shoulders.

Eloisa took a step backward, folded her arms across her chest and studied the things she had laid out on her bed. The sun was sneaking through the lace pattern of her curtains and throwing little spots of glimmering, shifting light over everything on the bed. She succumbed to her fantasies and continued to plan her evening, hoping that her dreams would come true.

For some odd reason, she felt as if she were following a recipe from a tattered, flour-encrusted, heirloom Betty Crocker** cookbook. The measured ingredients were coming out of her cupboards and drawers and going into the big mixing bowl on her bed, where they would later come together for what she hoped would be a wonderful night out on the town. She would mix cotton and nylon delicates beneath her cotton dress and slip on a pair of taupe stockings. Next, she she'd smooth and secure them to the garter snaps and slide her feet into a pair of modest heels.

Finally, she would bring a kitchen chair into her bedroom and set it in front of her dresser. Then she'd sit, lean forward, study her reflection and carefully apply her Revlon *Slightly Red* lipstick. Next, she would lacquer her nails, and when the time came for mascara, she would discover that it had dried and caked in the tray and needed softening with baby oil. When Nicholas came to knock in the evening, she would don her wool cape, grab her handbag and answer the door. She'd be ready. He'd whisk her away in his long black chariot to a destination that had been a long time coming.

Eloisa continued to build her castle in the clouds. Across the hall, she turned up the hot water heater and began to slowly to fill the tub. A hot bath and long soak in Jean Naté bath beads would give her flight of fancy some altitude. She could shave her legs, relax, close her eyes and give wings to her imagination.

Then she'd call her sister Ginny and make sure the kids were all right before she finished getting herself ready.

Fishin' For The Moon ...

The sun had gone to bed an hour earlier. Eloisa sat on the sofa, watching for headlights through the drapery liners. Nick didn't keep her waiting and arrived outside her house at exactly six. He had no sooner put the transmission into park than he spotted her coming through the doorway, backlit by a small table lamp down the hall. He watched her turn the key in the door, drop it into her handbag and take three steps down to the walkway. He reached across the front seat and opened the passenger door for her.

Although she briskly stepped toward the Oldsmobile, Ellie couldn't help but notice the forest green, US Government license plate on its trunk lid. Four, large white numbers and two letters caught her eye: 4307 BF. It was the type of oddity that occurs every so often throughout a person's life, and can give pause when it's recognized. For Eloisa, it did just that. She was born in Buffalo, New York on April 3, 1907.

She took her spot on the front seat and smiled, "You're right on time! Six o'clock on the button." The car door closed with a firm thump and she took a breath. The quick walk from the house and a flush of excitement had her heart pumping with exuberance.

"You look very nice, Ellie. Very nice."

The license plate prompted her to ask a question she would not ordinarily have asked, "I noticed the government tag on the back of the car, and guess what? It's the date and place I was born, 4-3-07-BF. How strange is that? It's like one of those strange but true stories out of Reader's Digest[**]. It's incredible; a license plate with my exact birth date and city. When were you born, Nick?" As soon as those words crossed her lips, she vowed that for the rest of the night, she would think before she spoke.

"I was born a couple years later, in '09. In Buffalo, too. In October of 1909. It's funny how numbers can pop up like that. It happens all the time, really. I used to see stuff like that when I would study flight maps during the war. Numbers can mean something when you want them to, and sometimes when you don't. And they can be good or bad. Like anything else in life, I guess. It is what you make it to be. Numbers or dates. It's all relative." He looked over his shoulder, pulled away from the curb, onto the street and started off northeast on Cayuga Avenue.

Eloisa was thinking aloud, "Numbers and dates. Like middle age." Again, she spoke without forethought, and again she vowed to be more careful. Spontaneous statements can lead any conversation down a bumpy road.

Nick questioned her comparison, "What's that you say? Middle age? The middle? I don't think so. I figure I'm past middle age. I'm forty-three and I don't think I'll make it to eighty. And I don't have that much faith in the future of the world."

She knew she was casting caution to the wild, "Well, I look at it this way: I'm old enough to know better but at least I know how. I need to start using all that knowledge."

Nick broke into a brief, bawdy laugh, fought back and quickly regained composure, "Good one, Ellie."

Her fear flew out the window. She felt relief, "Where are we going?" She turned slightly sideways on the seat, inched a bit closer and watched him steer the Oldsmobile around the parked cars along Cayuga.

Nick gave her a quick glance as he turned onto Mission Street. He knew it was nothing more than reflected streetlights, but her eyes seemed to be sparkling just for him. He answered, "At first, I was thinking we could go down to the docks and go fishing for the moon in the bay, but I wasn't sure what we could use for bait."

"I heard the moon is fickle. And moody. And it doesn't always respond to bait, no matter what you use."

Nick had begun to enjoy her company. Her wit teased him. Her will tempted him, "I'm staying at the Saint Francis Hotel up here on Powell Street, just a few blocks away and right off Market Street, if I remember right. After I got back from our morning visit, I found out that there's a whiz-bang restaurant right there at the hotel, the Maple Room. How's that? The clerk told me the menu's good and they got it all, from soup to nuts."

Eloisa toyed with her words again, "Great. I like nut soup."

He muffled a chuckle. He enjoyed her humor.

She moved even closer to him, to the center of the front seat and watched her evening come into focus through the windshield. The shimmering lights of downtown San Francisco were brighter than any other time she could remember. She allowed herself a mundane observation, "It seems to me that you know your way around for being the new guy in town."

"It's a knack, I suppose, Ellie. I learned how to read maps in the Air Corps and I'm lucky enough to be able to keep an image in my head of the important stuff. It's nothing more than that, and certainly nothing remarkable."

"It's reassuring to know that at least one of us knows where we're going."

They laughed together, enjoyed one another's company, and recognized the connection that was forming. The beckoning beam of the Yerba Buena Lighthouse drew them down Market Street, toward the Embarcadero waterfront and the brightly illuminated Ferry Building. Red and green Christmas lights ran along the roofline and spotlights lit up the two-hundred-fifty foot landmark clock tower.

Nick brought the Oldsmobile to a stop under the entrance portico of the Saint Francis. The valet asked, "Will you and your guest be dining or staying the night sir?"

"Both. I'm a guest at the hotel ... the name is Throckmorton ... and we'll be having dinner, thank you." Nick stuck a two-dollar bill in the young man's palm.

Eloisa's pulse quickened.

I've Heard That Song Before ...

Eloisa felt like a stranger in paradise. Nicholas gently took her arm and led her through the lobby of the Saint Francis to the maître d'hotel podium inside the Maple Room restaurant. A waiter escorted them to a candlelit table for two that was dressed with a deep burgundy tablecloth, sparkling silverware, twinkling glasses and gleaming china. The hotel, its restaurant and adjoining cocktail bar were not high society by any measure, but for Eloisa, they were part of an unfamiliar, cosmopolitan lifestyle.

Eloisa's last night on the town that could come close in comparison was nearly seventeen years earlier, in 1936, on Valentine's Day. She and her husband Leopold were proud new parents of their firstborn, a baby girl they had christened Shirley and marked the occasion with dinner and dancing at the Bayview Ballroom of the Golden Gate Hotel.

After some prater over the menu and observations of their surroundings, Nick ordered a neat Glenfiddich scotch and a glass of Hanzell Chardonnay for Eloisa. Half an hour later, following pointless chatter and innocent innuendo, she found it easier to breath, relax, and enjoy her situation and his company.

Appetizers were oysters Rockefeller and a shrimp cocktail, followed by the main course of Chinese roasted chicken, asparagus and baked potatoes. After their meal, Nick mechanically ordered a fresh Glenfiddich and another glass of wine.

Jumpy Nerves ...

The meal was delicious and the service superb, but the conversation over dinner was bland, innocuous and bordered on mundane. For her part, Eloisa could rightfully blame unfamiliar surroundings, jumpy nerves or her anticipation of intimate consummation.

Nick could only fault his senses. More than once, he thought he could hear ice cracking under his feet. He decided that he would stop second-guessing his choices, go ahead, and break that ice. He asked Ellie straight out, "How do you feel about spending the night?"

She tried, but couldn't fight the flush that overwhelmed her, and struggled for her first few words, "It's been a long time, Nick." She reached for his hand, held onto it and began searching for the right words and the ability to say them in the right order. He gently put his other hand over hers.

She explained, "I've already convinced myself that climbing under the covers and between the sheets with you was all right and I wouldn't be breaking any laws or violating the natural order of things; at least I don't think so. But it's just that all this ... all this uneasiness and self-doubt is knocking me for a loop."

"I understand."

"I don't think so. There's no way that you understand. I want you to. I really do. Goodness gracious I do. I'm confused myself and I'm looking for an excuse not to be confused, but I can't find one."

"There's nothing wrong with being human, Ellie. Human is what we are. We're here on Earth to do human things. Dogs and cats do dog and cat things and bugs do bug things. It's only natural for a human to act like a human. You're allowed to do human things."

"There's some kind of sweet confusion going on inside my head right now, Nick. I can't explain it. It's sort of a crazy dizzy feeling like you get from a couple glasses of wine, except my whole body feels that way and not just my head. I can't explain it any other way. It's a good feeling but it's one I can't describe very well."

"That's just what I was talking about, you see. You're human and experiencing human things. It's supposed to feel good. I've often been denied human contact one way or another, for one reason or another, and believe me; it's like dying of thirst. Somebody once told me that you should never try to drag your heart across a loveless desert, because you couldn't make it over the first dune. You would choke to death on drifting grains of sand full of regret, sorrow and loneliness."

He fell into her violet eyes. They glistened from what could either be tears withheld or the haze of a glass and a half of wine.

"To be absolutely honest, Nicholas, I would have been disappointed had you not invited me to share your bed."

He nudged his chair inches closer, leaned in, nuzzled briefly and tenderly kissed her lips. He whispered, "You smell magical."

"I confess. It's not magic. It's Max Factor's *Hypnotique* cologne."

"Magical, Ellie. That's what you are. It's not just the perfume."

She slipped her hand under the table, beneath the table linen and squeezed his thigh. He kissed her again, straightened in his chair and motioned for the waiter. For the next few minutes, there were no words between them, only glances. She dared him with every blink of her lashes.

Nick charged the meal and drinks to his room, and somehow they managed to walk, not run from their table and through the lobby to the elevators. When he opened the door to room 1100 and stepped inside, Eloisa recognized what was on the writing table and gave him a hip-bump hard enough to test his balance. He exaggerated his plight, bounced on one foot, rebounded quickly, and came to rest in the arms of a woman who was about to devour him.

He too, had anticipated after-dinner activities. There was a bottle of Inglenook White Zinfandel on ice and a Whitman's Sampler on the side table.

Over the next few hours, Eloisa rediscovered life and Nick willingly availed himself of her situation. The wine and the confections were left untouched.

(I Love You) For Sentimental Reasons ...
Wednesday, December 31, 1952

Nick was up, out of bed and in the shower before sunup. He came out of the bathroom with a plush hotel towel wrapped around his waist, and wiping Old Spice shaving cream off his face. It was not yet seven o'clock, and he didn't expect she would be awake.

"Good morning, Nick." Eloisa was sitting up, supported by six bed pillows propped against the heavy mahogany headboard. She was wearing her camisole, a single strap off the shoulder and smoking one of Nick's Camels. For years, she had struggled with pent-up emotion and lack of intimate human contact. For more than a decade, she had no one to share her worries, wishes and feelings. Her sister in Sacramento helped, but she wasn't a man.

"Good morning, Sweetheart."

She snuffed out the cigarette and broke a brief silence, "I thought about Leopold last night." Once again, she questioned her judgment. She worried that she had crossed a forbidden line and her words could be interpreted as too insensitive. Nervous and not knowing what to expect, she watched for a reaction.

His reply was matter-of-fact, "So did I."

She was relieved. She changed the subject and dared to continue, "I called room service and ordered breakfast ... coffee, some toast, orange juice, some over-easy eggs and bacon. I hope that's all right?" She didn't want to apologize, and felt she had no reason to. Regardless, again she wallowed in self-doubt.

He sat on the bed and gave her a soft kiss, "Of course, it's okay, Ellie. Thank you, breakfast is wonderful. Thank you."

She squeezed a single tear from her eye and Nick kissed it off her cheek. He brought her into his arms and held onto her. She was rocking ever so slightly. Suddenly, she stopped, pulled back a bit, and tried to explain, "No, *thank you*. Thank you, Nicholas Throckmorton, for being with me, and listening to me, and helping me live again. I worried and feared for your safety after you never answered my letter. I worried that I would forever be alone and never know a man again. I worried that your plane was shot down and you were dead or captured and little Albert would be the only Throckmorton left. Silly isn't it?"

"You had no way of knowing, Ellie. The enemy tortured all of us. It's the torture of war that nobody ever talks about. War doesn't always kill and tear up people in jungles or deserts. Back home, there's the loneliness and uncertainty and fear of being left alone."

Again, they renewed an enduring, yet gentle embrace. His kisses smothered her doubt and his arms wrapped her in security.

Her euphoria was short-lived. A knock at the door meant their breakfast had arrived.

Nick quickly pulled on his trousers, slipped into his shirt, signed for the meals, and set the oval Bakelite tray on the reading table along with the Sampler box and unopened wine. He noticed that Ellie had tasted a few of the Whitman chocolates while he was in the shower.

Over their breakfast, Eloisa's curiosity drove the conversation further into deeply personal territory.

"Have you ever been in love, Nick? I mean, really in love?"

He hesitated briefly before he answered, "I thought I was. Twice, I thought I was. The first time I was a scared kid ... eighteen years old ... lost without any family ... running away from tragedy, dumbstruck and numbed by what I thought was love. But I was mistaken, and got married anyhow. I had to. We had to. Sure, some people might call what Nora and I had 'love', but it wasn't soul-binding, knock-your-socks-off love by any measure. Nora gave me two things: our son Alexander and me. She's been a great mother to Alexander. And she was good to me. She gave me myself and allowed me to be me. She gave me enough rope to roam. And I did. I learned to fly and took off.

"I can't blame my wife Nora for the failure of our marriage. It was doomed from the onset. We were two kids and both of us knew we were young, dumb and hopeless. Of course, Nora's father had a huge influence on her and Nora's mother just went along with anything that her father said. I was the outsider in their world. And Nora's world too. I still am.

"Nora and her devotion to the Catholic Church ... well, I was an outsider there, too. I was born and raised a pig-headed Lutheran and I refused to convert ... I mean, what for? I'd still be the outsider and about as welcome as a beer and bratwurst fart in the front pew during High Mass."

He put a match to a Camel, inhaled and continued, "Like I said, I thought I was in love twice, but the correct answer is: only once ... and I realized it much too late... much too late. I should have snatched her up and held on. Her name was Guendolen Peate, an Aussie nurse I met in Sydney, and I allowed her to sail away from me. I watched her steam away to New Guinea, and never saw her again. Twelve hours later the bastard Japs torpedoed her hospital ship twenty miles off the northeast coast of Australia and sent it to the bottom of the sea."

His gaze had focused far away, out the window and somewhere deep in San Francisco Bay. He finished the last of his coffee and set the heavy, white china mug down on the table with a clunk. Eloisa refilled it from the stainless steel vacuum pot.

She decided it was her turn, "Your story is similar to mine, Nicholas. It's not similar in circumstance, but it's darn near identical in the way it all got started and all the physical emotional consequences. My life has been so full of tragedy; there have been times when I didn't think I could handle anymore.

"My parents were pretty strict Anglicans, and that's how I grew up back in Buffalo, but I drifted, you might say. Really drifted. Leopold and his girl Phryne left New York and I followed about six months later. When I got out here, I had a hole in my heart as big as all California. My life was a mess. As it turned out, so was Leopold and Phryne's. Their marriage was over almost as soon as the honeymoon ended. Then in 1934, by sheer coincidence, Leopold and I crossed paths here in San Francisco and you might say he saved me from falling into a bottomless pit. But he didn't save me with religion or anything like that ... you know that your brother wasn't too religious. His philosophy was *live and let live*, I think. He never talked about it much, but he had faith in me. He told me that I helped rescue him, but I've always thought that it was the other way around. We got married and you know the rest.

"Don't think bad of me, Nicholas. Your brother and I were in love. It wasn't the kind of romantic love that poets write about, or one of them soul-deep loves you see in the pictures, but it was a caring, enduring love-friendship or something like that. We loved each honestly, right up until the day he was shot and killed."

She mopped up the egg yolk off her plate with the last piece of toast, and finished her coffee.

"Thank you for dinner, Nick ... and last night. Thank you, I had a lovely time."

He leaned sideways, across the table and kissed her. "Thank you, Ellie. It was lovely, like you said."

She sensed it was ending. He looked at his watch, "I've got to go and report in, and let my boss know what I discovered at the crash site and where the investigation stands. And maybe find out where I'm going next."

"Of course."

He detected her mood, "No, no, Ellie. I'm not shuffling you off. Tonight's New Year's Eve, and I think we should celebrate, don't you? I mean, what else is there to do? You saw the posters in the lobby ... there's going to be a fireworks show over the bay, an open buffet and dance music with Kitty Cochenour and her Bob Kats. You said that your kids, Shirley and Al are at your sister's until tomorrow and here we are, in a decent hotel in downtown Frisco on New Year's. We can't waste this, Ellie. You're not running away on me now, lady ... not no way, not no how. I won't allow it. We're going to dance tonight, and it's going to be magic."

She brightened, "Really?"

"Really. I'll drive you home, then I'll scoot up to the Presidio**, cable my boss, maybe fill out some paperwork, and see if there's anything new I should know about, and come right back. And I'll pick you up at six o'clock again, just like last night. What do you say, Ellie? Can you fit me into your social calendar for one more night? It's New Year's, Ellie! We can dance past midnight! How special is that?"

How Long Has This Been Going On? ...

It was just past ten in the morning when Nick pulled up the Olds at Eloisa's home. They shared a quick kiss before she got out of the car and started up the walkway. Next to her pensive personality and willingness to take a dare, the standout trait that made an impression on him was the way she moved as she walked. Every turn of her ankle telegraphed its way up her calves and thighs, to her hips, neck, shoulders and all the way down to her fingertips. Her wiggle made waves that swamped his imagination. He loved it. She unlocked her door, turned and waved. He noticed her smile before the door closed behind her. He also spotted the new, forest green Chrysler New Yorker parked two doors down, but he didn't see anyone inside the vehicle.

Since his arrival in San Francisco the day before and his brief contact with the FBI in Moses Lake, Washington, he was aware that unseen Agency eyes could be watching every move he made. Nicholas believed that there was nothing for anyone to see. Eloisa was his sister-in-law and she was entitled to his company. It was as simple as that.

When the FBI and Air Force investigators told him that the crash site had been secured, that was the end of it. He half-expected to see Field Supervisor Munson at Moses Lake, but didn't consider it unusual when he didn't. Nick felt that he did his job just by showing up, and had no desire to pick a penny-ante fight. He knew that he didn't have the authority to break convention or question jurisdiction rights with the FBI. He would write it all down in his mission report back to Jovita and let her handle it. The Agency always yielded domestic jurisdiction to The Bureau when there was no evidence or suspicion of foreign influence. He didn't give the matter another thought, put the Rocket in drive and started down the street.

The traffic in the city was negligible, most likely due to the upcoming holiday. In less than half an hour, he could put a finger on the Agency's pulse and get a reading of the tealeaves and if need be, the tarot cards. He assumed that he would need to show his Agency ID to the MP at the guardhouse and with a nod and a wave, he'd be inside. A week earlier, when he left the Canal Zone from Balboa, Panama, he made certain that all the details of this trip were committed to memory. His contact at the Presidio Army installation was a supervisor named Donald Carlisle at the Inter-Agency Communications and Signal Corps Building on Sherman Avenue, just inside the Presidio gates. There he could pick up any messages and update Jovita on the C-124 transport kerfuffle. He expected that it could be an interesting conversation, given that not only hadn't he seen her since the spring of 1946, he hadn't heard her voice in nearly a year. Additionally, his current mission placed his feet on the continental United States for the first time in nearly two years.

Nick tiptoed around the truth when he told Eloisa that he had been investigating the December 20 crash of a transport plane in Washington State. As it turned out, he was at the crash scene less than an hour. Almost as soon as he displayed his credentials, he got the cold shoulder and was turned away. The FBI and Air Force had shut the CIA out of the investigation. They claimed that they uncovered enough evidence to deduce that human error had caused the death of eighty-seven soldiers and airmen and not foreign operatives. Regardless of the Second Red Scare** that was running through the halls of Congress and the Pentagon, the FBI agent in charge said that the bare-boned truth was that ordinary people make mistakes. The situation didn't smell right, but the Agency didn't pay Nick to use his nose. He would explain his doubts in his End of Mission report to Jovita.

Since he was already in San Francisco, alone with nothing better to do and a full week to do it, Nick concluded that he might as well visit his brother's widow. The FBI had no jurisdiction over his personal life, and to the best of his knowledge, neither did the Agency nor Jovita, as long as it didn't interfere with or jeopardize the mission. He was almost certain of it.

He would find out soon enough if his presumption was wrong. He cleared the guard post at The Presidio's main gate without fanfare, and parked at the Signal Corps building. At the Communications desk, he displayed his Agency ID to an Army Staff Sergeant who greeted him, "Good Morning, Mister Throckmorton, sir. Mister Carlisle is unavailable, but left this for you, sir."

The sergeant handed Nick a tobacco-brown 8 x 10 inch envelope. Inside was a cryptic, two-line cablegram: *You are to report to Corinth Street, Jacksonville for annual physical*[*]. *Transport departs Travis AFB Friday, 1400.*

An 'annual physical' was a mandatory mission briefing, but there was no need to disappoint Ellie. Their New Year's dinner and dance could go on as planned.

Oh! Look At Me Now ...

Eloisa closed the door behind her and immediately noticed the chill in her empty home. She set her pocketbook on the telephone table in the hall, stepped to the wall furnace, lit the pilot light and turned up the thermostat. Next, she telephoned her sister, exchanged pleasantries and mustered enough courage to tell her that she had an unannounced visitor the day before.

Ginny was genuinely surprised and happy to hear that Ellie actually planned to come out of her shell and go out dancing with Nicholas. It wasn't often that her sister welcomed male callers to her door. Of course, Eloisa only skimmed the surface and didn't tell Ginny the whole story. The main purpose for Eloisa's call was to talk with her children and not to engage in sisterly chitchat. If she felt the need, that could happen some other day.

Her son Albert was busy planning a game of sandlot football with his cousin, but Shirley was able to say hello. She talked briefly with her mother and reminded her that she and her brother would be coming home on Friday's noon train.

When Eloisa hung up the receiver, she paused and looked across the hall, into the living room and allowed her eyes to pass over Leopold's police portrait on the sideboard. She reflected on all the occasions in years past when she, Albert and Shirley would be sitting on the sofa, reading storybooks, listening to Little Orphan Annie on the radio, doing schoolwork or just gabbing away about nothing while her husband worked the night beat. She remembered birthdays, Neapolitan ice cream, the frosted birthday cakes, the silly paper hats made from bits of colored construction paper and Sunday dinners alone with the children. She thought about Christmases in Sacramento with Ginny, Geoffrey and the kids but couldn't recall any special New Year's Eve.

She returned to real time when she realized that this New Year's would be special. Eloisa could almost hear the kazoos**, tin horns, noisemakers and whistles of hundreds of New Year's revelers at the Saint Francis. She could hardly wait.

When Nick suggested that they make another night of it and welcome the New Year with dining and dancing, she looked back at the meager inventory of five dresses hanging in her closet. She had already rummaged through them and picked out the best of the shabby lot: the dirndl she was wearing. She determined that it was absolutely, positively necessary to buy a New Year's dress. However, such a purchase didn't warrant the pillaging of the family's passbook savings account.

She reached to the top shelf in the pantry, brought down a timeworn Peter Pan Peanut Butter can and set it on the kitchen table. She took a seat and pondered her course of action. In a flash, she removed the reusable, flexible plastic top and dumped the contents onto the grey Formica tabletop.

She immediately sorted, counted and stacked only the quarters and half-dollar silver coins. Next, she straightened and tallied the crumpled one and two-dollar bills. All totaled, Eloisa counted out one hundred, seventeen dollars and seventy-five cents in the peanut-butter-can-rainy-day-account.

She focused her eyes outside the kitchen window, out beyond the dwarf blackjack pine, and rationalized that after years of drought, she could tap the dam and afford a new dress. She placed fifty dollars into her pocketbook, twenty dollars in coin into her change purse, and put Peter Pan's can back on the top shelf.

Eloisa was so excited about her impending shopping trip, she got goose bumps just thinking about which store would be her first stop. She stood at the hallway mirror, ran a brush through her curls and applied a fresh coat of lipstick. With the impatience of an eight-year-old, she then fidgeted with the bodice and waistline of her old-reliable dirndl dress. After pulling this and adjusting that, she needed only to straighten the seam at the back of her stockings before she was ready. In mere moments, she was out through the kitchen door and backing her maroon 1940 Hudson out of the back alley garage. Still in the afterglow of the night before, she decided to drive uptown to Bullock's department store on Union Square. Although Bullock's was considered a bit pricey, it enjoyed a reputation for quality goods and service. Eloisa believed there was no reason to end her euphoria with a visit to Montgomery Ward or Sears and Roebuck. She wanted to ensure that the New Year would start out special.

After browsing through dozens of racks, studying countless mannequin displays and having a detailed discussion with saleslady Vicky, Eloisa selected a knee-length silk dress in mustard gold. It was a sleeveless, V-neck wrap with a pleated bodice, black velvet trim, cummerbund pleated waist, and full three-tiered skirt. Vicky consummated the sale when she pointed out that the fabric was genuine Chromspun silk taffeta and shimmered with every movement.

The dress, two pairs of stockings, a black, plush velour shawl, a kelly green handbag and matching three-inch pumps set the Peter Pan can back exactly thirty-four dollars and sixty-eight cents. Eloisa certainly wanted to shimmer.

She pondered one more purchase during her drive back home and stopped at the Glen Park Rexall at the corner of Santa Rosa Boulevard. There, she bought a new mascara kit, and made the daring purchase of eye shadow. Eloisa rationalized that it was time she tried something new. She paid the salesclerk two dollars and seventy-five cents in silver coin.

Yippee-i-o-ki-ay ...

For the second night in a row, it was exactly six o'clock when Nick arrived at 96 Cayuga Avenue and once again, Eloisa was ready to go. She was on her way down the front steps just as he placed the Oldsmobile in park. He made an honest effort to get out of the car to open the passenger door for her, but she beat him to it on both counts. If asked to say something positive about him, she could not deny that he was prompt.

Out of town visitors, early revelers and holiday dinner clientele swarmed throughout the foyer and lobby. The hotel was markedly busier than the night before.

One-half of the eleventh floor at the Saint Francis was permanently reserved for military and government agencies. Nick was aware that the biggest dividend of traveling on the Agency's dime was the special considerations that the Saint Francis Hotel afforded its regular clientele. He had reserved an intimate table for two in the Clock Tower Lounge outside the dining room, near the bar, bandstand and dance floor. The table linen was starched white linen with burgundy borders. A pair of tall-back chairs wore coordinating burgundy covers that also matched the napkins and two white, tapered candles flickered in the center of the table. There was a troupe of waiters and waitresses; all dressed in tuxedo style uniforms that created a flurry of black and white throughout the room.

Six-foot windows behind the bar and along the right side of the dance floor provided a panoramic view of San Francisco Bay. The Embarcadero, the cobblestone dock, the oak boardwalk, the Ferry Building and the landmark clock tower spread across a thirty-foot wall of windows like a giant picture-postcard. The city lights of Oakland flickered on the far shore and the reflected Bay Bridge marker lights danced upon the water.

Ellie and Nick sat like actors in a black and white, Paramount Pictures romance-mystery. They teased one another with inquisitive eyes, innuendo-laden conversation and subtle contact above and below the table. Each character trusted that the other had the script locked in memory, and wouldn't spoil the outcome of their private melodrama. Neither player wanted any suspense or changes to the plot.

They spent most of the time before dinner nibbling on hors d'oeuvres, talking about Ellie's work, management of the Mission Bakery and her two children. Nick filled the thorny quiet moments with doublespeak, insinuations and flat-out malarkey about himself and his flights around the globe.

Eloisa's curiosity drove her next question, "When was the last time you were home, Nick?"

He answered quickly, "The service is my home." His reply came as second nature. He heard that question countless times over the years and was always prepared when it popped up. Nick and his employer were coconspirators in deception with a common purpose: protect the mission. Where the mission ended and the truth began was a fuzzy line that led beyond eternity.

He sipped at his scotch and reframed his answer, "To be precise, Ellie, the last time I was in Detroit was in the spring of 1946, at the end of the war, right before I started working for the Department. I know that Nora has since left Mount Clemens to live with her parents in Oshkosh and our son Alexander is in the Navy." Although Nicholas hadn't had any contact with either his wife or son, his job gave him access to otherwise privileged information. Eloisa gently swirled the wine in her glass, watching it whirl within its crystal world.

For his convenience, Nick banked hard right, and sent the conversation in the other direction, "Where do you go when you get lost in your thoughts, Ellie? When you drift away like you do, maybe you could ask someone to go along for the ride. Right now, I'm available, you know."

She looked up at him, took a sip and set her glass down. For a moment, she had the hint of a smile, and then began, "I guess I travel back in time. So much has happened in the last twenty years, Nick. It's not all that hard to get lost in memories, and wonder about the way things could have been or would have been or should have been. I think my travels are daydreams. I mean, my daydreams are travels. And every single one takes me to some magical place, like the *Land of Never Was* or *Never Will Be* ... like *Alice in Wonderland* or some mysterious *Never-Never Land***. Everybody I've ever known seems to hitch a ride and tag along with me, and there always seems to be enough seats, so nobody gets left behind. You've followed along too, Nick. Back in Buffalo, you were only sixteen or seventeen when I first met you ... and you may not even remember, but I noticed you. I don't even think we said two words to each other back then, let alone anything more than *hello*."

Eloisa's words flowed like a woodland stream. She spoke as if she was hypnotized, "Back then, I was hanging on that Irish hoodlum's arm ... on Dylan Cafferty's arm. I was too busy living the life of a flapper. Me, Cafferty, your brother and his girl Phryne ... all we did was jazz it up and have a good time. Back then, I thought Phryne was my best friend. Wow ... it seems like yesterday ... Well, Cafferty raped me ... on the forth of July ... in Canada, believe it or not. He had me on the beach first and then on the front fender of his black Pierce Arrow. I found out after I came out here to California that he'd had his way with Phryne that night, too. Or, I should say ... she had her way with him. Anyway, he hoodwinked me good ... and so did she.

When my father and mother found out I was pregnant, they kicked me out of the house and into Lady of Victory ... the Lady of Victory home for unwed mothers in South Buffalo, in Lackawanna, right across the street from Father Baker's orphanage. I was raped by a bum who I thought loved me and I was shunned by my parents ... deceived by my friend ... pregnant ... cast out ... and alone. It sure wasn't an ideal start in life for a young woman. It was 1928 when I gave away my newborn baby girl to the nuns and I never held her or saw her. One of the nurse sisters told me that an older couple with money and a Negro wet nurse adopted her. They must have snatched her up from between my legs and straight off the table and maybe even before the nurses had me cleaned up. I think that there's a bench in the Basilica with a brass plaque with their names on it."

He interrupted. He decided to make an attempt to blow some wind into her sails and steer her away from the rocks, "I'm sorry. I didn't know about all that, Ellie. I wasn't there. I was long gone, in Detroit and married to Nora already."

"Oh, I know. Leopold and Phryne were long gone, too ... married and divorced by then too. You're only the fourth person I've told this story to: Phryne, my sister Ginny, Leopold and you. In that order."

Nick asked, "Nobody else?"

"Nobody."

Her story stirred Nick's empathy. "I'm sorry, Ellie."

She lit a cigarette off one of the candles and continued, "I can say that the nurse sisters made me feel welcome during my three months at Lady of Victory ... as welcome as I could feel, I suppose. I never thought it was possible to feel so damn alone. It felt like I fell into the deepest, darkest coal mine. It seemed like every day I fell further. I don't know where I'd be today if it wasn't for those nuns. I never really prayed until I was at the Protectorate. And I was raised Episcopalian." She puffed on the cigarette.

"I am what I am because of the paths I chose. Nothing more and nothing less. I have nothing to be ashamed of." The smoke from her cigarette danced gracefully upward, mixing with the warmth and flickering light of the candles.

"You asked where I go when I drift away. Now you know. And all the rest you already know. After the baby, I left the Protectorate and Buffalo, came out to Los Angeles, then to my sister's in Sacramento and just by sheer luck I finally met Leopold here in San Francisco, we got married and we had two kids ... and that's my life story ... the long and short of it, anyway."

Nick used three fingers, pushed his Zippo up and out of his pant pocket, and lit a Camel with a flash of flint, a flicker of blue flame and a final mechanical click. It was like a ritual: inhale, exhale and a swallow of scotch.

"You know what I believe, Ellie? I believe that life is merely a string of events strung together by the fabric that we, ourselves, and those close to us, weave."

"You're quite the inspirational speaker, Nick."

He finished his drink, leaned back in his chair and teased, "I'm good at what I do. My boss says that I can be a legend in my own time if I keep it up." A sly grin came across his lips, "Did I tell you that my boss is a good-looking dame?"

She understood he was making a joke, and it was okay to laugh. He was convincing, and she believed what he said. Her eyes sparkled with energy. She was having fun and teased him, "Really? You have a woman over you? Right over you ... on top of you ... and she's your boss?"

He laughed, nodded and played along, "Yes. Yes, I do. And like I said, I travel a lot so I rarely see her, and because her office is over on the East Coast, our only communication is by telephone and sometimes cablegrams. It depends on exactly where I am."

"Did you talk to her today?"

"No, but I've got my next investigation lined up. I think I told you that I'm leaving on Friday, tomorrow afternoon. I'm flying out of Travis Air Force Base, in Fairfield at 1400 ... two o'clock."

She seemed happy to announce, "I know exactly where that is. The Sacramento train goes right past it, but you didn't say that you were leaving on Friday. You said that you were here for a couple of days ... but I guess you're right. You got here on Wednesday morning, so Friday would be a couple of days. You're right."

"They don't pay me to sit around and do nothing, Ellie."

She feigned a frown, "I'm just kidding, Nick. I know you have a job and they pay you to do it. I know that. It's just that it seems everything that's fun and worthwhile has to end much too soon. Do you know where you're going on Friday?"

Of course, Eloisa was curious – it's human nature. Certainly, Ellie had no need to know whatsoever. Nick was doing his job when he wallpapered over one lie with another and said, "Badlands, South Dakota. Ellsworth Air Base, to be precise. I'm checking on an equipment order they fouled up. Routine, boring government paperwork stuff, that's all."

"South Dakota is full of cowboys, Indians and buffalo, isn't it? And with those wide open spaces and all that ... I think it sounds isolated."

"It is. They're sending me to the Badlands for good reason. I'm a bad cowboy and can't be trusted around women." His eyes laughed.

She poked back, "Yippee-i-o-ki-ay[**], Nick."

They attempted to mute their laughter, but still managed to draw the attention of a handful of neighboring patrons. Only slightly embarrassed, Nick and Ellie restrained themselves further, and laughed more quietly.

Eloisa dared to be playful, "You seem to know a lot about the world around you ... how many hats have you worn, Nicholas Throckmorton?"

"Not many, ma'am. I've only tried a few, but the most comfortable by far, is a leather flight helmet. It's not 100% waterproof but it sure as hell look good with a suit and tie."

She brought a hand to her mouth, held the back of her fingers over her lips and laughed. Her eyes sparkled. It may have been the wine.

The entertainment was well underway. The music was to start at nine o'clock.

Eleven Sixty PM ...

Eloisa's new dress was everything that she hoped it would be. More than just the glimmer and silky feel, it was a confidence booster. She hadn't danced in years, and reveled in the opportunity to be on a parquet floor. Likewise, Nick got to polish his footwork. His last jaunt with the two-step, foxtrot and waltz had been eight years earlier in Sydney, Australia. Throughout the evening, the dance floor seethed with a mass of moving humanity. The presence of one more couple could very well have triggered a cluster of earth tremors.

For the better part of three hours, Kitty and her six Bob Kats managed to make themselves heard over the noisemakers, laughter, and errant hoots and hollers. The anticipation on the dance floor and inside the lounge continued to intensify straight up until Kitty's eleven-thirty announcement. She thanked the crowd in advance and began to plead her case. Kitty feigned a passionate *meow* and purred that she needed to visit her scratching post, and that the catty music would resume in mere minutes. The drummer snared a little riff and ended it with a few selected punishing rim shots.

There were a few moans and groans from the crowd before the collective merrymaking continued. Celebrating for the sake of raucous revelry can test the patience of the young and inexperienced.

Nick kept his arm around Ellie's waist and walked her back to their table. The thought of saying goodbye flashed through his mind, and he immediately sent it into exile. Selfishly, he kept it to himself. She too, had to know this night wouldn't last. There was no need to dwell on it.

As Ellie and Nick took their seats, one of the wait staff appeared out of nowhere, and like the rest of the female crew, she was dressed in black and white. Her black rayon skirt flared out above her knees and rose to a beaded belt at her waist. Youthful breasts jutted proudly forward, punishing the buttons of her frilly pink blouse. "Hello, I'm Barbie. May I bring you folks some fresh drinks, cigarettes, cigars, noisemakers … horns, hats ... anything?" Her voice tinkled like translucent china.

Nick asked, "How long does the fireworks show over the bay last, doll?'

She responded, "It's scheduled to end at twelve-thirty, sir, but I heard that it can go on until one in the morning and a couple of years ago it went past that. I guess it depends on the weather and how many rockets they bring ... and how big the crowds on the docks are, I suppose." Her cheerful reply had the refreshing zing and bouncing zest of spring. Youthful innocence can be energizing, frightful or simply annoying.

Ellie caught Nick's eye and grinned.

Nick thanked the young woman, gave her a friendly smile and ordered another round of Glenfiddich for himself and a glass of chardonnay for Ellie. Barb turned on her heels and was off.

"It sounds like we could be in for quite a night, Ellie. I mean the fireworks and all."

"I think my feet are done for the night, Nick. I can't keep up with these kids today. Have you noticed the crowd in here? I mean, most of them are younger than you or me by more than just a couple of years. And that waitress who was just here ... goodness ... she looks younger than my Shirley."

He acknowledged her question with a smile, a nod and, "It's amateur hour, Ellie." He then leaned close, kissed her lips and suggested, "We can finish our drinks, blow our kazoo, watch a little bit of the fireworks show and go upstairs. How's that?"

"We don't have to stay down here to watch rockets go off. I remember yesterday's sunrise, and I know first-hand that your room faces the east bay. We can watch the fireworks from your room. I think the view from the eleventh floor is fantastic."

It was eleven forty-five when Barb returned with their drinks. Nick graciously thanked her and set a ten-dollar bill on her tray. At eleven sixty, upstairs in room 1100, the fireworks began to boom.

Lover Man ...

It was seven-thirty, New Year's Day. Nick and Ellie were sitting at the small table with their coffee. Dawn and its morning sun were cutting through the drapery liners. A tray littered with the remnants of their room service breakfast was on the bed. Heat from the floor vents softy wafted upward and pushed the white muslin into a ballet of dancing sunlight. Eloisa sat with her elbows on the small table, holding her coffee cup in both hands and warming her fingers. She glowed.

"Thank you, Nick. Thank you for spending some time with me, and showing me how much fun life can be. And sadly, how much fun I've been missing. I think I should try to loosen up just a little bit, don't you think? I need a push start downhill or something. Like an old Ford with a dead battery."

"I don't think you're an old Ford, Ellie. You're more like a Chrysler. And I can vouch that you sure as hell don't have a dead battery. I think you electrocuted me last night."

She smiled broadly, set her cup down and kissed his lips. "You're sweet."

Nick knew he was taking a chance when he inserted, "You're a good-looking woman and fun to be with. You must have men chasing after you, Ellie. Don't you? Don't you get the chance to meet men where you work, at church or at your children's school? There has to be someone waiting in the wings. Ain't there?"

"I've tried, Nick. I've tried to come out of my shell, but just like a big, fat bay oyster, I've kept myself locked up tight. There've been a few men, but none of them serious. Honestly, I just haven't been interested. I don't know what happened to me yesterday, the day before or even last night. I don't know what it was that you did to unlock me. Maybe I made up some imaginary connection between you and me, our distant past and your brother. God only knows. But now, I know that I've got to change what I'm doing, and change the way I'm living. I've got to. I'm afraid of just wilting away and drying up like a lily in the hot sun.

"Right after Leopold's death, the war was full steam ahead, you know that. Nobody, especially me, was interested in any kind of social life. I just lost my husband to a maniac. And for everybody else it was all war; you can imagine that, because you were in it. Some of the policemen came around, but I dodged them. A couple still dogged me and sort of stuck around, two of them to be exact. And over the years they got promoted. Sergeant Marty and Captain Barry still telephone and stop in sometimes, but they're goofs. There's been a handful of times that I've gone to Murphy's Diner or a Chinese restaurant after a Saturday matinee with Marty. And I've been to the pictures and dinner with Barry, too. We usually have Kung Pao chicken, Chow Mein, or meatloaf and gravy or turkey and mashed potatoes. The turkey comes with gravy, too. I really don't care for the rice or noodles."

She paused in thought and added, "Barry's good with them chopsticks."

Nick interrupted, "Like I was explaining to you last night about that fabric we weave, Ellie ... I think we all make our own blanket and we wrap it around us, around those we love, and those who love us. It's that fabric, that blanket that we weave that ties us together and keeps us warm at night and safe during the day. You can keep whoever you want under your blanket. If somebody or something brings a chill, you can kick them out from under the covers ... you should be under your blanket and comfortable with people and things that keep you feeling warm and safe. That's what I think. I think you should make your blanket bigger and warmer, Ellie."

She stopped and began studying him, as if she was in the middle of an art gallery, watching him paint a picture that she was trying to interpret. Certainly, he used the whole spectrum of color and there was a lot to read into what he just splashed on the painting. She knew that he wasn't finished.

He continued working on his stretched canvas, "You got to quit living like a hermit, Ellie. The world didn't stop spinning when Leopold died. You need to get back on, stay on, and keep spinning with it. Maybe you should give that Marty fellow or even Captain Barry another chance and go out on more dates or something with one or both of them and give them a piece of that fabric I was talking about and see what they do with it. What's the worst that could happen? I think you can take care of yourself all right, can't you?"

She rolled her eyes, smiled, chuckled quietly and explained, "Marty looks like Barney Google[**]. He's got the same big old googly eyes and big ears. And his last name ... I can't even pronounce it. It's *Gazagizahowitz* or something. And Barry Dunbar, well, I can say his name all right, but he might as well be Howdy Doody's[**] twin. He doesn't have the freckles, but he's got the same big nose and fat cheeks of that wooden-head puppet."

Eloisa paused again, took a sip of orange juice and smiled blandly at Nick before she began, "There's another man, Fred Gravitt, who comes into the bakery every Friday, on payday, and buys a loaf of pumpernickel and four Bavarian cream-filled croissants. He's nice enough, polite as all get-out and he's about fifty, I would guess. He's a teller at Mutual Savings Bank on Mission Street. About three months ago, we went to see *High Noon* with Gary Cooper and Grace Kelly, I think. He told me then that he was living with his mother and I wondered if he was grown up enough to even go out with me. He tried to kiss me goodnight and missed. He ended up between my top lip and nose, but to be honest, I feel more comfortable with him than I do the cops, though. It's like

Marty and Barry are more friends or co-workers than would-be admirers, and they're just checking up on me like busybodies or something. Do you think that's silly of me?"

He put a hand on hers, "This is just my opinion ... but from what I heard you saying, I think you should forget the matinees, rice, noodles and gravy for now. And I think you should tell that Fred fellow that you know how to make a tasty ham and cheese sandwich on a plain croissant with some mustard or mayonnaise, and if he stopped by the house, you could show him how. Then you should show him where your lips are. Maybe that would draw his attention away from his mom and the bank."

She briefly paused in thought and smiled at him. Nick perceived that her eyes were smiling, too.

They secured their connection that morning. It was much more than shared intimacy. They understood one another. Although it was never the topic of conversation, neither expected to see the other again.

Nick drove Ellie home after breakfast and walked her to the door of her Cayuga Avenue home. They kissed and shared a firm but brief embrace before they said their goodbyes.

He blew a kiss her way from curbside before he turned the key on the Oldsmobile and started toward Mission Street. She sent a return air kiss in his direction and doubted that he noticed. He didn't turn his head.

She looked to the North, towards Twin Peaks, and witnessed the morning sun starting to burn away the fog. It seemed to be a delightful day.

NICHOLAS ... 1953 – 1955

Havana Club ...
Saturday, January 6, 1953
Fernando's Hideaway, Jacksonville, Florida

During his eight-hour transcontinental flight from California, Nick had plenty on his mind. He wondered what could have driven the Agency or prompted Jovita to summon him to Jacksonville rather than returning him back to Panama. From his status reports, the Agency and Jovita certainly knew that there was substantial unfinished business in Panama, and that two of his closest confidants remained locked up in Colón National Prison. He guessed that Bolivia, Guatemala or Cuba could be the fly in the ointment. Knowing Jovita as he did, he was willing to bet it was Cuba. It was her first foreign assignment after her training and Nick sensed that she had a developed a secret fascination for the island.

Regardless of the real reason for his recall to Jacksonville, it was intriguing simply to wonder why. It wasn't whom he left behind in San Francisco, nor was it his assets Ramona or Enrique in Colón, Panama who occupied his thoughts. Sudden change was inevitable, and in fact, expected in his line of work. Sometimes it seemed that the Company could change a field agent's duty station willy-nilly, at any time for no specific rhyme or reason.

His boss and one-time lover, Jovita was the bug in his ear. He would be the last to admit it, but she was also the pang in his heart. Her memory danced a continuous airborne bolero during his flight from Travis Air Force Base to Naval Air Station, Jacksonville. He could hear the trumpets and castanets as if she was sashaying down the aisle next to his seat. He longed to see her and hear her voice. Nick knew fully well that she was alive and kicking, if only from her cryptic cable correspondence and intermittent, coded personal messages from contacts. Over the last half-decade, he had only a handful of telephone conversations with her, and those were always the distorted, time-delay, cipher-voice telephone calls. He wondered if she was still living at the Havana Hideaway, in her little *nest*, as she called it, next to her office. He fought the temptation, but just couldn't imagine her being intimate with her bartender-receptionist-bouncer Oliver or that Leonard fellow. He never had the opportunity to meet Lenny, and could only assume that he was short, sported a crew cut and wore milk-bottle glasses. After all, according to Joey, Lenny's only job was the teletypewriter, the cryptograph, writing and deciphering detailed, coded cablegrams.

Nick was already standing at the belly door of the DC-3 with his bags, ready to disembark when the pilot cut the starboard engine and came to a stop at Terminal D, NASJAX. He was down the ladder and on the tarmac almost before the control tower knew that the plane had landed.

He took a cab from the terminal, across the base to Corinth Street. He handed the taxi driver a five-dollar bill, stepped onto the sidewalk and unloaded his suitcase and valise. Nick stood on the corner, looked around and discovered that in six and a half years, nothing had changed at the Hideaway bar. It was as if he traveled back in time. It was familiar inside as well. The place was just as dark as he recalled and still smelled like beer and Spic and Span. He lifted his sunglasses off and stuck them in his shirt pocket. His eyes adjusted to the dim and he immediately recognized Oliver, despite the wire-framed glasses, goatee and twenty pounds. Before his backside hit the barstool, Ollie had a glass of beer sitting on the bar.

Nick asked, "How the hell you doing, pal? It's been a while."

The barman nodded, smiled and they shook hands across the bar. Nick lit a Camel and swallowed half the beer. Ollie never did have much to say and he rarely, if ever entered into a conversation.

"Is she in?"

Ollie nodded once again, and tipped his head toward the far end of the bar. Nick thought, *a man of few words is a master of less,* and said, "Thanks, Ollie. Thanks for the beer, too."

He slid off the stool, walked down the bar, through the cutout, down the hall and rapped twice on the green door to Jovita's office. His pulse quickened with anticipation and curious wonder. He wanted to jump out of his shoes and walk in.

"Come. Enter."

The door opened and closed with precision. At once, he noticed that a newer, large Persian carpet covered most of the wooden floor, and wondered if the floorboards underneath still squeaked with every footstep. He quickly discovered that it was as annoying as ever. Then he saw her at her desk.

He couldn't be certain, but he believed that he detected a camouflaged smile. Her coal-black hair was curled and styled differently, but still at her shoulders. Other than that, she hadn't changed. Her lipstick color wasn't as deep red as he could recall, but her lips were as inviting as ever. He heard her chair squeak and heels tap the floor. She stood, and used the backs of her knees to push her leather desk chair away. Her stockings whispered.

She was wearing a jade-green jumper dress with a white, lace-trimmed collar, and a half skirt that she cinched at the waist with a wide white belt. She was just as he remembered, and her shapely form attested that she hadn't been eating her dinners with Ollie. He held onto her with his eyes and saw that she still had that bottomless, deep brown sparkle in hers. She hadn't aged a day. He wondered how much the past six years had weighed on him. Although the image in his mirror hadn't changed, he wondered if she saw his reflection as he did. He convinced his vanity that he had endured a few more landings and seen a couple more years, that's all, but so had she. He was forty-four, and she was soon to be thirty-four. He reached into his memory for the glory of her form and found it. As far as he could tell, nothing had changed.

He fought the urge to test her with his presence, and to step forward to tease, tempt, and hold her. She defiantly stood there, seething with sexuality and watching him from behind the fortification of her desk. He felt the tension building between them, and wondered if she could feel it, too. Perhaps she was the one who was tightening the coils on the springs.

"Come in. Come in and sit," she said, and motioned to an upholstered armchair in front of her desk. "It took a few years, but I finally replaced that torturous wooden, World War I relic that used to be in here."

Her voice was just as entrancing as he remembered, and it softly caressed his heart. He dared to wonder if she still wanted and needed him to hold her the way she did so many years ago.

She held her ground and remained standing, waiting until he crossed the floor to the chair opposite her desk.

Nick took three steps to the chair and stopped. He endeavored to delay sitting and stood refreshing his memory of her appearance.

Jovita's body betrayed her nervousness, and he noticed. Her breasts pushed at the bodice of her emerald dress as she took a deep breath and said, "Please sit, Nicholas. We have things to discuss. Sit. Please." Her eyelashes flashed like the wings of a blackbird, and she smiled at him as he sat down. She seemed agitated, or vexed. He surrendered and sat.

There were pages of teletype and short stacks of cables on her desk. She pushed them aside and sat in her high-back leather chair. A few pencils stuck out from between pages of the messages like bookmarks.

"It's nice to lay eyes on you again, Boss."

She studied him for a flitting second and asked, "Did you enjoy your personal time in San Francisco with your sister-in-law, niece and nephew, Nick?" She was terse and not at all responsive to his casual remark. Although he realized that there could be no secrets between them, her question surprised him.

"Yes ... yes, I did. It was good to reconnect." The car parked on Cayuga was watching him. He suspected it and now he affirmed it. In case she was testing him, he added, "But I didn't get the chance to see my niece and nephew. They were with their aunt; Eloisa's sister in Sacramento ... Eloisa is my sister-in-law, of course. She was married to my brother when he was killed in the line of duty in 1942. He wasn't military, he was a cop. I think you know that."

Jovita kept her eyes on her desk and answered, "Of course."

She began combing through the stacks of paper, stacking them atop one another, and quickly sorting them in piles of alternating direction. As soon as she finished, she raised her head slightly, studied him from under her lashes and asked, "Tell me exactly what happened up there in Washington, Nick ... all of it. I mean with the crash of that C-124. Tell me everything you know. I read your report, but tell me what you uncovered ... every tidbit, every little ort that you were able to discover on your own ... without Munson or the FBI." With those words, she gave him her unflagging attention.

"I don't know what more I can say, Boss ... like I wrote in my report, as soon as I arrived in Moses Lake, they told me to beat feet. The FBI suits and Air Force brass said that the ground crew neglected to unlock the elevators and gust locks at take-off, and that there was nothing more to investigate and no evidence to suspect sabotage. That was it. They told me the mucky-muck about their sole CONUS[*] jurisdiction, showed me the door and closed it behind me. They didn't need to tell me twice. They may as well have thrown me out on my ear. I was *persona non grata*, so I left and then I notified you by wire and I took off for San Francisco. That's it. That's all she wrote and end of story."

She pressed him intensely, "What about our associate, Field Supervisor Munson? Did you see him or suspect that he could have been up there lurking in the shadows of the FBI and Air Force? Or did you make contact with him back at the Presidio?"

"No. I only saw the Feds and flyboys in Moses Lake. They didn't mention Munson, and I didn't see him at the Presidio, either. He didn't contact me and I didn't ask for him ... I only received your cable to report back here."

"Well, the bastard was there. The son of a bitch was up there in those woods in Washington. He left footprints behind as big as a Sasquatch[*]."

"What do you mean, Boss?"

"He filed reports from the crash site in Washington and he was at the Presidio. He was there, all right. And he put the screws to me. And he screwed you too, believe it or not. This time he crossed a line. I am disgusted with him, his innuendos, lies and rumor-mongering. He's been poking me with sticks and making me walk through mine fields ever since my first days at The Farm. This time the asshole went too far. He succeeded in pissing me off. I don't appreciate getting stuck without being kissed."

Nick dared ask, "He stuck you?"

She couldn't hide her burning anger and answered his question with a question, "Drink, Nick?"

Jovita reached into the bottom right drawer of her desk and brought out a bottle of *Havana Club* Cuban rum, set it down and brought out two highball glasses. One had lipstick tracks, but the other was clean. She sloshed two fingers of the Cuban libation into each glass and inadvertently pushed the stained glass across her desk to Nick. He put the glass to his lips, sipped the rum and imagined her kiss. He pressed her, "What did Munson do that crossed you, Boss?"

"I refuse to go into all the details with you, Nicholas, but I'll give you my cleaned-up, condensed version. Between Christmas and New Year's, before you took that time off in San Francisco, I took my first so-called vacation in years and travelled to New Orleans to celebrate with an old friend who I knew from my training days in Maryland. I'll call her Renée, and all I can tell you is that she's French and just returned from Indochina. Munson likes his fingers in everybody's business, and as soon as he found out that I was in New Orleans, he began spreading stories and claims that years ago, Renée and I were lesbian lovers back at The Farm."

Her story gave wings to Nick's imagination, and he interrupted, "You can tell me in confidence about that New Year's celebration in New Orleans, Joey. What kind of relationship did you have with her?"

"That's a double-barrel, two-part question, Nick. Number one: I can tell you that she's French and romantic and has that *je ne sais quoi*[*]. I'm Puerto Rican and sensual. Number two: It's none of your damned business."

He had tried to ruffle her feathers, but her retort quieted him. She continued, "When I got wind of it and contacted Section HQ in Frisco, of course, my facts blew holes in his bullshit story, but he didn't give up with his filthy muckraking. Then, when he found out about you being on the West Coast, he argued with the brass and started the rumor mill grinding about you and me doing the bedroom grind. He ordered somebody to follow you around in San Francisco and substituted me for your sister-in-law. He put me into his surveillance stories as she. And he put you grinding on top of me."

Of all the information that Jovita had given him, the thought of Munson's prying eyes burned the hottest. Nicholas silently vowed to burn him back when he had the chance.

She began again, "Days ago, after I heard all this, I contacted Wild Bill** himself in Washington. That worm Munson denied everything of course, but Donovan still demoted him from Field Supervisor to Field Agent, Grade 10. I'm not naïve enough to think Wild Bill believed everything I said, but I imagine he must have heard enough from other operatives about Munson and his shenanigans. Either way, Munson is working for me now, and that means that he'll be working on our next one."

Her eyes were on fire, and asked, "Heard enough?"

"That's enough. You're right, I agree. Years back, I figured out that Munson was an asshole, but I can accept that. I've worked with assholes before, plugged them and watched them suffocate in their own shit. But exactly why did you call me back for this *physical*, Boss? What's next?"

Jovita grabbed her glass, leaned back in her chair, and took a swallow of rum. Her anger was beginning to cool and she permitted herself to look into his brown eyes. Her tone went from frustration to triumph and replied, "You're holding the answer in your glass, Nicholas: Havana Club. President Batista's in the market for airpower that he can use against the growing number of socialist revolutionaries, and specifically the Castro brothers. They're swarming like locusts and flying out of the tobacco and sugar cane fields and into the streets of the cities."

"We have big fish nibbling on our line now Nick, but we need to be careful. There are storm clouds on the horizon and the sea is getting choppy, so it's likely that we're going to be reeling these monster sharks onto a slippery deck. It's slippery, but it's still a deck.

She took another swallow of the dark rum and formed her words carefully, "Take all of what I'm telling you as words of caution, Nicholas. Munson certainly is doing a burn about this and about me. Don't trust that son of a bitch. Be careful on this one. He'd stick his mother to get ahead in this bullshit game of legends and lies, so take this as a heads-up. We're playing both ends against the middle on this task.

"The Russkies* are flexing their muscles. Eisenhower just got sworn in as our new President and they're testing him already. They took the lid off a power struggle that's been cooking since the Yalta Conference** at the end of the World War. The new power players in Russia don't believe that further brutal, harsh Stalinization is the answer for the future and these young Russians alongside their new strongman Khrushchev are already starting to throw their weight around in our half of the world. They're casting their net of influence around Cuba and Central America farther and wider than the Nazis ever dreamed. They're working on *Five Year* master plans for everything from wheat collectives in the Ukraine to army and submarine bases all across the Caribbean. I predict that Ike* will end that mess over in Korea and then we can focus on the corruption of civilization and the poison of socialist Communism right here in our own back yard.

"You're leaving for Cuba the day after tomorrow. You'll carry ID for Thomas Armstrong, a procurement officer for the State Department, specializing in the disposal of war surplus aircraft. You'll bait the hook, cast the lines and set the nets for the big catch. You'll help place some assets like you did in Panama and El Salvador. You're good at that.

I have a room reserved for you tonight at the Aragon and I'll fully brief you here in my office, tomorrow morning at eight o'clock."

He finished his rum and looked down at his glass. Her lipstick stains had faded. "I'll see you tomorrow then, Boss."

He set the empty glass on her desk and asked, "I left behind some people in Panama. Two trusted contacts, a husband and wife team is still in the custody of the Federales* in Colón."

She was matter-of-fact, "It's already taken care of, Thomas."

"Thanks, Boss. See you tomorrow."

She stood, and again used her hips and legs to push her chair back. "There's one more thing that I need to mention; they tasked our friend Munson to follow you down next month, at the end of March, but it's likely you'll never see him. We're planting him with tap roots, way down deep, as Benito Pérez, a Bolivian academic. The plan is to get him and a few others inside with the Castro brothers and their rag-tag bandito recruits five hundred miles away in Oriente Province, on the eastern end of the island. It's like I said before, we're playing both ends against the middle on this one."

"Again, thanks, Jovita."

Nick dared to use her Christian name and walked out of her office with a smirk. Thomas Armstrong was looking forward to his assignment in Cuba.

Caribbean ...
Seven months later ... July, 1953
Hotel Nacional, Havana, Cuba

Like every other night in Havana, a party was going on inside the Starlight Nightclub at the Hotel Nacional on Wednesday, July 29.

Snowy-white, cotton sateen tablecloths, centerpieces of pink gardenias and shiny silver candelabras adorned each table. Reserved place settings in the front-row were set apart with flourished, hand-written name cards, gleaming silver utensils, crystal glassware from Spain, and gold-rimmed china. Every premier table had at least two bottles of aged Ron Santiago Cuban Rum, a bucket of iced Moët Champagne and a crystal compotier full of hand-rolled cigars.

Nick's legend, Thomas Armstrong earned a seat at the nightclub's head table with a personal invitation from Fulgencio Batista**. The Cuban President was jubilant over the lucrative deal he made with the American for the purchase of twenty-nine P-47 Republic Thunderbolt** fighter planes and spare parts. The newly acquired airpower could easily annihilate any rebel activity coming out of the sugarcane fields. Batista freely and consistently used power to protect what he considered his.

Armstrong was sitting next to Colonel Alberto del Rio Chaviano, four chairs away and directly across from *el Presidente*** and all of his glorious self. Generals of the Air Force Ernesto Pedroso and Carlos Padrón, Army Commander Marcos González and four captains of the Guardia Nacional were also seated around the large circular table. There was another reason to celebrate: Two days earlier, Batista's army, under the command of Colonel Chaivano squashed an armed attack on the Moncada Barracks** in Santiago de Cuba, Oriente. In the confusing aftermath, Batista's National Guard arrested and jailed Fidel Castro, his brother and fifty other revolutionaries. The day after the attack, BRAC** rounded up and executed dozens more. President Batista, his generals, captains, and commanders were wallowing in their victory.

When Nick first heard the news about the violence in Oriente Province and the Castro brothers' arrest, he wondered briefly about the fate of Angus Munson. Certainly, it was the nature of The Job, but like the third day of last November, Munson could be gone and forgotten. Nick consoled himself and reasoned that should worse come to worst, there would be no love lost, and certainly none from Jovita. Still, despite being a snake in the grass, Munson was a fellow agent. Nick's thoughts drifted stealthily into dark territory, and he pondered his mortality. He wondered if Jovita would carry a torch for him if he, rather than Munson, went toes-up.

A swallow of rum and a drag on a Camel quickly ended his macabre thoughts. He thought, *"It serves no useful purpose to wallow in that muck."*

Batista's table was merely fifteen feet from center stage and was alongside the catwalk route used by the club's showgirls as they pranced their way onto and off the stage. The floorshow featured high-stepping dancers moving to lively, rhythmic mambos powered by the sounds of trumpets and saxophones, chromatic marimbas, and the beat of conga* and bongo drums. Each of the long-legged, bikini-clad dancers had long false eyelashes, painted ruby-red lips and were adorned with billowing headdresses of ostrich feathers and well-placed, sequined appliqués on their taught tummies and thighs. Every moment they were onstage and lifting their legs in cabaret form, they broadcast huge smiles full of pearly white teeth toward the President and his guests. Everyone went overboard for *el Presidente*.

The wait staff was male, excepting those at the lead tables closest to the bandstand and stage, such as President Batista's. The hotel recruited beautiful young women of European mixed blood from all over the Caribbean island to serve the VIP tables. The dining room waiters wore white silk shirts, linen jackets, black bow ties, black silk trousers and heeled, black, patent leather half-boots. The waitresses at the upscale tables sported low-cut, white frilly blouses with linen jackets, cropped above the waist and buttoned tight just below their young, conspicuous breasts. Their black silk skirts ended above the knee, showing toned thighs and calves covered with fishnet hose. American twenty and fifty-dollar bills stuck out from garters barely under the hemline of their skirts.

Batista, his Air Force Generals and Colonel Chaivano boldly patted and caressed several inches of passing flesh. At times, there were more young jinetera* on the floor than the guests, dancers or waitresses. The hotel also commissioned dozens of young Latina consorts from across the Caribbean to stroll among the tables, chat up the clientele and offer casual companionship. The vast majority was women, but close observation disclosed the gigolos and froufrou boys. The entertainment-for-hire would either sit convivially at tableside or venture upstairs with paid guests of the hotel. The President had power to display and a reputation to protect. He would randomly select one of the young, enterprising women, grab a handful of flesh, pull her to his lap and let loose a bawdy, barrel-chested laugh that resonated across the dance floor. He preferred petite, big-breasted women, and would set them on his knee as if they were in fact, his puppets.

The fate of Angus Munson was unknown, and Thomas Armstrong sat tethered to Batista's trough of corruption, enjoying the show and drinking every ounce of intelligence that he could. The women, rum and music placed Cuba so high on his list of assignments; it was difficult to imagine a better posting. The women were delightful, the food was terrific, the rum delicious and the intelligence intriguing. The past seven months proved lucrative to Nick's legend and the Company, but that night, a shadow had darkened the room for Thomas Armstrong.

Try as he might, and despite his distain of the man, Armstrong's conscience grappled with by the possibility that Munson could be in trouble. One after another, Nicholas Throckmorton mixed bottles of Guantánamo pilsner with the taste of rum. He and Thomas Armstrong were one in the same, but sat side-by side as two separate identities with two distinct consciences. For the first time in his career of deception, he doubted his priorities. When the compass needle began to flutter between right and wrong, Nicholas regularly threw caution to the wind and purposely flew below the radar and set his course for wherever the Company needed him. He was extremely uncomfortable not knowing where the compass was pointing.

One attractive strolling consort caught his attention and he couldn't resist offering her an empty chair. She was spectacularly exquisite with the smooth, symmetrical shape of a classical Spanish guitar. Teresa Guerra y Calderón stood about five-foot-six with pert, proud breasts, a taut belly and a narrow waist yielding to ample hips. She was dressed in a clinging, black rayon skirt and semi-sheer white silk blouse. The young Latin beauty had soft brown, café con leche[*] skin and moved like a palm tree swaying in a breeze.

Thomas Armstrong poured her a glass of champagne, then another, and plied her with talk of his travels around the world. It started with shared glances, but when it turned into stares, he knew it was serious. Her hazel eyes didn't look very old, but they immediately burned her brand onto his heart. Twelve-year old Cuban rum and a twenty-something woman were navigating him to the point of no return. Their first dance was a conga line, and he playfully followed behind her, moving his hands up and down her hips. Teresa's gyrations, firm, rounded backside and tight skirt provided all the lift that his wings needed. They switched spots in line and she pulled him to her, then firmly held his waist, pressed her belly to his back and whispered words that tested his self-control. Thomas Armstrong gained altitude with each waltz and mambo that followed. He could hear Jovita's voice wrapped within every word that Teresa spoke and fantasized that it was his boss in his arms rather than a lend-lease companion.

A bit of reality and mental math affirmed that Teresa was younger than his son was. Despite the fact that Batista's wife, Marta insisted that twenty was the minimum age for club and casino companions, Thomas Armstrong knew he could be playing with fire. Months ago, he realized that the world was flying by faster every day. His mirror reflected the grey at his temples and the wrinkles around his eyes. The truth was staring back at him. He recognized the danger signs and knew that he was hell-bound for trouble, but he stubbornly engaged the supercharger. He was high enough to fully engage his target, pluck the feathers off this Cuban dove, take her under his wing and accompany her to the rarified air of high altitude passion.

However, Nick awoke alone the following morning and found himself struggling with a morning-after, roller-coaster, cotton-candy headache. In his alcohol haze, he briefly thought he was back in the Army Air Corps and wondered if everything back in Mount Clemens, Michigan was all right. He allowed his fogged mind to drift away yet again, and he was able to recall every mile he had ever flown and picture every face on every pillow from Kankakee to Cancun.

He looked across the bed and around the room. Teresa was gone. She had left him weak and alone. Once again, Nick swore off his one-night layovers, surrendered to the throbbing numbness, went back to sleep and dreamed of Jovita.

A few weeks later, the parties were still going on, but he received a cable from Jovita with a new posting. He was to leave Cuba for Central America.

Managua, Nicaragua …
August 20, 1953: 7:00 PM

From January until June, Nicaragua and Honduras are relatively dry. Much of the lush, green foliage dries up, turns yellow and awaits the rainy season. The rainy season begins in July and the next six months are wet ... real wet ... and it's always hot ... it's the tropics.

Drops as large as quarters pounded the tin roof of the hangar. The sky, blackened with clouds and driving rain, placed an uncomfortable blanket over the aerodrome. Nick could hear the twin Pratt & Whitney engines thundering through the darkness long before the landing lights of the Douglas C-47 Skytrain** were visible. Although Nicaragua was not the final destination of the passengers that Nick was awaiting, Las Mercedes airport, Managua, Nicaragua, was the only option for large aircraft. Southern Honduras' small airports and mountainous terrain were dangerously unfriendly and off-limits to any big aluminum birds flying in from America or the Caribbean.

For days, Nick had known that besides three crew and two United States Air Force officers, he could expect eight Honduran Air Force pilots fresh from P-38 Lightning** flight and familiarity training at Barksdale Air Force Base, Louisiana. As a courtesy, Barksdale had wired him that four Holy Cross Catholic Mission nuns along with two Episcopal Sisters of Charity and a Jesuit priest from Scotland were also aboard the flight from the United States.

Sheets of driving rain further blackened the night. Nicholas trained his eyes onto the aircraft's landing lights and watched the C-47 touch down, ending its 1700-mile, ten-hour flight from Bossier City, Louisiana. As a seasoned flyer, he imagined himself in the cockpit and felt a sense of satisfaction and completion once he heard the Goodyear tires screech and squeal on the wet tarmac three-quarters of a mile away. A time-tested and battle-proven Skytrain had made yet another safe landing and taxied to a stop fifty feet from the front of the arrival hall and open hangar. The pilot feathered the props and cut the engines of the unnumbered, insignia-free, olive-green aircraft. A ground crew of four dashed through the pouring rain, across the tarmac, and pushed the boarding ladder to the forward cabin exit. A pair of two-ton stake trucks parked at the belly cargo door of the aircraft to unload the cargo and baggage.

The first passengers down the steps and off the plane were the six missionary nuns and the Scottish priest. Nearly invisible in their black vestments and dark blue habits, they rushed across fifteen yards of asphalt holding hands to their foreheads, protecting their eyes from the pounding raindrops. They hurried through the downpour and dashed under the canvas portico into the hangar where a small reception committee of two parochial priests, a nun and about a dozen enthusiastic, local faithful awaited them.

The eight Honduran flyers were next, carrying brown duffle bags and dressed in nondescript blue denim coveralls and baseball caps. They were met by their commanding officer and the bus driver who was to drive them north on the Pan American Highway** to Toncontín Air Field, Tegucigalpa, Honduras, the next morning.

I'm A Big Girl Now ...

Their backlit forms in the cabin doorway were all that made them visible. From just inside the hangar, Nick gave the final two passengers, a man and woman, the high sign as they stepped out of the plane and started down the boarding stairs. One by one, they acknowledged him with a wave of their own and quickly walked through the rain, straight to their one-man reception party inside the building. Like Nicholas, they too, were in civilian attire. Dripping wet, they set their bags down, collapsed their umbrellas, brushed droplets of rain off their shoulders and stopped in front of him. The man was tall and lanky, perhaps thirty-five, with pronounced cheekbones and deep-set eye sockets. His wrinkled seersucker suit, wet with humidity, rain and sweat, appeared to be draped over broomsticks. Nick considered his rawboned appearance disconcerting.

Nick took his hand, "Nicholas Throckmorton."

"Captain Rupert G. Macklemore, United States Air Force … pleased to meet you, Colonel, Sir."

The woman moved a step closer, extended her hand and spoke, "Sir, I'm Lieutenant Hermione Purwerth, also Air Force." She was about the same age as her consociate, tall, perhaps five-foot-ten and carried the forced smile of a high school librarian during a Friday study hall. She wore a beige turban-wrap hat with a center cluster of burgundy silk flowers, a cropped tan jacket and high-waist, baggy, sienna-brown riding trousers that tapered to the ankle. Her handshake was firmer, stronger and warmer than the captain's. Her hands were also notably meatier.

Nick believed that he had read her straightaway and didn't hesitate before he asked, "Have you been flying long, Purwerth?" His curiosity won over propriety.

"Factually, yes, for a decade. Since '42. I'm one of them WASP[**] that they finally decided to convert into a real pilots. And now, today there's nearly a hundred of us flying around and buzzing the brass, just like our namesake, an angry wasp in their caps, so to speak. But I pull up my pants just like you: one leg at a time. I've been in this high-flying boy's club for a while now and the only reason I still wear a brassiere is to keep my spirits up. I know that it bothers some of you, Colonel, Sir, but be assured that this girl doesn't intend to crash land on your toes, occupy your hangar or burn up your ego."

Nick looked her in the eye. "You being a woman flyer doesn't bother me one iota. Not a whit. If I shoot straight, I expect you to. And let me say that you won't get any flak from me, not as long as you don't clip my wing. Do you understand me?"

"Yes, Sir. All right, Sir, all right, then."

He reached inside his shirt pocket for his pack of Camel, lit one and continued, "And around here, around civilian population, we're not military, no rank and no uniform ... as you were briefed ... and we use first names out in the real world, all right? We don't need to agitate or piss off the Somoza** politicos any more than we absolutely need to. This is all unofficial ... everything we do here in Nicaragua ... every place we go ... we fly under the radar whenever possible. We're here only with a wink and a nod ... it's all unofficial ... so, remember that until we arrive in Honduras."

Hermione spoke first, "I apologize. Like you said, we were briefed in Shreveport before we left and should have known better. I'm a big girl and understand. So, you can call me *Hermie* for short, then. While I'm here, I mean." It seemed that at least her smile was friendly.

The Captain stood stoical, emotionless, listening to their back-and-forth. He assumed it was his turn to say something, "I'm just Rupert, then. *Rupe,* if you must."

"Got it. I'm Nick. Let's get something to eat and wet our whistles and get you settled. At least for the night." He dropped the cigarette and crushed it underfoot. "There's a taxi just outside the hall to take us to the Hotel Ambassador where there's a room waiting for each of us. All you need do is show your passports and register, then we can get something to eat and drink right there at the restaurant before we call it a night. What do you think? Experience tells me that after a ten-hour flight you need to put your feet up, so I'll wait until tomorrow to fill you in on our destination, the flight and the mission." He didn't wait for an answer, picked up Hermie's smallest bag and turned toward the exit. Neither she nor Rupert broke silence. They were right behind him.

Rumors Are Flying ...

Their taxi to the *hotel del embajador* was a well-cared-for 1937 Maybach; a pre-war German luxury six passenger, four-door, extended saloon sedan. It had admirably withstood the tropic climate and chuck-holed streets of Managua for sixteen years.

The rain had subsided from a tropical drenching to a thundershower. The cab driver, a short round man with stout legs and a pork barrel belly, carried their bags inside the hotel and placed them directly in front of the desk clerk. He stood as straight as his stout, stubby legs allowed and waited as Nick thumbed through his wallet and handed him a 500-córdoba note, "Gracias, my friend."

The lobby of the Ambassador Hotel was cavernous, with a vaulted ceiling that arched majestically, gracefully to the second floor and a prominent, pristine white balcony directly above the front desk. The Stars and Stripes hung to the left of the blue-white-blue Nicaraguan flag with the British Empire's Union Jack to the right. The walls were yellow brick and bleached stucco; the ceilings plaster. Potted, twelve-foot cascade palms stood at the base of the stairway, angel wing begonias in pink and red along with blooming crab cactus filled nearly every unfurnished nook in the lobby. The clientele was international, sharply dressed in light summer suits and colorful dresses with mid-calf hemlines with either open collar, scalloped or daring décolleté necklines. The click-click of ladies' heels and the tap-tap of leather soles was heard dancing across the terrazzo floor of the central foyer.

Rupert and Hermione signed the hotel register, got their room keys and dispatched the bellhop with their bags and a 100-córdoba bill from Nick. Following his lead, without a single word or prompt they walked to the brass and glass doors of the Ambassador Restaurant and Lounge. Inside, the maître d' escorted them to a table with gleaming silverware, sparkling glasses and white linen. Notwithstanding their geographical location, the hotel, restaurant and its menu could very well have been anywhere on the Gulf Coast.

Dinner was broiled red snapper, roasted plantains, pineapple and rice. Afterwards, the waiter set an additional three bottles of *Carta Blanca* pilsner on the table. There was no substantive conversation during the meal.

Nick wanted to get to know these two new faces, if only to fill in the time, "How was the flight from Shreveport?"

Hermione glanced at Rupert, then offered her opinion without hesitation, "It was uneventful, really. No dings or dents, just a typical, noisy bone-rattling transport flight. But it was enough to shake up at least one of God's faithful. One of them young Scottish nuns was so scared, so afraid, she had beads of sweat on her nose. She could have peed herself for all I know. She kept her hands folded, wrapped around her rosary and clasped in a prayer grip so tight her knuckles were white, poor girl. One of the others sat close to her during the whole trip, wiping her forehead, whispering and praying right along with her. The whole thing was so intense, it even made me nervous, like they were having a divine premonition or something. I wish I could have helped. But I wouldn't know how. I mean in a religious way. Sure, I could have told them that I've flown a million miles, but I thought that maybe I would be interrupting their prayers or something. So I kept quiet.

"Anyway, I sat on a jump seat, right behind them two. There were a couple other Catholic and Episcopalian nuns on that gooney bird. We talked a bit and exchanged pleasantries and I answered some of their curious little questions about the C-47 and all. We didn't talk all that much, not having much in common, you see. I only communicate with God when I have to.

"I don't want it to sound like I'm grinding the rumor mill, but despite all the racket inside that bird, I was within earshot during the whole flight down here, and I got good ears, believe me. I managed to overhear the Holy Cross nun in front of me whispering about some outcast missionary priest from the Detroit area, Mount Clemency, I think, and she sort of warned the young Scot off and said she and the others should steer clear of him. I'm pretty sure that she said his name was Father John, and that he got himself banished and excommunicated a couple years ago for diddling with parishioners and going between the sheets and making babies with novice nuns, and for not practicing what he preached, so to speak. She said that finally the diocese archbishop had enough, cast him out by the collar and banished him down here, to some old Spanish mission church in a town named Leon, right where them Scots are going, I think. You can imagine that: tossed out of Detroit on your ear. He must have really pissed off some bishop or priest or rubbed some other mucky-muck pussycat's fur the wrong way. The dirty bastard."

Rupert sat emotionless, but the talk about the Church, nuns and priests prompted him to stick his own two cents into the conversation, "I remember back when I was just a kid, my father joked that the nuns have roller wheels under their habits just so it's easier for the priests to shove them around. And he used to say that they build orphanages next to convents just to keep the nuns' babies hidden."

Rupert let loose a raucous snicker as if he was a kid in grade school. His boorish comments showed that he was clearly disinterested and wasn't paying too much attention to the meat of Hermione's gossip.

Nick wondered what could have prompted Rupert to join the discussion with such off-the-wall remarks. He looked at Hermie and rolled his eyes in disbelief. The female pilot, however, had Nick's full attention and he encouraged her, "Go ahead, Hermie. Don't quit your purple newsreel now."

"The one nun really tried to make her point, warning them Scottish Episcopalians about this guy, I mean, because that's right where they were headed, that Leon place. That Holy Cross charity mission was mentioned more than once, and each time that Catholic nun said the same thing: *stay away from John*."

Nick interjected, "Hermie, was it *Mount Clemens*, perhaps, and not *Clemency*? Was that it? And you said *Father John*, am I right?"

"Right! You're right. It's Mount Clemens, not Clemency. That's what it was. But that's who she said: Father John. I'm sure I got that part right. And like she said, he's in exile down here in some church for being a devout womanizer. He sounds like a real sweetheart. A dedicated Catholic; an ordained priest helping women commit themselves to their unwavering devotion to the Faith, I bet."

Rupert seemed indifferent at the least and dreadfully bored. He took another deep drag on his Chesterfield, exhaled and swallowed the last of his beer, picked up his cigarettes, pocketed his Zippo, stood and pushed his chair back from the table. "I don't want to be impolite, but goodnight. Thanks for the dinner and drinks, Nick, but I'm done in and going up to my room. There's a bed and pillow up there with my name and a good night's sleep written on it in big letters. Tomorrow's another day."

"I must have bored you to death with all this chatter, Rupe. I'm sorry. Really, Rupe? You're that tired?" She was teasing him.

"No, no. You're not boring me. I'm beat, that's all. Bone tired. Goodnight. See you both in the AM ... for breakfast and the brief." He put the pack of Chesterfield in his shirt pocket.

Nick stood, reached out and shook his hand. "Goodnight, Rupert. Get some sleep and feel better. See you in the morning. We'll cover everything then."

The Captain did indeed appear to be travel weary. He turned and walked out of the lounge without another word. Hermie leaned in and spoke quietly to Nick, "He didn't seem well during the flight down here, didn't talk much and kept his eyes shut, and was trying to doze off most of the time. I think he probably caught a bug or something back in Louisiana."

A flyer's health is nothing to disregard and Nick had reason to be concerned about the captain. Regardless, the intrigue of Hermione's tale had weakened his worry about Rupert, and he purposely diverted the conversation away from what appeared to be a possible health condition and back to Hermie's story. He spoke sincerely, "Too bad. I hope the guy feels better; it's not good to be sick in this heat. I'll keep an eye on him tomorrow, but the good news is that we got three more bottles of beer between you and me, right? So, tell me more about your trip down here, Hermie. Did you and Rupert help train or interact with the Honduran pilots back at Barksdale?"

"No. We only met them last week, and they had their flight and familiarity training finished up by then. They know who we are, that's about it. We were introduced, but don't you ask me anything about them. During the war, I learned that it's best not to get personal. I don't remember too many names and don't care to. Rupert might, since he'll be stationed TDY with them.

"But, back to tomorrow's mission. I understand that Rupe and me are flying into Honduras and I will be turning around and flying out again. Am I right about this?"

Nick lit a Camel, and more as a matter of habit than anything else, looked around the room. "You're right, Hermie. You'll get all the particulars tomorrow. For you anyway, it should be in and out. Rupert and I will hang around Hondo[*] for a while."

His back-and-forth chatter with Hermione was meant to be placating. Nicholas Throckmorton had more than just the next day's mission on his mind. There were those new nagging, secondary thoughts he had to deal with: all those disconcerting things that Hermione had told him about Father John of Mount Clemens.

My Blue Heaven ...
Friday, August 21, 1953

The next morning, Nick, Hermione and Rupert found themselves once again inside the Ambassador's restaurant. With the first sip of their morning coffee, Hermie and Rupe knew it was nothing but serious from there on out. Rupert seemed to have had a good night's rest, and that abated Nick's immediate concerns about the Air Force captain.

After breakfast and a cab ride, they were back at Las Mercedes airport. Nick had the cabbie stop at a smaller maintenance building and hangar, a half-mile away from the arrival terminal at the opposite end of the runway. This time, Nick didn't help with the luggage, and kept a small leather satchel under his arm. Hermie and Rupe carried their bags from the cab to the half-round Quonset hut. They were met at the entrance by a pair of armed guards in nondescript, khaki military uniforms who recognized Nick, nodded, stepped aside and opened the door. Inside, two unmarked, North American T-6 Texan[**] trainers were parked and at the ready near the overhead doors. Nick led the way to a small office along the left side of the hangar. Inside, Nick closed the door behind him and Rupert and Hermione seated themselves at a small table. Nick went to a filing cabinet, unlocked it and brought out a folio, opened it and spread out flight charts. He then lifted the flap on his satchel and handed the assignment orders and operational assessment to Hermione and Rupert.

"You each have the topographical maps and our flight plan. We're flying into Toncontín, the only airbase in Tegucigalpa, Honduras. Flight time is about an hour and a half, about two hundred air miles. The approach at Tonco can be daunting and tricky, but very doable. There's one way in and out of this sweetheart. It looks ominous, but like most good-looking dames, she's easily conquered, but you need to treat her with kid gloves. She's got a surprisingly fast, steep, downward approach that comes upon you quick and gets your senses sharpened and your blood flowing. And just after clearing two volcanic mountains and her taller *el Picacho*, she gives you a short, 2000 foot, sloping runway to the finish line and concrete barriers... I'll take the lead ... Rupert on wing ... we'll circle ... get familiar and touch down. Copy?"

Rupert, "Yes, sir."

Hermione asked questions that she likely knew the answers to, "The Hondurans are there already? And I'm a backseat for this ride?"

"The Hondurans left by bus about two hours ago. We'll beat them. Like I said, Hermione, I'll lead. I'm familiar with Toncontín.

"You're backseating me because you'll be flying out again almost immediately. If the weather holds like it's supposed to, you're taking a P-51 Mustang[**] up to Punta Gorda, in Limey Hondo, British Honduras. Your flight plan is in your briefing jacket there in front of you. Where the Mustang goes from there, I do not know. These two T-6 Texans, however, the ones you see in the hangar here, the ones we'll be flying to Tonco, will stay in Tonco.

"Rupert, once we're there, it's your time to shine. There's five war surplus Lockheed P-38 Lightnings[**] on station that are currently the property of *Fuerza Aérea Hondureña,* the Honduran Air Force; four of them courtesy Uncle Sam and one from our friends at the Royal Canadian Air Force. These are Honduran aircraft and no longer part of any United States Air Force or any other contingent. Together, you and I will assist the Honduran command to make certain these aircraft are flight ready and able, and that's where our commitment will end. The State Department will be happy, the Air Force will be happy, the Hondurans will be happy and we can go on to the next one. Any questions?"

"No, sir," was echoed in unison.

Landing gear down in Tonco …

As they approached Toncontín, the weather was fair, with moderate to thinning overcast, intermittent drizzle, surface temperature 86°, winds ENE at 6 knots, and the cloud ceiling was nearly 12,000 feet. Nick broke through first, Rupert on his tail, up and to the right. The runway was deep within a valley, walled by volcanic mountains and tropic jungle.

The radio static cleared with words spoken in measured Oxford English coming from an anonymous, pasteurized voice breaking across the airwaves, "Welcome to Tegucigalpa, Honduras, Texas One, Texas Two. Traffic has been cleared. Acknowledge and proceed."

"Acknowledged, Tegucigalpa. Thank you. Out."

Nick switched the frequency, "There she is, Rupe. We're clear. Bank wide and watch my decent and turn. It can get windy ... so mind your yaw ... and pitch. Hell ... you know this shit. Keep the shiny side up, bud. See you down there. Beers on me. Out."

Nick cleared the radio, and spoke into the intercom, "Keep your eyes open, Hermie. Pay attention to the approach. It's tricky coming in, but easier on takeoff. See you down there. Hang on."

Behind him, Hermione was next to dumbstruck with what she saw. She immediately recognized that landing at this airstrip was akin to threading a needle at midnight with your eyes closed. She had previously believed that a night landing onto the moving deck of an aircraft carrier at full steam had always been the most difficult approach any flyer could attempt. She realized that her assumption was wrong.

She closely watched Nick's approach and felt her buttocks tighten. She could see his knees telegraph his adjustments to the rudder pedals and closely watched his left hand and fingers on the throttle and prop controls. Her heart was in her throat. Nick banked extreme left. She sensed the blood rush into her legs. She could only watch the artificial horizon and turn-and-bank dials in the rear cockpit as Nick controlled the plane. The engine coughed. He had dropped the air speed to under 80 knots. Her fingers, hands and arms felt helpless as if bound by the Devil. The Texan seemed to wiggle and joust about like a fish out of water only seconds before it quieted, smoothed, touched down and she felt the wheels on terra firma once again. She was relieved to be flying backseat, and wondered what the nervous nun would have experienced.

Nick braked, opened the exhaust manifold and turned the Texan hard left onto the taxiway. Small droplets of drizzle and fog danced across the windscreen and along the cockpit.

The roar of the engine quieted to a rumble. He taxied toward the fenced-off military quadrant of the airfield, past the control tower and arrival hall. The Texan came to rest 200 yards down the taxiway, in front of yet another Quonset hut. This one had no camouflage of any sort, and proudly bore the flag and emblem of the Honduran Air Force. Nick cut the engine.

The intercom crackled to life, "Touchdown, Hermie. We made it."

"Smooth, Nick. Smooth." She felt her heart in her throat.

Three ground crew scurried up to the plane. One hurriedly placed wheel chucks under the gear, front and back. The other two men scrambled up on the right wing and folded open the hinged cockpit. Nick and Hermie jostled up and out, down the wing and onto the tarmac. Their attention went to the southern sky. Deftly, nearly in unison, their fingers went to work on stripping their flight equipment. First off were the mask, goggles and goatskin helmets and finally the parachute harness at the chest, waist and crotch. They dropped their gear onto the cargo wagon, all the while straining their eyes at the approaching aircraft on the southeastern horizon.

Nick clenched his fists, "He's too low. Too fast. Too wide. Shit. Damnitall."

Hermie put two fingers to her lips and muffled a gasp. Her other hand found Nick's shoulder. Texas Two turned and banked hard, ninety degrees to the west. Then, no more than a half-mile away, the doomed flight ended with a sickening thud, followed a split second later by a fiery explosion, flames and black smoke billowing skyward. Captain Rupert G. Macklemore's life ended on a small hill; an outcrop covered by tropical evergreen forest on the west side of the Honduran capital city, Tegucigalpa.

"There's no explanation for that, Nick."

"Yes there is, Hermionie ... pilot error. That's what that was: pilot error. And it was a helluva waste of good equipment."

The Embassy of the United States of America, Tegucigalpa, Honduras
1 PM, Friday, August 28, 1953

It was Nicholas' first visit to an embassy of any nation. It was also his first investigation. The Air Force didn't call it that. Officially, it was labeled as an *inquiry*. Nick considered that it was inconvenient, annoying rigmarole and an exercise in futility at best. He also knew that the outcome was predetermined.

In the days leading up to the inquiry, Nick learned that Captain Macklemore's wife Molly had written and informed her husband a week before the crash of her intent to file for divorce. Air Force Military Police investigators found her letter in the Captain's barrack bag. Nick Throckmorton and Norbert Knudsen decided to keep that bit of knowledge confidential. The Hondurans and their air force had no need to know the full particulars or that their scheduled meeting was completely choreographed.

Nick showed his agency ID to the Marine corporal at the front desk, nodded and loosened his tie as he crossed the lobby toward the polished staircase. Outside room 210, he pocketed his sunglasses and removed his hat. Inside were two ranking, experienced Honduran Air Force officers, General Knudsen and his personal secretary Satcha.

The midday sun created sauna conditions within the plaster walls of the embassy's second floor conference room. An unbalanced, wobbling ceiling fan spun at full speed, churning the humid air into an uncomfortable, simmering bowl of steaming wet.

Brigadier General Norbert ('Nobby') Knudsen of the Panama Strategic Command, Albrook Air Force Station, Canal Zone, Balboa, Panama, had been dispatched to oversee the probe into the August 21 accident that claimed the life of Air Force Captain Macklemore. The general was pushing fifty, Nordic, fair-skinned, with sky blue eyes and blonde hair so light, it seemed he had no eyebrows. He motioned for Nick to take the chair on his immediate left and the mandatory, meaningless salutations began.

Satcha Diaz-Pretto, a Panamanian national, sat close to General Knudsen, at his right, with a thin folder of papers in front of her. As soon as he entered the room, Nick noticed a pair of small, delicate feet in black, open-toe, patent leather pumps and a perfect pair of legs wrapped in smoky-grey nylons. The young woman had an unusual, rusty shade of red hair curled and falling softly over her shoulders. She wore a bright floral dress, a green silk neck scarf and her only makeup was perfect mascara and deep red lipstick.

The Honduran Air Force officers were sitting directly across from Nick and General Knudsen. One was General Jorge Campos, base commander, Toncontín airport. He was a large, big-belly man with an imposing presence, in a dark brown uniform adorned with medals and ribbons in enough colors to fill a box of crayons. At his left was Major Amado Andrade, senior air traffic officer at Toncontín. He appeared as a smiling, amiable character, with much fewer medals upon his chest. He had thick, wavy, salt-and-pepper hair and a wide mustache that resembled a tailless house mouse.

The meeting was about to get underway. The table had been set. The Honduran officers had sealed, large brown folios in front of them on the table. Everyone had a pad, paper, pen and a full glass of water at their seat. Two large pitchers of water with chunks of vibrant yellow pineapple and ice cubes were at the center of the table. There were three empty chairs. Nickolas and the secretary were the only participants with a small manila folder of papers. Satcha sat with pen-in-hand and the hint of a smile on her lips.

General Knudsen spoke first, "Gentlemen, General Campos, Major Andrade, first let me introduce the others here with us; I present Señorita Diaz-Pretto, Embassy stenographer and translator, and Field Investigator Nicholas Throckmorton, United States Department of State." Nods, smiles and curious glances went around the table before Knudsen began again, "General, Major, if you open the packets in front of you, we can get started."

A few seconds ticked off the clock, envelopes were torn open and he began again, "I believe we would all like to finish this quickly, and I believe we can do that, considering what has come to light over the past few days and in particular, our inquiry into this unfortunate circumstance. Inside the volumes you just opened, you have found copies of our complete investigation.

"Investigator Throckmorton, please give General Campos and Major Andrade a brief outline of our findings."

Nicholas read from his prepared report, "The underlying cause of the crash of a T-6 Texan, type BT-9A, on this past Friday, August the twenty-first, can be clearly assigned to pilot error. When all the facts that we uncovered during our investigation into the accident are considered, there can be no other reasonable interpretation. Therefore, it is the position of the State Department, and of the United States, that a replacement aircraft should be provided to the Honduran Air Force at the earliest possible date and all Lend-Lease compensation for the new airplane be waived."

It was over.

Nick surveyed his company. Every forehead around the table had beads of sweat. He couldn't help but notice that Miss

Satcha was, without doubt, the most uncomfortable and he felt a measure of pity for the young woman. As she was making her notes, her hand, damp with perspiration, would stick to the pad of paper. She often brushed the curls at her temples, crossed and uncrossed her legs, and wriggled and fidgeted in her seat. Nick perceived that her stockings were certainly clinging irritably to her legs. Oppressive mid-day heat and humidity is something that a person either grows accustomed to or suffers through it.

A not-to-distant conversation brought a provocative paradox to mind. The previous year while in the Dominican Republic, he was sharing cigarettes, rum and stories with an attractive, intriguing local contact inside a sleazy Santo Domingo hotel bar. Under the table, he stealthily put a hand on her thigh. As if she expected his touch, she calmly told him, "I'm bare underneath. Only whores and American tourists wear panties and nylons in this heat". The dilemma was that Satcha was neither American nor a tourist. Nick clearly remembered that General Knudsen had introduced Satcha to him as a Panamanian.

That night, he wired the official results of the inquiry to Jovita and asked for a week of leave before his next posting. The next morning he had his reply: He was to remain in Tegucigalpa until the end of September to ensure that the Hondurans had a comprehensive operational grasp of their newly acquired aircraft and continue sending personnel and operations evaluations back to Jacksonville.

Next, he would be heading back to Havana again as Nicholas Throckmorton. Without specifically saying so, Jovita approved his time off by setting his "report by" date at October 7, but asked that he advise her in advance of his day and time of arrival in Cuba.

Civilization, Bongo, Bongo, Bongo ...
León, Nicaragua
3 PM, Friday, October 2, 1953

The city was starting to regain its heartbeat. The plenitud[**]
hours were over; the streets had awakened, and once again
they became the vibrant pulse of the city. Nicholas was in the
market district with a predetermined destination: The Church
of San Filipe, a modest community church that offered Friday
evening confessions. Confession however, was not his
intention. He was looking for a specific priest from Mount
Clemens, Michigan, and the obvious place to look for a
Catholic priest was in a Catholic Church. Nick simply needed
to find one that could help him find the path to his desired
objective. He hoped that the Church of San Filipe would
serve that purpose.

Stained a blackish green with mildew and algae, the timeworn
brick and tile exterior of San Filipe tarnished Nick's first
impression. However, inside he discovered an ornate, twenty-
foot arched ceiling, with gilded-edged paintings of biblical
references. A detailed, life-size wooden crucifix, standing at
the wall behind the altar and painstakingly painted to imitate
life, amazed him. From nooks and crannies, glowing candles
emitted a soft, flickering light. The walls had colorful bas-
relief wooden carvings of numerous saints. A silent priest
was standing near the altar and arranging some fresh bouquets
of cut flowers.

Nicholas felt lucky. Perhaps confession wasn't required to
get the information he desired. "Perdóneme, padre ... excuse
me, Father. I am Thomas Armstrong." He dared to use his
Cuban legend and the alias Joey had given him. The stage
was set.

"Good afternoon. I am able to speak the English some for
conversation."

"Very good, Padre, and I speak the Spanish."

They shared introductions, smiles and a handshake. After a few more words of congenial prate, they decided that Nicholas would speak in Spanish. It made things considerably easier.

Nick got right to it, "I apologize, Father. I am not of your faith, but a Presbyterian, and I am not seeking spiritual advice. Well, not spiritual direction, but I seek some help. I am from Detroit, Michigan, in the United States, and I was talking to a Methodist minister who mentioned that he believed that there is a Catholic priest here, in León, from Detroit. Is that true? I miss my home and family so much, it would be comforting for me to talk to someone who is from my home town in the United States."

The priest was visibly excited. Likely enthusiastic about being able to help this American stranger, he eagerly volunteered, "Father John from Detroit ... that's who are seeking. Tomorrow you'll find him at Restaurante Nuevo León. He's always there on Saturday afternoons enjoying his bowl of Sopa de Caracol[**]. Perhaps he can be of help and provide the comfort you seek."

Via con Dios (Go with God) ...
The missionary position ...
2 PM, Saturday, October 3

Restaurante Nuevo León was closer to a small, noisy cantina rather than a restaurant. At best, it was a run-down Latin American gin joint that served food and drink in less than sanitary conditions. Street noise and dust flowed through the open doors like city sewage in the Chiquito River.

Nick was at the bar, keeping an eye on the streaked, dirty mirrored wall for a certain priest to come in from the dusty street. He swallowed the last bit of tíck táck* vodka from his glass, set it down with a clunk and motioned the bartender.

"I think I'll switch to beer and have a bottle of Carta Blanca, thank you, *por favor*."

Nick wore a honey-colored panama hat**, low in front, with a black leather band. He had two-day stubble, but his entire dress was new: a white silk shirt, double-pleated, tan linen trousers and canvas deck shoes that he had purposely soiled.

He asked for, and received confirmation from the amicable, seasoned bartender that an American priest called *Father John* was a regular customer on Saturdays.

"Oh yes, he'll be in for his dinner. Every Saturday he appears from inside those thick walls of the Cathedral. He consumes his meal like a ritual, like he's about to perform a benediction, and he brings the wooden spoon up to his lips, closes his eyes and sucks it dry, noisy, like a pig at a trough, devouring every drop. He told me once that his soup and glass of wine are the only guilty pleasures he has."

"Really? His only guilty pleasures?"

"That's what he says. But I have also heard that the archbishop has him on a very short chord. There are so many rumors about him, I cannot know what's true. I do not know for myself. You must understand that I attend Mass at Church of the Calvary and I do not go near the Cathedral. It's much too dark and gloomy inside those old walls."

The time crawled for Nicholas, but half an hour later the wait had ended. Father John appeared through the open doors from the street and walked directly to a table at the window. It was sixteen years earlier, during his wife's hospitalization for appendicitis, that Nick had last seen the priest. Had he not known who he was, he certainly would not recognize him. Father John had acquired a considerable paunch and round, full cheeks like a chipmunk. Mission life had kept him fed at the least.

Nick remained at the bar, nursing his bottle of beer, watching the priest in the dirty mirror, patiently waiting for him to settle in and order his meal.

He used the time to elaborate his legend, formulate a plan, and to set the trap for his prey. Still in the planning stage, he was yet uncertain of an ultimate solution to the situation. The story he heard from Hermione a month and a half earlier seemed credible. With her tale and the bartender's words, he believed that he had found the vile vermin that had possibly defiled his wife and countless others.

He still he needed to be cocksure of the identity of the man wearing the reversed, starched white collar. After the barkeep delivered Father John's glass of wine, Nick knew the time had come. He walked over to the cleric's table.

"Father, please allow me to introduce myself. I'm Thomas Armstrong, a civil engineer working for TACA airlines, and I'm on my way to an extended assignment in Costa Rica to assist them in building a new terminal at San José airport."

Without lifting his head, the cleric glanced up at Nick, looking over the rim of his wine glass with aloof curiosity, "That's wonderful. You say your name is Thomas Armstrong ... like that Jack Armstrong[**] radio show ... the All-American Boy. But I bet you hear that a lot, don't you?"

Nick detected a tone of haughty sarcasm, and shot back, "No, I don't. Not at all."

The priest looked puzzled, and apologized, "I didn't mean to sound stuffy, please forgive me, and won't you please join me, for a glass of wine, perhaps."

Nick's pulse spiked. Visibility was unlimited and his target was on the horizon.

Nick accepted the priest's invitation with feigned reluctance, then fidgeted with his shirt collar and continued baiting the cleric, and attempted to instill nervous hesitation into his words, "Lately, I've been struggling with so much emotion and personal conflict, Father. I have family back in Detroit that I haven't seen in a long, long time and I feel so alone. I'm not a Catholic, Father, but I am hoping that I could talk to you about my isolation. I miss my family of course, but I long to hear news about the football Lions, baseball Tigers and hockey Redwings, you see. All that and so much more. Whatever I can glean from you would be Heaven sent, believe me. Sometimes, I find myself questioning my life purpose. I've tried talking to some of those Presbyterian and Methodist collars, but they just haven't been able to answer all the questions and doubts I have about my faith. I feel helpless sometimes."

The priest's pale blue eyes came to life. He took the worm, hook, line and sinker. Nick was about to pounce on his prey, and only needed to confirm it was Father John.

"I believe I can help you, my son. And it would be refreshing for me just to have a conversation in English, no matter how brief or inconsequential it may seem. Coincidently, I too, am removed from Detroit ... Mount Clemens to be exact. I have been on a medicinal posting since December of 1946, so I'm afraid that I'm unable help with any current news about the Detroit sports teams."

In a purposely convoluted, deceptive way, the priest had concisely admitted his punitive exile to a merciless hunter ready to pounce.

Nick gently set his hand down upon the priest's. He was about to release the safety, put a round in the chamber, pull back the hammer and cock his weapon. "Thank you, Father. Thank you ever so much. Bless you. It's too bad about the sports, but we can talk about so much more. Can we meet somewhere privately?"

The Priest's gave a spirited response, "Certainly. Most certainly. How about later? Would sometime after evening vespers be suitable? Perhaps about half past seven, Mister Armstrong?"

Nick tested him further, "That would be perfect ... simply perfect. Could we meet somewhere nearby, somewhere here in town? Perhaps some place where I could show my appreciation and buy you a nice glass or two of brandy?"

Father John's exuberance faded, "Unfortunately, as a guest of the Archdiocese of Managua, my presence is required on Church of Perpetual Mercy property after sunset. Archbishop González Robleto has drawn clear lines that I may not cross, but there's a well-groomed courtyard, private garden and sanctuary directly behind the Cathedral. I could meet you there Thomas, and we could talk."

"Church of Perpetual Mercy, you say?"

"That's correct. Down here they call it, *iglesia de la misericordia perpetua*. You can't miss it. Two blocks away on Avenida Bolivar. At the gate, tell the Portal Shepherd you have an audience with me in the rectory garden and he'll direct you to the courtyard."

Nick needed to nail down the priest's identity, "And you are Father ... ?"

"I'm sorry. I forgot to introduce myself, didn't I? I'm Father John. It's easy, and hard to forget: Father John."

"You're absolutely right, Father John. It's almost impossible to forget: Father John. I am looking forward to this evening."

Their conversation ended on an upbeat. So far, Nicholas was pleased with Thomas Armstrong's performance in Nicaragua.

Ave Maria (Hail Mary) ...
The Church of Perpetual Mercy
León, Nicaragua, October 3, 1953

Nick approached an ominous, black iron entry gate on the wall of stone that surrounded the parochial housing, cloister and courtyard of the Cathedral. It sat adjacent to the Church of Perpetual Mercy, which was an imposing mass of early Spanish Mission architecture on its own merit.

One of two guards who had been peering through the narrow windows of the watch house walked out and met him at the gate. He wore a black satin pillbox hat and dressed in a crimson red, double-breasted coat with brass buttons and epaulettes of gold braid. *This place is locked up tighter than a bull's ass,* Nick thought. *Who are they keeping out or what are they keeping in?*

Nick nodded a sterile greeting, touched the tip of his hat and spoke perfect Spanish through the iron bars of the gate, "Buenas noches ... tengo una audiencia con el padre Juan ... en jardin." *(I am meeting Father John in the courtyard)*

The gatekeeper kept a stoic, emotionless face and grabbed a large black ring of oversized keys from his bandolier. He unlocked the gate with precise movements, perfected by years of solitary repetition.

Blue-green lichen and years of viridian mildew clung to the brick, stone and stucco walls. Spanish moss dangled from the roof eaves and nearby tree branches.

The guard pointed the way for Nicholas, through a narrow portal into a garden that was quickly darkening in the twilight. He began to walk slowly along a mossy brick footpath, straining his eyes in the half-light of evening, looking for the priest. The cloistered garden seemed without bounds: a hidden sanctuary, a world within a world. A hundred yards to his left, mixed voices caroled a muffled, ancient Latin incantation. It drifted from deep within the 18th century stone and brick walls of the protectorate. To Nicholas' unfamiliar ears, it sounded like a ghostly chorus of *I can play dominoes better than you can.*

Abruptly from within the shadows, standing with crossed arms and a wide, aseptic smile, Father John appeared and greeted his visitor, "Welcome to my secret haven, Thomas. It's wonderfully, exclusively glorious, isn't it? For many hours, on many evenings, I have sat and languished in the solitude it offers. I've come to think of it as my own personal, private pathway to righteousness."

"Really? Perhaps it is, Father. Perhaps it is."

The priest reached out and they shook hands ever so briefly. They began to walk slowly further into the garden, taking measured steps. Nicholas had anticipated Father John's clammy palms and wet, feeble handshake. The man was a slug. His slimy trail went all the way back to Detroit.

The path became a cobblestone walk, bordered by twining, pink rock trumpets and crimson bougainvillea. They stopped at a stone bench nestled up against an ivy-covered brick wall, underneath an overgrown trestle of purple hyacinth.

Nick turned suddenly, and faced the priest, startling him. He stood toe to toe with John and stared into his eyes, searching for a soul, "I need to confess ... I need to tell you the truth, Padre. I am not Thomas Armstrong ... you don't remember me. Hell, I didn't even recognize you when first I saw you ... it's been so many years ... so many years. I am not Thomas Armstrong ... my name is Throckmorton ... Nicholas Throckmorton."

The stunned priest did not answer. His eyes opened wide.

Nicholas paused. Seconds ticked past before he continued, "I know the Church kicked your ass out of Mount Clemens,

Padre ... and I know why ... and I'm here to find out exactly what you did with my wife, Nora. Did you touch her?"

There was barren silence. Nick breathed the question again, "Did you touch her? Did you violate my wife like you did so many other women?"

Nick had given some thought to this planned encounter, but he did not expect to get the immediate confession that he was about to hear.

For Father John, it seemed that he was standing at the Heavenly Gates and awaiting Saint Peter's judgment. He worried that some form of dreaded eternal damnation could have already begun. He was teetering on the edge, writhing within his skin like a molting snake, and wishing he could slither away into the black abyss of night. The disgraced priest's toes painfully curled inside his calfskin slippers.

He started to ramble in a soft, liquid, almost harmonious tone, his words trickling from his lips like a woodland stream, "I have learned to receive the truth. I have transgressed. It's true. Years ago, I comforted Nora. Forgive me. I was weak, lost my direction and became lost. I have sinned and Nora shared my sin. I wrongfully tried to encourage her faith in His love. Certainly, I have sinned, but I meant no harm. And I have acknowledged my sin, and now I atone. I have examined my conscience; I pray and humbly seek exculpation. I am an avowed servant of our Lord Jesus Christ, and through penance and humility, I beg the Holy Father for mercy, just as I now beg for your most merciful forgiveness.

"I prayed for Nora to Saint Monica, Exemplary Mother of Augustine, patron saint of wives and victims of adulterers and wanton husbands. I prayed for her transgression and for her marriage. I prayed for my own guidance.

"When your death was reported, Nora and I grieved as one. We mourned as one and loved as one. We were weak and sinned as one. Together, Nora and I prayed to Saint Anastasia, the most Holy Martyr of widows, who understands the suffering of loneliness and knows what women such as Nora need, and we prayed for the Holy Martyr to intercede for Nora's urgent desires, her spiritual and material wants.

"And I have prayed to the most venerable Saint Jerome Emiliani for the orphans. I feel pity for them and I have atoned and I continue to send my offerings and blessings to the Sisters of Felicia Home for Children in Detroit. I pray for them daily and before I sleep at night.

"Yes, I have been excommunicated, but not as an expiatory penalty, but rather medicinal and not at all vindictive, not at all ... not at all vindictive, but with mercy from Our Heavenly Father and the Holy See. With time and the will of our Lord and Savior, Jesus Christ, my exile will end and I may receive the Sacrament of Reconciliation and hold the grace to resist further temptation. I am still of the Church and a man of God and deem myself worthy of your forgiveness as well."

John's revelations were as close to unbelievable as they were revolting and unexpected. Hermione's second-hand gossip proved to be true. The priest had openly confirmed his guilt, admitted to adultery and fathering orphans while he preached false faith. Nick's skin crawled. Although he was astounded by the priest's overwhelming flood of admission, he could feel no pity on him.

Nick's right hand grabbed the cleric by the collar, and twisted it tightly around the priest's throat.

He breathed into John's reddening face, "Bullshit, buddy. Bullshit. You can pretend to find redemption and forgiveness by plucking through your Bible verses and whispering your hollow prayers to your dead ancient Saints, but my copy of the Good Book proclaims vengeance as *an eye for an eye*."

Nick continued his vocal beating and condemnation of Father John, "I've been in the company of plenty of women in my lifetime, Padre, and I have known and I have comforted my dead brother's wife, but I never lied or pretended to be somebody I wasn't. You can't expect me to forgive you, buddy boy. You're a moral leper. A low-life lothario ... a rake ... a damn degenerate. You're far beyond forgiveness.

"You can't pretend to forgive yourself by just flushing your crap down the toilet. You can't call yourself a man of God ... you're a phony, and I know what you are. Your Church knows who you are. They might call you Father John, but you're not ... you're Johnny Boy ... Johnny Boy the lecherous leper. You're nothing more than a predatory, self-righteous, philandering prick. You seek out and put yourself upon the young ... the innocent postulants ... the doubting nuns ... the widows, the grieving women ... all the low-hanging fruit you can pluck. You might consider this garden of solitude to be your own little sanctuary, your private Eden. Well, maybe it has been ... but you're the damn evil snake in this garden, Johnny Boy and I'm going to throw you out.

"It seems to me if there's any truth to them sanctimonious sacraments of your church, there's an express elevator straight to Hell for bastards like you, Johnny Boy. And as far as I'm concerned, right now, you're on the ground floor, Padre, and you ain't got no place to go but down. You may suck your glorious snail soup for your Saturday dinner, but there ain't no place in the world for slugs like you. No damn place at all. Not even in this garden. Like the Lord said: *Vengeance is mine.*"

Nick's right arm and fist became a steam-powered pile driver that sent a punch deep into John's gut, just below the ribcage. The priest collapsed to the path gasping, writhing like a worm and vomiting like a dog. He strained to breathe. Insects shared his agony. Crickets screeched. Cicadas shrieked.

Enraged, Nick went to a knee, and once again grabbed the priest's frock at the neckline, wrenched the fabric tightly around John's throat and lifted him to his feet. The cleric's nostrils widened, struggling for air. His eyes bulged, worrying what was coming.

The priest struggled to keep his balance, his arms hanging limp, droplets of sputum bubbling at the corners of his mouth. Beaten and out of breath, he could not speak. Drained of strength, Father John could only stare at his adversary. His moans came from deep within his lungs.

Nick stood nose to nose with the wounded, disgraced and dumbstruck preacher, his left hand still holding him up and against the ancient brick trestle. He spoke intensely, roughly from deep within his throat, "I'm not through with you yet, Padre. I'm going to put a permanent fix on them blue balls of yours. So be patient, Johnny. Your problems are nearly over."

Nick jolted his knee upward and drove it diabolically into the preacher's groin like a jackhammer, sending the entirety of Father John's man-parts crashing up into his abdomen. The cleric's mouth hung full agape, reeking of intestinal stench. His tearing eyes were locked shut.

Agent Nicholas Throckmorton put his lips to the priest's left ear, and whispered, "Goodnight, Johnny Boy ... never again will you defile a woman. Never again, Padre. Never again." He jammed the barrel of his pistol into the center of Father John's breastbone and pulled the trigger. The muffled sound of a blowback Walther PPK[**] echoed through the garden like an uncovered cough.

Nick released his grip on the priest's collar and allowed the lifeless body to fall to the ground with an unceremonious, muted thump. He holstered his pistol, lifted the dead priest onto the bench and propped his body up against the trestle.

Nick looked around, his eyes piercing the dusk. He couldn't see a living soul.

From a cluster of ocote trees, the shrill, bewailing sound of a Great Potoo[*] rudely shattered the night. It was then necessary for all the lovesick kinkajous[*] and every creeping gecko to protest their rude awakening with piercing shrieks and clicking twitters. From beyond the thick walls of Perpetual Mercy and the confines of the city, the cry of howler monkeys cut through the tropic night like a conquistador's sword.

It was a normal night in León, Nicaragua. It was the natural order of things.

Nick brushed at his clothes, straightened his hat and calmly, methodically started down the cobblestone path toward the Cathedral gate. The mission bells in the rectory tower chimed eight times, and between each one, a lonely echo was lost within the brick, stone and stucco walls.

One of the guards saw him approaching and unlocked the portal to the world outside. The other gatekeeper peered through the narrow window of the guardhouse without expression. Oil lamps flickered on the gateway arches, barely able to tease the black of night. Thomas Armstrong tipped the brim of his hat with one finger, and spoke in flawless Spanish, "Good night and God bless you, gentlemen."

For an errant moment, he caught himself wondering if Nora was asleep.

Hours later, he arrived back at Las Mercedes airport just as the Nicaraguan sun warm began to heat the Earth. Inside the terminal, Nick retrieved his stored bag from the luggage locker and visited the men's lounge to splash some water on his face. He tore up and flushed Thomas Armstrong's passport down the toilet, discarded his cathedral clothes and changed into linen slacks, a white silk shirt with a thin, straight black tie, two-tone wingtip oxfords and a creamy-white fedora. Refreshed and dressed in fresh, wrinkled suitcase clothes, he purchased a one-way ticket as Nicholas Throckmorton for that morning's nine o'clock flight to Havana. It felt good to be himself again, regardless of his three-day stubble and haggard appearance.

In the distance, far north of the city, Mount Momotombo continued its deep, resonate volcanic rumblings. Clouds of sulfur, steam and ash rose through the tropic morning sun, wafting upward into the skies above Lake Managua.

At nine o'clock, a silver, blue and red Cubana Airlines DC-3 shook, rattled and rolled down the macadam runway. Nick felt the wheels leave the Earth as the plane climbed quickly and banked left. In his mind's eye, he saw the pilot set the bearing to 18.16°, North-northeast. Nick calculated just under 800 air miles to their destination with a flight time of about four hours. He asked the lone stewardess for a double rum, straight up.

Cuban Pete ...
José Martí International Airport,
Havana, Cuba, October 5, 1953, 2:20 PM

Jovita was waiting for him at the bottom of the boarding ladder. His thirsty eyes drank her image. It was unusual for a supervisor to be out of the office and in the field with the grunts. He was glad to see her, but certainly, something was in the air. He half suspected that the hammer was about to hit the anvil. Sparks could fly.

She was dressed in a cream, below-the-knee pencil skirt and a double-breasted, cropped jacket, flared from the waist and buttoned to her bust line. A puffed, white silk scarf was around her neck and tucked inside her jacket. An oversized, floppy beige beret sat off-center, giving stark contrast to her jet-black hair.

They shared an abbreviated handshake before a very brief, transcendental hug. He missed her company, however brief and infrequent as it was. She spoke first, "Nicholas, it's good to see you back safe and sound. I hope your trip went well, and tell me please ... did you enjoy your little time off? And don't you have any luggage? No bags?"

He defended himself, "No bags. I traveled light this time, and yes, I did enjoy my time off, Boss. Thanks for that. It was nice to sit around, sip some rum, relax and do nothing for a day or three."

Her upbeat mood eased his ominous premonition, but he was determined not to show his surprise at her presence.

They started across the tarmac toward the Arrivals Hall. She was walking at a brisk pace for whatever reason.

It was obvious that something was in the wind, and he needed to know what, but she teased him before he could ask. She poked his shoulder and prodded, "You're not going to tell me that you met up with your long-lost sister-in-law again, are you?"

He knew what she was doing but still, he deflected her question. "Nothing like that, I just needed a breather, that's all. Are we in a hurry, Boss?"

"There's a car waiting for us, and for goodness' sake, we're alone, Nick. You're making me nervous. You know that you can call me by name when we're alone. I told you that. And we're not in a hurry, but I'm on a schedule and yes, it's tight. It's the nature of our new assignment. We have things on deck that need to be done and done quickly." She gave him a sideways glance and added, "By the way, about your ragged tourist get-up: it's inconspicuous, and could possibly work to attract a certain type of woman in Honduras, but not here in

Havana. You can change later, before our meeting. You'll be with me, and you need to be presentable."

He recognized her jealous jabs for what they were: harmless vexing. True, they were dressed as if they were cards dealt from two separate decks. Together, they certainly weren't a pair and definitely not of the same suit.

They were approaching Immigration Control when he said, "Like I said, Boss ... Joey ... like I said ... I just needed a breather. It had little or nothing to do with a woman."

He suspected that she either didn't hear his words, or had ignored them. She was walking with purpose.

They displayed their State Department passports to the Border Police inside the terminal, bypassed Import and Customs, and walked through baggage claim directly to the street. The afternoon sun had begun to turn the previous night's rain into steam.

Directly outside the terminal, a black, US Government Cadillac stood at the curb waiting for them. Jovita kept her hand on the door handle and teased him further, "Honestly, Nick, considering our job and everything entails, I don't think I could trust a man who didn't cheat or drink."

She opened the car door, then took a half-step sideways, blocking him, and added, "It's nice to have you back, and I'd enjoy sharing a scotch with you, but first, you need to get out of those clothes and shave. We've got a five o'clock meeting at the American Embassy**."

The Embassy of the United States of America, Havana, Cuba

Barely six months old, the embassy stood as a gleaming, six-story mass of milk-white concrete and barely-blue plate glass towering above Havana's renowned, picturesque Malecón waterfront. At the entrance steps, a garrison size, 20 x 38 foot American flag was flying atop a lofty, fifty-foot flagpole between two shorter, thirty-five foot poles. The Cuban lone star and stripes was to the left and the State Department's blue and gold ensign flew on the right. The balustrade along the seaside parkway was a stage show of tourists, locals, swooping gulls and terns in front of a scenic backdrop of blue-green seas and rolling whitecaps.

Once past the Marine guards and main desk personnel, Joey slipped her ID card over her neck and Nick pinned his Visitor Pass to his lapel. As they started down the hall, he immediately sensed that the new building was air-conditioned; a rare, affluent luxury in the tropical Caribbean.

Their destination wasn't far from the foyer and only a few doors down the first floor hallway, but Nick, his hackneyed clothes and whiskers garnered more than a few glances as he walked alongside striking Jovita. Doubtless, he was the odd man out. Her gentle sway, measured steps and the click of her heels accentuated the glaring mismatch. She stopped in front of room 119 and opened the door. Inside was a long, empty table with a dozen vacant chairs. As the door clicked shut behind them, he noticed that the large Bendix wall clock across the room read 4:10.

"An electric razor and a change of clothes are in the washroom through that door to your right, Nick. There's a connecting shower room also, but shake a leg. When you come out, I'll quickly go over the mission and its projections with you."

Whatever it was, it was on the front burner.

Behind the fogged-up glass door of a stainless steel shower stall, he washed the sweat and dirt of the previous eighteen hours off his body. He completely cleared his conscience with a little help from the fresh scent of a bar of coral-red Lifebuoy medicated soap and watched the suds curl clockwise down the drain. Refreshed, he shaved and changed into a cream shirt, a lightweight, deep blue silk suit, with a maroon tie and oxblood Rockdale wingtips that were lying in wait for him. Standing in front of the mirror, he combed his hair with his fingers, and lamented privately, *She's got damn good taste and remembered my size, but she forgot the comb.*

He re-entered the conference room and discovered Jovita seated alone at the table, with a few documents in front of her.

"Sit here next to me, Nick. We have to be quick. Company will be here shortly."

In the ten minutes that followed, Jovita gave him an urgent, but shallow overview of his next posting. As an irregular, unusual twist, she was going with him.

She pushed Nick's new identification and passport across the table and began, "This is part of an operation named PBSUCCESS**, and comes directly from Washington, Nick ... authorized by Eisenhower himself. The Agency is going after the Communists with both barrels.

"Starting now, right now, I'm Carilla Ramírez, Provincial Attorney for the Argentine District of La Rioja, and you are working once again as Nicolás Tavarez, the Delegate-Designate for the Dominican Republic Foreign Office. You and I are at this meeting undercover with one legitimate Foreign Service officer, Miguel Ruiz of Bolivia. You'll meet him with the Ambassador and the Cubans in a few minutes. Remember: the Bolivian, he's real and we're not. He's as blind as a bat and we need to keep it that way."

Nick gave his papers a cursory look and pocketed them.

"The plan is that the three of us, you me and the Bolivian are going to get Munson and two others out of prison."

"No shit." Nick didn't feel emotion, and didn't care. The Agency's plans were always synonymous with urgency.

"I have used my mother's given name as my alias and your legend is the same one that I gave you back in 1946 for the extradition of those Germans from Argentina."

"I recognized it. I remember."

"We're playing the same game this time, but with a different twist. More details later this evening, but first we need to get through this meeting, and if all goes well with the Cubans tonight, you, me and the Bolivian can be on our way to get Munson and the other two out. You and I are unanimous that Munson's an over-officious nincompoop, but he's a damn good field operator and besides being one of us, six months is long enough for anybody to be in one of Batista's prisons. Follow with me, take my lead, agree with me and nod. Learn as you go. When we're out of here and the others leave, meet me at your hotel, the Aragon. Understand?"

"Yes, Boss. Understood."

"Sin sudar, Nicolás. No sweat." As Jovita's last words left her lips, the door opened and five men walked inside.

The United States' Ambassador Plenipotentiary to Cuba, Willard Beaulac entered the room with a mustached, thick-bodied man wearing a bad-fitting business suit, a soiled shirt and tie, and scuffed shoes. Jovita whispered to Nick that the big man was Miguel San Martin-Ruiz, Associate Consulate General of Bolivia, the man who should be accompanying them to free Munson and the others.

Three Cubans in full ceremonial military uniforms followed immediately behind. Their gold-braided epaulets, calfskin bandoliers and jackets full of colorful medals were prancing about the room inside of spit-shined, black jackboots. The Cuban officers took seats next to the American Ambassador across the table from Nick and Jovita. Nick considered meetings like this as glorified freak shows. He hated the

Circus, but he held season tickets. He had to be there. The ringmaster back in Washington signed his paychecks.

Other than a brief introduction and hollow pleasantries, Nick could only sit and listen through the meeting. He sat on his hands, watched the high-wire act, the dancing tigers and the clowns and let Joey do the talking. He had to. His knowledge about the mission was next to nil. Luckily, it was over in less than twenty minutes. The American Ambassador and the Cubans shook hands, congratulated each other, turned, smiled and walked out the door. Jovita, Nicholas and the Bolivian sat alone, stranded and ignored.

Jovita looked to Nick first, then the Bolivian and asserted, "I can only assume that freedom has been arranged for our countrymen. It seems to me that our presence here wasn't needed or appreciated."

Nicolás added, "I also believe that the prisoner release has been agreed. It appears that way, and I certainly hope so. What to you think, Delegate Ruiz?"

A young man in a shirt and tie entered, spoiling the Bolivian's chance to reply and leaving him temporarily speechless. The clerk smiled, nodded and said, "Your travel papers and tickets, gentlemen ... ma'am. Your flight will leave Havana from Playa Baracoa Airport tomorrow afternoon at one o'clock and arrive at Nueva Gerona Airport on the Isle of Pines** at fifteen minutes past two. Have a good flight." He set a small packet on the table and left.

Jovita's alias didn't hesitate, and became the assertive Carilla. She stood, snatched up the papers, brought out the plane tickets, passed them around to Nick and the Bolivian, and continued to check the contents of the packet. An excited smile crossed her lips and her expression telegraphed elation. Her words danced off her tongue in Argentine Spanish**, "The prisoner release is arranged! Señor Ruiz, and Señor Tavarez, we will meet here at the Embassy tomorrow morning at nine o'clock, and we will travel together to the airport, and board an airplane for the Isle of Pines and there we will free our citizens! They will be free!"

Carilla's words overflowed with authority and had taken control of the room. She did not wait for a response, and allowed Nick and the Bolivian only a brief exchange of glances before she started again, "Good. I will see you gentlemen tomorrow morning, here, at nine o'clock. Tomorrow we shall free our countrymen! Liberty! *¡Viva la libertad!*" She was in command and assertive, yet jubilant. Nick smiled in appreciation of her skillful finesse.

She gave the Bolivian a soft, flirtatious smile, then turned to Nick and rolled her eyes toward the widows, silently signaling him that she was hitting the air. She put her tickets and the other documents into her compact valise and left the room.

Nick tested the Bolivian, "Well, Miguel, I cannot speak our language as beautifully as she did, but I think she was telling us that she had somewhere better to be than in this room with you and me."

"I agree, Nicolás. There could be a man waiting for her. I think she must have a man waiting for her. I know that I would gladly wait for her." Miguel let out a small guttural laugh.

"I suppose that you are right, but I also think that she must have standards much higher than you or I possess. She seems to have high standards."

Again, Miguel chortled and Nick decided to change direction and play him. He began, "Miguel, I was thinking that perhaps I won't tell my government the news about the prisoner release yet. Something may still go wrong, especially with the way the Americans can sometimes stick their fingers into the mixing bowl."

Like a wet towel, a look of concern covered and weighed on the Bolivian's face. "I think perhaps that you could be correct, I think, Nicolás. Tonight I will also report that the negotiation is still going on."

"Good idea. I'll telephone home to Santo Domingo and tell them the same. Where are you staying tonight, Miguel, if I may ask?"

"The Tropicana, of course. In Havana, I must stay at the Tropicana. How about you?"

"The Dominican Republic will not pay for me to stay at the Tropicana! I have a room above a small cantina in a quaint tourist barrio away from the beaches called Paseo del Prado." Nick feigned a grunting scowl and added, "But they tell me the beer is cold."

The Bolivian pressed him, "Perhaps later you could enjoy dinner and drink with me at the Tropicana, Nicolás? In Havana it should be law that you have a party all night at the Tropicana! Right?"

"Not tonight, Miguel. I would enjoy it, but I've been awake for eighteen hours. I will leave all the beautiful women with tight skirts, stockings, high heels and no souls for you. I'm dog-tired."

Nick didn't wait for a reply from the Bolivian before he stuck his plane ticket inside his breast pocket and smiled, "See you here tomorrow morning, then, Miguel." He couldn't resist badgering him, "And if you see her, tell lovely Señorita Carilla Ramírez and all the pretty girls goodnight for me! And kiss them for me, too!"

Ritmo en la Habana (Rhythm in Havana)
Monday, October 5, 1953, 7 PM
Aragon Hotel, Malecón, Havana, Cuba

Joey and Nick were sitting at a small table at the edge of the second-floor dining room. A votive candle flickered inside a cherry-colored snifter and the distinctive scent of fresh-picked, white gardenias overflowed from a puckered milk-glass vase. The waiter had just cleared their dinner plates and brought their drinks.

Snuggled up alongside a white, quarter-wall railing overlooking the lively roulette, black jack, and craps tables below, their balcony table afforded them a teasing taste of privacy. The high-stakes poker games, high rollers and VIP's were out of sight, in a back room hidden behind a door next to the bandstand. The sounds of Antonio Orestes' mambo band had the dance floor throbbing. Somewhat secluded, they were able to temporarily relax and carry on a conversation spiced with playful innuendos and whispers.

Jovita confirmed that the meeting at the embassy ended well. The Cubans accepted fifty thousand dollars in munitions credits for the safe release of three political prisoners locked up on the Isle of Pines. The Agency had covertly arranged the tentative release of Agent Angus Munson and two others who were being held captive inside Batista's refurbished Presidio Modelo^{**} prison since July. BRAC, the Cuban Secret Police had captured them in the days following the Castro brothers' failed attack on the Moncada Barracks in Santiago de Cuba.

Nick's boss made good on her airport promise to buy a round of drinks, and had ordered two double, neat Cutty Sark scotch. Jovita was holding her glass just above the linen tablecloth, slowly rotating it counterclockwise and swirling the amber whiskey gently along the sides. She had that smile; the smile that nibbles at his heart and prickles the hair on his neck.

He teased her, "Next round, how about I buy the scotch? I'll order something other that Cutty, all right?"

She feigned surprise, "Is there something wrong with Cutty Sark? Am I missing something about the ship on the yellow label or the green bottle?"

He sipped at his drink, smiled and set it down. He said, "Cutty Sark isn't bad scotch. It's just fine, but during the war, I met a Scottish RAF* flyer, named Captain Boyd Donnan in New Guinea. He explained it all to me. It was the only hard liquor available on the airbase and he said, *'The Cutty is a taste of home. It tastes like it's been filtered through the purple heather that grows on the moors, and it smells like the peat, sphagnum and dirt found on the braes* with a disturbing hint of sheep shit. It's so bad, it's good.'*

"Boyd was one of them Brylcreem Boys**, talking in that thick, tartan-plaid Scottish tongue, you know. He told me that the stuff was so terribly delicious that a glass or two was all he could handle. And that meant that he never drank too much or got a hangover. And that's what's good about the Cutty ... and it makes sense if you think about it. It's never good to get too much of a bad thing, because it always comes back to bite you in the ass. And it's never good too get too much of a good thing either, because then you never know when your ass is about to get bit. Captain Donnan and his Thunderbolt flying bathtub never made it back to base the next day."

He was talking like a kid, but she understood. She reached across the table and put her hand on his. Her eyes danced in the reflected candlelight. "That's a wonderfully crazy story, Nick, and you've explained it so well ... but ... but we need to get down to business."

Those few words temporarily dashed his hopes of a romantic liaison with his former lover. "What's going on?"

She slowly drew circles on the back of his hand with the painted nail of a forefinger, "First off, I need to be back at the Embassy by nine o'clock for an enciphered, double-layer telephone call with Foggy Bottom[*]. This is a big deal, Nick. Right now, I'm going to quickly go over the mission with you in a little more detail before my telephone call and tomorrow morning's meeting at the Embassy." She lit a Chesterfield off the candle and leaned forward across the table. She whispered through her smile, "It's important that you hear this, so move your chair closer. And listen closely."

He sensed that her teasing touches and whispers were part of her acting in legend. She scooted her chair up against the balcony wall and Nick moved his next to hers. The casino and stage were in full panoramic view beneath them. They were as close as they could get without sitting on one another's laps.

She leaned slightly toward him and spoke quietly, "These men are on Isla de Pinos. To sum it up, the Cubans have agreed that you, the Bolivian and me can go to Modelo prison and bring three prisoners out with us: Munson, a young Dominican asset, and a murdering Argentinean lawyer.

"For the last ten months, Munson has been in legend as Benito Pérez, a Bolivian professor. He's been in jail for over three months now, for aiding in Castro's uprising and preaching the gospel of Communism to the Cuban masses. In addition to Munson and the Argentine, the Agency wants one of our implanted assets out as well. He's a 22-year-old Dominican kid, a college student named Pedro Pacheco, who has been working deep undercover and walking the tightrope for us long before Castro's Moncada attack."

Downstairs, the band started to play *Ritmo en la Habana*. The sultry Latin beat prompted Joey to begin moving her shoulders gently to the music, but her impromptu reaction was temporary. She shifted her body in the chair, moved back a bit, and sipped at her scotch.

She gave Nick a subtle smile, winked and continued, "As I told you earlier, this is a big deal in Washington. The get-away storyline is that you have been working to get Pedro home to his dying father back in the Dominican Republic. The Company has done the groundwork to free Munson and hand over the fugitive Argentinean, and now it's up to you and me to make sure everything goes smoothly from here on out."

Nick had a single question, "If Miguel believes that he's bringing out Munson as a Bolivian professor, and I'm pulling the Dominican for his sick father, who is this Argentinean fellow under your wing?"

"He's Diego Camoresi, a fugitive young lawyer from Argentina who is wanted for kidnapping and several brutal murders, but especially the torture and killing an assistant Chief of Police, his wife and four young children back in Buenos Aires. The Company knows that Diego holds the keys that can provide intelligence on a growing rag-tag gang of outlaws. The Agency is trying to get a foot in the door with a bunch of upstart Communist revolutionaries in Guatemala for reasons that you or I will never know or understand. It wasn't a hundred percent certain that the Cubans would release this Argentinean, that's why Washington sent me. I've been down here for the last week, passing out padded letters from the government of Argentina, smiling and using my talents of persuasion on Cuban generalissimos and trying to convince them to cut Camoresi loose to the authorities for trial back in Argentina.

"For years, Camoresi has had close ties to another hotheaded, radical Argentinen rebel named Ernesto Che Guevara[**], the leader of a violent new brand of revolutionaries. There's a whole bunch of these banana banditos[*] falling out of the trees deep inside the jungles of Guatemala and fighting the exploitation of the masses. This Guevara guerilla appears to have help from the East German intelligence network, an endless supply of Soviet money, and Czech weapons. The Company believes it can use Che's lawyer-friend Camoresi to provide information on Guevara's Guatemalan gang. Let's hope everything goes as planned and we're able to lasso Camoresi for ourselves."

Nick needed to pry, "So, are you telling me that we're not simply cutting Munson and the Dominican loose?"

In the moment that followed his question, Nicholas saw his field supervisor display an uncharacteristic air of smug confidence. She answered concisely, "Yes. We're not just getting them out. We're sending Munson and the Dominican undercover into Guatemala. To tell the truth, I highly doubt that Munson and the others know that they're getting out of jail or off the island. We have led the Cubans to believe that Munson and the Dominican will be released to Swiss diplomats and eventually back to their home countries. And tonight, courtesy of the Agency, our Bolivian friend will have his hands full of female company and his fingers around a glass of knockout drops. He'll wake up about noon tomorrow, won't know what hit him and completely miss tomorrow's flight. There may even be a woman still in bed with him when he wakes up."

She lit another cigarette, turned on her intriguing Argentine intonation and asked, "What do you think, Nicolás?"

"Maybe Munson will enjoy Guatemala."

Jovita scowled as her eyes teared from a flood of tobacco smoke. Disgusted with the discomfort and the habit, she crushed the cigarette into the ashtray. "I certainly hope so, but it gets better. Do you want to stay on the hook or are you ready for the rest of the story?"

"Go."

"Tomorrow, you and I are going to Isle of Pines, and will leave Nueva Gerona airport with Munson, Pacheco and Camoresi aboard a chartered Mexicana Airlines flight to Belize City, British Honduras. Once we land, we will be met by a Central American welcoming committee."

Nick playfully needled her, "No brass band?"

"No brass band and no castanets. This has been planned and plotted, and everything should end well, but as soon as we land in Belize City, our flight will be hijacked**. Pacheco and our man Munson will then be shanghaied* deep into the jungles of Guatemala."

She continued to play the vixen, leaned to him and, whispered, "Listen closely."

"I'm all ears, Boss."

Jovita refreshed her smile, and spoke quietly, "You and I will try to grab Camoresi before the plane takes off for Guatemala. Of course, we can't eliminate all the hijackers, because the plane needs to be stolen. We want to spare Munson, Pacheco, the cockpit crew, and hopefully one or two of the hijackers, but the others are expendable if need be. I don't expect any trouble tomorrow, but if you hear me exclaim '*Gun!*' I want you to reach under my dress and find the pistol holstered to my inside left thigh. Give me room, because I'll be in there reaching for the one on my right."

"Under your dress?"

"Correct. It's Fort Knox."

"And how do we get out of the plane?"

"Trust me. There's always a way out, a rabbit hole."

Nick saw the situation as his first chance to use Eloisa's exclamation of paradox, and said, "Yippee-i-o-ki-ay."

Jovita couldn't know exactly what he meant, and was at a loss for what to say or how to respond.

Instead, she had the last word, "Goodnight, Nick. I'm off to my telephone call, but I'll see you at the Embassy in the morning. Nine o'clock ... bright-eyed and bushy-tailed. We have a busy day on the books, so get some sleep."

She gave him a quick peck on the cheek. He could only watch as she stood, turned and walked toward the double staircase leading down to the lobby. Try as he might, he couldn't detect the outline of a gun under her dress.

She could feel his eyes.

In The Mood ...
Belize City Airport, October 6, 3:30 PM
Belize City, British Honduras

Mexicana flight 17 from Nueva Gerona landed as scheduled. The aged DC-2[**] rattled and growled along the taxiway toward the terminal, ending an uneventful two-hour flight from Cuba.

No sooner had the pilot set the hydraulic land brake and cut the starboard engine, four men dressed in short-brimmed ball caps and faded blue coveralls rushed up the eight steps of the boarding ladder and bolted through the cabin door. A large, barrel-chested man led the way. He fired three quick shots into the Cuban prison guard seated in the front row next to Diego Camoresi, unlocked his handcuffs, and pushed him toward the rear of the plane, into the empty row behind Munson and the Dominican.

Two hijackers sprang directly into the cockpit, pointed their weapons at the pilot and navigator and ordered the pilot to restart the quieted engine. They then ordered both crewmembers to sit with their hands folded behind their backs. The fourth hijacker scrambled down the center aisle of the plane with drawn pistol, jabbering nervously in bad Spanish, *"Hands on top your heads! Stay in your seats! You move and you die! We are now commanding this plane to Guatemala!"*

A nervous silence passed through the plane. Nicolás and Carilla occupied the two rearmost seats on the left side of the aircraft, with their fingers atop their heads and focusing their attention on the pair of gunmen inside the cabin.

The Argentinean had been moved two rows in front of them. The armed incursion came as no surprise to Nick or Jovita, but their hearts raced nonetheless. The large man who killed Camoresi's Cuban guard shouted, "Who are the other prisoners here? And who are not the prisoners? Answer now and no one else will die!" His big, hairy hands were holding a 38 caliber Beretta and his wild, steel grey eyes were looking for another target. Black, week-old stubble covered his rugged face, and his appearance brought back Jovita's troubling memories of her brutish uncle Horado.

Suddenly, things began to happen as quickly as corn popping in a hot cast iron pot. The DC-2's heavily idling Wright Cyclone engines were shaking the parked aircraft from frame to rivets and blanketing the cabin with a steady, grumbling drone.

Diego Camoresi twisted at the waist, turned in his seat pointed at Nick and Joey and spoke frantically, "Of course ... ¡porsupuesto! The man and woman wearing Yanqui* banker suits are politicos! I have not seen a weapon on them but they are the snakes and as dangerous as policía*! Of course!"

He didn't possess the sweet, melodic Argentine dialect that Jovita used masterfully, but rather, the harsh, excited, purpose-laden tone of a murderous, violent revolutionary.

Jovita sensed that the plot could be turning dangerously sideways. She slowly opened her knees.

Munson was in legend as Benito Pérez, and spoke flawless Continental Spanish, "Of course! ¡Porsupuesto! I have not seen weapons on the Yanquis, but it is clear that we prisoners are the ones dressed in the uniform of Batista's Modelo! We are all three together, and part of Fidel's glorious 26 July Movement!"

The Dominican spoke English, "We are three! The man and woman, they are harmless diplomats and they have liberated us from Batista's hellish island prison! The man and woman are diplomáticos, they are! They have liberated us and gave us our freedom and they are harmless, of course!"

The bearded brute with the Beretta took a half step toward Nick and Jovita. His comrade-in-arms remained standing nearer the front of the cabin, but kept his weapon pointed toward the action in the rear.

Without warning, the engines began to roar and sent strong vibrations throughout the aircraft. An intense command echoed from the cockpit, "The plane will now leave the airport. Now. Everyone must be seated! Now."

Nervous glances and curious looks spread between the participants like jelly on warm buttered bread. The Argentinean frantically surveyed his surroundings.

Jovita feigned shock, glared toward the cockpit, opened her eyes wide, and shouted, "Gun!"

An explosion of confused activity ensued. In shocking surprise, heads turned toward the front of the plane and heartbeats quickened. Together, Nick and Joey's hands went under her midnight blue silk dress and came out with a LadySmith** apiece.

Blackbeard recognized the trick, turned and hastily fired an errant round toward the rear of the plane that missed both

Jovita and Nick. Jovita instantly squeezed off two shots, both hitting the bearded brute squarely in the chest. Nick fired and hit the other gunman, dropping him in his tracks. Nick's second shot struck one of the cockpit hijackers in the back.

The aircraft began to jostle down the runway. Twin 700 horsepower Wrights roared. The remaining forward gunman slammed shut the cockpit door. The stack of dominos had begun to topple.

Joey ordered, "Time to go, Nicolás!"

Jovita was standing and holding onto the seatback in front of her. Nick dropped to his knees, pulled the ring on the floor hatch and pushed the round, two-foot cover aside. The Argentinean abruptly reached across the seats and tried to knock the gun from Jovita's hand. His attempt failed and Jovita fired. Diego was struck by two bullets; one into his armpit and another to his upper chest. The Dominican was on the floor with a wounded hijacker at the front of the cabin. Munson stood stunned, but managed a priggish smile.

Through the cargo door, the blurred runway beneath them signaled that the DC-2 was gaining speed.

"Go, Nicolás, go! Take Camoresi! I'm right behind you!"

Nick pulled the wounded Argentinean to the hatch, dropped him feet-first to the runway below and looked up to Jovita. "Don't dally, Carilla! Come on!" He slid to the open hatch, held the doorframe for a split second and rolled onto the runway.

Wind rushing through the hatch and into the plane whirled around Jovita's hair. She directed her attention to the front of the aircraft and focused on her nemesis Munson. She taunted him, "Hey Pérez ... pretty good shooting for a female cadet fresh off the Farm, right?"

She pulled the trigger and sent her final round cleanly through the flesh of Munson's upper arm. He glared at her in stark disbelief and watched as she kicked off her shoes and dropped down through the cargo door. The aircraft strained to bounce airborne.

Jostled, bumped and bruised, all three landed within a hundred yards of each other. Nick and Joey scrambled toward the Argentinean, tore pieces off his shirt and packed each of his two wounds. His left foot pointed sideways, likely the result of a shattered ankle. Bloodied and in shock, he was unconscious, but otherwise no worse for the wear. Safe and sound on the runway, Nick and Joey's emotions were in the clouds. He moved close, put an arm around her shoulders and said, "Good job, Boss."

She was lost in her thoughts and spoke without emotion, "I shot Munson ... gave him a stinging flesh wound."

"Why?"

"As a matter of principle, I suppose. But, now that I think about it, the wound will only help him in legend. It's likely that I did him a favor. Wounded, Che's guerillas will accept him as a hero and thanks to me, he'll have another war story to tell around the campfires in Guatemala.

"He's a slippery character, Nick. Ever since I first met him, he struck me as the type of man who could stumble face-first into a pile of crap, stand up, brush himself off and still smell like a fresh-picked rose."

Nick changed the mood and teased, "Maybe. But I don't think he'll ever have his hand under your dress."

Her eyes laughed and she said, "You're right. He won't."

She pressed her lips to his, kissed him, paused a second, and kissed him again. Although it was their first in more than seven years, it was over in mere moments. It was a sterile expression of relief; an emotionless release of stress. It saddened him.

The heat of the afternoon sun had baked the asphalt beyond tolerance, and forced them to drag Camoresi's body to a little patch of monkey grass and knee-high sedges between the taxiways. An RAF jeep with its annoying, high-pitched, two-toned siren bounced along the runway toward them. Aboard were two Air Force officers and a local Belize City policeman. A black Mercedes ambulance followed close behind with its flashing, cherry-red, bubblegum roof light. Five hundred yards away, the terminal began to flood with Army and Air Force military vehicles.

The jeep slid to a stop on the wiry grass next to them, and the RAF captain politely asked Jovita, "What happened here, Miss?"

"I believe our flight was hijacked. This wounded man is Diego Camoresi, an Argentinean, as am I. I am Carilla Ramírez, Provincial Attorney for the Judicial District of La Rioja, Argentina and this is Nicolás Tavarez, the Delegate-Designate for the Foreign Office of the Dominican Republic. We were aboard that Mexicana Airlines flight from Isle of Pines, Cuba that was just hijacked. I think that's what happened. Four armed men boarded the plane; two were in the cockpit and two in the cabin. There was shooting and I think that three, perhaps all four were shot. At least one was shot dead. A Cuban prison guard was shot. I think another prisoner besides this one was shot as well."

The ambulance pulled up and two medics scrambled out of the front. They hurried to open the rear doors and asked, "How badly wounded is he?"

Nick answered, "He's unconscious, but he'll live. He's got a busted ankle ... he took two bullets, one to the shoulder and one to the upper chest. We just covered them and controlled the bleeding. The chest wound doesn't appear to be sucking air."

The British officer abandoned the frivolous preliminaries and got down to business, "I'm Wilfred Towson, Captain, Her Majesty's Royal Air Force, and Adjutant General of Belize City Aerodrome. Welcome to British Honduras. We've been expecting you. "

As the world turns, the dust settles just as the wind kicks it up all over again ...

The hours following the hijacking were consumed by conversations with the Cuban Ambassador, an agent of the British Secret Intelligence Service[**] and encrypted telephone calls with the American Embassy in Havana and State Department Headquarters, Washington. By six o'clock, all interested parties seemed satisfied with what they had learned about what happened before, during and after the hijacking.

Although the newspaper account of the incident placed blame on the lack of proper security at Belize City Airport, it also indicated that the four hijackers were not only agents of the StB Czechoslovakian State Security[**], but were also plotting with the Guatemalan Workers Party. The commandeered Mexicana flight landed without incident at Guatemala City, Guatemala, where Communist guerillas spirited the two remaining passengers and two hijackers off the plane and into the surrounding jungle. The pilot and his navigator were permitted to leave unharmed and the Cuban prison guard's body was released to the Cuban Embassy. The report also noted that although three unnamed passengers were able to escape the aircraft from a rear cargo door before the hijacking began, two survived and one male Argentinean national was struck and killed by errant gunfire.

The next morning, October 7, Jovita left Belize City as a paying passenger aboard a TWA flight to Miami, Florida on her way back to Fernando's Hideaway. She promised Nick that she would buy dinner and a round of drinks at their next meeting. Their reunion would necessarily be sometime in the unforeseen future, because Nick needed to tie up some loose ends in Panama that had been dangling since January. He departed British Honduras later the same day aboard a US Air Force transport to Colón, Panama.

Diego Camoresi spent three weeks recovering from his bullet wounds and fractured ankle at the Royal Air Force Field Hospital located within Camp Ladyville, British Honduras. Members of Her Majesty's Secret Service kept him under armed guard, isolated and secluded behind blackened windows for the duration of his stay. His immediate future remained in the dark.

In late October, under the cover of night, US Army Rangers strapped him to an aged, rickety and noisy World War I era gurney, loaded him onto the bed of a two-ton stake truck, and drove him to Ladyville Airport. Camoresi was leaving British Honduras for an open-ended, undocumented incarceration courtesy of the Central Intelligence Agency. The first leg of his long journey would end at Albrook US Air Force Station, Balboa, Panama, on the Pacific side of the Canal Zone.

Yes, We Have No Bananas ...
One month later, November 9, 1953
Panama Federal Stockade, Flamenco Island, Panama

A scruffy, pudgy Panamanian guard unlocked the cell door, entered, stepped aside and folded his arms. Nick walked halfway into the cell with two burly American Military Police close behind him.

The prisoner glared at the intruders. Weeks earlier, when Nick dropped Camoresi's debilitated body from the belly door onto the runway, he did not expect to see him again, nor did Camoresi ever again expect to see Nick.

The Argentinean fugitive was leaning against the concrete block walls of a 6 X 9 foot jail cell and seated next to a pile of ragged, old burlap coffee sacks on a bed made of pallets and plywood. A cracked, dirty plaster cast covered his left leg from knee to toes. His right foot was shackled to an iron ring imbedded into the concrete floor, halfway between the bunk and a filthy, baked clay toilet. Camoresi was unshaven, wet with sweat and wearing threadbare cotton shorts and a t-shirt. His eyes burned with a stifled inner rage that strengthened his defiance.

"I knew you were a Yankee bastard as soon as I laid eyes on you!"

"We should at least try to be civil to each other, Diego. I'm here to take you to a much better place ... a place located a little bit north of here with softer beds and better food. And it's very likely that you'll be able to see daylight. I'm sure you'll like it. Even the cockroaches and iguanas hate this hole."

Camoresi had a brief display of futile, writhing violence before the MPs manhandled him into reluctant submission. The largest military cop was an Army Staff Sergeant who warned, "Your personal safety for the immediate future and during your trip north is dependent upon your behavior, Bud, so I strongly suggest that you cooperate."

The prisoner growled at Nick, "You're not taking me back to Argentina? They told me that I was going to Argentina! If I am going to die, I want to die as a hero in my home country, Argentina!"

"No, you're not going back to Argentina. We cannot allow them to stand you up in front of a firing squad, Diego. You don't want to die that way, and besides, we need you. You are much more valuable to us alive than dead."

Camoresi seethed with infected anger, "And where is that Río Plata Argentine whore? The whore who shot me? Tell me the revolution lives! Tell me the commandos killed her and I can die avenged!"

Nick poured salt into the open wound, "She's alive and well and looking forward to seeing you again, Diego."

There wasn't a grain of truth in Nick's words, but he found vindictive satisfaction in saying them. The Argentinean charged at Nick, spat at him but fell flat on his face when his leg iron reached its limit.

Nick wiped his face with his shirtsleeve, slammed his boot into Camoresi's rib cage and addressed the MPs, "Throw some soap and water on him, men. And see if you can find a pair of pants and a shirt that don't smell like a walking pile of shit. Thank you."

By the time Diego Camoresi regained consciousness, he was aboard a leased Panamanian COPA airlines DC-3 and an hour from his destination. He awoke approximately 20,000 feet over the Gulf of Mexico and 50 miles west of the Cayman Islands.

Mérida, Yucatán, Mexico
Prisión federal en Mérida

Camoresi awoke in a start, opened his eyes wide, studied his surroundings and discovered that the people aboard the flight were himself, Nick and the same two US Army Military Police from Panama. He was no longer in shackles, but handcuffed to a window seat in the row opposite his captor.

He asked, "Where are you taking me, Yankee? To Alcatraz or Sing Sing or another place for gangsters?"

At first glance, and judging by his intonation, Nick believed that the prisoner had controlled his anger and accepted his fate. He answered, "You're not a gangster, Diego. You're an unfortunate, misguided, misinformed and misbehaved Communist revolutionary. We only send the real gangsters to Alcatraz and Sing Sing. We take murderers like you to a charming detention center in Mexico, where you'll soon discover that there's more in Cancún than tourists, bars and brothels. The company took some jungle and carved out a special resort for bums like you."

Nick continued to castigate the indignant Argentinean further, "After we land, you're not going to see me again, Diego, so save your breath and don't spew any more of your Commie Bolshevik bullshit at me. I couldn't care less about your philosophy, fight or false revolution.

"Any idiot can go ahead and fight for a cause, but if you murder for it, expect consequences. A revolt that avenges itself by murder isn't a revolution. It's anarchy ... nothing more than lawless mob rule.

"It's damn near impossible for me to feel compassion for someone who murdered and tortured women, children and entire families for a bullshit cause, so allow me to give you a bit of advice, asshole.

"I know one thing for certain ... think about this ... that if it weren't for the Spaniards, your people would still be walking naked through the jungles just like your ancestors, hunting for half-naked, ripening females and chewing on coca leaves for a cheap buzz. And now, you think you have this new, evil, Capitalist enemy; the American and British land-owners, but their banana, pineapple and mango plantations give your people the clothes on their back, the food on their table and the roofs over their head. So don't think that you're some new kind of compassionate, democratic, champion-of-the-people revolutionary, Señor Camoresi. You're nothing more than an educated Troglodyte* who's been led to believe all the bullshit propaganda tripe that's thrown around by the Communists, their rag sheet newspapers and posters, and trumpeted by bought-and-paid-for, two-bit, hand puppet dictators.

"You would be best served to listen and learn, mister college-educated attorney. You can believe every word I say, because it's the Gospel Truth.

"Free yourself and confess your sins like the choirboy you are, Diego. Spill your guts on everyone in Guevara's merciless gang and ask for mercy. Redeem yourself and at the least, perhaps you can die a free man.

"Your hand-wringing worries and torturous nightmares about what the future holds for you, your family and your little band of gun-slinging Commie contrabandistas* are meaningless tripe. What's left of your family back in Argentina and your comrades scattered throughout these uninhabitable jungles are better off without you. This little banana republic that you're fighting will be around long after you're dead and gone.

"The United States of America is the best of the worst you could imagine ... the best of the worst ... believe me. America is your best option, asshole. It's your goddamned best goddamn option. Like I said: *Believe me, you slippery snake, I know.*

"I've been there and I'm going back."

Camoresi spat towards Nick and scowled, "You are going to Hell, Yanqui! That's where you will go! Straight to Hell! To Hell!"

Nick allowed Camoresi to stew, smiled and methodically brought his pack of cigarettes out from his shirt pocket, and slowly put the blue flame of his Zippo to a Camel. "Maybe ...

maybe not. I've sent a few men there on my own, but on the other hand, maybe you ain't going nowhere, Diego."

As he finished his sentence, the plane's landing gear moaned, jolted and locked into place. They were about to land.

When Jovita assigned Nick to escort Camoresi out of Panama and north to Mexico, part of the deal was that his next duty station would be stateside. She promised that it would be short, safe and sweet. Factually, he would be working in NOC* (non-official cover), carrying his military ID and wearing Air Force blue with the corresponding rank of Colonel on his lapels. He pondered the possibility that she was throwing him a meatless bone with such a gravy train assignment, but happily accepted her offer. Nick felt that he could trust her, and at the least, he needed a respite from the tropics. He considered bananas and mangos too mushy to be real food and oftentimes longed to sink his teeth into a two-dollar diner meal. He dreamt of a plate full of juicy pork chops, baked potatoes, steamed asparagus and fried apples.

Nick's hopes for an All-American, meat and potatoes meal soared the next day. His new duty posted him a few miles outside of Valparaiso, Florida.

He spent three and a half long months testing new panoramic cameras and high-speed film while logging 200-plus backseat flight-hours in Northrop F-89 Scorpion** jets out of Eglin Air Force Base. The newer, larger cameras had a high fixed focal length and used wide, nine-inch Kodak Verichrome film. His work was part of extensive research by intelligence agencies and military branches into airborne photographic reconnaissance. Although the assignment gave him the opportunity to experience flying jet aircraft, the monotonous repetition of cockpit photography became tiresome and left him alone on the ground and in the air.

Airborne intelligence was something that Nick had experienced first-hand during World War II over Burma,

China, Siam and islands of the Pacific Theatre. The marked difference between the *then* and the *now* was in the details. The new cameras and film made it possible to identify items the size of baseballs from an altitude of 40,000 feet. While he had no direct input into the project, his flying experience helped identify some operational quirks that occurred during multiple high altitude field tests over the Florida panhandle.

Nick's duty station was a mere three hundred miles from Jacksonville, but his only contact with Jovita during his time at Eglin was over the telephone. Years earlier, after a tempestuous one night stand, she had warned him off and reminded him of the restrictions that she placed on their relationship. Nevertheless, he still longed for her. His private hunger for her company morphed into a constant heartache and became a stark reminder that it was impossible to mix a personal and professional relationship in their line of work. Their kiss on the runway in Belize City highlighted his romantic frustrations. The equation contained so many variables that a workable solution seemed impossible.

It seemed that every escape hatch was booby-trapped and every lifeboat was full. Marooned by immature choices and stranded by a failed marriage, Nicholas Throckmorton was left thirsting for lasting companionship since 1938. Currently, there were no sails on the horizon.

From start to finish, his 600 miles-per-hour, high-altitude assignment at Eglin bore a volume of technical data, assessments and recommendations that Agency analysts transcribed onto an eighty-page report for Kodak engineers, designers and project managers. His obligation at Eglin ended in mid-March, when Nick traveled to New York State to hand-deliver the results at a guarded symposium for Defense Department contractors at Eastman Kodak headquarters in Rochester.

Rum and Coca Cola ...
Kodak Park, Rochester, New York
March 17, 1954

Grey skies, temperatures in the low thirties and a relentless northeast wind across Lake Ontario were a stark reminder that winter had not yet released its icy grip on Rochester. Many local residents considered it the *luck of the Irish* that Saint Patrick's Day in Upstate New York could invariably be synonymous with a blizzard or ice storm. Despite the blustery welcome, each visitor to Kodak Park[**] recognized their host as a hugely successful international corporation with manufacturing and headquarter facilities large enough to constitute a city within a city.

There were two levels of security at the conference, Kodak's and the United States Marshall Service. Of the two, the Kodak guards were the most thorough and particular. Once inside the main building, Nick assumed that Kodak likely had more on the line and much more to lose than the government. All things being equal, corporate espionage was evidently more important than Nick's portfolio of facts, figures and high altitude images of strawberry and bean fields in the Florida panhandle.

The product convention began at eight o'clock in the morning with coffee, pastries, slide shows and presentations. Shortly before midday, the meeting broke into smaller, product-specific discussion groups in the reception gallery, where everyone seemed to wither and wilt like daisies out of water.

For Kodak, it was a show-and-tell presentation allowing them to graciously exhibit and demonstrate their newest design innovations. For the Intelligence Services operatives and the foot soldiers of the Military, it was nothing more than a public relations parley with gratuitous palm-pressing, back-slapping and champagne-sipping.

The large reception hall and main gallery on Eastman Boulevard were inert twins, innocuous and as immaculately vulgar as disinfected white enamel bedpans. The cold grey light of winter flooded the large rooms through a south-facing wall of windows that stretched nearly from floor to ceiling. An elevated presentation stage was at the opposite end of the hall and fifty yards away from an array of buffet tables with white linen tablecloths. Singular, themed smorgasbords were neatly arranged with stainless steel warming pans, coffee urns, stacks of Buffalo China plates, cups, saucers and gleaming Oneida stainless cutlery.

The Army, Air Force, Navy and Marines had contingents in attendance along with the FBI, Secret Service, Coast Guard and Border Patrol. Colonel Nicholas Throckmorton was there as one of four Air Force personnel that included Major General Roger Welford, Second Lieutenant Mary Williams, and Brigadier General Owen McClusky, Commander, 27th Reconnaissance Squadron, Griffiss Air Force Base, Rome, New York. Other than Nick, only General McClusky had actual hours behind the controls of an aircraft.

He didn't realize it until hours later in the day, but when he arrived at Kodak Park that morning, he was about to embark on one of the most intriguing and personally precarious missions of his Central Intelligence career. He was in NOC legend as himself. Air Force Colonel Nicholas James Throckmorton was a difficult identity to assume and his gabardine uniform couldn't guarantee that he'd be comfortable in his own skin.

Nicholas had consistently tried to avoid such gatherings. Fortunately, such superficial, social soirées were far and few between and factually rare, but somehow, these boring buffet-style cocktail parties always seemed to pop up when they were the least expected. Whether the attendees were government grifters, military muscle, intelligence operatives, pompous politicos or corporate suits, these events were always the same. Nick resigned himself to the fact that there was naught else to do but accept the situation and all the discomfort it brought.

The only consolation was that the shutter was about to close on his picture-taking assignment and he would soon be back in the field. The free bar, chafing dish menu, good-looking hostesses, and a dozen or so female participants were an appropriate end to an uneventful, tedious mission. The affair was winding down, and the crowd was breaking apart into small clusters and scattering throughout the hall.

He considered that the sterile greetings, insipid introductions, forced smiles, and clammy handshakes were akin to a root canal. Nick decided to hold onto at least an inch's worth of liquid anesthetic and began to drift through the large room clutching his half-full glass of bourbon.

One markedly attractive Kodak employee caught his eye not long after he had refreshed his drink. His proclivity to temporary intimate liaisons was the hook and line that invariably led him on. Nick's thoughts wandered, giving him some glinting hope of diversion with either fetching conversation, casual company or, if lucky, a one-night stand. His senses sharpened as he walked toward the alluring young woman. He spotted her Kodak employee nametag pinned just above her left breast and guessed that she was in her mid-twenties.

From across the room, it was her shape and not her strategically placed nametag that captured his attention. She stood about five-foot-six, and had deep, shoulder-length brunette hair with auburn flashes and soft under curls. A dark green skirt hugged her form from her hips north to her waist. On top, she wore a button-front, white knit blouse with a wide collar under a black boat-neck sweater. As he got closer, he noticed that she had the bluest blue eyes he had ever seen. The woman was gorgeous and without a ring.

She beamed and asked, "Did you enjoy the displays and presentations, Sir?"

As if to tip his hat, he put a forefinger to his forehead and said, "Would it be rude if I said that I've seen it all before in one way or another?"

Her eyes laughed and her voice sparkled, "I know what you mean. So have I."

He nodded, smiled and offered his hand, "Colonel Nicholas Throckmorton, United States Air Force, Ma'am."

The young woman took his hand and held it for an eternity of two seconds. She struggled with her words and her tinkling voice cracked in mid-sentence as she spoke, "Pleased to meet you, Sir ... Katherine Dobbs, Sir. Assistant Section Chief ... Kodak Product Design and Development."

Nick was starkly aware of her nervousness and realized that something was amiss.

Her eyes studied him, searching for answers to questions that she didn't dare ask. She gathered her racing thoughts and apologized, "Pardon me, but please allow me to explain ... I'm sorry, but when you said your name was *Throckmorton*, it threw me for a loop. You surprised me and I had to catch my breath."

She began again, "I was in the Navy, a Lieutenant Junior Grade in the Signal's Information Services and I worked with a Petty Officer with the name Throckmorton ... Petty Officer Second Class Alexander Throckmorton was his name, and he was from Detroit, Michigan. Could you two be related in any way? Do you know him, Sir? Alexander Throckmorton?"

Nicholas sensed her discomfort and at first, he suspected that somehow, he was being tested for some unknown reason.

He quickly discounted that idea as absurd and accepted the reality that this woman knew his son. He had just been confronted by the Fates, the Gods themselves, and knew that he needed to exercise caution.

He answered, "No, Ma'am. Alexander, you say? I don't know an Alexander. I'm from Massachusetts. Pittsfield, Massachusetts, actually ... and that's where I grew up and most of my family still lives there, but I have heard of other people with the name of Throckmorton, though. They're all over the world, I guess. There's even some kind of royalty, a Duke or an Earl, named Throckmorton in England, I think."

He needed to know more of her story and pushed onward, plying her to continue, "But tell me more about you, please. You're not old enough to be a Navy veteran. Not by a long stretch. And please, stop calling me *Sir*. I work for a living. *Nicholas* or *Nick* or even *Mister Throckmorton* is fine."

"Oh, I'm old enough, Sir ... Nick. I signed on after college, went to OCS[*], received my commission and later sailed for Korea. I served at Joint Services, Sasebo, Japan and that's where I met him ... Petty Officer Throckmorton ... Alexander Throckmorton."

She paused, looked to the wall of windows and continued, "We worked together at a Signals Detachment for about a year before I got sick with the flu, returned Stateside and received a medical discharge. We lost contact then."

The stranger standing in front of her had stirred dormant emotions. The past fifteen months raced through her mind, kicking up muddied memories of her last moments with Alexander and the guilt-laden regret that their emotional separation had brought her.

Although it was nearly impossible to rattle Nick's cage, Katherine Dobbs had certainly ruffled his feathers. She had no way of knowing, but her words had wrinkled his senses and disheveled his thoughts. His scalp prickled.

Nick double-checked her nametag, threw caution out the window and asked, "Would you allow me to buy you dinner, Katherine? Please. You can help me escape this torturous monotony and I certainly would enjoy your company. We could discuss this wonderful winter weather here in Rochester and everything we know about the Throckmorton family. Obviously, it's not a whole helluva lot, but for me, at least, it's more than I know about cameras and film."

A smile came across her lips as she answered, "Yes. That sounds nice. I would like that." Her voice was cheerful and melodic, "First, I need to make one quick telephone call, and then I'll call for a taxi to take us outside the gates to eat."

Nick didn't expect that his informal invitation would be accepted so quickly. He was amused at her choice of words and her proclamation that they were going 'outside the gates' for dinner. It suggested that together, they were escaping the clutches of Kodak.

Inn At The Park Restaurant & Lounge,
Saint Patrick's Day, 4:30 PM,
Ontario Boulevard, Rochester, NY

In less than thirty minutes, there were seated in the dining room at a round table for two, decked with a brick red table cloth, a fluted white vase of yellow daffodils and a flickering flame of a candle from inside a five-inch, crystal globe. Twenty feet away was a wall of stacked grey Pennsylvania fieldstone wrapped around a glowing fireplace with snapping sparks and dancing flashes of orange and yellow light.

Nick continued to feel out of place as a blue-suiter[*], and felt constrained. He tried, but couldn't remember exactly the last time he had a woman on his arm while he was wearing his dress uniform. His best guess brought back visions from ten years earlier, in 1944, in Australia, with Nurse Sister Guendolen Peate. He shuddered at the memories: the good, the bad and the heartache. He cursed himself and wriggled in his chair.

Katherine noticed. "Are you all right, Nick?"

He quickly regained his composure, caught his balance, and returned to the tightrope. He simply needed to adjust altitude and get back on the flight plan. He wanted to hear everything this young woman knew about his son. "Yes ... yes. I just felt a chill, that's all. It must be a reflex reaction to the cold weather here. I'm used to much warmer climates."

"Really? Where?"

"I'm fresh from Florida, like one of those oranges on the television commercials. And before that, I spent some time in the Caribbean and Central America selling war surplus. So I suppose you could say that I've got warm blood in my veins. But, tell me about yourself."

"Goodness ... Central America ... is it as exotic as it sounds with all those jungles, monkeys, parrots and things?"

Their little back-and-forth was interrupted by an effervescent blonde waitress dressed in layered, black organdy cotton, "Happy Saint Patrick's Day! Can I bring you folks a cocktail ... or coffee? Miss?"

"Rum and Coke**, I think that's what I'll have, please. It's Caribbean! Why not?"

Two To Tango ...

They decided to pass on the traditional Irish holiday meal of corned beef and cabbage and ordered Cornish Hen off the brazier, roasted new potatoes, and green peas with pearl onions.

After two drinks, the small talk over dinner gradually leaned toward the substantive information Nick wanted to glean from Katherine. Bit by bit, one piece at a time, she put her past life onto the table for him to fit together. She was slowly offering him everything, but scattering it like a puzzle dumped from the box, and saving the most intricate, intimate pieces for last.

It was seven o'clock when he tempted her with key lime pie for desert, ignored her protest and ordered another rum and coke. He primed the pump, "This sailor you knew, Alexander ... you said he was from Detroit?"

He wanted to yank the missing pieces from her hand and discover all her secrets. He watched once again as she retreated inside her thoughts.

She sipped at her drink and answered, "Yes, he was. And he was the most honest man I have ever known. Ever." Again, she drifted.

He needed to be patient. "You must have been close."

During his years with the Agency, Nick may not have had direct contact with his wife and son, but he knew his military pay was still being sent to Nora in Oshkosh, and now and again, he would ask Jovita for an update on Alexander's duty status with the Navy, and was aware that his son's enlistment would end in less than a year. To be sitting across from a young woman who likely knew his son Alexander on more than a professional level was a treasure chest of information waiting to be emptied.

Earlier in the evening, he had lied about his age, and shortened it by five years. He audaciously felt it was necessary to deny any plausibility that he could be Alexander's father. Furthermore, his real age would also make him old enough to be Katy's father and he didn't want to unnecessarily nix the possibility an intimate encounter with the young Kodak designer.

Suddenly, the top came off the puzzle box, and the missing pieces tumbled onto the table in front of him. Katy looked him in the eye, blinked away a tear and said, "Yes. I had our babies in June. Twin girls, Sarah and Karen."

For the first time in his forty-four years, he was repulsed by his selfish lust and he shamed himself. In the past, he was able to justify his dalliances, acknowledge his moral missteps and errors in judgment, but he had never committed self-censure. The thought of intimacy with the woman who gave birth to his son's children burned through his conscience like the Devil's trident.

His stomach churned directly underneath the aching empathy in his heart as his hand covered hers. He dared to pry, "But you haven't married?"

Taken aback by the direct, abrupt question, she took the last sip of her drink before she answered, "No. It didn't come to that. I caught a bad case of influenza in Sasebo and Alex and I broke off our relationship because I was being transferred to hospital in Tokyo ... and anyhow ... I was about due to rotate back to the States.

"All along, Alex and I swore to each other that it was a romance of convenience with no strings attached and we vowed that we would keep it that way. It all started when we were pinned down together in Typhoon Ruth, then we spent the next year together courtesy of the United Nations. We broke the rules and took chances with our Navy careers and futures.

We were fully aware that it takes two to tango ... but the pregnancy wasn't planned ... we were always careful, but it was one of those accidents that happen. And after I got to Tokyo ... and they ran some tests and told me that I was pregnant ... President Truman's Navy discharged[**] me. I came home, had my babies and was lucky enough to get a job with the best employer in the world."

"We all know accidents happen, Katherine, but haven't you considered contacting your sailor? Shouldn't he know?"

"I struggled with my decision for over a year, Sir ... Nick. But I can't undo the past and can't hang that chain around Alex's neck after the fact. I didn't tell him then and sure can't tell him now. We parted as friends, I hope. Our whole relationship was based on the fact that it would end when the Navy ended it. We didn't dive in thinking that we would live happily ever after."

"So, that's it? You've decided to raise the children on your own? That's awfully brave. I'm sure you know what I mean."

She defended herself, "I'm part of Kodak now, and Kodak takes care of their own. Everything."

His curiosity pushed him to ask, "Are the girls with your parents tonight?"

She briskly took her hand back from under his, sat back in her chair and explained, "I was adopted at birth and raised as an only child by elderly parents. My mom passed away just over a month ago from a heart attack and stroke and my dad's in an institution for the old and senile in Honeoye Falls. But for tonight, my girls are safe and sound about three miles away in Brighton at my best friend Emily's house. She works with me at Kodak and we got to know each other right after I was hired and I trust her with my life. We met at the child care center there, so you can be sure that my Sarah and Karen are in good hands, Sir."

Several puzzle pieces had fallen into place, and Nick discovered two years of intimate history. While he was starting to digest some of what Katy had fed him, he finished his scotch, caught the eye of their passing waitress and signaled for another round.

Moments of tense silence passed before he said, "I have to admire you, Katherine. You have a lot on your plate but it seems that you're handling it well."

"I think I am. Thank you."

The waitress brought their drinks and a small crystal dish with a half dozen Andes after dinner mints.

Kate pulled the swizzle stick from her drink and dropped it to the table. She looked across the table at Nick, her blue eyes diving into his soul, "I want my girls to grow up knowing that they're loved and who they are."

Nick couldn't know what she was trying to say or what to expect, and asked, "What?"

I'm a Throckmorton

"I told you that I was adopted at birth. And as a child, I had a privileged life ... plenty of everything piled on top of nothing. But, as far as I'm concerned, my identity is false. The only connection that I have to who I really am is a piece of paper from Our Lady of Victory in Lackawanna, New York that gives my birth date, birth place and who adopted me. It may as well be blank."

Nick's senses piqued at the mention of Lackawanna, but he didn't dare interrupt.

Katy continued, "As a child, I remember being asked who my real parents were ... and my college applications ... and my Navy enlistment ... they all asked for the names of parents.

"Even though I believe that Mom and Dad loved me, I felt alone and abandoned. Like a lost soul. It's impossible to explain. And when I was ready to take Sarah and Karen home from the hospital, I was devastated when they wouldn't

262

allow me to name the father on their birth documents because I didn't have a marriage license or some kind of affidavit of fatherhood signed by the father. According to their birth certificates, my daughters' father is *'none listed'*.

"Before she passed away in January, I asked my mom if she knew who my birth parents were. All she said was that a Catholic nun told her that my birth mother was an assault victim ... a victim of rape."

She swirled the ice cubes in her rum and coke and took a drink, "I was born and adopted on April 2, 1928, all in one fell swoop."

Nick was overwhelmed. He was trying his best to sort through and make sense of all the blurry bits and pieces that had flown past at rocket speed. Instantly, like the flash of a lightning bolt, an idea thundered through his mind that broke the sound barrier. The words came from out of the blue, "I'm a Throckmorton. I could sign that paper. I'll sign it for you."

Katherine sat bewildered.

Nick paused in thought and sincerely offered, "I'll sign that paternity affidavit. What hospital were Alexander's ... I mean ... your daughters ... born at?"

A sparkling glint of hope erased Katherine's mystified gaze. She answered, "Sarah and Karen were born at Syracuse General Hospital. Downtown, on East Onondaga Street. But your name isn't *Alexander*."

He smiled across the table at the mother of his grandchildren and explained, "You're right. But like I said, I'm *A. Throckmorton* and that's just the way I'll sign it. I'm heading back to Florida tomorrow anyway, so I can make a little detour and stop by Syracuse General, sign that paper and mail it, or even better yet, I'll drop it off back here for you. Where can I leave it?"

She replied in an instant, "At the Visitor Center. You could leave it there for me ... Katherine Dobbs. D-o-b-b-s."

She was amazed at the offer and needed to ask, "You will do this for me? How? Why?"

Nicholas painfully swallowed his enthusiastic pride and said, "It won't be a problem. A uniform and a military ID can work wonders. After I get this done, your daughters will never see a blank space on their birth certificates. Don't think twice about it. I'm happy to help, Katherine Dobbs."

Katherine finished her drink, set it down and briefly studied the remaining bits of melting ice cubes in her glass before she asked, "This is our secret, right, Nick? Please. Between you and me. Please respect my decision, no matter what. And my privacy."

He put his hand over hers. "Of course, Katherine. I'm good at secrets. You have my word. There's nobody to tell."

The revelation and the revolution ...
March, 1954

At ten o'clock, after one final round of drinks, Nick arranged for a taxi and accompanied Katherine to her friend Emily Rutherford's home on Erie Station Road.

Although he had gallantly walked her to the door, stinging sleet pellets and a biting wind shortened their goodbye. They stood on the porch under a forty-watt bulb, fighting the freezing chill. He looked at her face and locked her image in memory, alongside that of his son.

"Good night, Katherine. I'm sure things will work out for you and that you'll be a fantastic mother. It was a pleasure to meet you."

She was smiling. "Thank you ... for dinner, Nick. And for everything. For helping me ... and Sarah and Karen. I won't forget you."

She reached out and they briefly held one another before he turned and walked toward the cab. He didn't turn around or look back. Somehow, from somewhere deep inside, he knew that he would never see her again. For a moment, he allowed his heart to ache.

He had tickets for a three-legged American Airlines flight from Buffalo to Jacksonville on Friday, March 19. He was to meet Jovita at the Hideaway on Saturday.

On Thursday morning, Nicholas drove a black, Buick Roadmaster with US Government license plates eastbound for ninety miles along the New York State Thruway and visited Syracuse General Hospital.

He kept his thumb over his first name when he displayed his ID and easily manipulated a records clerk to allow him to sign an Affidavit of Paternity as *A. Throckmorton*. One piece of paper and some sideways truth enabled him to successfully amend Sarah Elizabeth and Karen Ann Dobbs' birth certificates and list Alexander Throckmorton as their father. As promised, later that afternoon he placed the fruit of his deception into a Manila envelope and left it for Katherine Dobbs at the reception desk of Kodak's Visitor's Center.

If it were anatomically and physically possible to pat himself on the back, he would have dislocated both his shoulders. He was so proud of his solution to Katy's problem that he wallowed in the triumph of his efforts on his way back toward Buffalo.

Driving past the Henrietta, New York exit, something that Katy had said began to crawl and itch its way through his recollection of their conversations. He decided that a small detour was necessary before his departure to Florida and stopped at the Depew Service Area on the Thruway to change into civilian attire. He believed that the creases in his suit and the wrinkles in his shirt would add authenticity to his planned ruse. With his grey fedora and black tie, he convincingly fit the mold of a government agent.

He drove south through Buffalo and parked the Buick on South Park Avenue, just a few steps away from Our Lady of Victory Basilica in Lackawanna, New York. The offices of Baker Victory Family Services sat half a block away at the corners of Ridge Road and Melroy Avenue.

Once inside, he encountered more levels of security than the Pentagon. He needed to present his Government Driver License, Air Force and Department of Defense identifications along the way, but two offices, three desks and a half dozen nuns down the hall he was eventually seated in front of Sister Theresa Marie. After a cleverly concocted epic full of torturous Chinese labor camps, prisoners of war, survivorship and battlefield declarations, Field Agent Nicholas Throckmorton discovered that Katherine Dobbs' birth mother was Eloisa Ashworth.

It seemed the more he learned, the more he needed to forget or forever hold as secret. Once lovers, he and Eloisa became grandparents to children they were never intended to know.

Nick arrived at Fernando's Hideaway on March 20. Jovita couldn't be sure, but when Nick asked for an extended posting, he was in an unusually blue mood. His usual, controlled effervescence and wry wit were missing in action. She sensed something was amiss, but ignored her premonitions and dispatched him to Guatemala on March 21, 1954, the first full day of spring.

Three months later, unexpected events prompted Jovita to end Nick's mission and summon him back to Jacksonville. Despite her order for the mandatory annual physical, the command did not reach him for nine months. He was too far in legend as Thomas Armstrong and too deep undercover.

Nick was swallowed up by revolution and had virtually vanished. He spent a year flying recycled P-51 Mustangs[**] in and out of the steamy, secluded jungles of El Quiché Department, Guatemala antagonizing Che Guevara's communist revolutionaries. He fought alongside a rag-tag band of guerillas and mercenaries who called themselves The Guatemalan Exile Forces. The entire operation was a continuation of the Agency's PBSUCCESS[**].

After a long campaign of hop-scotch photographic surveillance around Guatemala City, nuisance bombing raids on weapons caches and fuel depots, false radio news broadcasts, and countless drops of propaganda leaflets, the Coup of 1954 was proclaimed a success. Guevara and ousted President Árbenz fled into exile as soon as Carlos Armas became head of Guatemala's new military junta.

Address Unknown ...
The year that never was ...
Fernando's Havana Hideaway, Jacksonville, Florida
Behind the green door, Thursday morning, April 14, 1955

Nick instinctively exchanged glances with the barman as he stepped from the sidewalk, through the open door and approached the bar. Ollie nodded toward the back hall and said, "She's waiting for you."

For nearly a decade, Jovita's office was the closest thing to a living room Nicholas had known. There was comfort behind the green door to her office. His job was his home. Over the years, Jovita became the only reason he wanted to go home.

She stood up as he entered, stepped out from behind her desk and quickly studied him. He had lost a few pounds and was bronzed by the tropic sun, but otherwise, he was as she remembered. She motioned to the leather chair in front of her desk, turned, walked back to her seat and said, "Sit down,

Nick. It's good to have you back home, but it wasn't easy finding you. You left me hanging, you did. You should have checked in. I needed to contact you."

"I was lost in the assignment, Boss. Lost track of time, I guess."

She was standing with one hand on her desk. "Bullshit. Whatever it is that you think you can say to clear your conscience, I don't want to hear it. You should have checked in. This will not happen again."

"I understand. I was wrong. No excuses, Joey." He was uncharacteristically humble. Now was not the time for explanations. He had expected that she would be upset, and he was right.

Seconds ticked off the Big Ben hanging on the wall before she sat down, reached into her bottom desk drawer and brought out the bottle of Havana Club and two glasses. "Two fingers?" she asked as she poured, not intending to wait for an answer.

Jovita had two analysts, one associate and five additional field agents in her charge, but Nick was the singular subordinate to whom she offered alcohol. She had wondered about it years ago and attributed it to the concept that old habits are hard to break. He was her first field agent and they had shared rum at their first meeting in 1946. They also shared an intimate slice of personal history following the death of her father. Nick was in her thoughts as much as she was in his.

"Yes. Thanks." Slightly relieved that she hadn't imposed the Geneva Conventions** upon him, he reached to her desk and picked up his drink. So far, there hadn't been any surprises. He sipped at the golden liquid and watched as she slowly pushed her chair back from her desk. He heard her stockings sigh as she crossed her legs. Her eyes locked onto his. Some things hadn't changed. There was communication without a word.

"I've got news, Nick."

He set his glass back on the desk. "Go."

"I'm sorry, but I did try to recall you as soon as I found out.

"All I can do now is spit it out.

"Your military pay isn't going to Oshkosh any longer.

"Your wife Nora passed suddenly in May of last year.

"Cancer.

"I'm sorry."

His heart stopped. Butterflies flew through his gut. He swallowed the rum from his glass, and set it on her desk. The booze had drowned the bugs. He fell into Jovita's mocha eyes and forced his heart to beat again. He asked, "When?"

Softly, she said, "On May 19th. Your son was by her side. But there's more." She refilled his drink and watched for a reaction.

He remained stoic and repeated, "Go."

"Your son Alexander showed up here ... here at the Hideaway ... in the middle of June. He walked in the door with his brand new wife, a waitress from Appleton. They walked right in the door. They sat at the bar, had beer and peanuts ... asked me if I knew you, then he wrote his address on a beer coaster and they left."

"A beer coaster?"

She finished her rum and answered, "Yes. A beer coaster. I'll give it to you later."

"It was Alexander who told you that Nora died?"

"No, he didn't mention it, not a word. Like I said, he and his wife asked if I knew you back in Chicago ... I told them that I did, and that you sell war surplus in the Caribbean, and that you're gone most of the time. Then they left. They drove away in a cream Packard.

"After they were gone, I got on the horn*, did some checking and found out about Nora's sickness and death. Somehow, they must have followed some little bread crumbs that you left behind in a safety deposit box at the Bank of Detroit and came down here. I've since verified that they live right here in Florida, in Chumuckla, north of Pensacola, on a horse ranch. He got out of the Navy in February of last year and runs an engine shop. His wife was born Maryanne Dahl in Appleton, Wisconsin, and she's twenty-three and she's very pretty. He called her *Annie*. They were married in Mount Clemens, Michigan one week after they met."

He lit a Camel and drank half of his second glass of Havana Club. He breathed, "That takes care of that."

Jovita snapped, "What?!"

He put up his left hand in a gesture of surrender, and said, "Let me explain."

After he had told her the tangled tale of Katherine Dobbs, his granddaughters, and his sister-in-law, Eloisa Throckmorton, they agreed that silence is golden. If Katy and Eloisa's secrets were to be told, they could jeopardize Alex and Annie's new marriage.

"I've given our situation a good deal of thought over these past months. You and I need to start over, Nick. We need too.

"You might think that you're living life for your job, but you're wrong. I've been helping you nurture a surreptitious tightrope career, and we've been living rent-free in the job for the last nine years. We've been getting paid to deceive and delude and now the lies we have lived have caught up with both of us. I don't know how, but Alexander and his new wife followed you down here. They figured it all out, found me out and now they know that you're alive and well. And now the legends that you and I have created have to end as well. The Agency is pulling the plug. They have to. This ends now."

"What exactly does that mean, Joey?"

"You have to stop being so damn selfish, Nick. You need to share your feelings and share yourself or you'll be forever alone.

"It means no more field work for you or me. I'll put you in Ollie's slot. If you want it, I mean. You're approaching your ten-year limit anyway. We'll get married and sit on the beach and watch the sun paint those beautiful sangria sunsets. We can be ourselves and let the novelists create the legends."

End.

SINCERELY ...
(AND IN THEIR OWN WORDS) ...

As I was researching and writing the Throckmorton series of books, I asked twelve of the most prominent players to write a few words about their lives. I was fortunate enough to obtain six mini-autobiographies. Three players eagerly agreed, two needed a gentle push and one stubborn holdout needed some persuasion, but a Waffle House breakfast and a 750^{ml} bottle of *The Famous Grouse* blended single malt Scotch Whiskey did the trick.

Unfortunately, I wasn't able to get all the character portraits I sought. One refused because of a possible copyright conflict, another declined due to a contractual commitment with a big-name Vancouver film producer, two could not be located and two had sadly passed on. The remaining six agreed to create their personal portraits, if I accepted them verbatim and unedited. What follows are their unique stories, dated and transcribed here, from either dictated sound recordings or written submissions. These little tidbits of personal insight should grant the reader an unprecedented view into the very intimate thoughts of each character.

Edward R Hackemer

Jovita ... August 3, 1963

I was born and raised in Puerto Rico and, like my parents, I'm very proud to be American. Mama once told me to *live American, and dream Puerto Rican.* I still have command of the Spanish language, but I think I dream in English now.

My parents grew up in poverty; my mother on a sugar plantation on the north coast and my father as the eldest son of a tenant field hand. My father joined the United States Army during the First World War to guarantee his American citizenship and escape the poverty of the San Lorenzo tobacco fields. I had a simple childhood, but there was always food and shelter. And although I have been away from my island home for many, many years, I hold my heritage dear.

My papa became my only family after my mother's death when I was almost 17 and I imagine that being young and motherless helped me fit in as an Army brat. During my last year of high school, the Army was my only home. It and Papa provided a roof over my head, fed me, clothed me and educated me. Maybe the military was my surrogate mother, making sure I never strayed far, didn't break curfew and didn't question discipline. I leaned on my father and he supported me more than I can ever explain. He gave me help when I asked for it. Following the death of my mother, he helped me escape my personal hell in Puerto Rico. One month after my mother's death, Papa arranged to be transferred to the Canal Zone as a signals translator. Without a doubt, I am what I am today thanks to my father and the United States Army. I know my mother would be proud. I have never had a desire to return to Puerto Rico, likely because there are too many bad memories.

My mother had two children, but I guess you could say that I was an only child. My brother, Felipe died two days after he was born. I was just two years old then, and of course, I don't remember anything about it. Mama never really talked about it, and I never asked. God, I still miss her when I think about her.

I graduated second in my class from Cristóbal High School, United States Canal Zone, Panama, in 1939. Please don't get any lofty image of me because I graduated number two ... there were only nineteen students in my senior class.

I was accepted at Louisiana State University, Baton Rouge, for a degree in Humanities. As the years passed, and especially now that I think about it, I strongly suspected that my father and the Army had some input into my situation at LSU. In my junior year, I was recruited by a fellow named Howard Vance into the Army's Intelligence Agency and went through six months of intense officer training at Fort Polk. Army Intelligence was swallowed up by the OSS and well, that's when my career at the CIA began. I was fascinated with the idea of becoming an intelligence officer and fighting the bad guys. Ever since that market day in 1937, and the weeks and months that followed, I have always wanted to right wrongs. Later on, one year after I became an operative, my father's death further hardened my resolve.

My next big milestone came in 1946 when Central Intelligence promoted me to Operations Supervisor and I became the immediate supervisor to a former airman named Nicholas Throckmorton. My life really changed that day. He turned out to be a good agent; hard-headed, but dependable and predictable. And again, Nick proved to be dependable. He was flawed, but we all are in one way or another.

On the personal level, I kept Nick on the back burner for many years, as a matter of necessity maybe, simmering on the warm up until the early 1950's. It wasn't until Nick's wife Nora passed away and he reunited with his son Alexander that our relationship really started to bubble up to the surface.

Driven by regulation, loyalty and the Company's restrictions, Nick and I had to lie about our jobs and ourselves. I especially lied to Alex and Annie when I first met them, about not only my job and its relationship to Nick, but also about my home and my youth. I have been able to survive the very personal abuse that my uncle Horado forced upon me all those years ago in Puerto Rico and I am happy that I never told anyone except my Nick. I could not give my father that burden so soon after he and I lost my mother. I couldn't. It would have poisoned him and poisoned me all over again.

My mother's murder back in '37 and my father's death after the war at the hand of the Philippine Huk Communists still upset me. I've known a lot of death and violence. All during my youth, Puerto Rico was embroiled in a nationalist struggle. And it still is. And, like my island home, I guess that I struggled with my past. I know that I told countless untruths attempting to avoid the uncomfortable, personal questions about my political beliefs, personal history and professional obligations. I have kept many secrets. Personal and professional. I suppose that I will always have some. Always. There are things that my husband and I can never reveal.

I believe that over the years I have learned that tolerance is a great virtue, especially if you accept the shortcomings of the people around you. I know that it doesn't involve much forgiveness but it sure takes quite a bit of patience. I think the reward is worth the effort. I found love with my Nicholas and it grew stronger with our children, Roberta and Hector. Nick's son Alexander, his wife Annie and their children, Sarah, Karen and Herbert mean the world to me. I love them all, every one. I love them all very, very much.

Nora ... January 13, 1952

I think the best way to describe my life is to start at the beginning. I was born Nora Jean Sterescu in Gödöllö, Hungary, in 1911 and came to this country when I was eight years old. My younger sister Marie and I arrived under the wings of our father, Dominik and our mother Gabi. We originally settled in Oshkosh, Wisconsin, up until the time that my father got a job with the Ford Motor company in Detroit, Michigan. I spent my childhood in a very modest home in the Delray neighborhood of Detroit. My father and mother scraped for every cent and made sure Marie and I had shoes on our feet and clean underwear. I left school after the sixth grade and worked alongside my mother at her lunch wagon which she had set up in Detroit's warehouse district off Gratiot Avenue. It was at that lunch wagon that I met a young man that would forever change my life: Nicholas Throckmorton. He pulled my string and set me spinning like a toy top, wobbling off-center and scooting across the floor in all directions.

We were way too young and naïve. I was pregnant at fifteen and married to Nick a week before I turned sixteen. He had his eighteenth birthday three days before our wedding, that's how young we were. We were married in the back of the church, almost in secret, because I was so young and he was a non-Catholic. It was Nick, myself, my mother and father and the priest. So I guess you could say our marriage of convenience was doomed from the start. When our son Alexander was born, he became my life and my reason for living.

I was raised to believe that a wife should honor her husband and make him proud. My mother, Jesus rest her soul, told me on the day I got married to always have my husband's supper on the table and he would come home at night. She didn't know that an airbase always has a cafeteria with a pretty young thing with a smile, a full pot of coffee and a meat pie on the warm.

I don't know why, I never dared to ask and he never told me, but I think Nicholas escaped. He learned to fly and took off. I resented that. A lot. Maybe too much. Our marriage was spoilt from the get-go and maybe I was jealous of him and his freedom and his ability to simply get up and fly away.

I prayed and I learned. I needed to reconcile my anger and fear. Yes, fear. I was often afraid before I forgave his absence and his transgressions. He took care of Alex and me, but it wasn't enough. People in prison have a roof over their heads and food in their belly and clothes on their back too. Once I believed that a false angel could wash me clean and crisp as a starched white shirt from a Chinese laundry. I found out much too late that there are devils with forked tongues that can drink you dry.

Alexander and my faith were my lights during my time of dark defeat.

After my father passed away, I began to reflect more and more on my life, my mistakes and the forces that influenced the choices I made or were forced upon me. I was ridiculed, then abandoned and tempted and shamed so much by men I thought I knew and trusted. I think it's natural to blame others for what went wrong in the past, but I came to realize that it takes time and grace to reset your life and start over. I prayed then and I pray now. Sometimes you don't get the chance until much too late. That's why I think that we should glorify our faith every day.

It's easy to look back and see the things that I did wrong and the wrong that others did to me. It's easy to have regret and it's work to forgive. Forgiveness is the Holy way. I don't think emotion warrants forgiveness. Only thoughts and actions can be forgiven. I'm not making excuses. We learn by our missteps and are forgiven as we forgive. Thank you. Bless you.

Alexander ... December 25, 1952

I'm twenty four years old, so there's not much to tell about my life. I grew up in Detroit and spent the last four years and ten months in this man's Navy. When I get out, I think I'm going to sit around and do nothing for a while. Maybe a whole year. Then maybe I'll get a place in Texas or Oklahoma and raise horses. My buddy Zeke grew up on a horse ranch in Waco. And Katy loves horses, too. Who knows? Maybe we'll cross paths again someday. I wasted a whole year thinking I was in love with somebody who loved me.

Here it is Christmastime and this so-called United Nations 'Police Action' in Korea is still a killing stalemate. Katy got a set of orders out of here, God bless her. My TDY is over and I'm back aboard the Valley Forge. *Happy Valley* we call it, but right now I'm not jumping up and down and clicking my heels. Not at this moment, I'm not. I miss her. A lot. Zeke says that I'll soon get over her.

I can't hold it against her that she got out of here. And it's too damn bad she had to get sick just before she left. It's the luck of the draw, that's what it is. We knew it could end one way or another and I know we never made any promises to each other, but damn it all. It's a sonufabitch being alone at Christmas after you've been close to somebody like me and Katy were.

I prayed last night. I was laying in my bunk, looking straight up at the bottom of my bunk buddy's mattress, just six inches from my nose and I prayed to God. I don't often do that, pray I mean, but I did last night. I asked Him to watch over Katy for me. It ended bad, but down deep she's a good person. I hope she gets well soon and can go on, finish her Navy time and have a good life somewhere with someone. I can almost bet that she'll have a horse ranch someday.

The idea of buying or starting a horse ranch has crossed my mind a few times. I still have that five grand in the bank that the Old Man left me for college and I could use the GI Bill for a loan if I need it. So it's possible, I guess.

I wish the Chinese army would go back home and then we could quit bombing the hell out of the North Koreans and maybe end this bullshit war. That's what I want for Christmas. We need to get serious about it. Ending it, I mean. Sooner or later, we got to let the Chinese know that we're the ones that carry the big stick. Like back in '51, General MacArthur wanted to get serious and bomb the Yalu River with some clean little Cobalt 60 nuclear bombs and end this. The little fishes might glow in the dark, but no big deal. It would have kept the Chinese out and the killing would have ended. I think we could all be back home by now if Truman didn't fire him. Maybe after General Eisenhower gets sworn in as President he'll end this damn winless war. Generals know how to win wars or they wouldn't be generals for very long.

I'll probably go see Mom when I get my rotation orders back stateside before my discharge and spend some time up there in Oshkosh. Grandmother Gabi died a couple months back and Mom's living in that big old house by herself. Mom tells me she's doing okay with everything, though. She surprised me when she finally got her driver's license last year and bought a tried and true '47 Plymouth. That tells me she's doing all right, I think. She deserves to take it easy. I tell her that all the time in my letters home.

The Army still hasn't changed my father's Missing In Action status and they keep sending his pay to Mom. But it's obvious to me that the Old Man ain't coming home. I hope someday that they find out what happened to him. Not that it means much, but at least I'd know.

It's funny how it seems that things work out for the best. If I didn't flunk my vision test and was able to be a pilot, I probably never would have met Katy. I like my job. Flying backseat in a copter[*] gets me up in the air anyhow, and it beats tearing engines apart all day. Katy might be home by now.

I bought a Christmas card for Mom at the ships store and one for Katy, too and sent it to her old Fleet Services address. I hope they forward it to her. I imagine they will.

Merry Christmas, everybody.

Katherine ... April 1, 1954

My birthday is tomorrow, so I imagine that April Fool's Day is as good a day as any to explain what winds my springs and makes me tick. I think this is a good opportunity for me to explain my life from my point of view. I'm not ashamed of anything that I've done, although there are some things I wish I could do over again. Please don't misunderstand me, I don't have any misgivings, but there have been instances in my past when I made bad decisions. Someone once said that life is a 'learning experience'. I suppose it is.

I've always wondered what circumstances could have made my birth mother give me up for adoption. It's certain she never really knew me, because Mabel, my adoptive mother, the only mother I ever knew, she told me years ago, before she died, that she and my dad, Roger Dobbs adopted me at birth. My adoption certificate reads that I was born at Our Lady of Victory Hospital in Buffalo, New York on April 2, 1928 and that's the same day that my parents adopted me. I think that it's highly likely that Buffalo is my birth mother's home.

I delivered my baby girls last year, on June 21, and couldn't imagine giving them away. They deserve to grow up together, under one roof. God entrusted their lives to me for whatever reason and I wouldn't dare break that trust. It would be wrong every which way to Sunday.

I was harsh and selfish with Alexander. I needed to be, or the mess we were in would have become worse. As I've mentioned, I regret some of my past decisions, but now I believe that I've done right with my daughters. I didn't know that I was pregnant when I broke it off with Alex, but I surely was ill. I was also younger, foolish and decidedly presumptuous. I thought it was best to simply break it off and say goodbye. Goodness, the Navy handed me my rotation orders back stateside on the day I came down with the flu. Alex and I discussed our situation at length and on countless occasions when we were seeing each other. We agreed up front, from the first time the subject came up, that we would part amicably and cut our ties when the time came for us to split up. I know I hurt him, but that was our agreement going in and he knew it. He has no way to know, but it also hurt me at the time. His Navy enlistment was about to end and mine was just beginning. Furthermore, when you think about our affair, the Navy's regulation about fraternization between ranks makes sense. If we had only obeyed the rules, we could have avoided a great deal of grief. Of course, we took precautions, and used either my diaphragm or condoms, but it's apparent that latex leaks.

The doctors in Yokosuka were just as surprised as I was; not about how I managed to get pregnant, but about the fact that I was already three months along. Maybe my influenza was a Godsend. Perhaps it was His way of letting me know. No matter, my pregnancy was cause for discharge from the Navy and I immediately left Tokyo for San Diego and home to Syracuse. I embarrassed my parents; I know I did, despite their welcome home and support. Briefly, I considered contacting Alex. The decision tortured me, but I felt that we couldn't build a future together, despite the lives in my belly. Alex and I couldn't mesh as one soul, we were simply too dissimilar in our perception of life. I believed that would be detrimental to the formation of a family unit. On a certain level, we certainly were in tune, but other than that, we could never be broadcasting on the same frequency. I didn't want to force him into a situation that he didn't ask for or see coming. After the doctors heard two heartbeats and told me that I was carrying twins, it seemed to justify my original decision.

The good news is that my life now seems to be on a path forward and the pieces seem to be falling together. Last year, my Bachelor of Science degree in design bore some fruit and opened the door to a new life for my daughters and me. I was lucky enough to find a decent job at Kodak of Rochester, New York in product development and design. It pays well and the fringe benefits are excellent. They offer employee stock options and treat all their employees fairly, both men and women. There's health care available on the campus for myself and the girls and even baby-sitting right here at Kodak Park during my work hours. Additionally, I'm able to give my father the care he needs for his senility just down the road in Honeoye Falls.

Don't ask me exactly how, but last month I was able to finagle a way to list the twins' father on their birth certificates. Unlike me, my girls will know the names of their birth parents.

Thank you for allowing me to explain my life my way.

Eloisa ... February 14, 1953

I used to get sentimental over Valentine's Day when I was younger, but not so much anymore. It's more for the kids nowadays. They exchange those little cards in school and make those big, goofy eyes at each other. It's all in fun, isn't it?

Most of the adults who I have held or hold dear to me are from Buffalo. And at one time or another, we've all had our hearts broken. I imagine some of us have managed to live fruitful lives even with a broken heart, but some haven't. I'm not sure, but I think my old friend Phryne may have died years ago from a broken heart and too many sleeping pills, although I think she broke a few hearts on her own terms.

I've noticed that everyone who tells me that they're from Buffalo don't live there anymore. My sister Ginny and her husband Geoffrey in Sacramento, my late husband Leopold, his ex-wife Phryne, his brother Nick and me; we're all from Buffalo. I think the world is getting smaller. Airplanes, telephones and the television are making it smaller.

It amazes me how quickly time drifts away unnoticed and then completely disappears without so much as a whisper. Thank goodness memories don't disappear like time does. Sure, memories can fade if you don't think about them for a while, but I think you have to keep remembering the good times and forget the bad ones. Once you forget them, they're not memories anymore. They disappear if you don't remember.

I've been nauseous lately. Maybe what I'm experiencing is nothing more than some kind of germ. I don't think it's fair to even think about telling Nick. Even if I knew how to get ahold of him, I wouldn't want him to think that I set a trap for him. But then again, if I am pregnant, I don't know how I'd explain it to Shirley and Albert. The truth is always best, but the explanation would be truly difficult, let alone being a mother again at the tender age of forty-six. I imagine it would be best to tell the kids that one of the cops from the precinct is the baby's father. Or maybe I can get Fred to pop the question and marry me. That's possible. We're going to the pictures tonight to see Marilyn Monroe in that new film *Niagara* with Joseph Cotten.

Nicholas ... July 4, 1960

After the war, you could say that I kept flying. I spent years helping banana republic juntas establish air forces to enable their penny-ante border wars. Our surplus fighter aircraft gave the generalissimos bragging rights and I've watched them smile ear-to-ear, stick out their chests like a strutting rooster and pop their buttons when they'd walk past a hanger full of American-made fighter planes.

Those people were born into revolution. It's in their blood. It's a genetic, violent, inbred way of thinking and it's the only life they've ever known. From the Mayans to the Spanish Conquistadors to the Bolivar nationalists to today's Communist revolutionary. Forget their bananas and pineapples. Upheaval, killing, corruption and cocaine are the basis for the whole goddamn economy in Central America.

I've learned that there isn't a single system of government that hasn't already been tried and there are only four kinds.

You got the *religious fiefdom*; where the populace follows the divine leader with blind faith. They believe, so they follow.

Next is the *economic kingdom*. The indentured servants and tenants obey because the royal family and ruling class control the purse strings. The peasants either follow or starve.

The third is *ethical tyranny*. The dumb masses follow because they believe the lies and rumors that their supreme leader spews. And the lies are constant; totalitarian and constant.

Finally, there's the *democratic republic*. That's what we Americans enjoy. Representative rule is honest and safe. The problem is access of information. If the people aren't informed by an honest press, then the third type takes over: moral, political, *ethical tyranny*. That Nazi Joseph Goebbels knew it. He said, "Think of the press as a great keyboard that the government plays" or something like that.

The 40's and 50's were a very eventful time in my life ... personally, professionally, and indeed, transformative in more ways than I could have ever imagined. At times, it was a bumpy flight regardless of the weather.

A few times I have second-guessed a decision that I made or a course of action that I took. Generally, I would just chalk it up as field experience or on-the-job training, file an incident report if they asked for one, and complete the mission as ordered. I have never given it too much thought beyond that. Joey delegated the work and my job was the mission. The rest was up to the brass. What is done is done ... and what is to be will be ... and what could be doesn't concern me.

When I think about all the people I have known, and think about all their personal tragedies, I could be run over by a freight train and it couldn't be worse. I'm not in bad shape for the shape I'm in.

Too many politicians and philosophers try to impose their will on the rest of the world. They get together as one big mutual admiration society and sit inside their white marble halls and pontificate about how the world should be. They got a favorite idiom that they love to throw around: *all men are created equal.* That's fine, well and good ... I agree, but the underlying problem is that systems of *government are not created equal.* That's why the League of Nations failed. And that's why the United Nations will fail. I'll bet a dollar to a doughnut, so mark my words. After the First World War the League of Nations invented Belgium out of land they stole from France and the Kaiser, signed a political abomination they called the Treaty of Versailles, created the Weimar Republic, and planted the seeds that allowed Hitler to grow tall and strong.

And after World War II, the United Nations drew border lines across Korea and Vietnam that created more war. You can see how that's turning out. Just you wait and see what kind of mess the Russians are making with the borders in Europe. And the UN's biggest boner was dividing up Britain's Palestinian mandate into Jewish and Arab sectors in 1948. Sooner or later the world is going to have to pay the piper. Those people have been killing each other since the sand started falling through the hour glass.

I've killed billions of bugs in my lifetime, from crawling Boll Weevils in Arkansas to airborne Cicadas in Guadalajara. And I've probably killed hundreds of men, and maybe more, during the war. After the war, I killed in self-defense. I'm not proud of it or screaming it from the rooftops, but it was my job. A few could be considered retribution or righteous capital punishment done in the Biblical sense as justice served for women who were wronged by evil men.

When I left Buffalo in 1927 I was looking for my destiny, and chased it for twenty years until I found it in a Chicago gin mill in 1946. I knew as soon as I met her. I knew that Jovita was the love of my life.

Just like in the movies, Nora ended up being the girl left behind who nobody ever came home to. I discovered early that we were wrong for each other, and I denied it. I was guilty but never knew it until it was far too late. Now I'm trying to give Alex and me the second chance I never got. I can't do anything more.

I'm living my life for my three children, Alex, Roberta and Hector and my wife Jovita. My granddaughters Sarah and Elizabeth are the diamonds that Kate entrusted to Alex and Annie who last month blessed me with a grandson, Herbert.

Living and working here at the Hideaway as a mixologist is a helluva lot easier than pretending to be somebody else for somebody else's sake. The most stress I've encountered while tending bar has been trying create the perfect tequila sunrise**.

Glossary

aluminium	(archaic) aluminum
annual physical	(espionage) return to base
apoplexy, apoplectic	stroke, pertaining to stroke
banditos	(Spanglish) bandits
babysitter	body guard
blue suiter	(Air Force) in dress uniform
braes	Scottish pastoral hillsides
bupkis	zero, nothing
café con leche	(Spanish) coffee with frothed milk
Commie	communist
conga	tall, narrow hand drum similar to the shorter bongo
contrabandista	(Central America) smuggler
CONUS	the continental United States
copter	helicopter
coup d'état	(French) illegal or forceful change of government
cuy	grilled guinea pig
ditty (case or bag)	(nautical) bag for personal items
Federales	(Spanglish) Federal police
Foggy Bottom	(metonym) State Department HQ Washington, DC
fortnight	fourteen days; two weeks
GI	Government Issue
growler	crank-operated telephone that makes a growling sound
head	(naval) toilet
Heinie	(derogatory) German

helo	(must-use naval term for) helicopter
Hollywood shower	(naval) long shower that wastes water in port or on base
Hondo	Honduras
horn	telephone
hotsy-totsy	flirtatious
Ike	(nickname) President Eisenhower
je ne sais quoi	(French) something special
jeep	**General Purpose** ¼ ton vehicle
jinetera	(Cuban Spanish) prostitute
John Wayne (officer)	(naval) tough, no B.S. boss
kerfuffle	fuss
kinkajous	Central American rainforest mammal (honey bear)
kraut	(derogatory) German
lack-a-nookie	lack of sex
legend	assumed, false identity
Mafioso	member of crime syndicate
malta	(Caribbean) sweet, barley and hops non-alcoholic soft drink
mantecadito	(Puerto Rico) sugar cookies
Mata Hari	femme fatale, female spy
mess (hall)	(military) dining hall
mess deck intelligence	(naval) consensus
moniker	assumed name
mortadella	(Puerto Rico) cold cuts
nasty bag	(naval) bag or box lunch
nave	pew area of a church
NOC {'knock'}	unofficial double identity

OCS	Officer Candidate School
off the cob	corny, silly
pendejo	(Puerto Rico) idiot, low-life
permanent	(military oxymoron) no such thing
pickle(d)	drunk, intoxicated; problem
policía	(Spanish) police
potoo	a predatory nightjar, bird
quesito	(Puerto Rico) small pastry
RAF	(United Kingdom) Royal Air Force
ratline (nautical)	rope ladder on sail rigging
ratline (political)	route for human smuggling
real world, outside world	not military; civilian life
Russkie	(derogatory) Russian
Sasquatch	Big Foot
scuttlebutt	(nautical) an open barrel of drinking water OR (slang) rumor
seabag	(naval) duffle bag
shanghai	trick, kidnap
snafu	(military) situation normal all fouled up
snazzy	sharp, well dressed
TDY	(military) temporary duty
telephone tree	(military & government) each office telephones the next in line
tíck táck	(Puerto Rico) sugar cane vodka
tightrope (walker) (tightroper)	undercover (agent)
Troglodyte	caveman
turista	(Spanish) tourist
Yanqui	(Latin America) Yankee
Elvis reliquit aedificum	(Latin) Elvis has left the building
Qui veniunt et vade	(Latin) They come and they go

** The End Notes **

JOVITA ... Chapter One

World War I prompted the US Congress to pass the Jones-Shafroth Act on March 2, 1917, which granted US citizenship to the people of Puerto Rico. A few weeks after the bill's passage, President Wilson signed a compulsory military service Act of Congress, which ultimately drafted nearly 20,000 Puerto Rican men into military service during World War I. Although the Puerto Ricans were segregated and served mostly in Puerto Rico and the Canal Zone, about one hundred served in France with the 396th Infantry Regiment, known as the Harlem Hell Fighters, an infantry unit consisting of Blacks and Puerto Ricans.

Bacalaítos are deep-fried salt cod pancakes or fritters, crunchy on the outside and dense inside. They remain a staple street and fast food in Puerto Rico.

La Borinqueña is Puerto Rico's anthem and has a history back to 1867. *Boricua* is the original name given by the Taíno Indians to the island that was renamed *Puerto Rico* by the Spanish exploration and occupation. The song's lyrics were oftentimes deemed too radical and revolutionary for public gatherings. After decades of countless revisions, it was made Puerto Rico's official song in 1952.

The Ponce Massacre occurred on March 21, 1937 in Ponce, Puerto Rico. What precipitated the event was a march organized by the **Puerto Rican Nationalist Party** to protest  of the imprisonment of their leader, Pedro Albizu Campos, on charges of attempting to overthrow the government. Initially, the march organizers had asserted that it was a commemoration of the abolishment of slavery by the Spanish Assembly in 1873. There were 19 deaths: 17 civilian and 2 police. More than 230 were injured in the violence. Blame for the initial gunfire has gone back and forth. Regardless, the American-appointed governor, Blanton Winship, was removed by President Franklin D. Roosevelt in 1939. From its inception in 1922 until the death of its leader Pedro Campos in 1965, the Puerto Rican Nationalist Party believed in the concept of armed violence to overthrow of the American colonial government in Puerto Rico. In 1952, the current flag of Puerto Rico was officially adopted. Previously, both flags pictured here were illegal, considered revolutionary, and flying them was a felony.

The American Red Cross has held a strong presence in Puerto Rico since it established a Nursing Corps in 1898 and during its expansion for the World War I effort in 1917. The Spanish Red Cross was first on Puerto Rico in 1893.

Canal Zone, Panama was a territory of the United States from 1903 to 1979 when it was abolished by the Torrijos-Carter Treaty (Presidents of Panama and USA) of 1977. Interest in building a canal connecting the Atlantic and Pacific oceans started in 1826, spurred by the success of the *Erie Canal* that was dug between Albany and Buffalo, New York. Actual construction of the canal began in 1904 and was completed in 1914. Under treaty from 1903, the US paid Panama $10 million with annual payment of $250,000. All of which were to be invested in Panama. During the time as an unincorporated territory, the United States kept a strong military presence in the Canal Zone. Panama has the strongest economy in Central America and the US dollar is the official paper currency. Panama does mint their own coinage, based on the Panamanian *Balboa*, which is traded on par with the US dollar.

Segregation (by sex) in the armed forces of the US Military still exists, often blamed on structural and mechanical design. For example, the space restrictions for separate sleeping, rest room or bathing accommodations.

Pink and green army dress uniforms (1942-54) were olive drab wool jackets and light brown shirts and slacks for men and knee-length skirts for women. The brown was of a shade of color that if seen in odd light, it appeared to be pink.

Office of Strategic Services (OSS) was officially established by President Franklin D. Roosevelt) on June 13, 1942. The idea was to centralize the uncoordinated intelligence agencies of the Army and Navy intelligence branches. The agency recruited anyone from anywhere for anything and used them where their skills warranted. The OSS was officially disbanded on October 1, 1945 when it was fragmented back into the Department of State and War Department. It reappeared as the **Central Intelligence Group (CIG)** in January, 1946 when President Harry S. Truman created the National Intelligence Authority. With the passage of the National Security Act in September, 1947 the **Central Intelligence Agency (CIA)** was created. The agency's unofficial motto is: *You shall know the truth and the truth shall make you free.* (John 8:32).

Mata Hari (Margaretha Geertruida Zelle) was a Dutch-born exotic dancer who traveled freely throughout Europe during World War I. She gained her fifteen minutes of espionage fame given her reputation as a femme-fatale. She married at age 18 to a man 20 years her senior, bore two children, both of whom died from syphilis and/or its treatment. Thought to be a double-agent, she was executed at age 41 by a French firing squad in 1917 for spying for Germany.

The National Park Service worked with the OSS to establish top-secret training centers throughout the country. The remote locations of parks such as The Badlands of South Dakota, the Catoctin Mountains in Maryland and the Florida Everglades, helped disguise the clandestine activity. One specific location named *Camp X* was dubbed the 'school of mayhem and murder'. Located near Toronto, Canada, it was where paramilitary, hand-to-hand and commando tactics were taught. It has been said that some attendees of the camp were Ian Fleming (author of the *James Bond 007* novels), Roald Dahl (the author of *James and the Giant Peach* and *Charlie and the Chocolate Factory*), General William J. Donovan (head of the CIA), and Paul Dehn (screenwriter of *Murder on the Orient Express*, *Goldfinger* and *Planet of the Apes*).

DGER (Direcion Generale des Etudes et Recherches) was the General Directorate for Studies and Research, the Free French spy agency of World War II. Post war, in 1943, it morphed into the DGSE (General Directorate for External Security).

The Doolittle Raid was the first bombing of Japan's mainland in WW II. It occurred on April 18, 1942 and was carried out by the Army Air Corps with fifteen B-25 Mitchell bombers taking off from the deck of an aircraft carrier, the USS Hornet. It was a morale booster for the United States and a blow to the Japanese. Although the military consequences were insignificant, it was the first ever air raid by bomber aircraft made from a carrier. The B-25's met no Japanese resistance and because they were unable to land on the carrier, fourteen planes purposely crashed in China or the sea, and one landed in Russia. Three crew were killed in action and eight captured by the Japanese in China as POW. Three were executed and one died in captivity.

Ballpoint pens were patented in 1943 by brothers László and György Bíró in Argentina. The pen was marketed in October, 1945 at Gimbels department store in New York for $12.50 apiece. ($170US - 2016 dollars). Ballpoint popularity sky rocketed and the price dropped dramatically by 1946. The popular throw-away ten-for-a-dollar Bic pen of today was introduced in 1953 by Marcel Bich.

War Surplus was a burgeoning business after World War II. Millions of dollars worth of equipment went for a fraction of its original cost to the American taxpayer. Everything from typewriters to fighter aircraft made their way to clearing houses and high bidders around the world. Flamethrowers used in the Pacific and Europe to clear enemy bunkers were sold as "weed killers and underbrush removal tools" for a mere $40 apiece. Powerful diesel generators went for $200-$400. Latin American governments were the largest customers of used American aircraft.

Operation Paperclip was initiated by the OSS (soon to be the Central Intelligence Group) in 1945. President Truman specifically wanted to exclude members of the Nazi party who had committed atrocities. That policy was difficult to enforce, given the underlying purpose of the program: get as much information as possible on Germany's rocket program. By the end of 1946, more than 1,800 German scientists were "evacuated" from German soil to Fort Bliss, Texas. After further investigation and *de-Nazification*, about 3,700 family members were brought to the United States. Great Britain and the Soviet Union had similar programs but the American effort was the most successful.

Bariloche, Argentina (officially known as San Carlos de Bariloche) is located in Patagonia, Argentina, just east of the Chilean border. In the early 1900's it became known as an Alpine ski and recreation center in South America and had the nickname of 'Little Switzerland'. Beginning in 1939, a flood of German and Austrian immigrants began to fill the town. After the World War II, it was discovered that several Nazis had escaped post-war imprisonment and fled to South America. There were reports that Adolf Hitler and his lover Eva Braun lived about three miles east of Bariloche until the early 1960's. US President Dwight D. Eisenhower visited

Bariloche in 1960, while on a tour of Brazil, Argentina, Chile and Uruguay. All of these South American nations were known to grant 'off the record' asylum to Nazi fugitives. Some have suggested that the President's visit to Bariloche (indeed an out-of-the-way destination) was to attend Hitler's funeral. Bariloche, as picturesque as it may be, is no Buenos Aires.

Berchtesgaden is a location in Bavaria, Germany. It was the vacation spot favored by German Chancellor, Fuehrer Adolf Hitler.

Ratlines were multi-national networks established after World War II had ended in Europe. There were several operations in various countries carried out by governments, spy agencies, political and religious groups (one of which was the Vatican). Ex-Nazis, Italian fascists and other various expatriates were smuggled across borders and found their way to Central and South America. The trip oftentimes took months, avoiding capture or execution.

Böblingen is a city in the Baden-Württemberg district of Germany where large underground facilities were located that provided cover for Nazi tanks and aircraft. Jet propulsion research was said to have been conducted there as well. The Nazis sabotaged and destroyed many of the caverns and tunnels after the Allied invasion and prior to the American occupation. Field Marshal Erwin Romel (The Desert Fox) once commanded a Panzer (tank) company in Böblingen and the Luftwaffe operated a squadron of fighter aircraft that was able to safely take off and land from a neighboring section of the Autobahn highway system.

British Honduras was located south of Mexico and east of Guatemala on the Gulf of Mexico, and was the last colony of Great Britain in the Americas. It became a crown colony in 1862, a self-governing colony in 1964, renamed **Belize** in 1973 and totally independent in 1981.

Hukbalahap was a Communist guerrilla movement active in the Philippines from 1940 to 1965. Rag-tag units on the island of Luzon harassed and fought against the Japanese occupiers during WWII. After 1946, their ranks swelled and the *'Huks'* violently promoted the overthrow of the Philippine government. At their peak, they controlled 75% of the island of Luzon.

NASJAX is the acronym for Naval Air Station Jacksonville. It was built in 1940 and became an important part of the US effort in the Caribbean during WW II. During the war, the base was home to 1500 German prisoners.

NORA ... Chapter Two

Harry (*Slug*) Heilmann played major league baseball with the Detroit Tigers (1914, 1916-29) He played right field and first base, and is one of only five American League players to bat .400 in a season, with a lifetime average of .342. He was nicknamed *slug* because of his slow running speed. From 1942-50 he was the official broadcast voice of the Detroit Tigers.

Western Union was formed from competing companies and in 1856, Ezra Cornell of Rochester, New York touted its service of sending telegraph messages across the country in two days. In 1843, the nation's first telegraph line from Washington, DC to Baltimore, Maryland had been commissioned by Congress at a cost of $30,000. It opened on May 24, 1844, when Samuel Morse keyed the Biblical message *"What hath God wrought"*.

The company that once employed an army of young men on bicycles across the country also has a storied list of commercial innovations. From stock exchange ticker tapes, the first commercial credit card in 1914, teletypewriters, microwave communications, to singing telegrams and the candy-gram, Western Union has spread worldwide news and information. On Friday, January 27, 2006, Western Union's last telegraph was sent. Because punctuation cost more than letters of the alphabet, periods were oftentimes omitted. The word *stop* was free, and was commonly used to end sentences. The company now specializes in money transfers.

Woolworth was the common reference to America's premier five-and-dime store, *F.W Woolworth*. It was founded in 1878 in Utica, New York by Frank Winfield Woolworth and grew to become the largest variety store in the United States. By 1912, the chain was America's largest retailer with nearly 600 stores.

Oshkosh Motor Truck Manufacturing Company was founded by William Besserdich and Bernhard Mosling. It has been headquartered in Oshkosh, Wisconsin since 1918, and employs about 13,000 worldwide. The company makes heavy duty construction and specialty trucks as well as military vehicles. The rugged dependability of Oshkosh equipment has nurtured a loyal following among construction and snow removal customers.

ALEXANDER ... Chapter Three

"Pomp and Circumstance" It would be an anomaly if any high school — or college — graduate in the United States didn't march into the auditorium or onto the field to this song, either blasted by a household stereo system or played by the school band. Composed by Sir Edward Elgar but named for a verse in *Othello*, "March No. 1 in D Minor" is the typically performed American version. "The Graduation March" is the *Trio* section of the song, originally called "Land of Hope and Glory," first played at a graduation ceremony at Yale in 1905, the year Elgar received an honorary Doctorate of Music from that school.

Good Humor ice cream company was founded by Harry Burt in Youngstown, Ohio in 1920 and by the 1930's, it was a nationwide distributor of ice cream novelties. Their chocolate covered 'ice cream on a stick' was sold from 'sales cars' across the country. At the company's peak, more than half of their customers were under the age of twelve.

Sophie Tucker was widely known as "The Last of the Red-Hot Mamas". A star of vaudeville and burlesque halls in the 1920's, she began her career wearing burnt-cork blackface and miming Southern black singers. In the 1940's she promoted "fat girl" humor in her act with songs such as *I Don't Want to Get Thin* and *Nobody Loves a Fat Girl, But Oh How a Fat Girl Can Love*.

The Life Of Riley was an extremely popular 30-minute radio soap opera that aired from 1941 until 1951. It was a situation comedy that centered on a hapless, middle-class family (Riley). In 1949, a TV series was developed that originally stared Jackie Gleason and later William Bendix as Chester A. Riley, a riveter at a California aircraft assembly line. The television show lasted six seasons. The show was truly a groundbreaker and molded many television classics: *The Honeymooners, The Flintstones, Married With Children, All In The Family and The King Of Queens.*

Subic Bay, Luzon, the Philippines was home to the largest overseas US military installation outside of the United States. At 260 square miles, the Naval Installation at Subic Bay had the largest Navy Post Exchange in the world and dispensed more fuel than any other US military post. The city of Olongapo and the town of Barrio Baretto played host to American servicemen on R&R leave from 1899 until 1992, when the US relinquished control of the base to the Philippine government.

KATHERINE ... Chapter Four

Sasebo, Japan first became a naval base in 1883 when Admiral Tōgō Heihachirō established a hub for the Japanese Imperial Navy. During WW II, about 60,000 Japanese personnel were stationed on the base. After the Japanese surrender, the US Seventh Fleet began using Sasebo as a deep-water port and for Naval Fleet Services. Kim Il Sung (Supreme Leader of North Korea) ordered the invasion of South Korea on June 25, 1950 and effectively started the Korean War. Sasebo instantly became a central staging area and supply hub for United Nations forces in Korea. Currently, Japan Self-Defense Forces occupy the base along with US Naval 7th Fleet Support Services.

Fanny Hill* and *Lady Chatterley's Lover are erotic novels first published in 1748 and 1928 respectively that were considered pornographic in their time. *Fanny Hill* is the popular name used for the actual title of *Memoirs of a Woman of Pleasure.*

Chi Omega (XΩ) is the largest woman's fraternity and a member of the National Pan-Hellenic Conference with over 180 active chapters on campuses nationwide.

Carrier Corporation is the heating, ventilation and air conditioning company founded by Cornell University graduate Willis Carrier, a mechanical engineer from Buffalo, New York. He built the first working air conditioner in 1902, formed the Carrier company in 1915. Carrier employed thousands of workers in their Solvay factory, which is a suburb of Syracuse, New York. Currently, the company is headquartered in Charlotte, North Carolina.

Recruitment of women for service in the Army, Navy, Air Force and Marines peaked during the early 1950's. The Armed Forces faced personnel shortages at the onset of the Korean conflict. Regardless, women had restricted career opportunities. The vast majority of women were nurses, while the remainder worked in "pink collar" personnel and administrative positions. Basic training and boot camp instruction included stereotypical classes in acceptable application of makeup and etiquette lessons. A 1950's Army pamphlet stated, *'In authorizing job assignments for women, particular care must be taken to see that the job does not involve a type of duty that violates our concept of proper employment for sisters and girlfriends. For example, in the military transport field, women will not drive heavy trucks.'*

Female enlistees had a poor rate of retention. In fact, one third (33%) left service before completing their first year. Of that number, more than 90% were due to pregnancy. On April 27, 1951 President Harry S. Truman signed Executive Order #EO 10240, directing all branches of the military to discharge females if they became pregnant, gave birth to a child, or became a parent by adoption.

The recruitment effort to enlist more women did not produce as much success as desired. Also in 1951, as an attempt to enhance female enlistment, Secretary of Defense George Marshall created a panel of civilian women called the Defense Advisory Committee on Women in the Service (DACOWITS). You honestly cannot make this stuff up. As of this writing, this committee is still in existence.

TWA (Trans World Airlines) began as Transcontinental and Western Air 1925. Howard Hughes acquired the company after World War II and expanded service to Europe, Asia and the Middle East. It was then the world's second largest carrier next to Pan Am (Pan American Airways). Competition and the 1978 Airline Deregulation Act during the Presidency of Jimmy Carter led to its demise.

Wings cigarettes, along with other brands that include Camel, Chesterfield, Old Gold, Phillip Morris and Lucky Strike were included in US Military C-rations, army field kitchens and bagged lunches up to 1975. It was then that some concern was expressed over the health effects of smoking. During the 1940's and 50's, Wings advertised a pack of twenty cigarettes with the slogan "fifteen-cent quality for ten cents". Marine Corps, Navy, Army and Air Force planes and pilots were extensively used in advertising.

The United States Air Force was established in September, 1947 from the US Army Air Corps.

Nissen huts were developed by the British armed forces during World War I. They are very much like American-made Quonset huts, consisting of corrugated steel bent and formed to arched girders to create a building that resembles a half-circle. Their largest asset is that they assemble fast, are portable and study. They can be built on a concrete slab, wooden pallets or directly on the ground.

No man's land usually refers to the deadly battle zone located between trenches occupied by opposition forces during World War I.

Dungarees were the US Navy uniform worn by enlisted sailors in grades E1-E6 from 1917-2000. It consisted of a blue chambray shirt, white t-shirt, denim bell-bottom pants, the white Dixie-cup hat, or blue baseball cap. Blue, wool-knit watch caps were authorized for cold weather wear. Footgear was low boots, deck boots or flight boots.

General Orders 5370.2B Prohibits unduly familiar relationships between officer and enlisted personnel that do not respect the differences in grade or rank. Transgressions are punishable under Article 92, Uniform Code of Military Justice, up to and including incarceration and dishonorable discharge.

Typhoon Ruth was a Category 4 storm that struck Japan and rolled directly over Sasebo on October 15, 1951. It had maximum sustained winds of 140 mph and created 30-40 foot waves. The storm killed 1300 people in its path and destroyed more than 30,000 homes during its ten-day, October 9-18 rampage.

Batten down the hatches is an idiom with naval origins. 'Batten' are small strips of wood that were nailed over the edges of canvas that was spread over deck hatches. The secured canvas kept swells of seawater out of the bowels of the ship.

USO is the acronym for the United Service Organization that was founded in 1941. It worked with the War Department (now the Department of Defense) and coordinated private and non-profit funding for the entertainment of American troops. Hundreds of celebrities like Bob Hope and Marilyn Monroe have visited countless GIs during war and peace from Korea to Iraq to Japan and over a dozen more countries.

C-rations were individual pre cooked, prepared rations for military forces in the field from 1938 until 1958. A typical box of rations consisted of:

- **canned meat entrée** (such as Meat Chunks and Beans or Vienna Sausage and Beans)
- **bread components** one packet each of powdered milk, coffee & sugar, 5 crackers, 2 cookies, a 1½ oz tin of jam, and one 12 oz can of fruit cocktail
- **accessory pack** (typical contents: Wrigley's gum, 4 sheets of toilet paper, salt, wooden spoon, a pack of 4 Old Gold cigarettes)
- **(one) p38** thumb-and-finger can opener

Anti-psychotic drugs such as Thorazine (chlorpromazine) were part of a first generation of drugs introduced in the 1950's used to treat psychotic disorders such as schizophrenia. When first introduced, some physicians prescribed these new anti-psychotics for symptoms of "housewife fatigue" and "feminine lethargy".

The Occupation of Japan was the only occupation of the defeated Axis powers of World War II that excluded the Soviet Union. It took the United States and Great Britain six years to transform the Empire of Japan into a parliamentary democracy. Termed "Operation Blacklist", the occupation ended on April 28, 1952 with the San Francisco Peace Treaty.

Vicks VapoRub was developed in 1894 by Lunsford Richardson and manufactured by Richardson-Vicks in the USA. Its primary uses are as a cough suppressant and decongestant. The 'active' ingredients are listed as menthol, Eucalyptus oil and synthetic camphor. 'Inactive' ingredients are nutmeg oil, turpentine oil and petrolatum (such as Vaseline).

ELOISA ... Chapter Five

Betty Crocker was a character originally developed in 1921 by the Washburn-Crosby Company, which later became General Mills. She was created to personalize the brand and promote sales. In 1924, fictional Betty began a career as a teacher in an on-air radio cooking school. Betty Crocker cookbooks were first published in 1930 and continue to be popular to this day.

Reader's Digest magazine is a popular general interest monthly magazine that features articles culled from other major publications, reader-submitted wit and experiences. In 1950, the company began publishing condensed books as *Reader's Digest Condensed Books* by direct-mail advertising in their monthly periodical. A hardcover volume of sharply abridged popular novels or non-fiction stories was marketed four times a year. Generally, there were five separate titles in each edition. Reader's Digest magazine was first published in 1922 and currently has a circulation of about five million.

The Presidio is a tract of land on the northern tip of San Francisco, California, on the southern terminus of the Golden Gate Bridge. It was a United States Army installation from 1848 until 1994 when it was transferred to the National Park Service. Of all American military bases, the Presidio was by far the most prestigious, scenic, well groomed and picturesque.

The Second Red Scare lasted roughly from 1950 through 1956. During that era, strong suspicion and fear over communist activity in the United States created what later became known as *McCarthyism,* named after Republican U.S. Senator Joseph McCarthy of Wisconsin. Concern over Soviet and Chinese espionage and sabotage led to scrutiny of members of the communist party. Much of the paranoia during the 1950's can be traced back long before Senator McCarthy to the **First Red Scare** of the early 1920's, when the communists were successful with infiltration efforts into the early labor movement, and the infatuation of the intellectual community with the burgeoning political ideology and its promise of a workable Garden of Eden.

Kazoo is a hand-held music instrument that makes timbral, or

buzzing sounds from a vibrating membrane of rubber or thin metal. The first patent for a 'kazoo' was in 1883 by Warren Frost, but did not resemble the modern kazoo. George Smith of Buffalo, New York patented the metal kazoo of today in 1902. In 1916, the Original American Kazoo Company began manufacturing the instruments in Eden, New York, a small rural community south of Buffalo. The Kazoo Factory is still in operation today, makes about 1.5 million units a year and houses the Kazoo Museum. The fun instruments measure about five inches long and have a worldwide following of musicians and performing bands. While the instrument has no connection to the city, Kalamazoo, Michigan has the nickname "Kazoo".

Never-Never Land is a real place. The term was first used in the late 1800's when early settlers described the vast uninhabited areas if Australia which now occupy parts of Queensland and the Northern Territory as the "Never-never". In everyday conversation, the term can relate a form of dismissive attitude, a disconnection from reality, or some sort of Utopian paradise.

Yippee-i-o-ki-ay is an expression found in the lyrics of the song *I'm an Old Cowhand (From the Rio Grande)*. It was sung by Bing Crosby in his starring role in the 1936 film *Rhythm on the Range*. Roy Rogers and the Sons of the Pioneers popularized it further a few years after the movie's release. In 1988, Bruce Willis somewhat altered the phrase in the film *Die Hard*.

Barney Google is a comic strip character created by Billy

DeBeck in 1919. Big-eyed Barney and his sidekick Snuffy Smith spread their antics across two dozen different countries. The strip coined many terms popular to this day, including *doodle bug, hotsy-totsy, great balls o' fire, horsefeathers* and *googly eyes*. The word *google* was first introduced in Vincent Vickers' 1913 book "The Google Book" which was about a make-believe place called *Googleland.*

Howdy Doody was the wooden puppet star of the Howdy Doody Show produced by E. Roger Muir. The children's show ran on CBS television from 1947 until 1960. Howdy was created by radio personality *Buffalo Bob Smith*, who hailed from Buffalo, NY and ultimately became Howdy's 'handler' and co-star. An integral part of the show was a studio audience of about forty children who made up *The Peanut Gallery*. Buffalo Bob opened every show by asking, "Hey kids, what time is it?" The Peanut Gallery would then answer in unison, "It's

Howdy Doody time!" Howdy's twin brother was *Double Doody*. He also had an adopted sister named *Heidi Doody*.

NICHOLAS ... Chapter Six

(Wild Bill) William J. Donovan was the man behind the creation of the OSS. A native of Buffalo, New York, Donovan served honorably in both World Wars. He is known as "Father of American Intelligence" and the "Father of Central Intelligence". He is only person ever to receive all four of the highest honors for an American: The Medal of Honor, the Distinguished Service Cross, the Distinguished Service Medal (3), and the National Security Medal. He was also awarded the Silver Star and Purple Heart (2). He was an advocate for fair treatment of women in the workplace.

The Yalta Conference was held in February, 1945 in the resort city of Yalta, Crimea on the Black Sea. Roosevelt, Churchill and Stalin met to discuss the end of World War II. The controversial meeting divided Europe into spheres of influence controlled by Russia and the Western Allies. Nations were built, borders were redrawn and the Cold War began.

Fulgencio Batista was President of Cuba from 1952 until his overthrow in 1959 by the revolution of Fidel Castro. His rise to power began in the 1933 Revolution of the Sergeants. As the de facto leader, he empowered puppet regimes until his election as President in 1940. After World War II, Batista formed strong alliances with the United States government, American organized crime and multi-national control of Cuba's sugar and tobacco industries. His rule was marked with corruption, payoffs, bribery and brutal enforcement. He was identified with moniker: *el Presidente.*

el Presidente (Spanish for "the President") is a cocktail that originated in Havana, Cuba during the United States'

Prohibition era of the 1920's. It consists of 2 ounces of rum, 1 ounce of Curacao, 1 ounce of dry vermouth, and a dash of grenadine. It is served straight up, without ice and has the soft burgundy color of cranberry juice.

Moncada Barracks is a national historic site in Cuba. A group of revolutionaries led by Fidel Castro attacked the Cuban army garrison at Santiago de Cuba on July 29, 1953. The attack is considered the beginning of the Cuban Revolution. Fidel and his brother Raúl were among 51 captured revolutionaries to stand trial and sentenced to prison.

BRAC (Buró de Represión de Actividades Comunistas) The Bureau for Repression of Communist Activities was the brutal Cuban secret police set up by President Batista to combat the revolutionary *26th of July Movement* of Fidel Castro. It was commanded by Mariano Faget, who also ran a counter-espionage unit for Batista during WWII that hunted Nazis and fascist agents.

The Pan American Highway was a long dreamed-of road project connecting North, Central and South America that finally got underway in July, 1937 with a treaty signed by Bolivia, Chile, Colombia, Costa Rica, El Salvador, Guatemala, Honduras, Mexico, Nicaragua, Panama, Peru, and the United States. By 1930, only Mexico had completed construction of its section. Currently, it is still not complete. Its unofficial length is measured at 19,000 miles from Alaska to Argentina.

WASP & WAFS were non-combat units of the Army Air Corps during World War II from 1942 until 1944. More than 1000 members of the Women Airforce Service Pilots and Women's Auxiliary Ferrying Squadron were used as flight training instructors, glider tow pilots, test flying, and transferring aircraft all over the globe or for towing targets during air-to-air and anti-aircraft gunnery practice. Nearly 85% of the women stayed in service after the units were disbanded in December of 1944.

The Somoza family ruled Nicaragua from 1927 to 1979 as a military dictatorship in a quasi-democratic society. Assassinations, land seizures, kidnapping and political corruption were the accepted norm.

Plenitud is Spanish, and translates into English as 'wholeness', 'completeness' or 'quiet time'. It is a term that Latin cultures equate with midday naps (siestas) or rest.

Sopa de Caracol is traditional, hearty Nicaraguan seafood chowder made from large chucks of sea snails (conch), onions, carrots, green bananas and coconut milk.

Panama hats originated in Ecuador and are traditionally made of woven palm leaves. They remain popular today in Central and South America.

Jack Armstrong, the All-American Boy was a syndicated national radio show from 1933 until 1951. Boys during the Great Depression years and World War II had their ears glued to radio receivers for fifteen action-filled minutes each week. General Mills sponsored the program, encouraging all American boys to eat their *Wheaties* for breakfast. During its final season of 1950-51, it ran in a full thirty-minute format with the title "Armstrong of the SBI". Jack had graduated to an adult government agent for the fictitious "Special Bureau of Investigation". The show entered the Radio Hall of Fame in 1989.

Walther PPK is a double action, self-loading pistol first manufactured in 1908 by Waffenfabrik Walther of Thuringen, Germany. It became the preferred weapon of the military and law enforcement because a round could be safely kept in the chamber and ready to fire. Modern production of the legendary PPK (Polizeipistole Kriminalmodell – Police Pistol Detective Model) began in 1952 by French manufacuturer Manurhin. Walthers are available in various sizes but the semi-automatic, 7.65mm is a favorite of law enforcement and military users. Ian Flemming made it James Bond's weapon of choice. The pistol is currently manufactured under license in the United States by Smith & Wesson.

The American Embassy, Havana, Cuba is located on Havana's picturesque Malecón oceanside parkway. It is six stories of concrete, steel and glass designed and built in 'Brutalist' style and first opened in March of 1953. The building was air conditioned by Carrier Corporation of Syracuse, New York.

After the Cuban Revolution, President Eisenhower ended US diplomatic ties and the embassy was closed in January, 1961. From 1977 until 2015 it housed the US Interests Section under the authority of the government of Switzerland, who ran the Swiss Embassy in the original building. The United States and Cuba resumed diplomatic relations in 2015 and once again the building is used as and American Embassy.

Isle of Pines (Isla de Pinos) is the seventh-largest Caribbean island (850 square miles) and the second largest island of the nation of Cuba. It lies in the central Caribbean about ninety air-miles directly south of Havana. During its history, the island was also known as *The Island of Parrots* and *Treasure Island*, based on neighboring pirate activity. In the early 20th Century, either American logging interests, or private American citizens owned 95% of the island. The 1904 Hay-Quesada Treaty between the US and Cuba ceded control of the island to Cuba, but the treaty wasn't ratified by the US Senate until 1925. In 1978, Fidel Castro renamed the island as *Isla de la Juventud* (The Isle of Youth).

Argentine Spanish (Rioplatense Spanish) is a dialect spoken in and around the Río de la Plata Basin of Argentina, Uruguay and parts of Bolivia. It was highly influenced by Italian, Basque, Portuguese and French immigrants. American and

British English also helped influence the language in the fields of business, education, agriculture and industry.

Brylcreem Boy was a slang term used by US Army Air Corps flyers during World War II when referring to British (Royal Air Force) pilots. Brylcreem is a British men's hair dressing introduced in 1928 made of water, mineral oil, and emulsified bees' wax. The Brits had a propensity to use a little more than "a little dab will do you".

Ernesto (Che) Guevara was an Argentinean Marxist revolutionary. A 1958 CIA report described Guevara as "quite well read" and added the distinction "Che is fairly intellectual for a Latino." In the early 1950s, he rallied a band of rebels against the United Fruit Company's perceived abuse of land and native labor at its banana plantations in Guatemala. He was behind armed revolutions in Cuba, Bolivia and the Congo and a founding driving force in the Marxist ideology of armed revolt. In 1967, assisted by intelligence from the CIA, Che was captured by Bolivian rangers and on October 9, Bolivian President René Barrientos ordered his execution. Although much of the concept of armed uprising has dwindled to a trickle, the Progressive Labor Party of the US still pursues the global goal of worldwide Communist revolution.

PBSUCCESS was a covert operation of the CIA that US President Dwight D. Eisenhower authorized in August of 1953. President Truman first initiated the clandestine program as *PBFORTUNE* in late 1952. It ended on July 27, 1954 when coup d'état[*] replaced the democratically elected Guatemalan President Jacobo Árbenz with the military dictatorship of Carlos Castillo Armas, the first in a series of US-CIA-backed authoritarian rulers in Guatemala. Some sources have interestingly suggested that the "PB" acronym is the shortened form of "Pineapple Banana". Years after the overthrow of the Árbenz government, the leader of the Guatemalan Communist Party, José Manuel Fortuny proclaimed, "The (Americans) would have defeated us whether or not we grew bananas."

Official CIA documents released on May 23, 1997 revealed that the operation intended to overthrow the government of Guatemala by any means deemed necessary by CIA field operatives, up to and including assassination. At the conclusion of the initial campaign, the CIA launched operation *PBHISTORY* to justify the results and counter international criticism.

(This author encourages the interested reader to do additional research on this topic. It is too deep, twisted and disturbing to attempt disclosure within the pages of this novel. In the 1940s and 50s, United Fruit Corporation held strong interests throughout Guatemala, as did US Secretary of State John Foster Dulles and his brother, CIA Director Allen Dulles.)

Presidio Modelo was a prison on Isle of Pines (*Isla de la Juventud*) built between 1926-28. The "model garrison" was built to be a modern, humane prison that consisted of five, five-story circular buildings of individual jail cells capable of housing up to 2,500 inmates, each cell with windows to the outside world. It was where most of the survivors of Castro's failed 1953 attack on the Moncada Barracks were incarcerated. Fidel Castro and his brother Raúl were inmates from 1953-55. As a twist of fate, Castro began to fill the prison with more than 4,000 of his political enemies after the fall of Batista's regime. Revolts and hunger strikes plagued the jailhouse after the Cuban Revolution of 1959, so much so that Castro had tons of dynamite placed in the underground passages of the prison just prior to the Bay of Pigs invasion as a threat to the unrest. Castro closed the institution in 1967 and converted it into a museum.

Hijackers first struck the airline industry in 1931, when a group of armed revolutionaries commandeered a Ford Tri-Motor off the runway in Arequipa, Peru.

LadySmith® (Centennial) is a lightweight series of handguns manufactured by Smith & Wesson since the early 1900s. Short, three-inch barrels, aluminum or stainless steel bodies, concealed hammers and a five-round, 22 long-rifle or 38 caliber cylinder has made the model a favorite of government or law enforcement personnel whose primary weapon is concealed.

Secret Intelligence Service is the foreign intelligence service of the United Kingdom. Formed in 1909, it is commonly known as MI-6, however, its existence was not publicly admitted until 1994, eighty-five years after its founding. The announcement destroyed the organization's motto *Semper Occultus* (Always Secret).

Czech State Security (StB) was a harsh plain-clothes secret police force in the former country of Czechoslovakia from 1909 up until its dissolution in 1990. The StB had a long history of brutality, bribery, assassinations, kidnapping and torture long before it came under the sphere of Soviet influence. It was one of the earliest East European, Communist intelligence agencies to become involved in the politics of Central America and assist in the importation of weaponry for revolutionary forces. In 1993, Czechoslovakia was divided into the Czech Republic, Slovakia and the Ukraine.

Kodak Park is a 1,300-acre city within a city. Located about five miles north of downtown Rochester, New York, Kodak Park grew steadily with the company. The company's founder, George Eastman believed in people. One of his most significant quotes gave a unique insight to his world view: *"A good reputation is measured by how much you can improve the lives of others - customers, employees, and community."* To prevent anything from going wrong at the first levels, he gave his employees almost unbelievable benefits. Not just excellent pensions, he made available doctors, dentists, optometrists, drug stores, dispensaries, restaurants and one of the nation's first pre-school childcare centers on-site at Kodak Park. Dinners could be had for a few dollars and medical care at nominal cost. The employees were treated extremely well and were given not just benefits, but options to purchase stock. There were over 50,000 people working at Kodak Park, Rochester in 1960; an almost unbelievable total in a city of about 300,000.

Rum and Coke is an alcoholic cocktail made from light or dark rum, cola and a dash of lime juice. It is also widely known as the *Cuba Libre (Free Cuba)*. It is the consensus that the drink originated in or around Havana, Cuba at the beginning of the 20th Century, when Cuba became independent of Spain after the Spanish-American War.

Pregnancy in the armed forces was reason for immediate medical discharge "resulting from a condition incurred not in the line of duty". In 1951, President Harry S. Truman signed an Executive Order (EO 10240) granting the armed services permission to discharge a woman if she became pregnant, gave birth to a child, or became a parent or stepparent by adoption. The military took it as an ironclad mandate. Regulations were written and military women who became pregnant were summarily discharged.

Geneva Conventions comprise four international treaties signed by 196 countries in 1949 (some with reservations) that define the treatment combatants, prisoners, civilian populations and the wounded or sick during times of war.

Tequila Sunrise is a cocktail made from tequila, orange juice and red grenadine syrup. It was originally created in the late 1930s from tequila, crème de cassis, lime juice and soda water. Its name is derived from the various shades of red that appear after preparation.

The Aircraft and Warships

Beechcraft C-45 Expeditor was a twin-engine light passenger plane made by Beech Aircraft of Wichita, Kansas. During WW II, 4500 units saw military service with the Army Air Corps. After the war the "Twin Beech" was the primary business aircraft and 'feeder' for the airline industry. It had a range of about 1200 miles and a cruising speed of 160 mph.

Siebel Si 204 was a twin-engine transport with a maximum crew of two and a capacity for eight passengers or 3,500 pounds of cargo. It was manufactured for the German Luftwaffe in Czechoslovakia by Böhmisch-Mährische Maschinenfabrik AG. It had a cruising speed of 160 miles per hour and a maximum range of 1000 miles. About 1200 aircraft were built.

Messerschmitt me 262 was the world's first operational jet-powered aircraft. Very fast (550 mph), with outstanding firepower and maneuverability, it was the most deadly force in the German Luftwaffe. Its late introduction into World War II in April, 1944, however, reduced its effectiveness. The allied air forces could not compete with 262 in the air, but attacked it on the ground during takeoff and landings. Heavy allied bombardment of Nazi jet fuel facilities also limited the Messerschmitt's effectiveness.

USS Valley Forge (CV-45) was an 888 foot, Essex Class aircraft carrier built for the US Navy at the Philadelphia Naval Shipyard. She was laid down in September, 1946 after World War II had ended. Fully manned, it had a crew of 3,448 and carried 80-100 aircraft. The ship's nickname *Happy Valley* stuck. The Valley Forge had 4 deployments during the Korean War, earned 3 Navy Unit Commendations, 8 Battle Stars for Korea, and 9 for service in the Vietnam War. The ship was decommissioned in January, 1970 and sold for scrap in October, 1971.

Sikorsky H03S was the US Navy's version of the Sikorsky H5 helicopter. About 100 units were built  in Stratford, Connecticut, powered by a five-cylinder, air-cooled Pratt and Whitney engine. As built, it had a total capacity of 4: pilot, co-pilot, 1 crew and 1 passenger and a range of 360 miles. There were many modifications made for other US military services.

Lockheed Constellation (Connie) was a propeller-driven four-engine aircraft produced in Burbank, California from 1943 until 1958. Initially designed after Lockheed's highly successful fighter plane, the P-38 Lightning, it underwent further modifications by TWA owner Howard Hughes. A total of 856 planes were built from eight variants. It was initially designed for 60-90 passengers, 5 flight crew, and a cabin crew of 3. Cruising speed was 340 mph with a range of 5400 miles. Flying times: NY to Los Angeles = 7¼ hours; NY to London = 10¼.

Haven Class hospital ships served during World War II, Korea and Vietnam. A total of six were built and served from 1944-89. A full complement was 95 officers, nurses and doctors and 606 crew and corpsmen. At 520 feet long and a beam of 72 feet, the ships had a capacity for up to 800 patients and one evacuation helicopter. While anchored in port, helicopter landing pads could be moored alongside at port and starboard.

Douglas C-124 Globemaster was a large capacity, heavy lift,
 four-engine aircraft used by the US
Air Force from 1950 until the early
1960's. Nicknamed "Old Shaky",
the plane initially endured growing
pains and ultimately suffered through several fatal crashes
during its use. 440 units were built at Long Beach,
California.

Republic P-47 Thunderbolt was a highly functional single
engine, oval cowl fighter manufactured in Farmingdale, Long
Island, NY and Evansville, Indiana from
1941 until 1945. More than 15,500 units
were made at a cost of about $85,000 (1944
$) apiece. Pilots referred to this sturdy, heavy aircraft as the
flying bathtub. Post-war, many of the planes were sold as
surplus. Cuba and numerous countries throughout the world
used them in active service until the 1970s.

Douglas C-47 Skytrain was a military version of the proven,
solid DC-3. It was first flown in 1941 and was initially put
 into service by the USAAF in the
Southwest Pacific and CBI (China-Burma-
India) theater of operations. It also saw
extensive service in Europe and Africa. Many of the 10,000
built are still flying today.

North American T-6 Texan was a tandem-seat trainer first
into service in 1935. A rugged flyer, many are still in service
today. It was used as a fighter in the 1948
Arab-Israeli War, the Greek Civil War of
1946-49, the Korean War, Argentine
Naval War, by the Portuguese in Angola and Mozambique
during 1961-75 insurrections and in Vietnam as forward air
control for US ground support. More than 15,000 units were
manufactured.

North American P-51 Mustang was a long range, high speed fighter used extensively in WWII and the Korean War. Originally designed with an Allison engine, the powerful Packard V-1650-7 with twin superchargers became standard equipment. At more than 1700 horsepower, the Mustang had a maximum speed of 430 mph, and cruised at 360. The Mustang's speed, armament and dependability were the reasons that hundreds were still in military use well into the 1980's. The plane was used extensively by air forces throughout the world. Mustangs were the pride of the Guatemalan Air Force from 1954 until 1975. The Dominican Air Force was the last to retire them in 1984.

Lockheed P-38 Lightning was a twin-engine World War II fighter plane developed for the Army Air Corps in 1938. It was nicknamed *two planes - one pilot* by the Japanese and the *fork-tailed devil* by the German Luftwaffe. After initial 'growing pains', the P-38 proved to be a versatile aircraft, and was used in numerous roles including dive bombing, ground support, night fighting, long-range mission escort and photographic surveillance. 10,000 were built in Burbank, California from 1941-45 at a cost of $87,163 (1942 $) apiece. It was the first fighter to fly at 400 mph and the only one manufactured throughout the war. The cockpit windows did not open, which forced pilots in the tropics to fly in tennis shoes, shorts and parachute. Scores of used aircraft were exported to Central and South America as War Surplus.

Douglas DC-2 was a rugged 14-seat passenger and military transport plane. It was  one of the very first all-metal airliners and featured retractable landing gear, tapered wings and twin, 9-cylinder Wright radial aircraft engines. Douglas produced over 500 planes from 1934 until 1939 when the need for higher passenger and cargo capacities prompted the company to produce the wider, longer DC-3. It measured only 3 feet, 6 inches from the belly cargo door to the runway.

Northrop F-89 Scorpion was the first American jet-powered interceptor aircraft designed and built for the United States Air Force. Its performance was limited due to the early straight-winged design, but it was the first aircraft armed with unguided air-to-air nuclear missiles. First introduced in 1950, Northrop produced over a thousand aircraft at a cost of nearly a million dollars apiece. The planes were retired in 1969.

Music To Consider

A Tisket, a Tasket	Ella Filtzgerald
La Borinqueña (Puerto Rican girls)	The Jose Negroni Orchestra
Heart and Soul	The Blue Barron Orchestra
Daddy, won't you please come Home	Annette Hanshaw
Panama	Bob Crosby and His Bobcats
Hot and Anxious	Duncan Whyte & His Orchestra
South America, take it Away	Jane Morgan & Bernard Hilda's Orchestra
Down Argentina Way	Irene Daye, Gene Krupa Orch
Das gibt's nur in Berlin	Die Vier Casanovas
Bésame Mucho	Kitty Kallen & Jimmy Dorsey Orchestra
Please don't talk about me when I'm Gone	Mills Brothers & Tommy Dorsey Orchestra
I can't begin to tell You	Betty Johnson
It's been a long, long Time	Helen Forrest & Harry James Orchestra
How can you say No	Leah Ray & Lou Harris Orch
All by Myself	Martha Wainwright
Pomp and Circumstance	Royal Philharmonic Orchestra
To each his Own	Freddie Martin
Alexander's Ragtime Band	The Boswell Sisters
I've got rain in my Eyes	Teddy Grace with Bob Crosby and His Bobcats
Let me call you Sweetheart	Bing Crosby

Whoa, Sailor	Don & Rose Maddox
As Time Goes By	Dooley Wilson
Rockin' Rollin' Ocean	Hank Snow
East of the Sun (West of the Moon)	Billie Holiday
Between the Devil and the Deep Blue Sea	The Boswell Sisters
Stormy Weather	Lena Horne
Take it easy Greasy	Trixie Butler
Slipping Around	Floyd Tillman
Don't fence me In	Bing Crosby
A fool such as I	Hank Snow
What's New	Helen Forrest & Artie Shaw Orchestra
Till the real thing comes Along	Thomas 'Fats' Waller
Fishin' for the Moon	Liza Morrow & Benny Goodman Orchestra
I've heard that song Before	Helen Forrest & Harry James Orchestra
Jumpy Nerves	Wingy Manone
(I love You) For Sentimental Reasons	Eddy Howard
How long has this been Going On	Peggy Lee & the Benny Goodman Orchestra
Oh! Look at me Now	Helen Forrest & Benny Goodman Orchestra
I'm an Old Cowhand (From the Rio Grande) {Yippee-i-o-ki-ay}	Roy Rogers & The Sons of the Pioneers
Eleven sixty PM	Pied Pipers & Axel Stordahl Orchestra
Lover Man (Where can you Be)	Billie Holiday

Havana Club	Ottmar Liebert Orchestra
Caribbean	Hank Snow
Managua, Nicaragua	Gloria Wood , Kay Keyser Orch.
I'm a big girl Now	Betty Barclay, Sammy Kaye Orch.
Rumors are Flying	Marjorie Hughes
My blue Heaven	Gene Austin
Civilization, Bongo, Bongo, Bongo	Louis Prima
Vaya con Dios	Les Paul & Mary Ford
Ave Maria	Deanna Durbin
Cuban Pete	Amanda Lane & Desi Arnaz Orchestra
Ritmo en la Habana	Senén Suárez
In the Mood	Glenn Miller Orchestra
Yes, We have no Bananas	Louis Prima
Rum and Coca Cola	The Andrews Sisters
Two to Tango	Pearl Bailey
Address Unknown	The Ink Spots
Sincerely	The McGuire Sisters
The Green Door	Jim Lowe

The Telegram

A. N. WILLIAMS
PRESIDENT

CLASS OF SERVICE

This is a full-rate Telegram or Cablegram unless its deferred character is indicated by a suitable symbol above or preceding the address.

SYMBOLS
DL=Day Letter
NL=Night Letter
LC=Deferred Cable
NLT=Cable Night Letter
Ship Radiogram

The filing time shown in the date line on telegrams and day letters is STANDARD TIME at point of origin. Time of receipt is STANDARD TIME at point of destination.

79 GOVT WUX WASHINGTON DC 213 JUN 1 1946

MRS NICHOLAS THROCKMORTON
12 SECOND ST MT CLEMENS MICH

MRS NORA THROCKMORTON STOP

THE SECRETARY OF WAR DESIRES ME TO EXPRESS HIS DEEP REGRET THAT YOUR HUSBAND MAJOR NICHOLAS J THROCKMORTON USAAC HAS BEEN LISTED MISSING IN SERVICE AND MISSING AIRCREW SINCE APRIL 29 1946 IN THEATER SOUTHEAST CHINA STOP

IF FURTHER INFORMATION OR DETAILS ARE RECEIVED YOU WILL RECEIVE PROMPT NOTIFICATION STOP

LETTER OF CONFIRMATION FOLLOWS STOP

SIGNED CAPT JA ULIO ADJUTANT GENERAL STOP
END OF TRANSMISSION

WA - 5

Image Credits

Aircraft & warship silhouettes: United States War Department Manual #30-30 (1934-1945)

Barney Google: ©Billy Debeck; courtesy King Features

Howdy Doody: Detroit Institute of Arts

Women's Auxiliary Ferrying Squadron badge: United States Army Air Corps

Post Script

The Title Spring:

"We'll get married and sit on the beach and watch the sun paint those
beautiful sangria sunsets."
~ Jovita Maria Vasquello, April 14, 1955

"Tiptoe, tango or two-step? Truth be told, you got to dance
barefoot if you want to feel the earth move."
~ Edward R Hackemer, 2012

This novel was created with 100% recycled thought.
Some of it was green ... some of it wasn't.
The ink is fossil. It's carbon-based. (Oops.)

Thank you!

"qui veniunt et vade* *"*

Made in the USA
Columbia, SC
15 May 2017